THE
TRAITOR

When Jonathan Holt first travelled to Venice, he found it shrouded in thick fog and flooded with high water. This experience inspired him to write the Carnivia Trilogy: a series of thrillers based on Italy's hidden history which capture Venice's unique combination of glamour and decay.

The books in the Carnivia Trilogy have now become international bestsellers, published in 16 countries. The second novel in the trilogy was longlisted for a CWA Steel Dagger Award.

Discover more at
www.carnivia.com

THE TRAITOR

—

JONATHAN HOLT

HEAD *of* ZEUS

First published in the UK in 2015 by Head of Zeus, Ltd

Extract from 'Cities and Thrones and Powers' by Rudyard Kipling,
first published in *Puck of Pook's Hill* (1906).

Extract from 'The Hacker Manifesto' by The Mentor (Loyd Blankenship),
originally published in *Phrack* (January 1986).

9 7 5 3 1 2 4 6 8

A catalogue record for this book is available from the British Library

ISBN (HB) 9781781853757
ISBN (XTPB) 9781781853689
ISBN (E) 9781781853740

Printed in Germany by GGP Media GmbH, Pössneck

Typeset by Ed Pickford

Head of Zeus, Ltd
Clerkenwell House
45-47 Clerkenwell Green
London EC1R 0HT
WWW.HEADOFZEUS.COM

For we wrestle not against flesh and blood, but against principalities, against powers, against the rulers of the darkness of this world, against spiritual wickedness in high places.

– Ephesians 6:12

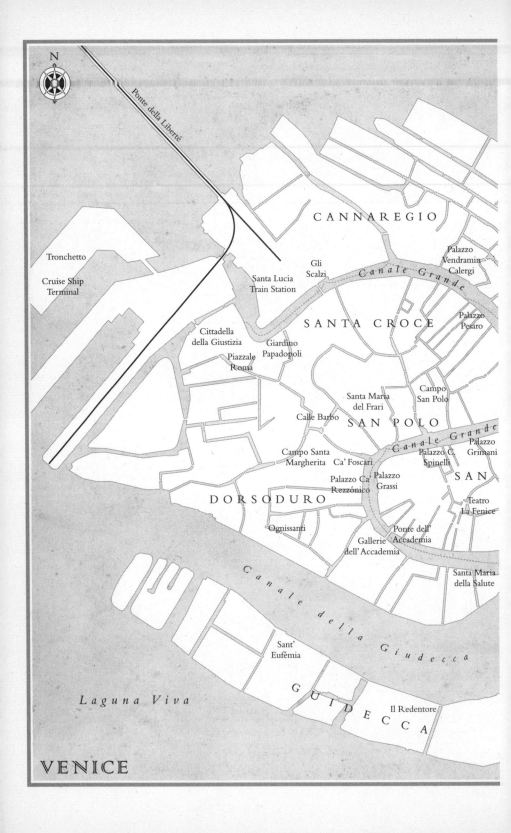

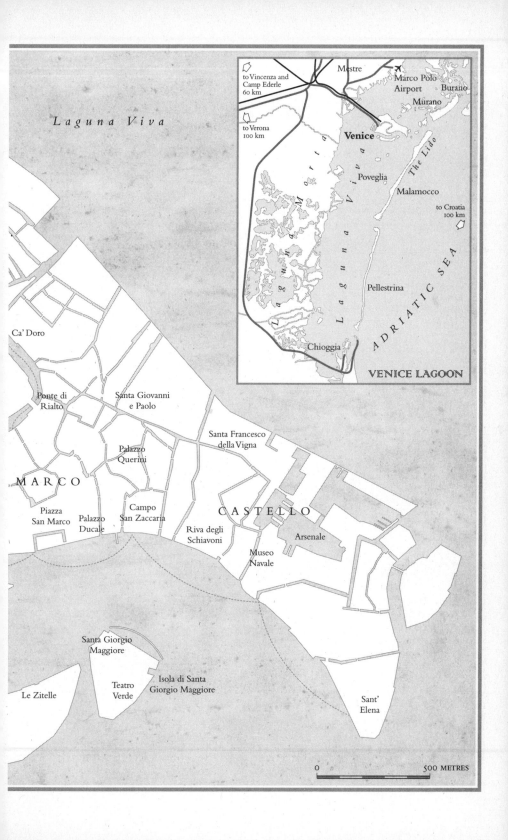

Laguna Viva

Ca' Doro

Ponte di
Rialto

Santa Giovanni
e Paolo

Palazzo
Querini

Santa Francesco
della Vigna

MARCO

Piazza
San Marco

Palazzo
Ducale

Campo
San Zaccaria

CASTELLO

Riva degli
Schiavoni

Arsenale

Museo
Navale

Santa Giorgio
Maggiore

Teatro
Verde

Isola di Santa
Giorgio Maggiore

Le Zitelle

Sant'
Elena

0   500 METRES

Mestre

to Vincenza and
Camp Ederle
60 km

Marco Polo
Airport

Burano

Murano

to Verona
100 km

Venice

L a g u n a   M o r t a

Poveglia

L a g u n a   V i v a

Malamocco

The Lido

to Croatia
100 km

A D R I A T I C   S E A

Pellestrina

Chioggia

VENICE LAGOON

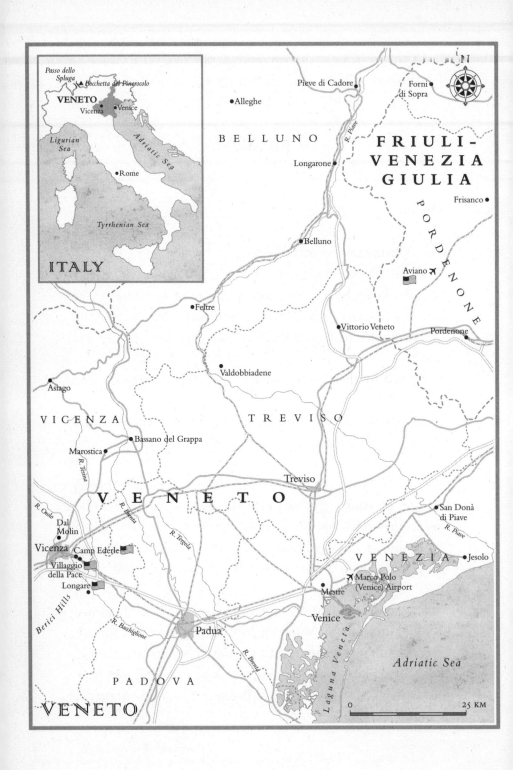

PROLOGUE

THE CANDIDATE WAS in darkness.

He heard three loud knocks as the two men either side of him struck the heavy door, followed by the response, "Who goes there?" And he heard the answer, confidently given, the words of the ritual flowing in unison from his companions' tongues.

Guided by their hands on his shoulders, he stepped over the threshold into the room beyond. Although he could see nothing, he sensed that it was large and cool. He smelt burning candle wax, along with the scent of polish from the flagstones under his bare feet.

"Brother, you will step off with your left foot, and bring the heel of your right foot into the hollow of your left," a quiet, purposeful voice in front of him said.

He did as he was bidden. The instruction was repeated twice more, before the voice said, "Now bring your heels together."

The candidate kept his face impassive, knowing that those around him would be watching him closely. Inwardly, though, he was exultant. Being told to take the third step was a sign that he had reached the very highest degree of what they liked to call their Craft. All of its so-called secrets would be revealed to him.

But, more importantly, it meant he would be trusted utterly by the silent watchers now gathered round him in a circle. He could ask any favour, and if it was in their power to grant it, it would be his.

At last, he was safe.

It had been a close-run thing. There had been times recently when he had felt as if he was staring into an abyss of panic and terror. But now, finally, he had something to trade with those who had been pursuing him.

He stood meekly as a length of rope, coarse and hairy, was wound around his arm and shoulder. "The candidate is in order, Worshipful, and awaits your further will and pleasure," one of his companions said when they were done.

"You will cause him to kneel on his naked knees," the Worshipful Master responded.

The candidate knelt. His knees were bare because his loose cotton trousers – the only clothing he was wearing – had been rolled up to his thighs. There was a cushion on the floor, and when he had positioned himself on it he reached forward to grasp the heavy oak table he knew was also there.

"Candidate, how came you hither?" the Master asked.

"I came neither naked nor clothed, neither barefoot nor shod, deprived of all moneys, means and minerals, blind-folded, and led by the hand of a friend to a door," he replied.

"Are you willing to make your sacred obligation, and take the oath?"

"I am willing and eager to take the oath."

"Detach your hands and kiss the book. Then speak your obligation, beneath the gaze of the Great Architect and of us all."

As the candidate spoke the stark words of the pledge, he fancied he could just make out, through a tiny chink in the antique mask that covered his eyes – the "hoodwink", in the arcane jargon they loved so much – the flame of a nearby candle. In a few moments, he knew, he would be asked what he most desired. "More light," he would reply. The Master would reach down to press a lever on the hoodwink, and the velvet-lined eye-covers would spring open to reveal in front of him a chair holding a human skeleton, its ancient, mis-coloured bones illuminated by the flames from a dozen silver candelabra. A dramatic piece of ritual theatre, as well as a symbolic reminder of the consequences of betraying his fellows.

Betrayal... To the candidate, the concept was meaningless. A man looked out for himself. What else was there? But just for a moment the words he was uttering, words that detailed the exact penalty for such a crime, took on meaning. Involuntarily, he faltered.

In the long silence that followed his declaration, the candi-date shifted uneasily on the cushion. He must be careful not to make such a mistake again. But if any of the watchers had noticed, they gave no sign of it. In fact, they made no sound whatsoever. For a moment he wondered how many were really there. But why would they hold an initiation to the Third Degree and not invite the full assembly to witness it? He forced himself to relax.

The point of something sharp pressed against the right side of his chest.

"Brother," the Master's voice said, "on entering this place for the first time, you were received on the point of a compass pressing your right breast, the moral of which was explained to you. On entering the second time, you were received on the angle of the square, which was similarly explained. I now receive you on both points of the compass."

The sharp object was lifted away from his chest, then pressed six inches to the left. It felt heavier and sharper than on previous occasions. He must remember to ask about it later, when they were enjoying the convivial drinks that always followed these initiations. They liked nothing better, he had discovered, than to discuss the finer details of their ceremonies and what they signified.

"As the vital parts of man are contained within the chest, so the most excellent tenets of our institution are contained within these two points – which is to say, secrecy and honour," the Master droned.

The sharp point was lifted away again. The candidate tensed a little. Next, he knew, the point of the compass would be pressed against his skin hard enough to draw blood. Then the ritual would be almost over.

He certainly wasn't expecting the long, hard-bladed shiv that thumped with sudden violence between his ribs. With a choking gasp he fell backwards. Waiting hands caught him and set him upright again. He put his hand to his chest and felt the handle of the knife, its blade lodged solidly within him; felt his skin already running with blood, blood that was pumping from his heart in abrupt, jerky spurts. He tried to reach up, to tear off the hoodwink, but his hands no longer obeyed him.

And then, even more terrifyingly, he felt the spurting stop, and knew that his heart was gone.

ONE

IT WAS GOING to be another beautiful day. Although it wasn't yet nine o'clock, the sun was fierce and the sky clear, with just a few wisps of cloud trapped over the Dolomites to the north. Kat Tapo felt the welcome coolness of the spray on her face as the Carabinieri motorboat bounced down on a wave. She opened the throttle even wider.

In the stern, Second Lieutenant Bagnasco gave a startled gasp as cold seawater slapped her face. She stumbled forwards to the relative safety of the cockpit. As well as being wet, she looked, Kat noticed, somewhat green. She'd been that way even before they neared the Bocca di Lido, the narrow opening or "mouth" in the line of sandbars and islands that separated the calm of the lagoon from the choppier open waters of the Adriatic.

"How long have you been in Venice, Sottotenente?" Kat called over the noise of the engine.

"A month," the other woman answered dutifully, although she looked as if even speaking was physically difficult right now.

"And you're still getting seasick? Even when it's calm like this?" Kat said, surprised.

Bagnasco didn't reply. It wasn't the swell making her sick so much as the ridiculously tight turns her superior was executing as she ducked and weaved between the boats going up and down the shipping lane to San Marco. But she knew that telling the *capitano* that wouldn't make any difference. Captain Tapo was clearly relishing the opportunity to turn on the launch's flashing blue light and break the speed limit. It had been like this ever since they'd left the pontoon at Rio dei Greci, next to the Carabinieri headquarters in Campo San Zaccaria: Kat had jumped in, as steady on her feet as a gondolier, and got the engine started while Bagnasco was still clambering cautiously down the steps.

The launch veered sharp right as they cleared the artificial island in the middle of the *bocca*. The island was a recent construction, part of the system of giant underwater gates known as MOSE that would – if the politicians were to be believed – protect the city against globally rising sea levels. Like many Venetians, Kat was sceptical. So far fourteen people connected to the construction consortium, including the mayor of Venice, had been arrested on corruption charges, and the project was running years behind schedule as well as billions over budget.

Once beyond the *bocca* the boat continued turning until it was travelling parallel to the long sandy seafront of the Lido. Kat scanned the beach as she steered. Even though they were only a few kilometres from Venice, in these closing days of August the Lido still had the lazy feel of a bathing resort from a different century. Here was Nicelli, the tiny airport where Mussolini once welcomed Hitler to Italy, now only used by the helicopters and light aircraft of the super-rich. Here was the hulking, Fascist-era cinema built to glorify the Italian dictator's pet film festival, in front of which she could make out a cluster of tiny figures; although why anyone would want to spend a morning as glorious as this watching a movie was beyond her. Here were the endless rows of sun-loungers, as closely packed as graves in a cemetery, topped by bodies in every shade from maggot-white to caterpillar-brown. Here too was the elegant Liberty-era façade of the Hôtel des Bains, once Venice's most famous hotel, where Winston Churchill had begun each day painting a water-colour by the sea's edge, wrapped in a bathrobe and puffing on a cigar. The hotel was closed now for conversion into apartments, just one more victim of the global recession, while its once-exclusive beach was covered with yet more sunloungers. The hotel *capanne della spiaggia*, the striped Edwardian bathing tents amongst which Visconti had filmed the closing scenes of *Death in Venice*, were still there, towards the rear of the beach, but these days you had to be a million-aire to rent one for the season.

Death in Venice... As if on cue, Kat spotted a white tent, only slightly larger than the *capanne*, placed incongruously on the shoreline. Blue tape cordoned off a large area around it, from one breakwater to the next. As she watched, a figure in a white bodysuit, complete with mask and hood, stood up and stretched, then crouched down again.

"That's the forensic team," Kat said. She turned the motor-boat towards a nearby jetty, slowing to a crawl as she did so. Dr Hapadi, she knew, wouldn't appreciate having his delicate handiwork ruined by her wash.

It was less than thirty minutes since General Saito had called her at her desk. "How busy are you, Captain?" he'd asked without preamble.

"Colonel Piola and I are wrapping up the paperwork on the Murano investigation," she'd said cautiously. "Another two or three days' work, we estimate." Tedious work, and probably pointless too. For months now, cheap coloured glass from China had been turning up in the tourist shops on the traditional glass-making island of Murano, labelled with fake "Made in Venice" stickers that quadrupled its value. A Carabinieri raid on a warehouse in Mestre had netted over fifty thousand pieces, along with half a million stickers waiting to be fixed to future consignments. Needless to say, the glass-making families who had been selling these imports were blaming an "administrative error".

"That's all right. I've spoken to Colonel Piola and he's happy to finish up without you. It was the prosecutor who suggested your name, actually. But the colonel and I both agree you're ready to run a major investigation on your own."

"May I ask what it concerns, sir?" she'd asked, trying not to let her excitement show.

"It's a homicide," Saito said tersely. That in itself was surprising – in the early stages of an investigation, such terms were usually prefaced with the words "possible" or "alleged". "We'll discuss budgets and manpower later, but it's clearly going to be a large and complex case. In the meantime, I'm assigning Sottotenente Bagnasco as your assistant. She comes highly recommended, but given that she's new to the team, let me know how she gets on, would you?"

"Of course, sir." Kat wondered if it would sound inappropriate to say thank you. "And thank you. I'm grateful for the opportunity."

There was a moment's pause. "I doubt you'll be grateful for this one, Capitano," Saito said darkly. He rang off before she could ask him any more.

She edged the boat up to the jetty and cut the engine. Most junior officers would have jumped out to help by securing a line, but Bagnasco still appeared to be too seasick, although she recovered a little once she was on dry land.

It seemed as if every sunbather on the beach raised themselves up on one elbow to watch the two women as they walked towards the blue tape. Kat was used to being stared at – female officers of the Carabinieri were a rarity even now – but it felt odd to be fully dressed, and in uniform at that, amongst so much bare flesh. Sun *and* murder: it was hardly surprising nobody was bothering with their paperbacks this morning.

At the tapes they paused to put on the microfibre suits, gloves and masks that would prevent any of their hairs or DNA from contaminating the scene. The tapes were being manned by three regular *carabinieri* on crowd control. Kat recognised one of them, a *maresciallo* from the station on the lagoon side of the Lido at Riviera San Nicolò. Nodding a greeting to him, she ducked under the tape and walked across the sand to the forensic tent.

Inside, it was incredibly hot. The combination of the blazing sun, the tent's plastic roof, the humidity and the overalls instantly made her long for the slight breeze that had been coming off the sea. She felt sweat prickle down her spine and forced herself to concentrate.

Noticing her, the medical examiner, Dr Hapadi, got up from where he was squatting so she could see. The corpse was lying on its back, half in and half out of the water, just where the waves ran into the sand. It was a male, middle-aged, dressed in bloodstained cotton trousers that were rolled up above the knees, as if he'd been wading. His chest was bare and a length of rope was wound over one shoulder. His throat had been sliced open, all the way from one clavicle to the other – the head rolled sideways at an angle, resting on one ear, so that the wound gaped obscenely wide: she could see the severed white tube of the oesophagus, ridged like a vacuum-cleaner hose, already half-filled with sand from the receding tide. But shocking though that was, it was what covered the man's face that drew her gaze. Beneath the sodden, greying hair, he was wearing a curious-looking mask of leather and cloth, like pre-war motorcycle goggles but with solid metal cups where the eyepieces should have been.

To one side, on a sheet of plastic, was a sandy object the size of a tennis ball. It was this Hapadi had been examining with the dental probe in his gloved hand.

"What kind of mask is that?" Kat's voice was muffled by her own mask.

"It's called a hoodwink," Hapadi said. Normally immune to the sights and smells of death, today he seemed almost dazed, though whether by the stifling heat or the condition of the body she couldn't have said. "A kind of blindfold. Here."

Reaching down, he pressed a small lever above the eye-pieces, which flipped open. Behind her, Bagnasco jumped as the dead man's eyes, piercingly grey, stared up at them.

"Who found him?"

"The younger of those two men, I believe." Hapadi nodded to where, behind the tapes, a good-looking man in his twenties was talking to one of the local *carabinieri*. He, too, looked very pale. An older man stood next to him, one hand protectively on the younger one's shoulder. There was a small lapdog, some kind of dachshund, tucked under his other arm. They looked like a couple, Kat thought. That was no great surprise: the Lido had long been one of Venice's most gay-friendly areas. "He was walking his dog. The animal found this and took it back to his owner." Hapadi indicated the sandy object.

She still couldn't work out what the object was. "What is it?"

Hapadi crouched down and unrolled it with the tip of the dental probe. "The victim's tongue," he said quietly. "It's been pulled out, probably with pliers."

Kat heard a choking sound behind her. She turned to see liquid spilling from the sides of Bagnasco's forensic mask. Yanking the mask from her face, the second lieutenant bent down, retching. Vomit tumbled into the sea.

"You'll need to give Dr Hapadi a DNA sample," Kat said when Bagnasco had finished. "For elimination purposes."

"That's all right," Hapadi said resignedly. He indicated where some of Bagnasco's breakfast had splashed onto the damp sand. "I'll take a swab from this, while it's fresh."

"Sorry," Bagnasco whispered. "I just…"

"It's hot in here. Go and get some air," Kat ordered.

When Bagnasco had gone, she turned back to the medical examiner. "Sorry about that. I think it's her first." She gestured at the body. "So the implication is that he was killed elsewhere and brought here by boat? And that the tongue was deliberately placed next to the body?" That would explain why the trousers were bloodstained but the sand wasn't. "But if you've got him in a boat, why not just throw him over the side in deep water and get rid of the evidence? Why bring him all the way to the beach, where you might easily be seen?"

"Because of the oath," Hapadi said quietly.

"Oath?"

The medical examiner wiped the sweat from his forehead with his sleeve. "I do most solemnly promise and swear," he recited heavily, "without the least equivocation, mental reservation, or self-evasion of mind whatsoever, binding myself under no less penalty than to have my throat cut across, my tongue torn out by the roots, and my body buried in the rough sands of the sea at low watermark, where the tide ebbs and flows twice in twenty-four hours, never to divulge the secrets I shall learn amongst this brotherhood." He looked at Kat, and she saw that his gaze was troubled. "I don't know who this man is, Capitano, but I'd lay good odds that he was a Freemason."

TWO

DANIELE BARBO STEPPED onto the balcony of the Doge's Palace. Below, in Piazza San Marco, a thousand masked faces looked back up at him expectantly. Many more, he knew, would be watching on computers and tablets all around the world. Never before in the history of Carnivia had its founder made a public appearance, let alone a speech: for the last two days, ever since he had announced his intention to address the website's users directly, the blogosphere had been awash with speculation about the reason.

Many believed Daniele was going to announce that Carnivia was finally being sold. Both Google and Facebook had made no secret of their desire to acquire it. Analysts were talking about a potential price in the region of half a billion dollars, pointing out that although Carnivia currently carried no advertising, the lack of a revenue stream was more the result of its founder's idiosyncrasies than any inherent lack of commercial viability. Alternatively, the encryption algorithms it employed would be worth a small fortune to the defence industry.

Others believed Daniele was going to announce curbs on the very thing that made Carnivia what it was: its anonymity. Each of the masked figures in the square below him was an avatar, the online representation of an individual user, their real identity and location hidden from everyone but them-selves. Uniquely, though, the anonymity only went one way – Carnivia itself could access all the data in your contacts list, allowing you to interact with your Facebook friends, your neighbours, classmates or colleagues without them knowing who you were. Not surprisingly, it was often controversial. In one recent case, a fourteen-year-old girl had killed herself after being taunted by a gang of anonymous cyberbullies. In similar situations, most websites gave law-enforcement agencies the perpetrators' details. Only Carnivia consistently maintained that even the site owner – Daniele Barbo – simply did not have access to that information.

As he looked down from the balcony – which was an exact simulation of the balcony on the real Doge's Palace, right down to the tiniest detail of crumbling stone – Daniele hesitated. He had planned the substance of what he was about to say, but had neglected to consider how he might begin. He was aware, of course, that it was customary to preface a speech with some kind of greeting. But what? "My fellow Carnivians" seemed like the wrong tone. "Hi", on the other hand, sounded too casual.

It was exactly the kind of difficulty that led many, he knew, to label him socially dysfunctional.

The silence dragged on.

Hello world, he said at last.

A ripple of amusement went around his audience, transmitted via tweets, emoticons and murmurs, as Carnivia's own internal communications were called. For those in the know, Daniele Barbo had just made a brilliant joke. A "hello world" program was a hacker's way of demonstrating proof of concept on a piece of coding. By using those words, Daniele was not only reminding his listeners that everything around them was his creation, but also acknowledging that they were sophisticated enough to appreciate such references.

Up on the balcony, Daniele glimpsed some of the responses as they fluttered past. He sighed. He had meant no such thing, of course. But at least he had started now. The most difficult part was over.

As many of you are aware, this website started as a mathematical model to help me understand certain aspects of computational complexity. But over the years, it has grown into something I never anticipated, he said.

Technically, he was at a computer screen, typing rather than speaking, but one of the many strange things about Carnivia was that such distinctions soon ceased to matter. The murmuring fell quiet as his listeners concentrated on his words.

That is, Carnivia has become a community.

Ten years ago, when he'd built the site, few had seen the point of its elaborate encryption. After all, wasn't the internet anonymous enough already? More recently, though, rising concerns about data privacy and online surveillance had meant that Carnivia was no longer just a haven for hackers, cypherpunks and crypto-anarchists. The site now had more than three million regular users, and that number was growing all the time.

Keeping that community free, peaceful, and safe from the interference of governments and regulators has taken up a great deal of my time, he continued. *Too much time, in fact. I have done no useful work for over a decade.*

As a result, I have decided that the burden of running Carnivia should be devolved to you, its users. You will decide, for example, what the correct balance should be between your privacy and your public responsibilities. You will decide what

*constitutes acceptable behaviour, and what should happen to
users who infringe those rules. You will decide whether there
should be investment in the site, and if so, how it must be generated. You will decide – your most pressing task – how these
decisions themselves are to be made, choosing your own system
of government by whatever process you collectively see fit.*

As of today, I will take no further part in those discussions.
He looked down at the multitude.

Does anyone have questions?

Several hundred did, it seemed. From the clamour he
selected one. *Yes?*

But you as owner will always have the final say, right?

*No. The ownership of the site, along with its servers, will
be transferred to whatever body you, Carnivia's users, decide
on. I will no longer have any legal claim to it.*

Why? What are YOU going to do?

There was a pause as Daniele struggled to articulate his
answer. Eventually he said, *I have recently become interested
in writing a piece of software to simplify seating plans for
weddings.*

Again there was a ripple of amusement, although it was
rather smaller this time. Daniele's joke was barely funny.

Will you continue to use Carnivia yourself?

*I don't know. But then, Carnivia's users have always been
anonymous. Assuming you wish to maintain that principle, I
suppose you will never know whether I'm on Carnivia or not.
Whatever happens, I will no longer be an administrator, or
reserve for myself any special privileges.*

His audience seemed almost more stunned by this final
demonstration of his seriousness than by anything else he had
said. To become a Carnivia administrator was a privilege
most of them could only dream of. There were no tweets now,

no murmurs, only the occasional exclamation mark that floated over the heads of the crowd and was lost in the faint breeze that rippled the waters of the Bacino di San Marco.

I wish you the best of luck, he added, stepping back. Closing the balcony doors, he sensed the hubbub starting up below as they began to debate what it all meant.

In the music room of the real-world Palazzo Barbo, where Carnivia's massive servers were housed, Daniele pushed his chair back from the screen and breathed a sigh of relief. Taped to the wall in front of him was a short To-Do list. Reaching out, he crossed off the first item with a single stroke of his pen.

Leave Carnivia.

As he turned back to the computer and closed the program, a message flashed up.

Are you sure?

He clicked "Yes" and felt a great load lifting from his shoulders.

THREE

"I WANT YOU to take the statement from the witness who found the body," Kat said, going over to where Bagnasco was rinsing her mouth with a water bottle. "I'll listen in, but it'll be good training for you."

"Thank you." Bagnasco gestured at the tent. "In there… I'm sorry. It won't happen again. I was still a bit seasick, that's all."

"Forget it. But for future reference, it's better to speak up and leave a crime scene than to throw up all over it. Ready?"

They made their way over to where the young man was standing. Bagnasco did a good job of putting him at his ease, Kat thought, turning occasionally to involve his partner in the conversation, and even reaching out to stroke the dog, although she recoiled involuntarily when it tried to lick her fingers with its moist, sandy tongue.

The young man, it transpired, was an actor, in Venice for the film festival. His partner was a director, drumming up finance for his next movie.

"I brought the star with me," the older man interjected, squeezing the younger man's arm.

The actor gave him a devoted look, then continued, "Anyway, I couldn't sleep, and Dauphin was awake too, so I took him for a walk."

"I'd taken a sleeping pill," the older man said. "I said to David, why don't you take one too? But you don't like pills."

The young man nodded. "They make me groggy. Anyway, when we came back, Dauphin found that... that *thing* and I saw there was a body." He shuddered, and the older man patted his shoulder.

"What time was this?" Bagnasco asked, writing it all down in her notebook.

The young man hesitated. "It's hard to say. Pretty early."

"And the body wasn't here when you first went past? Only when you returned?"

"I think so. I mean, it was only just light."

Kat waited until Bagnasco had finished, then asked politely, "Could you fetch your ID documents from your hotel, please?"

As she'd hoped, the older man said, "I'll get them. It's too hot for Dauphin out here, anyway."

When he'd gone, she addressed the younger man. "Now would you tell us what actually happened last night?"

He blinked. "What do you mean?"

"Was it really an early-morning walk? Or a late-night cruise?" Bagnasco was giving her a puzzled glance. "Look, I know what goes on in the woods at Alberoni at night," she continued. "It's fine, but I need to find out what time that body was actually placed here."

The young man looked shamefaced. "I'd have told you, but it was difficult with Milo listening. I thought if I took the dog he'd never know. And I only meant to be gone for an hour or so. But it was... busy last night, and all of a sudden I realised it was past four. So I headed back, and that's when Dauphin found the tongue."

"So it was dark when you first went past this spot? Meaning that you might have walked right past the body?"

He nodded.

"Thank you. I'll have that written up as a statement for you to sign."

When they were alone, Kat turned to Bagnasco. "Weren't you ever told to take statements one-on-one?"

The *sottotenente* looked mortified. "Yes, but…"

"Why didn't you?"

"I wanted… That is, I suppose…"

"You wanted to show that you weren't homophobic," Kat said. "So that's the second lesson learnt: get over it."

She went over to where the three local *carabinieri* were guarding the tapes. "Morning, boys," she said pleasantly. "Please tell me you've already questioned everyone on this beach in the hope of turning up a witness."

The three men exchanged glances.

"What?" she demanded.

One of them, the *maresciallo* she'd recognised earlier, said, "We've talked to the guys who put out the sunloungers. And the tractor driver who cleans the beach first thing. And the builders working at the hotel."

"And?"

"No one saw anything. More than that, no one was even here. The sunlounger guys were sick. The tractor driver had an engine problem. And the construction workers were all off shift, though they can't tell us who was on."

"What about this lot? Any of them get here early?" She gestured at the sunbathers.

"They're all tourists," the *maresciallo* said. "If there were any locals here, they've decided to call it a day."

Now that Kat looked again at the sunloungers, she saw how many were empty. And more were emptying all the time. Like a flock of starlings taking fright at a distant hawk, the people on the beach had decided that it would be better to forego a day in the sun than be associated, however loosely, with whatever it was that had happened here.

She sighed. "Try the builders again, will you? And come back tonight, in case there's anyone uses the beach late who was here yesterday."

By tonight, she suspected, the ripple of silence would have spread right across the Lido into Venice itself. But it was worth a shot.

While the scene-of-crime team finished up, she and Bagnasco took the boat down to the pine woods at the southern end of the Lido. Known as Alberoni, or simply "the dunes", this was Venice's unofficial naturist beach as well as its only gay one, the exact demarcation between the two shifting almost as fluidly as the sands themselves.

They had little luck in finding any witnesses there either, however. The woods were quiet at this hour of the morning, and the sight of two uniformed Carabinieri officers sent the few men who were still around scurrying into the trees.

Then, deep in the woods, Kat caught a flash of red. A tent. Camping was illegal outside the official site at San Nicolò, but she wasn't surprised to find someone ignoring the regulations. Going up to it, she called, "Anyone in there?"

After a few moments the door was unzipped. A grizzled face peered up at her.

"Carabinieri," she said unnecessarily. "Would you mind stepping outside?"

The man did so, and she added hastily, "But would you mind putting some clothes on first?"

"Why?" he said belligerently.

It was on the tip of Kat's tongue to say that he was committing a crime of indecency in addition to disrespecting the uniform of the Carabinieri, but she decided to play this a different way. "You feel more comfortable like that?"

"Yes. What of it?"

"Well, let's see how it goes," she said amiably. "We're trying to establish what boats were in the area in the early hours of this morning. Say around four a.m.?"

The man considered. "As it happens, I was up early this morning. There was a big cruise ship, but that was some way out. And a *motoscafo* as well."

"A water taxi? You're sure?"

"Pretty sure. It was one of those old motorboats, the nice wooden ones with a cockpit and a long hull."

"Any flags? Side markings?"

"None that I remember."

"Well, if you remember anything else, give us a call. That's my number." Kat handed him a card. As an afterthought she added, "The cruise ship – which way was it headed?"

"That way." He pointed north.

Kat looked out to sea. There were two or three ships out there, in the shipping channel. Otherwise the sea was empty all the way to the horizon.

For the first time since leaving her desk she felt the enormity of what she was faced with. A man had been brutally murdered in cold blood. But it was more than that. The dumping of his body on the beach had been designed to convey a very public message. Whoever they were, the murderers clearly believed they could deliver it with impunity.

Binding myself under no less penalty than to have my throat cut across, my tongue torn out by the roots, and my body buried in the rough sands of the sea at low water-mark...

Despite the heat, she felt a shiver go down her spine.

FOUR

SECOND LIEUTENANT HOLLY BOLAND flipped the catches on her father's old footlocker trunk and pushed open the lid. Inside, under a layer of lining paper, was her childhood.

The first thing she saw was a drawing she'd done of her favourite *piazza* in Pisa – not the overcrowded Campo dei Miracoli where tourists congregated round the Leaning Tower, but the much smaller square at the end of the street where her own family had lived, where their Italian neighbours chatted over purchases in the grocery store, drank espressos propped against the zinc counter of the bar, or sat on the backs of parked Vespas eating ice creams and flirting, depending on their age and gender. The drawing was signed *"BUON COMPLEANNO PAPÀ!!!* HAPPY BIRTHDAY LOVE HOLLY!!!"

She noticed that she'd mixed Italian and English. It must have been done when she was eleven or twelve, the two languages still overlapping in her head.

Beneath the card was a class assignment in a clear folder, titled, "What it's like to be an American officer's daughter in Italy." It was illustrated with a photograph of her and her brothers at a barbecue at Camp Darby, all three of them in swimwear. She'd been as lean and wiry as her brothers even then, her hair even blonder than theirs after weeks in the

Italian summer sun. Behind them, a group of Marines jogged along the beach in PTs and fatigue caps.

"Hi!" the caption read. "*Io amo la mia vita in Italia!* I love my life in Italy!"

Smiling, she put it down and moved on. A *Certificato di Eccellenza* from the Scuola Secondaria di Madonna Dell'Acqua attested that student Signorina Holly Boland had swum eight hundred metres. Another card, also handmade, bore the words, "*Per il miglior papà del mondo!* For the Best Daddy in the World!" It was dated *marzo 19*, the Feast of St Joseph, when Italian children wore green clothes and baked *frittelle* in honour of their fathers.

She wondered when she'd stopped giving him cards on the third Sunday in June, Father's Day in the US. Had she even noticed that she'd ditched the customs of her homeland for those of the country she was being raised in? Had he? And if he had, had he been proud, or concerned? Or a little bit of both?

Fascinated and nostalgic in equal measure, she continued digging through the layers. Every card she'd ever made him, every homework assignment she'd ever proudly passed on, every certificate she'd earned and postcard she'd sent home – he'd kept them all. Like most military personnel, always ready to move at short notice, his most precious possessions were stored in trunks rather than cupboards or drawers. That he'd devoted most of this one to mementoes of her childhood moved her almost to tears.

Further down, she found a photograph he'd taken of her. She was sitting on the back of a Vespa, grinning like a cat who'd got the cream, about to be driven somewhere by a handsome youth in sunglasses, his teeth gleaming in his olive-brown face. She must have been about fifteen. Her long, adolescent legs ended in the briefest pair of denim shorts she'd ever seen.

"How are you doing?"

Holly turned round. Her mother had come into the garage. "Hey, Mom. Look what I found." Holly showed her the picture. "Did I *really* go out dressed like that? And did you really think it was OK?"

Her mother smiled ruefully. "I don't recall us having much choice – you were always so determined. And the Italian boys were always very respectful."

"They may have seemed that way round you and Dad. I remember some very persistent wandering hands. It's a wonder I wasn't—" She stopped abruptly.

Her mother said nothing. Holly had told her a little of the events that had led to her taking extended leave from her posting at Camp Ederle, near Vicenza. A US colonel had incarcerated her in an underground military facility and tortured her, that much she knew. But she had also learnt that it was best not to press her daughter for details unless she was in the mood to talk about it.

Turning back to the trunk, Holly took the upper tray out. Underneath was her father's "formal", his dress uniform – a four-pocket green jacket, complete with insignia and shoulder braid; tan trousers with a black stripe down the seams; a peaked, braided hat – and, alongside, a small case of medals. Medals for achievement and diligence rather than combat. Her father had been a conscientious officer who loved and believed in his country and his job, but he was no bloodthirsty warrior.

Beneath the medals was a sash. She lifted it out. It was designed to fasten around the neck like a waistcoat and bore a series of embroidered symbols: a compass, a set square and an eye inside a triangle. "I didn't know Dad was a Mason," she exclaimed.

Her mother took the sash from her, nodding. "Oh, yes. He'd been in the Oddfellows before we moved to Europe, and when we settled at Camp Darby he got himself elected to a lodge near there. He always said it was for your sake – you and your brothers."

"For our sake? How come?"

"He claimed it was a good way of getting to know the locals. But actually I think he just liked being around men and uniforms. As if he didn't get enough of that on base. It was his friend Signor Boccardo who proposed him, I think."

"Boccardo..." Holly remembered a neighbour by that name, a pharmacist whose daughter had been in the same class as her. "Wasn't he the one who was killed in a car accident?"

"He was, yes." Her mother handed the sash back. "Do you want to shave your dad? Dr Hammond will be here soon."

"Sure. I'll just finish up in here."

At the door of the garage her mother paused, looking back at the crates and trunks stacked around the walls. "Thanks for doing this, Holly. I haven't touched any of this since we came home – I just can't tell which of his old army things are important and what can be thrown away." She was silent a moment. "Not that any of it's really important now, I guess."

When she was gone, Holly turned her attention back to the trunk. Under the uniform were more cards and photographs, some dating back to pre-Pisa days when the family had hopped around Europe, moving from base to base every few years. She pulled out a picture of her parents at a dance. They looked young and carefree. Germany, she guessed. That was where they'd met.

Reaching down again, her fingers encountered a small

bump in the trunk's cotton lining. The cloth was old and fragile, and when she prodded it a second time it ripped. Her fingers closed around the ends of a few sheets of paper, pushed down inside the lining. She pulled them out.

The first thing she saw was a copy of a poem – she thought she recognised the typeface of her father's clattering old electric IBM.

Cities and Thrones and Powers
Stand in Time's eye,
Almost as long as flowers,
Which daily die:
But, as new buds put forth
To glad new men,
Out of the spent and unconsidered Earth,
The Cities rise again.

This season's Daffodil,
She never hears,
What change, what chance, what chill,
Cut down last year's;
But with bold countenance,
And knowledge small,
Esteems her seven days' continuance
To be perpetual.

It was Kipling, one of his favourites. The family used to roll their eyes whenever he recited it, but that had never stopped him.

The next sheet bore a few short paragraphs, typed on the same machine.

Re: The Attached Memorandum

This memorandum details concerns reported to me by an Italian civilian, a fellow brother of the Aristarchus Lodge in Pisa, regarding remnants of the NATO clandestine network codenamed "Gladio".

The command structure of Gladio having been abruptly terminated along with the rest of the network in 1990, I was unsure who to report these concerns to. I have therefore passed the memorandum to a US intelligence officer of my acquaintance who, I knew, had previously been involved in the neutralisation of terrorist organisations such as the Red Brigades, in the hope that he will be able to distribute it to those best placed to take action.

This copy I am placing here, for safekeeping.

Major Edward R. Boland

March 12, 1991

The memo itself consisted of three pages, stapled together. It was stamped "COPY" in red ink and titled:

Highly Confidential.

She turned to the first page.

Since the public exposure of Operation Gladio in October of last year, those of us involved on the NATO side have been working at speed to roll up the network and transfer operational resources back to Allied hands. However, I have recently been made

aware that some former Gladio agents may not only
be resisting this process but may be actively
regrouping, using Masonic fraternities as their cover.

"Holly?" It was her mother, calling from the house.

"On my way," she called back. She flicked to the next page, skimming the text, then put the document down. So her father had been connected to the infamous Operation Gladio, one of the strangest and most controversial episodes in Italy's post-war history. She'd been aware, growing up, that he couldn't talk about some of his work, but she hadn't realised he'd actually dealt with intelligence matters.

Going into the house, she went into what had once been the dining room. "Hi, Dad," she said. "Guess what? I've just been reading that memorandum you wrote, back in the day. And I found all those certificates of mine from Pisa High School."

From his bed by the window, her father gazed up at her with eyes that were dark and troubled. She moved into the centre of his field of vision so he could see her better.

"And that drawing of Piazza Martraverso brought back so many memories. Remember the *gelateria* on the corner? They did a mandarin flavour I still swear was the best thing I've ever tasted."

He continued to gaze at her soundlessly.

"OK if I shave you now?" She waited for him to respond, and when he didn't, went on, "I'll just run the water to get it warm."

She scraped the white bristles from his cheek with the razor. It reminded her of all the times as a child she'd kissed his rough end-of-day stubble after he'd come home late from work. "If you want to move a little to the right…" She reached around and did the far side of his face. "No problem. We managed, didn't we?"

"It's good that you talk with him," a quiet voice said behind her.

She looked up. Dr Hammond was standing in the doorway. He was young and good-looking, which always took her by surprise – since when were doctors barely older than her, let alone handsome? – but he'd been her father's physician for almost five years now.

"It feels disrespectful if I don't. Besides, you said yourself there's a chance he understands more than he can show."

"A small chance," he reminded her. "While there *are* stroke victims with locked-in syndrome, your father's scans show vascular damage to his right hemisphere. Even if he could follow some of what was said to him after his first episode, it's unlikely he can now."

"Even so," she said. Turning back to her father, she wiped his face carefully with a towel. "There, all done. Dr Hammond's going to look you over, then I'll come back and we'll chat some more. OK?"

His expression didn't change. Standing up, she said, "All yours."

While Dr Hammond got to work, she washed the razor under a tap. As she did so, something occurred to her.

She went and found her mother in the kitchen. "That neighbour you were talking about – Signor Boccardo, the one who died in a car crash. When was that, exactly? Was it round about the same time Dad got sick?"

"Oh." Her mother made a face. "That horrible business. Yes, it was a little before your father took ill. He was very upset, as I recall – he liked Mr Boccardo."

Going back to the garage, Holly pulled out her father's memorandum and went through it, more slowly this time, searching for the name she'd glanced at earlier and only half-registered.

There it was.

It was Gianluca Boccardo, a neighbour and good
friend of mine, who first spoke to me about an
influx of new members at our lodge. He asked
whether I, as an American officer, could tell him if
there was any truth in what some of them were
claiming...

Another thought, an even bigger one, hit her suddenly like
a blow to the head. Through the open door of the garage she
saw Dr Hammond walking to his car. "Doctor?" she called.
"Do you have a minute?"

"Of course, Holly." His smile was friendly. For the first
time, she realised that he probably fancied her a little.

"Answer me a hypothetical question, would you? Is it possible – in theory, at least – to *make* someone have a stroke?"

"Well, if a person drinks, or smokes, or has high blood
pressure—"

"I don't mean their lifestyle," she interrupted. "But say
there was someone who already had those risk factors. Is
there any substance or medication that would make a stroke
more likely?"

He considered. "Warfarin, I guess. It's used to kill rats, and
it's sometimes prescribed for people with blood-clotting problems. But no doctor would ever prescribe Warfarin to a patient
who might already be at risk of an intracerebral haemor-
rhage."

"Because those risk factors would show up on their medical
records, right? You'd know to avoid that class of medica-
tions."

He nodded. "Exactly."

Or not, she thought.

Or someone would know from that person's medical records exactly what was most likely to kill him.

The possibility was unthinkable, yet having been thought, there was no dismissing it. Her father and his friend had stumbled on something, something her father had considered serious enough to pass on to his superiors. Within a short time Boccardo was dead, and her father had suffered a stroke.

Someone had decided to silence them both. And the reason for it was right there, in her hand.

FIVE

"WE WON'T BE able to perform the autopsy until tomorrow at the earliest," Dr Hapadi said apologetically as he led the two Carabinieri officers through the mortuary. "We had two deaths in the hospital last night and they'll have to take priority."

"That's all right," Kat said. "It was you we came to speak to, actually."

"I thought it might be," the pathologist said quietly. "Let's go in here."

He took them to his office, off to one side of the morgue and almost as cold. Through the glass wall Kat could see Spatz, the technician, leaning over the corpse with a camera, taking photographs of the victim's face. The pictures, she knew, would be uploaded via a specialist program to Google Image Search in the hopes of finding a match. It wouldn't replace a formal identification, but it might give them a starting point.

Hapadi handed Kat a sheet of fax paper. "I spoke to our Worshipful Master earlier. Those are the names of every member of our lodge."

"How long have you been a Mason?" Kat asked, scanning the list.

"Almost seven years. People have the wrong idea about us,

you know. Most of what we do is charitable. And since Anselmi, it isn't even secret."

Kat nodded. The Anselmi law, introduced a decade earlier, required any club or group to produce a list of members on request. Effectively, it made secret societies illegal.

A name jumped out at her, then another. "My God," she said. "I know him. And him." There were at least half a dozen senior Carabinieri officers here. She turned the page. Listed under "S" was General Saito, her *generale di divisione* and the man who had assigned her to this case.

Hapadi nodded. "It was General Saito who proposed me. Major Flavigni was my seconder."

Kat put the list away. "But you don't recognise our victim?"

The pathologist shook his head.

"Are there any other lodges in Venice besides yours?"

"Not that I know of." He hesitated. "Not official ones."

"'Not official ones'? What does that mean?"

"The Anselmi law... It was very unpopular with some Freemasons. Sometimes you hear talk of 'black' lodges – lodges outside of the Grand Orient, the official Masonic federation. Technically, they've no right to call themselves Masons, but they justify it by saying that they hold true to an earlier, more rigorous set of rites. That stuff about having your tongue torn out, for example – that hasn't been part of the official oath for decades."

"So having that done to him might suggest that our victim was indeed a member of a black lodge?"

"I suppose it might, yes," he said reluctantly.

"And how would I set about finding such a lodge, if there is one here in Venice?"

Dr Hapadi shook his head. "I don't know anyone who would have dealings with something like that."

Just for a moment, she thought she saw a flash of fear in

his eyes. "But you might have heard gossip?" she pressed him.

"Rumours? Anything would be useful at this stage."

He seemed to come to a decision. "I don't know whether it's relevant. But there's a man, a wealthy man, who collects Masonic memorabilia. I've heard he can be quite... pushy."

It seemed to Kat a fairly small transgression, but since she suspected Hapadi might have other reasons for mentioning this individual, ones he'd rather not divulge, she said only, "And his name?"

"Tignelli. Count Tignelli."

Kat raised her eyebrows. "The one who bought La Grazia?"

Count Tignelli was a well-known figure in the Veneto. As the title suggested, his family were old money, the makers of a well-respected brand of *prosecco*. More recently, under his leadership, the once-staid family firm had through a series of daring expansions succeeded in turning itself from a mere wine label into a fashion brand to rival the likes of Armani or Benetton. These days you could buy Tignelli luggage, Tignelli sunglasses or Tignelli cologne; she herself owned a cashmere Tignelli scarf that she brought out every winter. The man behind all this, meanwhile, had gradually moved from the business sections of the newspapers to the front pages, his opinions sought on everything from the latest corruption scandal to the failings of the politicians in Rome – not least because those opinions, and his vociferous calls for reform, were rarely watered down for publication. Not long ago he'd bought the lagoon island of Santa Maria della Grazia from the cash-strapped city council; the sell-off of several islands being, it was rumoured, part of the deal struck over the endless government bailouts for the MOSE project.

"Thank you," she said, mentally tucking the name away for future reference. There would be little point in going to speak to Tignelli at this point. Interviewing someone with that kind of influence was hard enough even when you had some evidence. "And if I wanted to know more about Freemasonry in general? Who could I ask?"

"I'll give you the name of our archivist," Hapadi said reluctantly.

"Captain?" It was Spatz, calling from the morgue.

They went through to the larger room. On Spatz's computer screen were half a dozen images from local newspapers. All showed the same middle-aged man in a variety of expensive-looking suits. She leant forward to read the captions: "Signor Alessandro Cassandre at the inauguration of the new Mestre arts centre…" "Alessandro Cassandre, Senior Partner of private bank BCdV, alongside donors to the Save Venice fund…" "Alessandro Cassandre hands a cheque for one million euros to the children's home…" "Alessandro Cassandre and his wife were among the honoured guests at the gala evening, which was sponsored by BCdV…"

"Alessandro Cassandre." She glanced at Hapadi. "Still sure you don't know him?"

He shook his head. She pulled out the official list of Masons he'd given her and checked. No Cassandre there either.

She typed "BCdV private bank" into Google and clicked on the first result.

Welcome to Banca Cattolica della Veneziana.
Who we are. What we do. Meet the team.

She clicked on "Who we are."

Banca Cattolica della Veneziana is the fourth oldest bank in Italy, one of only a handful of surviving private banко. Originally a aolf holp organiaation, londing money in ways compatible with religious principles, it now manages over thirty billion euros on behalf of a range of private clients and institutions.

In 1904 a minority stake in the bank was acquired by l'Istituto per le Opere di Religione, formalising an alliance dating back over two centuries.

"The IOR," she said aloud. "The Vatican Bank. Our man had some serious connections."

Clicking on "Meet the team" brought up photographs of the senior partners. Under each one was their name and a short description of their specialisms. Cassandre's was listed as "Wealth management and tax planning".

She looked across at the corpse, comparing his face with the photograph on the screen. "What do you think?" she asked Bagnasco.

The second lieutenant had barely spoken a word since they'd been in the morgue – trying to make sure there was no repeat of that morning's mishap, Kat suspected. "I'm not certain," she said hesitantly. "He looks different, somehow. Younger."

"That's because he's dead. And he was lying in seawater. The skin starts to tighten within a few hours. Like a facelift, only more temporary. It's definitely him, although we'll need a formal identification from his wife."

"So we go and speak to her now?"

Kat looked at the dead man again. Now that he was cleaned up and lying on his back, the likely cause of death was clear – not the gaping wound in the throat, but a small, neat puncture beside the left nipple. The blade had been perfectly positioned above the heart. But then, she reflected, Cassandre would have been kneeling, bare-chested, blindfolded by those peculiar goggles. The killer would have been able to take his time, getting the spot exactly right.

Even so, there were no hesitation wounds; no second blow just to make sure, or to vent a killer's anger. This was a cold, precise death, inflicted by an expert.

So: a professional killer. A dead Freemason who was not a member of the official local lodge, left on display at Venice's most crowded beach. And now a Catholic bank... Already this case had all the hallmarks of one of those crimes that were never solved, the ones people talked about for years with shrugs and knowing looks; just one more instance of the spider's web of corruption and influence that still, after so many scandals and clean-ups, plagued her country.

And for some reason, she – the least experienced investigator in the Carabinieri – had been assigned to it, along with this joke of an assistant. For the first time she wondered if that could have been deliberate.

"No," she said. "We go to the prosecutor and apply for a warrant."

SIX

HOLLY SPENT THE rest of the day on the internet, reminding herself about the strange episode in Italy's history codenamed Operation Gladio. Although she'd only been a child when it had first come to the public's attention, the main facts of the story were already familiar to her.

In 1990, pre-empting the efforts of a determined prosecutor, the Italian prime minister, Giulio Andreotti, had made a statement to parliament revealing the existence of a secret army of Italian civilians, recruited, trained and equipped by NATO, which had been intended to act as a paramilitary resistance in the event of a communist invasion; or, for that matter, a communist victory at the ballot box. It seemed extraordinary now, but she knew that in the paranoia of the Cold War, when the Italian communist party routinely polled more than thirty-five per cent of the vote, such a scenario had been considered quite possible.

The outrage that greeted Andreotti's revelation had been compounded when it subsequently emerged that some of the "gladiators" – whose name derived from the "*gladio*", or short sword, carried by Roman centurions for close-quarter combat – were very far from being the disciplined army-in-waiting the prime minister had described. Instead, they had used their training, and their NATO-supplied explosives, to intervene violently in Italian politics, part of a coordinated "strategy of tension" that they hoped would lead to the public demanding tighter security measures from the government. Over the years, many atrocities of the turbulent seventies and eighties – the so-called *anni di piombo*, or "Years of Lead" – had been shown to be the work of gladiators; although even today, forty years later, actual convictions were still rare.

From what she could glean from his memorandum, it seemed her father's role in all this had only been incidental. Most of the gladiators' practical training, he wrote, had taken place at Capo Marrargiu, a remote corner of Sardinia, with NATO personnel at Camp Darby only contributing theoretical knowledge in such matters as secure communications and tactics. Even so, she thought she could discern, behind the bland, official tone of his report, a sense of unease at what he'd been ordered to take part in.

It was not for those of us at Camp Darby to question how the network was being disbanded, any more than it had been our place to express opinions about arming those whose ideology might be fervently anti-communist but whose practices, professionalism and sense of honour were sometimes demonstrably at odds with that of the US Army.

If she was to find any direct evidence linking the memorandum to his stroke, she realised, she wouldn't do so from her parents' house in Florida, five thousand miles away.

Despite what had happened to her when she was last in Italy, it was time to go back to the country she still thought of as home. She logged into the Delta Airlines page and booked herself a flight.

*

That done, she noticed a story in her newsfeed: "Carnivia Creator Steps Back". Reading the article prompted mixed feelings in her. She was one of the few people who could claim to know Daniele Barbo well, having had a brief affair with him that she'd only ended after her ordeal in the underground cave complex at Longare. She doubted they'd ever resume that relationship now. She found him fascinating, but he was both too difficult and too vulnerable for someone who was still damaged herself. And whilst like everyone else she marvelled at the obsessiveness that had enabled him to create an exact 3D digital replica of Venice, she'd always found Carnivia itself somewhat creepy. She knew her Venetian friend, Kat Tapo, disagreed, considering that Daniele's much-vaunted encryption technology was simply the modern-day equivalent of the masks her ancestors had worn to gamble, gossip, or conduct liaisons. But Holly was made of more puritan stock.

She was curious, though, as to what had prompted Daniele's announcement. She clicked on a few links and found no shortage of speculation. Many were calling it the most spectacular abdication since Dong Nyugen had taken his game Flappy Bird offline after receiving hostile comments about the gameplay, even though at the time it was the most popular game in the world. The general consensus was that Barbo must have suffered some kind of breakdown.

The suggestion that he had genuinely become interested in wedding seating plans was, of course, dismissed by most as a rather strange joke.

Holly knew better: Daniele didn't do jokes. She kept digging. Eventually she came across a post written by a young mathematics professor at the Massachusetts Institute of Technology, headed:

Holy c**p – Daniele Barbo thinks he can solve P=NP

P=NP, the professor explained, was one of the most important mathematical problems of the computer age, as well as one of the six remaining unsolved Millennium Prize problems. Put simply, it asked whether there was an algorithm that would allow a computer to find answers to complex mathematical problems as quickly as it could check them.

Aware that even a simple statement like that might go over the heads of some of his readers, he gave a real-world example.

Suppose you want to go to Disney World, and you know there are long queues for the most popular rides. So you try to work out a route that will cut your waiting time to a minimum. There are 21 attractions on the One-Day Touring Plan – that's 51,090,942,171,709,440,000 possible itineraries, six times as many as the estimated number of grains of sand in the world.

But here's the thing. If you generate two itineraries, and you know the estimated wait at each ride, you can very quickly see which one is better. In other words, the solution is easy to check. Why can't we devise a computer program that can work out the best itinerary just as easily? At the moment we can only generate solutions one by one and then compare them – what's sometimes called a "brute force" program, a fancy name for trial-and-error. When the number of possible solutions is as big as 21 factorial, as it is in the Magic Kingdom example above, that would take longer than a human lifetime, even for a computer.

A seating plan is just another version of the same problem. Let's say you have fifty couples coming to your wedding, and each table seats ten people. How do you break those couples up so everyone's sitting next to someone who isn't their partner? And – let's complicate it – how do you simultaneously make sure that every couple from the groom's side sits on a table with at least one couple from the bride's side? Then let's say the groom has invited all fifteen members of his rugby team, who tend to get drunk and sing rude songs if they're placed on the same tables... People usually figure out an acceptable solution to these kinds of problems, because it's pretty easy to see when you've got it right. But why isn't it possible to write an algorithm that will do it for you?

An algorithm isn't magic – it's just a set of instructions for carrying out a calculation. You used an algorithm every time you did long multiplication at school. But in the examples above, no one has ever found an algorithm that would allow a computer to generate an answer in what mathematicians call polynomial time, or P – that is, an amount of time that isn't ridiculously long.

The point is, if such an algorithm did exist, it would revolutionise the kinds of tasks we ask computers to carry out. We could use machines to solve every remaining mystery of our existence, from why a wave breaks where it does to how a jet vapour trail over New York affects the chances of rain in London. It would mean that computers could scan every detail of our personalities and find the one person in the world most likely to be our soulmate. It would mean that instead of needing an infinite number of monkeys and an infinite number of typewriters to come up with the works of Shakespeare, a computer could generate plays that were Shakespearean in every respect other than the actual authorship. It would even mean, in theory, that Amazon could write books specially for you, based on your favourite passages and characters in other authors' works. Or, on a more altruistic level, it would mean that if you had fifty kidney donors and fifty people on dialysis, you could find the most efficient match between them in seconds.

And it would mean – perhaps ironically – that encrypted websites like Carnivia or PayPal would be in real trouble, since hackers would quickly be able to generate the private keys on which such sites depend.

Many people, it has to be said, think that a world in which P equals NP would be a more sterile, less interesting place; one where creative leaps, intuition and instinct have almost no role. For that very reason, many also believe that P can never equal NP – that we've effectively reached the limits of what mathematics, and therefore computers, can do for us.

Daniele Barbo isn't a well-known figure in the mathematical world – he's no Perelman or Yau. But his early work on Kullback–Leibler divergence was startlingly original. Perhaps it will take someone who thinks more like a computer than a human being to help computers move one step closer to thinking.

Then again, that paper of his was published almost twenty years ago, and he's done nothing of any real note since. It was 357 years before Andrew Wiles found a proof for Fermat's Last Theorem, and over a hundred before Perelman solved the Poincaré Conjecture. The P=NP problem was only formulated in 1971 – just articulating it earned Steve Cook a Fields Medal. I wouldn't be placing any bets on Daniele Barbo claiming that Millennium Prize just yet.

There were fourteen comments, all agreeing with the writer. Holly was tempted to add one as well, before deciding to keep her thoughts to herself. The MIT professor might know about mathematics, but he didn't know Daniele Barbo.

SEVEN

"IF WE WAIT until his wife's made a formal identification, any useful evidence at his office will almost certainly have been whisked away," Kat said patiently. "A warrant to search the place now is the only way we can be sure of getting whatever's there."

The prosecutor, Flavio Li Fonti, turned to his number two, a lawyer called Melissa Romano. "I imagine you'll have something to say about that, Avvocatessa?"

"Indeed I do," she said crisply. "As I understand it, Captain, you have no probable cause that any such evidence exists. It would be a fishing expedition, pure and simple."

"The man was a banker, and his death is linked to Freemasonry," Kat argued. "Given his wounds, it's highly unlikely to be a domestic dispute. Therefore, searching his office sooner rather than later is just a sensible precaution."

They were in Flavio Li Fonti's office in the Cittadella della Giustizia, the Palace of Justice, one of Venice's few strikingly modern buildings. Both prosecutors had already been in court and were wearing the formal black robes and white cravats of their profession. Kat and Bagnasco sat opposite them, on the other side of Li Fonti's desk.

"There's no suggestion he was killed at his workplace. It would be more logical to search the nearest Freemason's lodge," Li Fonti said, crossing his legs.

"He's not listed as a member of the official Venetian lodge."

"Which makes the link to Freemasonry even more tenuous," Melissa Romano interjected. "Your argument defeats itself, Captain."

Kat knew from experience that these objections, although couched in a tone that suggested she was wasting her time, actually meant nothing of the kind. Good prosecutors were no pushover, particularly when you were asking for something out of the ordinary. They would test your argument to destruction, and only then make a decision.

And Flavio Li Fonti was a very good prosecutor. Proof of that could be glimpsed through the open door of his office, where two plain-clothes bodyguards sat in the vestibule, toying with their mobile phones. The long series of trials, lasting over eight years, which had cracked open a major 'Ndrangheta drugs network had been a spectacular success, with convicted *mafiosi* turning *pentito* one by one and incriminating others in return for a lighter sentence. But the 'Ndrangheta weren't the type to forgive and forget. While the *pentiti* were able to disappear to new lives abroad, the price of Li Fonti's success was that he now had to be guarded around the clock, never spending more than one night a week in the same place, never travelling by the same route to the courts or his office. It had cost him his marriage, his wife adopting a new identity and fleeing abroad just like the *pentiti*. It was said that he saw his children no more than half a dozen times each year. He couldn't have been more than forty, but his face was deeply lined and his brown eyes had a permanent sadness in them.

"Of course, it might be different if you were arguing that the killer could have contacted him via his office computer," he said thoughtfully.

"That's exactly what I'm saying," Kat said quickly, grateful for the steer. "As a banker, he would have worked long hours, and his personal and professional lives would certainly have overlapped. There could well be information on his computer that could help identify his killer."

"Tell me, Captain," Melissa Romano said. "You appear to have discounted the most logical explanation for a man being killed in such a manner – that he had revealed Masonic secrets connected with their rites, and that his fellow Masons exacted the literal penalty. Why is that?"

Kat thought. "I suppose I have trouble in taking all that mumbo-jumbo about ancient rites seriously myself, so I'm inclined to doubt that anyone else would care about them enough to murder for them. Besides, there have been Masonic scandals in Italy before, haven't there? Banco Ambrosiano, P2, Roccella Ionica, Catanzaro... the list goes on and on. And in almost every case it's turned out to have been about power, corruption and the bribery of public officials. I don't doubt that Cassandre was killed as a warning to his fellow Masons. But whatever he betrayed, I suspect it was to do with influence and money, not some threadbare ancient ritual."

Li Fonti came to a decision. "Very well. You can have a warrant to seize his computer and phone records. But nothing else. Come back in twenty minutes for the paperwork."

As the two *carabinieri* stood up, Li Fonti addressed Bagnasco directly. "You're the new *sottotenente*, I take it?"

"Yes," she said. "It's my first posting in Venice." She smiled at him, clearly grateful to have been noticed. The handsome prosecutor with the tragic life story was something of a heart-throb amongst the younger female officers.

"Well, stick close to your captain," he said, nodding at Kat.

"You can learn a lot from her."

"I will," Bagnasco said, although she sounded a little doubtful.

When they were outside, Kat turned to her. "You recall our nudist saying he'd seen a cruise ship heading north? That means it was coming into Venice, not sailing away. So the chances are it'll still be moored at the cruise terminal." Like most Venetians, Kat disliked the way these massive floating skyscrapers were allowed to sail right through the heart of Venice, across the Bacino di San Marco and along the Canale della Giudecca, on their way to the terminal at Tronchetto. Many claimed that their thunderous *moto ondoso*, the wake from their mighty propellers, was damaging the city's ancient buildings. Even at her own desk at Campo San Zaccaria, Kat could sometimes feel the vibrations as the behemoths passed by. A campaign to limit their size and number had been rumbling on for years, but the tourist dollars they brought in were simply too important for them to be banned.

"Every ship over twelve feet that sails in or out of Venice is given an identifier, a LOCODE, by the port's navigation system," she continued. "If the other boat our witness saw really was a water taxi, it might have been picked up by the cruise ship's radar. It's a long shot, but I want you to ask the captains of all the cruise ships currently moored at the terminal for a copy of their radar logs."

Bagnasco nodded. "Of course."

When she was gone, Kat turned and re-entered the building. Going back up to Li Fonti's office, she found the door closed. She knocked. The bodyguards gave her an incurious look, then went back to their phones.

"Enter," Li Fonti's voice said.

He looked up from his desk as she came in. "I thought it might be you."

She undid her jacket and took it off.

"What are you doing, Captain Tapo?" he said, raising an eyebrow.

She unbuttoned her blouse. "Taking off my clothes."

"I realised that. But why?"

"So that I can do what I promised I'd do if you got me a homicide of my own."

"I must admit, I wasn't sure if that counted as a legally binding contract," he said, watching her undress. "Since it was made in circumstances that might be construed as coercive."

"You mean, because you were fucking me at the time?"

"I should also point out that there was no impropriety whatsoever about the decision to appoint you. General Saito was most insistent that you were the right woman for the job."

"Even so, the offer stands," she assured him, stepping out of her skirt.

He crossed to the door and locked it. "It looks like I'm in an urgent conference, then."

"You were right, by the way," she said as she moved towards him. "What you said earlier. Once we start looking for evidence without reasonable cause, we're on the way to becoming a police state." She reached up and unpinned her hair, shaking it loose so that it fell over her shoulders, an unruly black mane. "But I had to try."

"And you were right to," he said. "If you'd waited for a formal ID, that office would be clean by the time you got there."

"It may well be anyway."

"At least letting you seize his computer gets you in there. I imagine you'll ask all the necessary follow-up questions at the same time? This case stinks worse than the water below that window." He picked up her Carabinieri hat and placed it on her head. "I think you should keep this on, by the way."

"All right," she said, pushing him back against his desk. "Now shut up, will you?"

EIGHT

Is it true?

Daniele scanned the attachments Max had sent him. *Which bit?*

Any of it. The stuff about P=NP. Or what they're saying on the Huffington Post, that you've had some kind of breakdown.

Not that I'm aware of, Daniele answered cautiously. On the side of the screen, three more avatars popped into the chat room, which was reserved for the exclusive use of wizards. These were Carnivia's administrators: Eric, Anneka, Zara and Max.

They were probably also his oldest friends. Zara had even helped him with some of the coding for Carnivia, back in the early days when it was still an open-source, collaborative project. He'd met her only once in the real world, and had discovered that she was profoundly deaf and almost mute, her speech an unintelligible mumble. Online, she was the most quick-witted and articulate of any of them. Max he had encountered a couple of times at conferences in the US: he had turned out to be obese and painfully shy, his gut straining at an ancient Nirvana T-shirt. Anneka and Eric he had still never met in the physical world. He sometimes wondered what hidden handicaps their confident online personas were concealing. He supposed he'd never find out, now.

It was Max who normally acted as their spokesman. But today he seemed unusually incoherent.

I just can't believe it. I can't fucking believe it.

Believe what? Daniele replied.

That you've fucking BETRAYED us like this.

I don't understand, Daniele wrote, mystified.

I think what Max means, Zara interjected, *is that we were all taken by surprise by your announcement. None of us had any idea it was coming.*

Of course. I hadn't told any of you.

DIDN'T YOU THINK YOU OWED US THAT FUCKING COURTESY AT LEAST? That was Max again.

Daniele was confused. *Why?*

If you're going to give Carnivia to anyone, Eric wrote, *did you consider even for one moment that it should have been to us?*

Daniele looked back and tried to recall. *No, I didn't.*

He's not literally asking whether you did or didn't give any thought to the question, Daniele, Zara explained. *He's saying that, in our opinion, you should have done.*

Because???

BECAUSE WE DO YOUR SHIT FOR YOU, THAT'S WHY, Max thundered.

Daniele, I'm not sure you realise just how much time being a Carnivia wizard takes up. Dealing with lost passwords. Resolving disputes. Remonstrating with trolls. Answering complaints—

There are complaints? He hadn't known.

Of course there are complaints, Eric snapped.

We also patch up holes in your coding, Max put in. *You probably didn't know that either, did you? Places where the great Daniele Barbo's code is beautiful but just a tiny bit impractical. Like the functionality that was allowing users to send anonymous text messages to other people's phones. A lovely, elegant piece of script. We disabled that after a teacher received rape threats from her entire class.*

If it was from the entire class, why didn't she just punish them all? Daniele wondered.

The point is, we clean up, Max said. *Sometimes we don't sleep for days. We've never asked for anything in return. But we always assumed that if Carnivia WERE to become commercial, we'd be given our due.*

It's not becoming commercial.

Oh, come on. Once it's owned by its users, how long before they cash in? Already stockpickers are telling investors to get themselves an account. It costs nothing and it might just net you a fortune when Google buys you out. We've gained half a million users since your announcement.

Then why don't YOU stand for election? Daniele wrote. *As an administrator, who better to run Carnivia than you? Then you could put safeguards in place to make sure it stays independent.*

So you'll endorse me? I've got the official backing of Daniele Barbo?

Daniele thought. *I'm sorry, Max. I just don't want to get involved in all that.*

Screw you.

I'm sorry you feel that way.

No, you're not. It's all right for you, sitting in your father's Venetian palace. Your lifestyle's pretty good, isn't it? Whereas I look out of the window, I see a trailer park.

I didn't realise you cared so much about money, Daniele wrote sadly. *I thought we all believed in the same things.*

Me too, Daniele Barbo. Me too.

Daniele logged off. He knew he'd do no work for the rest of the day now. His brain was too clouded – not just by the row with the wizards, but also by what the MIT professor had written. The man knew what he was talking about, and his frank assessment of Daniele's chances of solving P=NP had depressed him.

Not that Daniele had been underestimating the task. Some of the finest minds in the world, men whose achievements dwarfed anything he had ever accomplished, had spent years puzzling at the P=NP conundrum. Most had concluded it was impossible. But he found himself inexorably drawn to it, all the same.

It was also true, as the professor had written, that many mathematicians believed a world in which P equalled NP would be a world that had lost some of its wonder. It would be a world in which breakthroughs such as Einstein's $E=MC^2$ or Newton's law of gravitational force would be generated not by once-in-a-generation flashes of inspiration but by computers, patiently scanning the furthest corners of mathematical notation, crunching numbers and sieving the resultant torrent of integers like a probe trawling through deep space.

But in such a world, Daniele believed, he would have a place. He knew that other people saw him as strange: his disfigured face, the legacy of his kidnap as a child, when the kidnappers had cut off his ears and nose in order to pressure his parents into paying the ransom, would have been reason enough for that. What few realised was that he saw them as equally incomprehensible. Perhaps in a world where P=NP, a world without ambiguity, the anxiety he felt whenever he tried to fathom out others would finally disappear.

He sighed, and picked up a piece of paper that was lying next to the computer. It was a letter from his guardian, Ian

Gilroy, requesting that Daniele vacate Palazzo Barbo in order for essential repairs to be carried out. The masonry in the lowest storey, the part that was regularly flooded by Venice's rising tides, had been eroded further by a leaking septic tank. Daniele wasn't surprised: it stank of fetid sewage and crumbling stone down there. You could see the damp slowly creeping up the walls, and many of the stone pillars which supported the higher storeys were soft to the touch.

Following an engineer's assessment, the letter said, it had been decided that the only solution was to slice the whole palace open at the waterline, hydraulically raise it by several metres, and create new foundations. It would cost millions and take years. During that time, the *palazzo* would be uninhabitable.

If Daniele had sold Carnivia to the highest bidder, he could have paid for the repairs out of the small change. But he would still have had to move out while the work was done.

He let the letter drop to the floor. He intended to go on ignoring its contents for as long as possible.

NINE

THE BANCA CATTOLICA della Veneziana was housed in the magnificent surroundings of Palazzo Dolfin-Manin, just east of the Rialto bridge. If they were a relatively small bank, as their website had implied, it certainly wasn't apparent from the splendour of their surroundings. The vast entrance hall was decorated with extravagant eighteenth-century murals, and bust after bust of solemn Venetian nobles peered loftily down their noses from niches in the walls.

Kat showed her warrant to a startled receptionist and asked to be taken directly to Alessandro Cassandre's office.

"He's not in," the receptionist said. "He doesn't usually come in at this time of day. And it'll be locked—"

"Then call your security manager and open it," Kat said equably. She pointed at the four-man team of *carabinieri*, one armed with a door-ram, that she'd brought along to show she meant business. "Please ask him to hurry, though. Those old doors of yours look rather valuable, and I'd rather not break one down unless it's absolutely necessary. You've got five minutes."

Cassandre's office, when it was unlocked for her exactly four minutes and thirty seconds later, turned out to be as elegantly appointed as you might expect an office on the first floor of a *palazzo* overlooking the Grand Canal to be. More to the point, there was a laptop open on the ornate old *scrivania* that served as a desk. She touched it to see if it had been left on standby and discovered that was as far as her luck went: it had been properly shut down.

Amongst the framed photographs on the desk was one of Cassandre being presented with a medal by the previous Pope. She picked it up. A caption on the back read: *Presentation of the Cross of Honour Pro Ecclesia et Pontifice to Sig. Alessandro Cassandre, September 1997.* The picture had been placed further forward, and more centrally, than the photograph of the expensively dressed middle-aged woman who was presumably Cassandre's wife.

The warrant, she had been pleased to find, authorised her to take away "computer equipment" rather than just a laptop, thus legitimately allowing her to search Cassandre's office for anything fitting that description. In the first drawer of the desk she found eight identical memory sticks, which struck her as being unusual. There were more in an envelope, while another bag contained high-denomination chips from the Casino di Venezia. She put the memory sticks into an evidence bag but left the chips where she'd found them.

The next drawer contained two boxes of business cards. One gave the address of the bank and Cassandre's title of Senior Partner. The other set, which appeared to be newly printed, bore the words:

Alessandro Cassandre

3°

Grand Lodge of the Venetian Order De la Fidelité

Underneath was a symbol she vaguely recognised, a cross inside a circle, like a sniper's sights.

They looked like some kind of Masonic calling card: the first actual evidence she'd had that he really was a Mason. She slipped a few into the evidence bag as well.

"May I ask what you're looking for?"

She looked up. The security guard who'd unlocked Cassandre's door had gone off to locate a higher authority; the man hurrying towards her now, buttoning up his expensive suit as he did so, was presumably the result. Without stopping what she was doing, she said calmly, "Carrying out a search to locate and remove Signor Cassandre's computer equipment."

"I'm Hugo Speicher, the bank's chairman. Do you need any help?"

Surprisingly, he didn't get angry or bluster at her, as many people might have done on finding a senior partner's office being searched by the Carabinieri. But then, she reflected, the bank's chairman was presumably no fool. He'd know there was little point in arguing with a warrant. Better to give the appearance of cooperation and hope to find out what she was after that way.

"When did you last see Signor Cassandre?" she asked, opening the next drawer and methodically going through its contents.

"Three nights ago, just before our last board meeting. Why? Is he in trouble?"

"A body answering his description was found this morning at the Lido," she said, looking up to catch Speicher's reaction.

"My God." His shock certainly seemed genuine. "And you think his death was connected to the bank?"

"It's too early to say. But tell me, what exactly was the nature of Signor Cassandre's work here?"

"Well, he was…" Speicher frowned. "It's quite hard to explain to a layman, actually. Essentially, he dealt with sophisticated financial instruments for off-setting risk. Along with tax planning for high-net-worth individuals, charitable institutions and so on. But he was on the brink of retirement. Most of his day-to-day work had long since been taken over by younger staff."

"How old was he?" Kat asked, surprised. The man on the mortuary table hadn't looked much over fifty.

"Fifty-four, I believe. But he had other interests besides banking." Was it her imagination, or did she detect the faintest hint of distaste in the chairman's tone?

"Your receptionist seemed to know his daily routine quite well," she pointed out.

"She's got a very good memory," Speicher said blandly. "I wouldn't read too much into that, if I were you."

She recalled the name Dr Hapadi had given her as a possible member of the black Masonic lodge, and decided to do some fishing. "Did Signor Cassandre still deal with Count Tignelli's accounts?"

Speicher hesitated. "Unless your warrant specifically covers it, we can't confirm any details of Signor Cassandre's clients."

She noted that he hadn't denied it. "I quite understand."

Back at Campo San Zaccaria, she took the bagged laptop and the memory sticks to Giuseppe Malli, the Carabinieri IT technician. Long ago, when the Carabinieri headquarters was a convent, this attic had been the novices' dormitory. There was even a faded fresco depicting the Annunciation along one wall. Now the room was a mess of computer equipment. Leads and connectors dangled from pegs that had once held coifs and scapulars, while shelves built for vestments contained a jumble of hard drives.

"In theory, we're looking for anyone who might have had a reason to murder the man who owned these," she told him. "In practice, I want to find out everything about him that I can. His chairman just did a very slick job of distancing his bank from whatever it was he did for them, and I'd like to know why."

"Any idea where I should start?"

"Apparently he worked for both charitable trusts and high-net-worth individuals in need of advice on tax planning, which strikes me as an odd combination."

He considered. "Well, I'm no expert, but that sounds like money laundering to me."

"What makes you say that?"

"Charities collect donations in cash. That's the first stage in cleaning dirty money – having a legitimate explanation for where it came from."

"Could money laundering also involve casinos?" she asked, remembering the chips.

He nodded. "You take the cash to a casino, you buy some chips, then after a few bets you go back to the cashier to redeem them. But this time you ask for an electronic transfer instead of cash. It'll look to anyone following the money trail as if you won it at the tables."

"And the memory sticks?"

"Let's take a look." He took one of the USB sticks and

plugged it into a reader attached to his computer. "I'm just making an optical image, so I don't actually disturb the contents," he explained. "Ah—"

"What is it?" She watched his fingers fly over the keys.

He turned the screen towards her. It contained a row of numbers. "It's money. Electronic money. Easy to transfer, impossible to trace."

"How much?"

His fingers tapped again. "The exchange rate for bitcoins is pretty volatile at the moment. But at today's rates, there's the equivalent of about a quarter of a million euros on this stick alone."

Bagnasco, meanwhile, had brought back printouts from the cruise ships' radar logs and started to identify the boats entering or leaving Venice. The logs showed one boat with no LOCODE: either its transmitter was broken, it was too small to require one, or it had deliberately turned off its equipment in order to avoid identification.

Two separate records, twelve minutes apart, showed it moving from south to north along the Adriatic shore of the Lido shortly after 3 a.m. Another, thirty minutes earlier, showed what looked like the same boat *inside* the lagoon, heading south towards the Bocca di Malamocco, the more southerly of the two openings into the Adriatic.

In other words, Kat thought, it had set off somewhere south of Venice but north of Malamocco.

She looked again at the map. There were around half a dozen small islands in that area. Most were long since abandoned, the sites of former military garrisons, plague hospitals and leper colonies. One of the very few that was inhabited was La Grazia, the island owned by Count Birino Tignelli.

It wasn't enough for a search warrant, not by a long chalk. But at least it meant she now had a legitimate reason for calling on Count Tignelli and asking if he'd seen anything.

But not today. Today she needed to set up the operations room, assemble a larger team of *carabinieri* and put out requests to other crime agencies for information. She also needed to arrange for Cassandre's wife to identify the body at the mortuary. Unlike some officers, Kat had no problem with doing that; in fact, she found it strangely satisfying that even in the midst of such raw emotion she could stay detached and professional. It was one of the things that made her believe she was in the right job, but it nevertheless required some thought on how best to approach it.

In this instance, she concluded, the person she was trying to put pressure on wasn't just the wife but the forensic examiner too. She had a suspicion that at some point she might well need more information from Dr Hapadi about his Masonic brethren.

"Can I ask something?" Bagnasco said as they grabbed a couple of tuna *tramezzini* at the bar round the corner. Without waiting for a reply, she continued, "Do you have any feedback for me?"

"Feedback?" Kat said, surprised.

"I know I've made some mistakes," Bagnasco said. "I really want to improve, and I think continuous assessment is the way to do it. Plus I'm really pleased that I'm being mentored by a woman. I'm very ambitious, and I think the prosecutor's right: I could learn a lot from you as a role model – how to get ahead in the Carabinieri as a female officer, I mean."

Kat waved the suggestion away. "You're doing fine. Don't worry about it." She never knew what to say when people described themselves as ambitious. You got promoted because you were good, not because you announced to everyone that you wanted it.

"But on a score of one to five?" Bagnasco persisted. "It's good to have a number. That way I'll be able to keep track of whether I'm improving or not."

Kat sighed. "Look, let's get one thing clear. You work for me, not the other way round, and the job we're both trying to do involves finding out who stabbed a man through the heart, cut his throat open and ripped out his tongue. If you're doing something wrong, I'll tell you. But I haven't got the time or the energy to review your performance on a day-by-day basis. And the fact that we're both women is pretty irrelevant to me, frankly." Although a male assistant, she thought wistfully, would surely have been a lot less needy than Bagnasco was proving to be. Or did all the younger officers spout management-speak like this? The idea made her feel old and cynical.

She thought back to something Hapadi had said earlier. "Don't be too hard on her," he'd said quietly, when Bagnasco was out of earshot. "She wouldn't be the first officer to vomit at a crime scene." And he'd given her a pointed look. Somehow, she realised, he must know about the time when she herself had done exactly that. It had been an equally gruesome murder: a fisherman, killed and tipped into a concrete holding tank for his own crabs to feast on. On that occasion, Aldo Piola had sluiced the vomit away before the forensic examiner got there. He must have mentioned it to Hapadi later.

Even Flavio had said something similar about Bagnasco, just as Kat was leaving his office. "Go easy on her, won't you?" he suggested. "It'll be tough on her, being your number two."

65

"Why? Am I such a monster?" she'd demanded. He'd only laughed.

She glanced at the second lieutenant, who was now looking somewhat crestfallen. "Look, I didn't mean to sound harsh. But I've made far too many mistakes to be a role model for anyone. The best advice I can give you is to concentrate on doing your job. Oh, and not to sleep with any senior officers."

"Like you did with Colonel Piola, you mean?"

So people were still talking about that. "Like I did with Colonel Piola, yes."

"Is it true he left his wife for you?" Bagnasco asked curiously. "And that you sent him back to her, because you weren't interested any more?"

Kat was fairly sure a male officer would never have asked such a personal question, but she swallowed her irritation and said mildly, "I believe the colonel and his wife have separated and are currently going through a divorce. It's not something he and I ever discuss. These days we keep our relationship strictly professional."

"Isn't that difficult? Given that you still work together quite closely?"

"No," she snapped. "It's actually a lot easier than gossiping like a couple of old women." She pulled out a ten-euro note and threw it on the counter. "Come on. We've got work to do."

TEN

THANKFULLY, BAGNASCO PROVED more adept at filling in Budget Requisitions, Overtime Projections, Evidence Collection Protocols and all the other forms needed to make the Carabinieri's labyrinthine bureaucracy creak into action than she was at inspecting crime scenes or interviewing witnesses. Kat left her to it, and went to break the news of Cassandre's death to his wife.

Signora Cassandre turned out to be a more elegant woman than the photograph on her husband's desk had suggested, impeccably dressed and well mannered even in the midst of shock. At one point she clutched Kat's arm and asked what would happen to her apartment. It was a curious thing to mention at such a time, so Kat asked what she was concerned about.

"The mortgages," Signora Cassandre whispered anxiously. "I had to sign them. But he said it was only for a short time."

Kat made a mental note to have an officer go through Cassandre's personal bank accounts. If he *was* money laundering, where had the proceeds gone? His lifestyle, she surmised from the elegance of his apartment, along with its location in one of the most fashionable parts of San Marco, was lavish, but hardly more so than one would expect of a senior partner in a Venetian bank. And then there had been all that money on the memory sticks. If that wasn't Cassandre's, whose was it? A client's?

She escorted Signora Cassandre to the morgue for the formal identification. Hapadi had placed wooden blocks under the victim's head and a folded cloth over the gaping wound in the neck. Even so, the removal of the tongue had caused the cheeks and mouth to swell and twist grotesquely. Signora Cassandre took a careful look before confirming in a steady voice that it was her husband. One should never underestimate, Kat reflected, the sang-froid of old money. Hapadi, by way of contrast, looked deeply uncomfortable.

Back at Campo San Zaccaria, she checked over what Bagnasco had done and had to grudgingly admit to being impressed. She did spot one glaring mistake, however.

"I asked for five officers and twenty *carabinieri*. That's standard for a homicide. You've listed three officers and eight *carabinieri*."

Bagnasco nodded. "Allocation are saying that's all that's available."

Kat went straight to General Saito. "As you said yourself, this is clearly going to be a big and complex investigation," she reminded him. "We'll probably need to bring in financial experts from the Guardia di Finanza. And because of the Masonic angle, people may be reluctant to talk to us – we'll need more resources than usual, not fewer."

Saito held up a hand to forestall her. "It's August, Captain. In case you hadn't noticed, everyone's away. But when you mention Freemasons... Let me caution you against jumping to conclusions. There's no direct evidence yet that Freemasonry had a bearing on your victim's death, as I understand it."

"You're probably not aware of the latest developments,

sir." She filled him in on the calling cards they'd found at Cassandre's office and the USB stick full of electronic money. "My working hypothesis is that he was involved in financial crimes, in the course of which he may have swindled or otherwise betrayed some of his fellow Freemasons. That's why they killed him in a way that reflected the wording of their oath."

"Was he wearing a watch when he was found?"

"No," she said, puzzled by this sudden change of tack.

"So a far more obvious hypothesis, Captain, is that he went for a late-night swim and was mugged," Saito said blandly.

"Whilst dressed for a Masonic ritual?" she said incredulously.

He shrugged. "It's your first solo investigation. All I'm saying is, be careful not to get carried away."

"Of course, sir," she said. "Am I right in thinking that you yourself are a Freemason?"

His expression gave nothing away. "How is that relevant?"

"Only that in circumstances such as these we have to be seen to be completely objective. There may be people who will imagine that we might try and steer the investigation away from Freemasonry, in order to deflect attention from the number of *carabinieri* who are Masons." She kept her tone as neutral as his had been.

"Only if we draw their attention to the issue in the first place. Which is precisely my point, Captain. Putting a more... *melodramatic* interpretation on events than is strictly warranted by the evidence might be counterproductive. It might even be seen as an attempt on the part of an inexperienced officer to sensationalise the case and thereby draw attention to himself. Or, indeed, herself. Do I make myself clear?"

"Thank you for the warning, sir. I'll bear it in mind."

Softening his tone, he said, "Look… running an investigation like this effectively gives you the rank of acting major. Get it right, and promotion will surely follow. But you have to understand what getting it right means, in this context."

"Identifying the killer and getting a conviction," she said. "Obviously."

"We always aim to do that, Captain. But there is another, equally important aspect to this case." He raised his eyebrows. "I'm talking about maintaining public confidence in the Carabinieri. A diligent and carefully managed investigation, one that's proportionate to all the circumstances, is what's required here."

She went downstairs still seething. Saito was as good as telling her to keep a low profile on this one, dangling the prospect of a promotion if she obliged. But at the same time, he was covering his arse by appointing an investigating officer who demonstrably wasn't a Freemason. If Cassandre's killers had hoped to create a climate of fear around his murder, they had certainly succeeded.

Bagnasco was waiting for her, looking anxious.

"What is it?" Kat said.

"Have you been to the female officers' locker room recently?"

Kat sighed. "No, and I really can't be bothered to right now. What is it this time? Someone's decided to tell us that we're lesbians? Or that we're whores? Or that we're lesbian whores?" Ever since she'd joined the Carabinieri, her locker had regularly been defaced with graffiti, none of it very imaginative. She added, "You wanted career advice earlier, so here's some: lighter fluid gets rid of it just fine."

"I know," Bagnasco said impatiently. "I've had plenty of stuff like that, and usually I ignore it. But I think you should see this one."

Kat followed her to the changing room. There, sprayed across her locker, was a cross inside a circle – the same symbol that had been on Alessandro Cassandre's Masonic calling cards.

"What does it mean?" Bagnasco asked.

"It's a warning," Kat said at last. "A warning that they're watching us. And that's fine. Because now we're also watching them."

Her final interview of the day was with the archivist whose name Dr Hapadi had given her. It turned out that he worked in a library attached to the hospital complex, just a few hundred yards from the morgue. She trudged up a narrow stone staircase to the first floor. There she found a long, well-lit room under a magnificent gilded ceiling. It was unexpected, but she had learnt over the years that Venice was full of such tucked-away treasures, too many to be listed by the guidebooks and consequently all but forgotten.

A figure was bent over one of the display cases. "Signor Calergi?" she called.

The figure turned, and she got her second surprise: he was wearing a dog collar. "Monsignor, actually. And you must be Captain Tapo – Dr Hapadi told me you might be coming. You want to know about Freemasonry, I understand?"

"That's it," she said, wondering what else Hapadi had told the cleric. "We have a corpse who's had his throat cut and his tongue torn out. He was left on the beach, to be washed by the tides... That relates to a Masonic oath, I understand?"

"Some Masonic rites make reference to such a scenario,

yes," he said quietly. "I've never heard of it being enacted before."

"Our victim was also wearing an unusual mask. Dr Hapadi called it a 'hoodwink'. And he had some rope wound around his arm."

Monsignor Calergi nodded. "These are symbols connected with a Mason's initiation into a new degree – that is, a higher level of the organisation. The hoodwink represents the mystical darkness, or ignorance, of the uninitiated.

"And the rope?"

"The cable-tow symbolises the secret obligations that bind one Mason to another. Masons believe their first duty is always to help a brother, no matter what."

"Forgive me for asking, Father. But are you yourself a Freemason?"

"I have an academic interest in the Craft," Calergi said with a slight smile. "But the Vatican's position is that one cannot be both a Mason and a practising Catholic."

"Why not?"

"To understand that, you have to know a little about Freemasonry's origins. Back in the thirteenth century, Venice was dominated by a number of powerful guilds and cofraternities. It was one such organisation, in fact, the Scuola Grande di San Marco, which built this very hospital. At that time, the Freemasons were little more than a trade guild for the itinerant stonecarvers who travelled from country to country building Europe's cathedrals. Their symbols – the set square, the keystone, the plumb line – depicted the secrets of their craft, mysteries they were careful to keep from outsiders.

"Then, in the eighteenth century, the first men of science found in the almost-forgotten secrets of the stonemasons a kind of allegory for their own rationalist beliefs. To them, the masons' craft represented everything the Church was not – a brotherhood of equals, where man listened to his fellow man instead of the dictates of an autocratic pontiff; progress and reason, instead of medieval superstition and conservatism; mutual prosperity and self-help, instead of sacrifice and charity. In their rituals, Masons replaced the Bible with the Volume of Sacred Law. Their oaths were dedicated to the Grand Architect of the Universe. They weren't denying God, not explicitly; but they were open to the heresy that the divine wears many masks, of which the Catholic deity is but one."

"And from rejecting the authority of the Church to questioning the authority of the state wasn't such a great leap either, I imagine?"

"Exactly," he agreed. "It was a group of Masons, for example, who were responsible for betraying Venice to their fellow Freemason, Napoleon Bonaparte, without a single shot being fired. A century later, an offshoot of the movement, the Carbonari, was accused of trying to overthrow the government and seize power for themselves. In many ways, the Masons were a white-collar version of the Mafia, and followed a similar trajectory. What began as a network of self-help organisations that depended on secrecy for their survival gradually became a magnet for criminality. In our own century that has been particularly true, of course, with so-called black lodges like P2."

"P2. That was Propaganda Due, wasn't it?" She recalled Piola telling her a little about the P2 scandal, but was interested to hear the archivist's view.

He nodded. "A black lodge that existed from about 1960 to 1980. Over two hundred government officials, military leaders, journalists and businessmen were listed as members. The Grand Master fled abroad and was charged *in absentia* with conspiracy against the state. But the truth is, no one really knows what P2's purpose or political agenda was, even today."

"Do you have any knowledge of a black lodge like that operating here in Venice?"

Father Calergi's expression gave nothing away. "Such a thing is always possible. But if so, it has no contact with any of the lodges I know of."

She took out one of the cards she'd found in Cassandre's desk. "Does this look like the card of an official lodge to you?"

Father Calergi examined the card, visibly surprised, then shook his head. "'De la Fidelité' was the name of an ancient Venetian lodge, long since vanished. They must have resurrected the name to lend themselves an air of authenticity. 'Third Degree' is a reference to Cassandre's status – it means he was a fully fledged master Mason, a member of the innermost circle. Cards like these were once an important part of a Mason's paraphernalia – when visiting another lodge, he would hand one to the Tyler, the official guarding the door, to prove his bona fides. But this symbol isn't Masonic, or not specifically."

"I have a feeling I've seen it before. But I can't recall where."

"A few years back it was banned – it had been appropriated by some unpleasant far-right thugs for their own purposes. It's sometimes referred to as 'Odin's Cross'. But long before that, it was known as the *carità*, and it was the symbol of the oldest of Venice's *scuole grandi*. You can still see it today, carved into the side of the Accademia, which occupies their former headquarters."

"Why would a present-day lodge adopt an ancient Venetian symbol as their emblem?"

Father Calergi looked troubled. "I don't know. But given

that the symbol has political associations now, it's surely worrying."

Once again she thought she caught a flash of fear in the archivist's eyes as he turned back to his books and cabinets. And once again she was left with a sense that the person she was speaking to wasn't telling her everything. The message that had been left on the sands of the Lido had done its work too well for that.

ELEVEN

"GATE OPENS IN approximately twenty minutes," the check-in clerk said, sliding Holly's boarding pass and passport across the counter. "Have a great flight to Italy, Second Lieutenant."

Holly nodded her thanks. The last time she'd made this journey in uniform, the clerk at JFK had added a fulsome thank you "for the amazing job you guys do to keep America safe". That had been during the so-called Surge, when people were feeling more optimistic about the war on terror. Since the long, slow withdrawal from Afghanistan – a defeat only loosely masquerading as a victory – ordinary civilians hadn't been quite so supportive. Or perhaps it was the revelations of whistleblowers like Bradley Manning and Edward Snowden that had eaten away at their certainties.

On the other hand, serving military still got to use Delta's First Class lounge free of charge. She found herself a space among the businessmen tapping at their laptops and pulled out her father's memorandum again. She'd read the three double-spaced pages more than a dozen times now, googling every reference. It was hard going in places: her father had been writing for an audience familiar with the shadowy code-names, military acronyms and long-dismantled committees that he referred to. It was also clear that Andreotti's announcement to the Italian parliament about the existence of the

Gladio network had taken NATO's military intelligence by surprise: her father described a state of near panic as they scrambled to roll up the organisation before the Italian media got to it. But it was another section in the memorandum that she kept coming back to.

It was Gianluca Boccardo, a neighbour of mine and brother Mason, who first spoke to me about an influx of new members at our lodge. He asked whether I, as an American officer, could tell him if there was any truth in what some of them were claiming: that they were members of a paramilitary network dedicated to saving Italy from the left, and that following their betrayal by Prime Minister Andreotti they had been ordered to regroup in this manner and await further instructions.

I knew Signor Boccardo to be a reliable man, not inclined to jump at shadows, so made it my business to ascertain whether what he had told me was true. The new members, in turn, immediately recognised me as one of those who had been involved in Gladio and – to my consternation – began to speak openly with me about what they called "the crypsis".

"Crypsis", she knew, was a term used in the intelligence world for anything that concealed a person from detection, from a sniper's camouflage jacket to a field agent's cover story.

This plan, they said, had been suggested at the very highest level, quite possibly by "Caesar" himself. I formed the impression that this was an informal

nickname rather than a NATO codeword, since that
name had never cropped up in any of the reports
that passed across my own desk.

Without exception these men had nothing but scorn
for the NATO command, which was, they said,
abandoning them now that NATO's own objectives
had been achieved, whilst leaving Italy itself in a
state of political chaos, ineffectual government, and
deeply entrenched corruption.

"Delta Airlines Flight 169 to Venice," a metallic voice high in the roof girders interrupted. "Please proceed to Gate 18." Holly blinked. She'd been staring at her father's words for over thirty minutes.

He'd taken the rudimentary precaution of making a copy of his report. It struck her that she should do the same. She went over to the desk. "Do you have a photocopier here? And envelopes?"

"Of course." The attendant pointed towards a business centre to one side of the lounge.

Going to the machine, she made two copies. Then she noticed something. The machine was a modern one that offered a range of options, from printing documents to sharing them on Facebook.

She pressed the menu on the touch screen, and from the options selected "Email".

TWELVE

THE NEXT DAY, too, dawned bright and hot. Even at 8 a.m. Kat could feel the sun's heat searing her face, and once again she was grateful to be escaping the humidity and stink of Venice for a few hours. She thought of one of her favourite Venetian sayings: *D'istà, anca i stronsi gaégia,* 'In summer, even the turds float.' It was used to describe the way a mediocre person could shine when surrounded by other mediocrities, but it also contained a literal truth about her native city: at this time of year, every canal and *rio* gave off a faint whiff of warm sewage.

With no excuse to turn on the blue light, she piloted the Carabinieri motorboat a little more sedately today. But it was also because she was in a reflective mood. Freemasons, Catholic banks, money laundering... and, if Father Calergi was right, politics as well. In Italy it seemed there were always these shadowy forces at work, the tentacles of corruption reaching so deep into ordinary life that they became almost invisible; until, that is, the tentacles gave a slight squeeze, and ordinary life was shattered. Small wonder that most people didn't try to fight those forces when they came across them, but simply turned a blind eye, or stuck their own hand out for a share of the action. But exactly who was being corrupted here? And who or what, besides the unfortunate Cassandre, was its true target?

It took twenty minutes to reach La Grazia, the island that Count Tignelli had bought. As she approached, she could see that it contained pretty woods of tamarisk and pine as well as vineyards and a formal walled garden. All were immaculate. There was a newly built granite sea wall to protect against flooding, and the jetty was of new oak, lined with brass rails. Clearly, money had been no object. Beyond a long, sloping lawn stood the former convent after which the island was named. Once little more than a ruin, it had been heavily rebuilt by its new owner. Its Gothic marble-framed windows were turned towards the city across the water, a Venetian palace in all but name.

She tied up to a huge brass ring set into the mouth of a carved lion, one of several positioned along the jetty. Next to her, a sleek eighty-foot yacht, a rich man's plaything, made the Carabinieri boat look as tiny as a dinghy. Beyond it was a smart private launch, the kind of thing a luxury hotel might use to ferry guests around. Unless you were a Venetian, and knew the subtle differences, you might well have mistaken it for a water taxi.

As she stepped onto land, a stocky man in a dark blazer, crisp white shirt and dark tie appeared from between the trees. A curly wire ran from his collar to his ear.

"May I help you?" he asked politely.

"I've come to speak to Count Tignelli," she replied, equally polite. She'd worn her Carabinieri uniform for this trip. Although homicide investigators usually wore plain clothes, she'd decided it would do no harm to keep things more formal.

"May I ask what it concerns?"

"A murder investigation."

The man's expression didn't change. "Please wait here."

Within minutes he was back. "The count apologises that he's too busy to come to the house. But he would be pleased to speak with you at the *peschiera*. Please follow my colleague."

He beckoned to a second, equally muscular bodyguard, who accompanied her down an immaculate path. There were water sprinklers everywhere, even on the helipad she glimpsed through the trees, and all around a small army of gardeners were trimming, weeding and cutting. One was carefully clipping the grass around a statue of an athlete holding a golden rod. The face seemed somehow familiar.

"The Emperor Napoleon," the bodyguard said, seeing her looking at it. "He rejected that particular statue because the sculptor had tried to be too flattering. After Napoleon's defeat at Waterloo, the Duke of Wellington had it displayed at his residence in London, as a reminder of the greatest opponent he ever faced in battle. Count Tignelli acquired it five years ago for his collection." The man recited all this as if he had said it many times before, an anecdote to entertain guests.

She recalled the archivist mentioning that Napoleon had a connection with Freemasonry. "What collection is that?" she asked.

"Count Tignelli has one of the most extensive collections of Napoleonic memorabilia in private hands." The bodyguard nodded. "Please go ahead."

By the edge of a large stone-walled basin that jutted into the lagoon, two figures were engaged in animated conversation. The taller of the two looked like a workman. The shorter man was giving him orders, gesturing at the basin with quick, sweeping gestures. He was about fifty, quite stocky, his thinning hair brushed forward over his temples. As he turned, Kat saw that he was actually even smaller than he'd first appeared, his riding boots – which were presumably only for show, here in the middle of the lagoon – built up to give him a few extra inches. She wondered if that was why he had a flattering statue of the famously short Napoleon.

"What do you want, Captain?" Count Tignelli's greeting as he turned towards her was as abrupt as the bodyguard's had been polite.

She decided to be equally blunt. "I'm investigating a murder that took place two nights ago. The body of a man named Alessandro Cassandre was discovered yesterday morning on the Lido."

"And why do you think I can help you?"

"First, because the body was almost certainly moved by boat from a location not far from here. I'm wondering whether you or any of your staff saw anything."

"And secondly?" he said, without bothering to answer her first question.

"Secondly, because the death appears to be connected with Freemasonry. I understand that's an interest of yours?"

Count Tignelli shrugged. "I collect artefacts relating to the liberator of Venice, Napoleon Bonaparte. He happened to be a supporter of Freemasonry. So yes, you could say that I have a passing interest."

"The liberator of Venice!" she repeated. To a Venetian, that was not unlike calling Hitler the liberator of Poland. Even today, Napoleon's legacy was still so controversial that when the city museum obtained a statue of him, it had been subjected to a mock trial before it was put on show.

Tignelli nodded; a curt, almost military inclination of the head. "At the time of Napoleon's arrival, Venice was mired in decadence and corruption. Just as it is today, although for very different reasons. As a Carabinieri officer, you will surely agree with that. But that's as far as my interest extends."

"So you don't know Signor Cassandre?" she persisted.

The count made a dismissive gesture. "I meet many people. I really couldn't tell you whether any of them share that surname."

"Do you have an account with Banca Cattolica della Veneziana?"

He looked thoughtful, as if the connection had only just occurred to him. "Oh, of course. There's a Signor Cassandre there I've had some dealings with."

"That's who's been killed," she said, watching him closely.

His expression didn't change. "How terrible. I must tell my assistant to send flowers to his family."

"You know them socially?"

"I really can't recall. Zuane!" he called. "How are you doing?"

"Almost done," the workman said in a thick Buranese accent.

"This may interest you, Captain, as a fellow Venetian," Tignelli said, nodding at the basins. "I've been restoring this fish farm to its original condition – a not insubstantial project, given that each basin is lined with over two thousand ancient bricks. Our investigations show that they survived intact for over eight centuries, only to fall victim to damage from cruise ships in the last three decades. I've had to replace over half of them."

The man he'd addressed as Zuane was opening a sluice gate. A torrent of silver poured into the basin – water, catching the morning sunlight, but in the water, she saw, another kind of silver as well: eels, hundreds of them, released from a holding tank.

"When this was a convent, the nuns would have eaten eel every week," Tignelli said conversationally. "But the farm actually dates back to Roman times. Did you know, Capitano, that wealthy Romans used to make pets of their favourite eels? They'd decorate them with jewellery, pit them against each other in fights, and feed them on unlucky slaves to increase their ferocity. *Bisati* were one of the things Napoleon liked best about Venice, incidentally. He took the recipe for eel stew back to France, and insisted that his cooks learn how to prepare it the Italian way."

He called an instruction to Zuane, who reached into the cascade of silver and deftly tossed two eels onto the bank, where they lay for a moment, stunned. Pulling a tattered plastic carrier bag from his pocket, the workman quickly wrapped it over his hand like a glove, grabbed the eels, then turned the bag inside out to trap them.

"For you, Captain Tapo," Tignelli said, waving Zuane forward. "A small recompense for your wasted journey. So that you can cook *bisato in umido*, and toast the Emperor. But be careful to tie a knot in that bag. They're slippery little creatures."

"Thank you," she said, accepting the bag from Zuane. "Though personally I prefer my eel cooked *su l'ara*, with bay leaves. As for not letting it escape, you don't have to tell a Venetian how to deal with an eel, however slippery."

And as for how Tignelli had known her name, she reflected, when she hadn't actually told him; or that she was a native Venetian; or why he'd been so unbothered by her questions, almost as if he'd known in advance she was coming – that, perhaps, was an even slipperier mystery.

THIRTEEN

HOLLY CAME OUT of the Customs Hall at Venice airport and turned right, towards the car-rental booths. The very last booth, discreetly tucked into a corner, bore a small sign: "Welcome, Vicenza Community".

The first time she'd made this trip, the sign had said "SETAF Personnel Report Here". But even the vague-sounding acronym of the Southern European Task Force was now deemed insufficiently bland for her employers' purposes.

The desk was no longer manned, either. She followed the instructions taped to the wall and picked up the desk phone. When it was answered, she gave her name and ID number. "You just missed a shuttle, Second Lieutenant," a voice on the other end said. "There'll be an hour's wait."

At the coffee shop, she bought herself a *macchiato* and a copy of *Il Giornale*. America was on the front page again. Ever since Edward Snowden had revealed that the US was intercepting data from its biggest internet companies and using it to spy on the rest of the world – an intrusion that, if it had been directed at its own citizens, would have been in breach of the US Constitution – Europe had been smarting. To add insult to injury, as far as the Italian government was concerned, several of the "splitters" were actually located on Italian soil. Three of the internet's busiest underwater cables – SeaMeWe3,

SeaMeWe-4 and Flag Europe-Asia – made landfall in Sicily, where there just happened to be a cluster of US signals instal- lations. Over two billion intercepts, the newspaper said, had been forwarded to an Anglo-American facility on Cyprus for analysis.

"Excuse me?" a voice said.

She looked up. The man sitting next to her at the counter gestured at her uniform. "I can't help noticing how many American soldiers there are round here." His accent was British. A tourist, from the look of his wheeled hand luggage, en route for a weekend in Venice.

"There's a few of us, sure," she said neutrally.

"How many, if you don't mind my asking?"

"Here in the Veneto? Around five thousand. Ten thousand, if you count the families."

He looked amazed. "Why so many?"

"Not so long ago, the Iron Curtain was just over there." She nodded east, towards the lagoon. "If the Russians decided to invade, someone had to stop them."

"OK. But the Cold War ended twenty years ago. How come you're still here?"

She opened her mouth to reply, then closed it again. How come indeed? Answers flitted into her head, but they weren't ones she could speak out loud. *Because we decided our foreign policies have to be imposed on the rest of the world through force. Because we exchanged the enemy beyond the Urals for the enemy beyond the Bosporus, with barely a beat in between. Because somewhere along the way, we stopped being the opti- mistic, youthful superpower of old and turned into the weary, paranoid giant we are today.*

"There's always bad guys somewhere," she said lamely. "I guess it saves on gas if we're already in the region."

A woman came out of the baggage hall, putting away her iPhone. "All done," she told the man. "Shall we go?"

As they left, he said to Holly politely, "Nice talking to you."

When they'd gone she exhaled thoughtfully. It struck her that, for the first time in her life, her automatic response hadn't been to spring to the defence of her country.

She was a soldier. More than that, she was an army brat. Growing up around Camp Darby, loyalty had never been a conscious decision so much as part of the air she breathed.

And yet it could only have been someone within the military who had decided to silence her father.

The more she thought about it – and on the plane she'd thought about little else – the more certain she'd become. Only an insider would have had access to his medical records. And only an insider would have had sight of that memorandum.

So her start point had to be whoever he'd given the memorandum to.

I have therefore passed the memorandum to a US intelligence officer of my acquaintance who, I knew, had previously been involved in the neutralisation of terrorist organisations such as the Red Brigades, in the hope that he will be able to distribute it to those best placed to take action.

She sat bolt upright. Pulling out her phone, she made a call. It went straight through to voicemail.

"Daniele, it's Holly," she said. "I need to speak to you. Call me back, will you?" Just to be sure, she sent a text as well.

She waited twenty minutes to see if he'd reply. Then she

dialled another number. This time it was answered immedi-ately.

"Holly," an American voice said warmly, before switching to Italian. "*Come stai? Così sei tornata in Italia?*"

"Fine," she said hesitantly. "I just got back. Look, could we meet?"

A few kilometres away, in the music room of Ca' Barbo, Daniele looked at his phone as it displayed, first, Holly's caller ID, then the voicemail alert, and finally the text.

Holly Boland.

Holly Boland voicemail.

Holly Boland message.

Glancing at the To-Do list still taped on the wall, his eye rested on the second item.

Finish with Holly.

He had slept with the wiry blonde American just once, but the experience had disturbed his dreams for weeks. Sometimes he found himself entertaining crazy fantasies of domesticity, in which they lived together like any other ordinary couple. Then he would catch sight of his face in a mirror – the horri-bly truncated nose, flat-tipped like a pig's, the white rose buds of scar tissue where his ears had once been: the twin legacies of his childhood kidnap – and he loathed himself. Not for what he looked like, but for his weakness in not accepting that cosy domesticity would never be his lot. Whatever Holly's motives for going to bed with him – and in his bleaker moments he believed she had been pushed into it by his guard-ian – he knew it hadn't meant the same to her as it had to him.

Reaching for a pencil, he crossed the second item off. Then, abruptly, he pushed back his chair and stood up.

FOURTEEN

KAT CALLED FLAVIO from the boat on her way back from La Grazia. "I may not have any leads, but I have got some eels. Can you come round tonight?"

There was a long silence at the other end.

"Or we could meet at a hotel," she added, mentally kicking herself for her stupidity. As part of his security arrangements, Flavio wasn't meant to spend more than one night a week in the same place, and he'd last been to her apartment just a few nights ago.

A couple of times recently he'd tried to warn her that she shouldn't get too involved, that his life wasn't one that anyone could share, but she didn't care about that. If snatched encounters in hotel rooms or his office was the price of a relationship with him, it was one she was willing to pay.

But as it turned out, that wasn't why he was hesitating.

"Captain, I think you should come and see me straight away," he said formally. "There's been an important development."

By which she took him to mean, first, that he wasn't alone, and second, that the investigation was about to get even murkier. Had Tignelli been stirring up trouble already?

She turned the Carabinieri boat hard to port, towards Santa Croce and the Palace of Justice.

As well as Flavio, there were two other men in his office. One was Benito Marcello, a prosecutor she'd worked with before. He was young, bright, impeccably dressed and, she knew, utterly craven, especially when it came to making any decision that wouldn't directly further his own career. The other was a short, grey-haired man she didn't know.

"This is Colonel Grimaldo," Flavio said, introducing him. "Prosecutor Marcello you've already met. We thought it best to inform you straight away."

"Of what?"

It was Grimaldo who answered. "Responsibility for the investigation you are currently working on is being transferred to AISI."

"To the Intelligence Service!" she said, astounded. "Why?"

"It impacts on a parallel operation by the anti-terrorist division. That's all I can say."

Marcello tapped his pen self-importantly on the desk to gain her attention. "You will hand over any evidence you have gathered so far to Colonel Grimaldo and his team. That includes records, forensic reports, and physical evidence such as Signor Cassandre's laptop. His body has already been moved to the hospital in Milan, where Grimaldo's team will conduct the autopsy. General Saito has been informed."

"An anti-terrorist operation?" she repeated slowly. "I don't understand. All the information we have so far suggests that Cassandre was involved in financial crimes."

"Then perhaps," Marcello said smoothly, "the secret services have done their job, Captain, and managed to keep their involvement, and by extension the operation, *secret*."

She got the implication. "So he was an informant?"

Colonel Grimaldo gave Marcello an annoyed glance. "*All* details of our involvement with Signor Cassandre remain subject to operational secrecy. Although I'd be interested to know, Captain, what makes you reach the conclusion that he was engaged in criminal activity."

"We recovered a large amount of money in electronic form from his office. We also found a number of high-denomination casino chips."

"Well, we will follow the leads you've developed to the very best of our ability," Grimaldo said. "My thanks for all your efforts." He stood up and addressed Marcello. "Avvocato, can we speak in your office?"

When they were alone, she turned to Flavio. "Terrorism? *Really?*"

He shrugged. "Cassandre was registered as an informant on the AISI database. Marcello showed me the entry."

"But there has to be a financial angle," she said, thinking aloud. "And what about Tignelli? I suspect he's involved somehow, but there's surely no way he can be part of some terrorist plot." It was only just sinking in that she had been removed from her first homicide investigation as casually as a moth being brushed off a coat. Disbelief was rapidly giving way to anger. "I bet those fucking pricks at AISI have got this all wrong, as usual. Either that, or they're part of the cover-up as well."

"Why do you say that about Tignelli?" Flavio said, going straight to the point as usual.

She told him about her visit to La Grazia. "I'm sure he knew exactly why I was there," she concluded. "There was all this fancy misdirection with the eels, but he'd clearly been pre-warned. Plus he's the only person I've spoken to so far who hasn't seemed frightened by what happened to Cassandre."

"Those are the eels, I take it?" He pointed at the bag she'd left by the door. Every so often it gave a violent wriggle, as the eels tested the limits of their confinement.

She nodded. "Can you come round tonight?"

"I can't ask the bodyguards to stay outside your apartment all night," he said quietly. "Not again."

"Just for an hour or two, then," she said reluctantly.

He made a decision. "All right. I'll be there at eight."

As she turned to leave, he added, "And Kat? I'm sorry about this investigation. But there'll be others. Grimaldo was impressed at how much you'd found out in a couple of days, I could see that."

"Thanks," she said. She didn't bother to tell him that, in her opinion, Grimaldo hadn't been so much impressed as alarmed.

FIFTEEN

"THANKS FOR MEETING me," Holly said.

"Not at all – it's good to see you. And, if I may say so, looking rather better than on the last occasion we met." Ian Gilroy's piercing blue eyes scrutinised her carefully. "Are you quite sure you're up to returning to duty?"

Ian Gilroy was seventy-two and long retired from his job as chief of the CIA's Venice Section. He kept his mind agile, as he put it, by teaching classes on military history at Camp Ederle, the US base near Vicenza where Holly was stationed. But the main reason he'd become her mentor and confidant was because he'd been a friend of her father's. One of her earliest memories was of a barbecue at Camp Darby, when she was eight or nine years old. She'd stood on Gilroy's feet, one foot on each shoe, and he'd marched her round the party like she was a general. All the officers had to salute her in turn, while she barked nonsensical orders that they'd pretended to carry out.

"You must think I'm stupid," she said, shaking her head. "Me an intelligence analyst, and I never realised my dad was part of that world himself."

They were sitting outside a café in the centre of Vicenza, in the cool shade afforded by Palladio's grand basilica. Gilroy stretched his legs out and looked at her thoughtfully.

"I never think you're stupid, Holly. Quite the reverse. It takes a special kind of detachment to question the assumptions we grew up with, and your father was too conscientious to tell his family the details of what he did. Why don't you tell me what you've discovered?"

She told him about the memorandum, and the realisation that someone might have tried to kill her father because of it. Gilroy heard her out, nodding occasionally.

"And the document itself?" he said when she'd finished. "Where is it now?"

She indicated the backpack at her feet. "In there."

"May I see it?"

She took it out and handed it to him. For a while he was silent as he read, occasionally flicking back to a previous page to check something. When he was done he placed it on the table and looked at her.

"You've seen it before," she said.

He nodded. "You father gave it to me soon after he wrote it."

"I thought it must be you. But you never mentioned it."

"I had no idea it might be significant." He frowned. "Though actually I did bring it up with you once. I tried to be oblique – I wasn't sure how much you knew of his professional role, and I didn't feel it was my place to reveal it if he'd chosen not to."

It was true, she realised. Almost the first time they'd met, Gilroy had told her that her father had raised concerns with him about an aspect of Operation Gladio. But she'd never put two and two together and worked out that her father was part of the same shadowy world as him.

As if reading her mind, he said, "NATO, Military Intelligence, CIA – during the Cold War, we were all part of the same chess game. But that didn't stop NATO from running its own, sometimes ill-advised, sideshows."

"Like Gladio."

"Like Operation Gladio," he agreed. "As you know, that was an operation its creators in NATO were careful to keep well away from the real spies. And what a mess it turned out to be."

She indicated the report. "What did you do with this?"

"I passed it up the line to my superiors." He shrugged ruefully. "What else could I do? Camp Darby was outside my remit, and as your father says, everyone was in a panic after Gladio was exposed. NATO went into damage-limitation mode. That some of the gladiators felt betrayed would hardly have been a surprise, let alone a priority."

"Do you think it could be true, what he wrote – that they were being encouraged to regroup by people within the intelligence agencies? Maybe even organised by them?"

He made a very Italian gesture, a back-and-forth wobble of the hand, to indicate the impossibility of knowing such a thing for certain. It was a reminder that, whilst he might not have grown up in Italy as she had, he'd been living here since before she was born. "Again, it wouldn't surprise me. There were NATO staff officers whose whole careers were built on that operation. There would have been some, I'm sure, who would have found it hard to give up."

"And what he said about you – at least, I assume it was you – was correct as well? That you were involved in tackling the Red Brigades?"

"Yes." His eyes took on a faraway look. "I spent almost a decade finding a way into that organisation, Holly. When we talk about terrorists today, often they're as nothing to the Brigate Rosse. They were well run, well financed and completely ruthloss. If they were caught, for example, they refused to be represented by state-appointed lawyers, on the grounds that the state was nothing but a collection of imperialist corporations. If a lawyer persisted in trying to defend them, they had the lawyer assassinated."

"That's pretty hardcore."

"Indeed. Eventually, of course, we managed to bring the ringleaders to justice. Why do you ask about that?"

"Because of Daniele Barbo," she said simply.

"Ah." He nodded thoughtfully. "Again, you're quite correct – that was how I came to know Daniele's father, Matteo. After the boy was kidnapped, as the local Red Brigades specialist I was asked by our government to offer any assistance I could, not least because Daniele's mother was American. Despite the unlikely circumstances, his father and I became friends. Afterwards we kept in touch, and when it became clear that as well as disfiguring his son's face, the terrorists had done something even more terrible to his mind, I found myself becoming involved in Matteo's plans for the boy's future. It's a responsibility I still feel today, although as you know, Daniele has never welcomed the fact that I'm his guardian."

"'A responsibility'?" she echoed quietly. "Or guilt?"

He sighed. "Perhaps a bit of both. We should have been able to get him out sooner than we did. The Italian operation was a travesty from start to finish. But you know how it is in this country."

They were both silent for a moment, thinking their respective thoughts. "So," he said at last. "What will you do with this?" He indicated the report.

"I'm going to find out who tried to kill my father, and why. That means finding out who these people were who were infiltrating his lodge."

"Is that wise?" he said gently. "You're still recovering from a major trauma yourself. And even if, by some miracle, there's anything left to find after so long, it can't help your father now."

"Even so," she said stubbornly. "I need to do this. Will you help me?"

"I'm not sure you know what you're asking."

"I think I do." She tapped the report. "If this is right, when Prime Minister Andreotti told the Italian parliament about the existence of the Gladio network and in almost the same breath said it had already been dismantled, he was lying. But the implication is even bigger than that. It's now well established that dozens of bombings and other atrocities during the Years of Lead were actually committed by Gladio agents. If my dad was right, and Gladio didn't go away, what did they get up to after they were supposed to have disbanded? When did they disband? Did they *ever* disband?"

"There are many people, even today," he said quietly, "who won't want those questions asked, let alone answered."

"I'll be ready for them. And I'll have a head start." She indicated the report. "According to this, the Gladio headquarters was in a remote region of Sardinia called Capo Marrargiu. I'll look there."

"What makes you think there'll be anything left to find after so long?"

"I've got to begin somewhere. And in the meantime, maybe you could find out who else read that report."

He looked worried. "I don't like stirring things up while you're out in the field. It's bad tradecraft."

"It's the surest way to get a response," she pointed out.

"Hmm." He thought. "Are there any duplicates of this?" He nodded at the report.

"I made a paper copy at the airport, just before I flew back. And I emailed one to myself as well."

"Good," he said, although it seemed to Holly that he said it almost with a sigh. "I'll see what I can do. Be careful, won't you?"

"Of course." She stood up. "I'd better go."

After she had left him, Ian Gilroy sat for a long time, thinking. He reread the memorandum one more time, although he was already familiar with its contents, and had been ever since he received the original, many years before. He had never imagined that it would come back to trouble him after so long.

Reaching for his cell phone, he dialled a number. It was one he'd committed to memory long ago. For reasons of security, though, he had never stored it as a contact.

"I need something done," he said when it was answered. "To be carried out immediately."

He spoke for just under a minute. The call over, he removed the SIM card from the back of his phone and snapped it in two. Then he beckoned to the waiter for another coffee.

SIXTEEN

THE EELS WERE in Kat's sink now, waiting to be cooked. She got hold of the first one using the same method Tignelli's workman had, wrapping her hand in a carrier bag to get a firm grip just below the head. Even so, it writhed vigorously around her fist as she carried it over to the counter, head and tail thrashing in opposite directions.

She'd already laid out a sharp knife, a chopping board and a cleaver. In one decisive movement she stabbed it through the top of the head, pinning it to the board. Then it was a simple matter to lop it off just above the gills with the cleaver. The eel's long tail wriggled away across the counter, scattering blood. She dropped it into a bowl of water and vinegar, then repeated the process with the other one before cleaning up.

Skinning them was equally straightforward, thanks to a trick she'd learnt from her grandmother. Looping a piece of string behind the gills, she tied both bodies to a doorknob, then got hold of the skin at the severed end and pulled, peeling it away from the flesh like a stocking. A real traditionalist would have told her not to bother – in days gone by, eel cooked *su l'ara* wouldn't even be washed, since fresh water would have been too precious a commodity for the glassblowers of Murano, in whose furnaces the dish originated, to waste on anything except drinking. Kat didn't think of herself as a traditionalist, but she did use the customary five handfuls of bay leaves to line the bottom of the pot. The eels would roast quickly in their own juices, the bay leaves both flavouring them and protecting them from the heat.

She opened a bottle of white wine, a Ribolla Gialla from the mountains to the north: its sharp acidity would cut through the richness of the meat. Then she sent a text.

You've got twenty minutes. If you're late, I'll do to you what I just did to the eels.

She knew, though, that Flavio would never be so rude as to show up late for food. Sure enough, almost immediately the answer came back.

Better let me in then.

Crossing to the window, she saw a car pull up outside. Flavio climbed out of the back and bent down to say something to the man at the wheel. It would only be going around the corner, she knew: the bodyguards were never more than a short sprint away.

The water for the pasta was already boiling, while in another pan she'd prepared a simple sauce of anchovies, chopped parsley and onions softened in butter. She threw a couple of handfuls of buckwheat *bigoli* into the boiling water, and opened the door just before he knocked on it.

It was good to be able to kiss him properly, so unlike their snatched moments in the Palace of Justice. Good, too, to be alone. She considered herself too thick-skinned to be put off by the bodyguards' glances when she entered or left his office, but it was a welcome relief not to have them there all the same.

As their kiss deepened, he ran his hand up her hip and

cupped her buttock, pulling her body into his. "Uh-uh," she said sternly, pulling away. "Eat."

"Eat first," he corrected with a wolfish grin.

"Eat first," she agreed, her insides fluttering with anticipation.

They sat at her tiny table, their legs companionably tangled, and ate the pasta while the apartment filled with the deep, almost medicinal aroma of the bay leaves. Not until the eel was on their plates did they discuss the case.

"I stopped by the casino this evening," she told him as they ate. "I've got a contact there, someone who's given me bits of gossip in the past."

"And?"

"Cassandre had been coming in for months, buying chips with cash, then placing a few small bets before taking the chips back to the cashier and asking for a cheque. Money laundering, in other words. The cashiers would get a couple of chips as a tip, so they weren't going to call him on it. But recently, my contact said, he'd also been gambling for real. He'd spend twenty, thirty thousand euros a night on the tables. Losing it, mostly, but winning just often enough to make sure he kept coming back."

Flavio raised an eyebrow. "For a banker, that sounds remarkably stupid."

"Or desperate. Then, about a week ago, he stopped coming in."

"From which we deduce…?"

"That either his luck had changed, and he wasn't desperate any more. Or he'd realised he was drawing attention to himself."

Flavio got up and fetched the bottle. "Even if Cassandre *was* laundering money, that doesn't mean Grimaldo's story about using him in an intelligence operation isn't true. Cassandre wouldn't be the first white-collar criminal to do a deal with the security services."

"But what if the truth is the exact *opposite* of what Grimaldo is saying?" she persisted. "What if they're actually part of it? And this is something AISI is trying to cover up, not investigate?"

"This is beginning to sound like *dietrologia*," he said, his smile robbing the words of any offence. To many Italians, there was always a hidden truth that lay *dietro*, or behind, the official explanation of events. *Dietrologia* was the faintly disparaging term for taking it too far. Although Flavio came across many bizarre conspiracies in his work, he always made a point of not jumping to fanciful conclusions without having explored the simpler alternatives first.

"Father Calergi made the point that all Freemasons think their first loyalty is to their fellow Masons, not to the law. What if these people are all protecting each other?"

"Then we'd need some evidence," he said gently. "Investigations come to court because someone has assembled a cast-iron case, not because of hypothetical speculation."

She nodded. "I know. That's why I asked Malli, our IT expert, to take another look at Cassandre's computer."

Flavio looked startled. "I thought he'd handed the laptop over with all the other evidence?"

"He did. But he'd previously made a copy, an 'optical image', as they call it. After they took the laptop, he asked me what he should do with the copy. I told him to go ahead and examine it."

"Which you had no right to do. Kat, anything you find will be inadmissible. It'll have been completely compromised as evidence."

"We don't have to tell anyone else what we find. But something about this smells, and I can't think of any other way to find out what it is."

He was silent a moment. "And when will this Malli get back to you?"

"He said he'd email me tonight."

Flavio threw up his hands. "You'd better find out what he's said, then."

She crossed to the counter where her laptop was and opened her emails. Malli's was at the top.

Subject: Is this what you're looking for?

There's a lot of stuff on here – I can't be sure what's important and what isn't. A lot of it is technical: spreadsheets, lists of numbers, what look like banking details.

But I'm sending the attached document as Cassandre had deleted it recently, or thought he had.

The attachment was headed "Insurance". She opened it.

It was a list of names, running to several pages. She spotted the names of dozens of local politicians. Others were industrialists or businessmen. Many had titles – General, Archbishop, Prince, Deputy, Judge.

"This doesn't look like terrorism to me," she said. "More like a list of his fellow Masons in the black lodge."

"You don't have any evidence for that," Flavio said, reading over her shoulder. But she could tell by his tone that he was no longer quite so unconvinced.

"Father Calergi mentioned the P2 conspiracy. Remember how they called it the 'government within the government'? What if this is something similar?"

"All right   so perhaps these are the members of an illegal society." He gestured at the document. "That doesn't mean they're conspiring. No prosecutor could launch an investigation merely on the basis of a list of names." Even so, he scrolled down the list, occasionally shaking his head when he recognised one.

"So what *do* we need? Whatever happens, I can't do what Grimaldo's asking and just forget that I was ever put on this case."

"You know, Kat," he said quietly, "if I'd realised, when I first began those Mafia trials, how much of my life it would take up, and at what cost, I would never have started."

"But you did start. And you're still doing it. You're the most fearless prosecutor I know."

"Not any more." He turned to meet her eyes. "Until recently it seemed like I had no alternative. There was nothing in my life but my work. But things are different now."

"What's changed?" she said, although she'd already half-guessed the answer.

"You," he said simply. "Lately I've found myself thinking... what if we went abroad? To Brussels, say. You could transfer to Interpol, I could be a prosecutor for the European Commission. It would be dry work – dull, even. But we could live together, stroll to a café every morning like normal people do, eat together every night... I'd be sharing my life with you, instead of with my bodyguards." He gestured at the screen. "Kat, if there *is* a conspiracy here, and by some miracle we get to the bottom of it, you know we won't touch the real problem. Corruption is just too endemic in this country. We're like housewives trying to shovel snow off the front step while the blizzard's still raging. Maybe the answer is just to go where there isn't so much snow."

Or so much water. When he'd said the work might be dry, she had immediately thought that her surroundings would be, too. Like every Venetian, she hated the way tourists took over her city for ten months of the year; hated the way there was never enough money to stop the canals from stinking, the foundations from sinking, the bridges from crumbling. But there was lagoon water in her veins. Could she give that up for any man? Even a man like this?

As if reading her thoughts, he said, "Or Amsterdam. There are canals in Amsterdam, you know. They call it 'the Venice of the north'. We could work at the Hague."

"I bet Amsterdam's canals don't stink like Venice's."

He looked perplexed. "That's a good thing, isn't it?"

She was torn. She'd never come across a man like him before – a man she was quite certain of, whom she both respected and lusted over; a man to whom she could say anything, or nothing; a man of fierce moral integrity who nevertheless seemed to disapprove of her, or try and make her into something she wasn't.

"Mind you," he added, "I never heard of anyone calling Venice 'the Amsterdam of the south'. So perhaps they're exaggerating a little."

She kissed his jaw. She loved the rough sandpapery feel of his end-of-day stubble, the faint aroma of courtrooms and business that lingered on his collar. "Then let's do it," she said. "But let's do both. Sort this case out, as best we can, and then run away to Amsterdam and pretend it's just Venice on a cold day. And now for God's sake take me to bed, before your bodyguards start hammering on the door."

Much later, she crept to the window wrapped in the bedcovers and watched him climb into the car. *If he looks up, he loves me, she told herself, then, a moment later, Don't be such a schoolgirl.*

He looked up and blew her a kiss. Her heart melted.

Amsterdam it is, my love.

SEVENTEEN

HALFWAY ACROSS THE world at JFK airport, the attendant at the Delta Airlines First Class lounge reception desk looked up as a man approached her. Although he was wearing a suit and carrying a briefcase, he looked somehow different from the other passengers in First – the suit too cheap and too grey, the briefcase boxy and made of plastic. Although she smiled automatically, there was just a touch of challenge about the way she said, "May I see your boarding card, sir?" It wouldn't be the first time an Economy passenger had tried to slip in here.

Instead of a boarding card, though, it was an HP Business Services ID the man laid on the desk in front of her. She squinted at it. *Steve Simmons. Network technician.*

"Photocopier's reporting a fault," he explained. "I'm booked in for a repair."

"Really?" she said, confused. "I wasn't aware of a problem."

"It's all automatic," he assured her. "These new machines are so smart, they send us an email when they're going to need fixing. Good thing it's not smart enough to mend itself too, or I'd be out of a job." He tapped the case, which she now realised contained his tools. "It's a five-minuter, then I'll be out of your hair."

She pointed. "The copier's over there, in the business centre. Can I get you a coffee?"

"I'm good, thank you, ma'am," he said courteously.

She watched from the desk as he carefully spread a dust sheet on the carpet next to the machine, to prevent any stray toner from staining it. Pretty soon he had the photocopier open and was delving around in its innards.

The last repair man had explained to her, when she'd taken him a coffee, that modern copiers didn't actually photocopy any more. They were now scanner-printers: every document placed on the glass was recorded as a digital image before being either printed, or – more frequently these days – emailed.

"Which also means," he'd added, "that modern machines keep everything. You'd be amazed how many people don't realise that when they photocopy their naked ass at the office party and email it to their boyfriend, that image and address is stored on the copier until we delete it." She hadn't known that either, and from then on she'd never quite trusted photo-copiers the same way.

In a remarkably short time Steve Simmons was finished. Again, she was impressed by the efficiency with which he cleaned up after himself. He'd been wearing disposable gloves, but even so he produced a polishing cloth and meticulously wiped down the copier's glass and sides after putting it all back together.

"Many thanks, ma'am," he said cheerily as he left.

Half an hour later, when she was on her break, she saw him again, queuing for a domestic flight to Washington Dulles. She thought what an expensive business it must be, flying a repair-man all the way from Washington just to fix a copier. But the people who decided these things must know what they were doing.

By the time she came back from her break, she couldn't even have told you what he looked like.

EIGHTEEN

THE HACKER WAITED patiently in the internet café. He had planned tonight's demonstration down to the last detail. It was now two in the morning in Misrata, Libya's third-largest city, and the streets were deserted, but even so the café had been closed all day as a precaution. No one would see the commander or the cleric arrive.

He was waiting for the sound of a car, but when they came it was on foot, opening the back door and silently slipping inside. The hacker, whose name was Tareq, saw the commander glance uneasily over to where Hassan, the café owner, was standing.

"It's all right," he said. "Hassan will make tea, then leave us."

The commander nodded. He was wearing an old camouflage jacket and a turban that had been washed so many times its colour was indeterminate – the same one he had been wearing ever since 2011 and the War of Liberation. The cleric, by contrast, was wearing a black woollen *chechia*, a Tunisian imam's hat, although, so far as the hacker knew, he wasn't from that country. He spoke Arabic with a strong Egyptian accent.

They waited in silence while Hassan made thick, syrupy black tea, pouring it repeatedly from one glass to another to produce the *regwhet*, or foam, that proved how clean the utensils and water were. Then, with a respectful "*Ma as-salama*", he left them.

The hacker turned back to the computer in front of him. The other two men came to stand behind him, looking over his shoulder as they sipped their tea. The screen showed what appeared to be a security camera's view of a road tunnel. Traffic was relatively light: mostly big commercial trucks, each one with a tail of three or four cars, unable to pass them on the single-lane carriageway.

"Of course, this is just a demonstration," the hacker said quietly. "If it were a real operation, it would be done when the traffic was heavy."

"What are we looking at?" the commander asked. "What country?"

"The Fréjus road tunnel," the hacker said. "It runs under the mountains between France and Italy. Thirteen kilometres long – not the longest, by any means, but enough."

He typed in an IP address and a crude menu appeared, asking him for a user name and password. He typed again and the menu was replaced by a list of numbers. To the commander, whose technical knowledge was limited, it looked like the menu of an internet router.

The hacker turned some nodes from "On" to "Off". Then, typing a second IP address, he accessed another menu and checked "Disable".

"Now we wait," he said, almost to himself.

"How long?" It was the cleric who had spoken.

"Ten minutes. Perhaps twenty."

"Time for a second glass, then."

The commander poured them all more tea, and brought over the bowl of almonds Hassan had left.

"By the end of this year," the hacker said in his soft, precise voice, "there will be more *things* connected to the internet than computers. By 2020 the world will have more 'smart devices', as they are called, than people: over twenty billion of them. Security cameras, traffic lights, ovens, baby monitors... not to mention automated stock-trading networks, power stations and defence systems." He tapped the screen. "Or in this case, air turbines."

The commander and the cleric listened respectfully. The hacker might be thirty years younger than either of them, but they had travelled a long way to hear what he had to say this evening.

"These days computers have relatively sophisticated security systems," the hacker continued. "Firewalls and anti-virus software that are constantly updated as new vulnerabilities are discovered. But the Internet of Things generally runs on the simplest, cheapest software each manufacturer can find. In many cases the devices don't even require passwords, or they're set to one of a few factory defaults." He gestured at the screen. "The air turbines in that tunnel, for example, were set to require the username 'admin' and the password 'password'. But even if the engineers who installed them had thought to change the passwords, it would have been a relatively simple process to bypass them."

"So that's what you did?" the cleric asked. "You turned the turbines off?"

The hacker nodded.

"And that's it?" The commander couldn't keep the disappointment out of his voice.

He had already recounted to the cleric the story of how, during Libya's War of Liberation, Colonel Gaddafi's troops had shut down the national cell-phone network to deny the rebels a means of communicating. Someone had brought this skinny kid to see him. He claimed he could hack into the network and restore their communications. It had seemed worth a try, so he'd told the kid to go ahead.

Within a day, they not only had a phone network but the kid had also somehow fixed it that they didn't have to pay billing charges.

He had the kid brought back to him. The young hacker looked at him as if he was expecting thanks, but the commander had something else in mind.

"What else can you do?" he'd asked.

A week after that, Gaddafi's troops had towed two trailer-mounted batteries of Patriot missiles up to their forward positions and prepared to fire them at the rebels. Within an hour, one of the batteries had loosed off a rogue missile that exploded on top of the other battery instead of its designated target. The skinny kid had hacked into the missiles' electronic firing systems, changed the coordinates around, and then activated the firing protocol.

The commander hadn't even known that a Patriot battery was connected to the internet.

"It's not, in the conventional sense," the kid had explained. "But the manufacturers built in an uplink so that it periodically sends maintenance data back to head office via satellite. With machines like this, it isn't even a person the data goes back to – it's machine talking to machine, via sensors and microcontrollers that communicate between themselves, using simple, low-cost networks."

His words meant almost nothing to the commander; he was just vastly relieved to have the Patriots out of action. "Come up with more ideas," he said.

The next thing the hacker did wasn't even hacking. He

devised a plan to get the local schoolchildren to mark the regime's sniper positions on Google Earth using their mobile phones, thus enabling the rebels to target them more effectively. He also came up with a way to improve their mortars' accuracy using videogame controllers.

When the regime sent in tanks, the hacker built a simple GPS spoofer to fool the tanks' satnavs into thinking they were in one part of the city when actually they were in another. It took the tank commanders an hour to realise what was happening, by which time their advance was in chaos.

After the regime fell, many of the rebels formed Libya's new administration. Others went into the army, or returned to their farms and villages. Some, though, went on to fight a different sort of war.

The commander was among the latter. He wasn't sure if he really believed in jihad, or if it was simply that, somewhere amongst the bombed-out ruins of Misrata and Sirte, he had found his vocation. He knew how to fight; but more importantly, he knew how to lead. Men trusted him.

He sought out the hacker and asked him what he planned to do next.

The hacker shrugged. He didn't know.

By now the older man knew something of what motivated the boy. "The tyrant who killed your father is dead," he told him. "But the people who kept him in power for so long are still alive. We make jihad to glorify Allah. But we also fight to destroy the power of the West, so that Arab countries can at last be free from their interference."

"How can I help?" the hacker said.

"I don't know. Go away and think of a plan. But make it a big one. When the twin towers of New York fell, *al-hamdulillah*, it inspired a movement. But ever since, we have been biting them like fleas, when what we need is to roar at them like lions."

"Give me a target."

The commander had glanced at him, as if trying to decide how much to tell him. Then he pulled out a map of the Mediterranean.

"A decade ago," he said, "America had more bases in Germany than in Italy. Soon, it'll be the other way round. Do you know why?"

The hacker shook his head.

"Because of us," the commander said. His finger traced Italy's coastline, where it jutted deep into the Mediterranean. "If they control the Italian peninsula, they control North Africa." He pointed at Sigonella, on the west coast of Sicily. "This is where their new Alliance Ground Surveillance system will be based. Two billion dollars' worth of high-altitude drones, capable of flying for days at a time, spying on the whole of Africa. They intend to expand it so that it eventually covers all of the Middle East as well."

"We want to attack the bases?"

The commander shook his head. "We want to *remove* the bases. If we attack them, the Americans will simply make them stronger. But the bases have a weakness."

"What?"

"They are actually owned by Italy."

He waited to see if the hacker understood the implications of this. The younger man was nodding thoughtfully.

"In other words," he continued, "if Italy were to *demand* the removal of the bases, then legally they would have to go. There would be no American drones spying on us any more. This would be a major breakthrough for our fighters on the ground."

"And Italy would insist on the bases going," the hacker said, "if the price of being America's ally was too high. If something happened – something as great as the Twin Towers, but on Italian soil."

The commander nodded. "Exactly. I am in contact with a group of our brothers in Italy. They have raised funds for such an attack. All that is needed is for someone to come up with the right plan."

The commander heard nothing for over a year. Then he received a request for money, so the hacker could travel abroad for some specialist training. He paid it immediately with funds from his backers.

Six months after that, the hacker finally sent word that he had a plan. This evening was meant to be the night he explained it, by way – he had said – of a demonstration. But so far, all he had done was turn off some turbines in a road tunnel. The commander had hoped for something better.

The hacker looked at the clock on the computer's taskbar. Ten minutes had gone by. "Not long now," he said quietly.

On the screen, an articulated truck was thundering down the tunnel's right-hand lane. Half a dozen cars followed in its slipstream, impatient to get back on the dual carriageway. As they watched, a car coming in the opposite direction veered sharply across both lanes and drove straight into the front of the truck. The truck jammed on its airbrakes, jack-knifing. Its cab scraped along the right-hand wall, trailing sparks, while its rear wheels swung outwards, towards the other lane. Just ahead was one of the emergency lay-bys – which, with its sharp concrete corner, brought the cab abruptly to a halt. The vehicle's momentum caused the back end of the trailer to continue, skidding around the mangled cab's axis, until it struck the tunnel's opposite wall, crunching under the impact. A

minibus coming the other way tried to brake but only suc
ceeded in broadsiding it, while the cars directly behind the
truck had no chance at all. The screen flared white as vehicles
on both sides of the crash exploded. Moments later, the whole
pile-up was engulfed in flame.

"There are sprinklers? Alarms?" the commander asked.

"There were," the hacker said. "I turned those off too."

"And the one who started all this? The driver coming in the
opposite direction – a brother seeking martyrdom? You had it
all arranged?"

The hacker shook his head, although his eyes remained
fixed on what was unfolding on the screen. "Just a tired businessman seeking sleep. And finding a tunnel full of carbon
monoxide instead of fresh air."

"You mean…" The commander was trying to get his head
round this. "*You* did this? Just by turning off some switches
on the internet?"

"Exactly." The hacker still spoke softly, but his voice
throbbed with passion. "This is their weakness – their soft
underbelly. Imagine a day when all their so-called technology
suddenly rises up against them. Not just road tunnels, but air-
traffic-control systems, electricity plants, sewers, oil refineries
– all malfunctioning at the same moment, and in the most
dangerous ways possible. Their computers turning into fire-
bombs, their transportation networks into weapons of
destruction. Their financial systems selling and buying at
random, paralysing their economy. Their cash machines emptying, their plastic cards no longer working in their shopping
malls and supermarkets. Their hospitals, their food-supply
chains, all breaking down at once. And at the centre of it all,
while they are preoccupied with everything else that is going
on, a spectacular gesture of destruction, unmatched by

anything since 9/11. It will be focused on Italy, just as you requested. But its effect will be felt far beyond Italy's borders." He gestured at the screen. "On that day, *Insha'Allah*, even a few burning cars will pale into insignificance."

"This is possible?" The commander's voice was equally quiet. *Allah, what have I done?* he was thinking. *What have I unleashed?*

The hacker nodded. "There are many details still to be arranged. And it will be expensive. But the capability, the framework – that is all in place."

The commander turned to the cleric, who hadn't spoken since the pile-up had started. His eyes, too, were glued to the monitor. At the rear, behind the main collision, other cars were still screeching to a halt, the drivers struggling from their crumpled vehicles only to flail around, clutching at their throats, their mouths gaping in unheard screams.

"The fire has consumed what little oxygen was left," the hacker said. "The tunnel has become a vacuum." At the back, fire engines were approaching, their flashing lights blossoming and fading on the monitor. There was no way for them to reach the centre of the conflagration: too many cars were already involved. A moment later, the camera failed too. The screen went blank.

The cleric turned to face the other two men. His eyes shone with excitement.

"Allah be praised," he said. "What do you need?"

NINETEEN

DANIELE BARBO WALKED along the Fondamenta Záttere, deep in thought. Across the Canale della Giudecca, the lights of San Giorgio Maggiore twinkled in the distance.

It was only in the small hours that he wandered like this, when Venice's narrow *calli* were deserted. Although the day had been scorching, a night breeze coming in off the lagoon had cooled the stones of the buildings, and the temperature was now almost comfortable.

Not that he noticed the temperature. He was thinking about the nature of beauty.

When James Watson and Francis Crick set out to unravel the structure of DNA, they were convinced that they would know it when they saw it because anything so important must surely be beautiful. And when they first blocked out the famous double-helix pattern, they realised immediately what it was.

To Daniele's mind, there was a similar beauty in perhaps half a dozen mathematical formulae, from the fundamental theorem of calculus to Newton's constant of gravity. Yet the irony was that one could not arrive at such truths by deduction, only by intuition. Einstein formulated $E=MC^2$ long before he was able to prove it. Newton glimpsed gravity in the path of a falling apple before he worked out the mathematics it embodied. You couldn't hope to calculate the algorithm that would prove P=NP; you could only hope to recognise it when it arrived.

It would be simple, and it would be beautiful. That was all he knew.

Half-closing his eyes, he tried to make himself see the world around him as if it were nothing but numbers. The movement of the waves against the sea wall – that was determined by the Navier–Stokes equations of fluid dynamics. The relationship between the moon and the tides – that was so mysterious, even Newton had failed to understand it fully. And the architecture of the church on his left, Spirito Santo, was all Euclidean geometry, the Gothic arches and rose-windows deliberately fashioned to express a beauty which, its builders believed, echoed the perfect mathematics of God. Its proportions were based on the Golden Section, the mathematical ratio found in everything from pine cones to snail shells, from the seed of a sunflower to the swirl of a galaxy.

He turned the corner of Punta della Dogana, the old Custom House. Ahead of him, the curious octagonal structure of Santa Maria della Salute stood sentinel at the mouth of the Grand Canal, its huge dome resting on the skyline like a massive royal crown, given a rime of silver frost by the moonlight. There were some, he knew, who believed that its design had been inspired by mathematics of a different kind: the numerical mysticism of alchemy and ancient Hermeticism. It was said that alchemy sent Isaac Newton mad, so that he spent his last years filling notebooks with strange speculations about the transmutation of matter. Leonardo da Vinci became obsessed with the ancient conundrum of "squaring the circle" and even Galileo, the arch empiricist, had devoted much of his life to astrology and star charts.

You'll know it when you see it, Daniele promised himself. *It will be beautiful. But it will be real, too.*

He had emptied his life. Now he must try to empty his mind as well.

TWENTY

AS THE PLANE banked over Sardinia, Holly saw through the window a long vista of grey, treeless mountains that looked hot even from up here, their rocky slopes plunging almost vertically into the Mediterranean. Below her, where the peaks ended, was a crescent of sand fringed with white hotels. That would be Alghero. A sleepy resort, tucked away in the island's quietest corner. Even from this height, she could make out the scattering of black dots in the sea where tourists were paddling.

She picked up *Il Giornale* from where it lay in her lap. The paper's front page was dominated by the freak accident in the Fréjus road tunnel. Investigators were still unable to reach the wreckage: cars and trucks had fused into one solid mass, along with a section of tunnel roof that had melted in the heat. At least twenty people were unaccounted for, including twelve schoolchildren returning from a school trip in a minibus. It wasn't the worst road tunnel disaster in history – the Gotthard crash in 2001 had caused one hundred and thirty-nine casualties, the 1999 Mont Blanc fire killed over forty, and twenty-eight died in the 2012 Sierre tunnel disaster – but it was already shaping up to be one of the most baffling. The Fréjus tunnel had a good safety record, and had been further upgraded after the Mont Blanc fire. There were no reports of any technical failures, although investigators were looking into allegations that the automatic sprinkler system had failed to come on. A spokesman for the tunnel authority said they weren't ruling out any possibilities, including driver error.

The row over the taps on the undersea internet cables was petering out, relegated to the middle pages. The United States was now proposing that Italy reinstate them voluntarily, as part of a new information-gathering alliance called VIGILANCE. "VIGILANCE, short for Virtual Intelligence Gathering Alliance, will be the most effective anti-terrorism measure the West has, while taking into account legitimate concerns about privacy and data security," a White House spokesman was quoted as saying. The Italian government had rejected that suggestion out of hand – which was hardly surprising, Holly thought. Surely no country, having discovered it had been spied on, would choose to submit to exactly the same scrutiny of its own volition.

"Ladies and gentlemen, we will shortly be landing at Alghero," the stewardess said over the PA, her voice as mechanical as a recording. There followed the usual warnings about not getting out of your seat until the seatbelt sign had been switched off – warnings that, as usual, everyone ignored except for Holly. This too, she reflected, was the product of being an army brat. The instinct to obey authority to the letter had been ingrained in her since childhood.

She'd read somewhere that army brats had rules where others had principles, which was why, when they did go off the rails, they often did so in spectacular fashion. She'd seen it with some of her own contemporaries. Daddy's little princesses on base, once away at college they'd become the sluttiest, wildest girls on campus.

Somehow, she'd gone the other way. Sometimes she wondered if she wasn't just storing her rebellion up, waiting for a trigger.

Was *this* the trigger? Supposing she did find something that proved her father had been deliberately silenced because of what he'd found out about Operation Gladio, what would she do with that knowledge?

She sighed. *Cross that bridge when you come to it, Boland.*

As she filed off the plane, she noticed a group of half a dozen men. They looked familiar – not the individuals, but the type. Burly, well built, with the broad chests and inflated biceps of those who spent too much time working out. They weren't in uniform, but their buzz haircuts were a dead giveaway. Sure enough, as they walked towards the Arrivals hall, they unconsciously fell into step, their legs hitting a perfect parade-ground stride. You could take the man out of the base, she thought, but you couldn't take the base out of the man.

By the time they'd been through baggage reclaim, most of the group were toting golf bags. Master sergeants, she guessed, getting in some seaside R&R.

She rented a car from Sixt and drove to a climbing shop she'd found on the internet. Everything was pre-booked, but she lingered for a chat with the heavily tattooed and dreadlocked young owner, knowing from experience she'd learn more from him than any guidebook. Sure enough, he spent a good half hour telling her about the island's best climbing areas. It confirmed what she'd hoped: her destination was well away from the spots usually favoured by recreational climbers.

From there she drove south along the coast towards the small town of Bosa. The road, she knew, had been built only a decade or so ago; in the seventies and eighties, when the

Gladio network used this area as a training ground, It had
been accessible only by boat. Even now, it was one of the
most spectacular drives she'd ever made. On one side craggy,
jagged mountains soared vertically into the shimmering sky;
on the other, they fell away into the sparkling sea. Her car felt
tiny and insignificant, sandwiched between the immense
masses of rock and water. There were no buildings, no farms
or crops; no side roads to towns or villages even. A couple of
coaches passed her, coming in the opposite direction, but
otherwise the road was eerily quiet, her only companions a
few mouflons, wild brown sheep with extravagant curly
horns, nibbling the scrub on seemingly inaccessible ledges.

She felt, deep down in her soul, a sharp tug of love for this
sea, this sky. Did people back in America feel this way about
the landscapes of the US? She imagined they must do. But a
part of her was now as deeply Italian as it was possible for
someone not actually born here to be.

Eventually she saw a rusted chain-link fence next to a small
turning, and pulled off the road. Even though she'd seen no
one, she parked behind a rock, out of sight.

Getting out, she discovered that it was very still and very
hot. The turning was little more than a track, zig-zagging
down the side of the mountain towards the sea, two hundred
feet below. If there were any guards or surveillance devices,
she couldn't spot them.

Fifty yards from the track, she hammered an iron peg into
the ground, then clipped a rope to it. She'd brought a simple
friction hitch to slow her descent, along with climbing shoes
and kneepads. Although the US Army insisted on helmets and
gloves when abseiling, Holly, like most real mountaineers,
disliked them: the gloves because they increased the

likelihood of getting your fingers caught in the friction hitch, and the helmet because it impaired upward vision.

As she cleared a small overhang, the base came into view below her. It wasn't much to look at: no more than half a dozen windswept concrete buildings, so ugly they could only be military. Everything seemed derelict. She abseiled another hundred feet before reaching a ledge. There she waited, making sure no one was around.

Satisfied, she dropped the last fifty feet. A second fence bore a warning that this was a military zone and that trespassing, photography and mapmaking were forbidden under the Italian penal code. A smaller, more recent sign warned that it was also in danger of collapse. A graphic of a snarling guard dog needed no explanation. But there were large rusty gaps in the chain-link and what looked like rabbit holes pocking the ground on either side. If there had ever been dogs here, they'd long since departed.

She'd read online that the site was still officially used by the Italian Intelligence Agency as an observation post – observing what, she wondered? – but if so, she couldn't see any signs of it.

She walked to the nearest building and peered through the broken window. It contained twenty or so bunk beds. But the mattresses and everything else combustible had long since been burnt, only the iron frames and charred bedsprings remaining, strewn across the floor.

She moved on to the next hut. This one looked more promising. Old papers and bottles were scattered around, as if it had been vacated in a hurry. In the middle was the burnt-out carcass of a billiard table.

She went inside. On one side of the table was a small metal plaque. "To the men of Gladio, with my warmest admiration, Giulio Andreotti." Well, at least she was in the right place. She wondered at the personal gift of appreciation from the same prime minister who'd subsequently revealed the network's existence. It was surprising the departing gladiators hadn't ripped the plaque off in disgust. Or had leaving it here for others to see been the more pointed comment?

In a room at the back her heart quickened when she spotted a small safe. But there was nothing inside, only some charred fragments. The Gladio clear-up, if that was what had happened here, had been thorough.

Or perhaps, she thought, the clear-up had been carried out later, by the Italian security services, when they were handed the site as an observation post.

She checked the other huts, but the story was the same. In the former mess hut even the empty wine bottles had been smashed, the broken glass crunching like gravel under her feet.

Well, what did you expect after so long? Documentary evidence? But even though she'd known it was a long shot, she couldn't help feeling disappointed. She'd been hoping for something – anything – that told her the trail wasn't completely cold.

Her ears caught the sound of an engine. Going outside, she saw a military truck coming down the track towards her.

Shit.

Quickly, she retreated back inside the hut. She watched through the window as the truck pulled up by the buildings and two soldiers in Italian uniforms climbed down, pulling out packets of cigarettes as they did so. Leaning against the truck's side, they smoked and chatted in the sunshine. Then one of them walked straight towards the building she was hiding in.

She ducked her head back from the window and held her breath. A moment later, she heard the splash of urine against the wall. "They need to play him in position," a voice said, suddenly very near; he was still chatting to his companion over his shoulder. She was close enough to smell the sharp reek of his urine. When he'd finished, the men got back in the truck and drove off.

A routine patrol, she guessed. Just one more pointless duty in a day filled with pointless duties, carrying out an order given by some panicked bureaucrat a decade or more ago and never rescinded.

She didn't bother to climb back up her abseil rope but simply walked up the track, the sun blasting off the rock and crumbling tarmac onto her face. High above her, a griffin vulture swooped around the mountaintop and then, without apparently moving a wingtip, floated down to inspect her more closely.

Pausing to enjoy its magnificent five-foot wingspan, she thought, *Well, at least I saw you. So it wasn't a completely wasted trip.*

Something flashed in the corner of her vision. A windscreen, catching the sun, as a vehicle pulled off the coast road where it snaked round the same mountain, high above her. She could just make out that it was a Land Rover. Tourists, most likely, stopping to admire the view. She waited for them to set off again before she moved.

After she'd waited ten minutes, she realised they weren't coming. Which meant that they'd stopped to take more pictures. Or…

Or they were watching her, waiting for her to move. If she hadn't paused to look at the griffin vulture, she'd never have spotted them.

She drove back to the climbing shop, checking occasionally in her rear-view mirror to make sure she wasn't being followed.

"Think I chose a bad route," she said noncommittally to the owner. "Look, do you happen to have a map of the military installations here on Sardinia?"

The man gave her a look. "You mean, a map of the places we're not allowed to map?"

"That's the one." Just as nautical maps showed seabed channels and underwater reefs, so climbers needed to know which parts of the mountains were off limits. If anyone had a map like that, it was likely to be him.

He considered. "As it happens, I do."

He pulled out a cylinder of thick paper and unrolled it, weighing its corners down with coffee mugs to reveal a large-scale map of the island. Parts had been hatched with thick red lines. "If you're worrying about DP, you're right to." He pointed to an area in the south-east with one heavily tattooed, muscular arm. "This region here, Quirra, is the largest weapons-testing facility in Europe. Leukaemia levels in the surrounding area are running at up to sixty-five per cent of the population. The shepherds had so many deformed lambs they couldn't make a living, so they've all moved to other parts of the island."

By "DP", she realised, he meant "depleted uranium", the residue of shells made from radioactive metals.

"But that's not the only area they've contaminated." He tapped the island's north-east corner. "There was meant to be an EU scientific study into Lake Baratz, here. They found so much unexploded ordinance the scientists had to pull out for their own safety. The point is, the Italian government charges international weapons manufacturers a million dollars a day to use these mountains. That money goes straight to Rome. When our regional president managed to get a compensation fund of ten million euros, it was hailed as a great victory. But actually it was less than two weeks' income for the people who run this place." He spoke matter-of-factly, as if his anger at these manifold injustices had long since been exhausted.

"What about other bases?" she said, squinting sideways at the map.

"Take your pick. Down in the south you've got Decimomannu. The largest airport in Italy, and it doesn't host a single civilian flight. And Capo Taluda." He pointed again. "That's where they test white phosphorus. This whole island's just one big playground for the international military."

"Any bases that have been closed or mothballed in, say, the last fifteen years?"

He considered. "There's the old US–NATO base on the island of La Maddalena. That was closed about ten years ago."

"What's it used for now?"

"Not a lot. The base was turned into a fancy hotel. The rest of the island's just a bird sanctuary. Though I did hear they use it for military exercises from time to time."

"What kind of exercises?"

"Who knows. It's pretty remote. Whatever they do up there, there wouldn't be anyone else around to see it."

She thought. "Any climbing?"

"Some. Bouldering on sea cliffs, mostly. But what with the contamination and everything, why would you want to go there?"

She flashed him a smile. "I like birds, I guess."

TWENTY-ONE

ONCE AGAIN VENICE had dawned hot and humid. Kat had to share the *vaporetto* from the train station at Santa Lucia with a mass of tourists, who shuffled slowly around the deck at each stop like penguins instead of going down inside the boat to make room. Nor was her mood improved by the article she found on page four of *Il Gazzettino*, headed: "Night Swimmer Found Dead on Beach". According to the unnamed reporter, a body "wearing goggles and partially undressed" had been found on the beach at the Lido. It was thought, the article went on to say, that the dead man might have decided to sleep outside in the hot weather, and fallen victim to muggers. Even before she saw the quote from Avvocato Marcello, reassuring tourists that Venice was generally a very safe place to visit "so long as sensible precautions are taken to avoid areas with a large itinerant population", Kat had discerned the prosecutor's fluttering hand, airily rewriting history.

On the next page, another article caught her eye.

NAPOLEON'S IMPERIAL SUITE REOPENS
AFTER €3M REFURBISHMENT

After a century of neglect, the Imperial Apartments of the Royal Palace, commissioned by the Emperor Bonaparte after the fall of the Venetian Republic, reopen this week following a €3m refurbishment.

The refurbishment of the rooms overlooking Piazza San Marco marks the completion of an ambitious programme of restoration for the Royal Palace. The project's sponsors, who include the Tignelli fashion brand, will mark the occasion with a spectacular gala in the Imperial Ballroom on Monday night.

At Campo San Zaccaria, the operations room so efficiently set up by Bagnasco had just as efficiently been dismantled, the manpower already allocated to other investigations. Kat went and found Colonel Piola, still dealing with the paperwork from their previous case.

"How's it going?" she asked.

He grimaced and stretched, glad to have the chance to lay down his files for a few minutes. "The usual. The lawyer representing the glassblowing family has come up with the ingenious explanation that they made the glass themselves and shipped it to China, before realising they couldn't sell it there and returning it to Murano. A failed business venture, in other words, not an attempt to fleece Venice's tourists. Oh, and the prosecution's own expert says the Chinese fakes are probably better quality than the stuff the family was knocking out in any case. I wouldn't be surprised if they drop the whole thing. You?"

She hesitated. The room was filled with Carabinieri officers tapping at their computers. "Can we do this somewhere else?"

They went to a small bar on Fondamenta de l'Osmarin. As well as coffee, Aldo ordered a *cornetto*, a croissant dusted with icing sugar. He was putting on a little weight, she noticed. She wondered if he was looking after himself now he and his wife had separated. She didn't ask. Their personal lives were off limits to each other now.

"This is about your Freemasonry case, I take it," he said, when they'd found a quiet corner.

"That's the problem – it's not my case any more, at least not officially." She told him about Grimaldo's intervention, the list Malli found on Cassandre's computer, and the Masonic cards in his desk.

"May I see?"

She took out one of the cards and passed it to him. "I've seen this symbol before," he said immediately.

"Where?"

"You recall that Romani case I dealt with a few years ago?" She nodded. It had been not long after she'd joined the Carabinieri. There had been a national panic about the number of gypsies coming into Italy, with the press full of scare stories about pickpockets and white babies being stolen to order. "The city council in their wisdom decided to put all the Romani in one place, the *campo nomadi* on Via Vallenari. Some wild rumour started doing the rounds, something about an Italian schoolgirl being dragged there against her will... We never found out who started it. But the upshot was that a mob of vigilantes went down to the camp, cut off the power, then set fire to the Romani caravans." He shook his head. "Three gypsies died, including a bedridden old lady whose son was on a night shift at a local factory. No one was ever arrested. But I remember seeing that symbol sprayed on one of the burnt-out caravans."

"That's horrible."

"And that's not all. It cropped up again when some gay tourists were beaten up in Mestre a couple of years ago. Someone had sprayed it on a wall, along with the words '*Morte ai culatoni*'. Death to queers."

"Father Calergi told me it was banned because it was being

used by right-wing extremists. But he said it was also the sign of an ancient Venetian confraternity."

"Then perhaps that's why they chose it," he suggested. "Because of the overlap. Has it occurred to you that your Masons may not be Freemasons at all, at least not primarily – that their lodge may have been formed for some specific criminal purpose, and they're simply using the rituals and structure of Freemasonry to disguise it? After all, what better cover for an illegal conspiracy than an organisation which already exists in the shadows, one where absolute loyalty to your fellow members is a given?"

It made sense, she realised. Like a partygoer at Carnevale, Cassandre had stepped onto the stage wearing a mask, and they had all obligingly looked at the mask, not the person. Even those like General Saito, who wanted this whole business hushed up because it might bring Freemasonry into disrepute, were thinking about the trappings rather than the crime.

"Father Calergi hinted at much the same thing," she said, remembering. "He said that even today, no one really knew what P2's political agenda had been."

"What are Count Tignelli's political leanings?"

"Also to the right, I think. He hero-worships Napoleon, of all people. Called him the 'liberator of Venice'. He's even sponsored the refurbishment of Napoleon's Imperial Apartments."

"Perhaps he sees himself as Napoleon's political heir."

She nodded thoughtfully. "He almost said as much, actually – that Venice today is mired in corruption and vice, just as it was in the last days of the Republic. He suggested that I, as a Carabinieri officer, would surely agree with that."

"I'm sure many of our colleagues would." Piola dusted his lips with a paper napkin and gestured to Viliberto, the owner, for the bill. As usual, Villiberto waved the suggestion away, indicating that it was on the house; and as usual Piola pulled out a five-euro note and dropped it on the counter – probably more, Kat reflected, than the bill would have been in the first place. Piola's refusal to accept kickbacks, however small, was one of the things that had made her fall for him, back when they did their first investigation together.

"I'll ask around," she said. "Someone will know something." Venice might be one of the world's most popular holiday destinations, but it was also a village. Take away the tourists and you were left with just sixty thousand residents, many of whose families had been there for generations. She might not have come across Tignelli before, but he would almost certainly be known to some of her contacts.

"I take it you won't be involving General Saito's niece in these unofficial investigations?"

She stared at him. "Who?"

"Lieutenant Bagnasco. Saito's niece." He laughed at her horrified expression. "Didn't you know? You should feel honoured – he could have assigned her to any investigation, but he chose yours."

"He wanted to keep an eye on me," Kat said slowly. "Even if he's not involved in the black lodge himself, he doesn't want any scandal that might discredit the Carabinieri."

"Or perhaps he wanted to keep an eye on you because it looked like being a big case, and you're still relatively inexperienced," Piola said mildly. "Besides, Bagnasco has the makings of a very good officer."

"You know her?" Kat said. It was her turn to be surprised: Bagnasco had said she'd only been in Venice a few weeks.

Piola nodded. "She's asked me if I'll mentor her. We've had a few chats, that's all."

"Chats? Over dinner, I suppose?"

"Over dinner, yes. Why not?"

Because she's using you, Kat thought sadly. *Because she knows you're lonely, and she's seen an opportunity to advance herself.* Bagnasco would never make the mistake she had, of sleeping with a more senior officer, but she might well let that officer think she wanted to.

She saw from the look Piola gave her that he thought she was jealous; saw, too, that he found the idea rather pleasing. "I'm not jealous," she said angrily. "I just think she's trying to run before she can walk."

"Well," he said, still amused, "you'd know all about that."

As they left the bar she saw how he glanced automatically at his reflection in the mirror behind the counter. His hair was greying at the sides, and his face had a lived-in, crumpled quality that was part of its charm. There was no doubt: he was still a very good-looking man. And not just physically, either. It occurred to her, not for the first time, that he wore his principles proudly, like one of his Brioni suits; as if he knew how attractive they made him.

Back at Campo San Zaccaria, she went up to Malli's attic. The usually ebullient technician gave her a sombre look and scooted his chair over to a table piled high with evidence bags. "Here," he said, handing one to her. "I have a feeling I should never have looked at that."

"I was hoping I could persuade you to look some more."

He shook his head. "No, you can't, and besides, there's nothing much there."

"Nothing much?" she echoed. "So you did find something else besides that list?"

He hesitated, then rummaged around on another desk until

he found a printout. "He'd deleted his search history as well. But what people don't realise is that a deleted browsing history isn't erased – it's stored in a system file called *index. dat*. Getting it back can be as simple as doing a System Restore."

"Have you taken a copy of this?" she asked, skimming the list quickly.

He shook his head. "And if you've got any sense, you'll put it straight in the shredder."

"You're right," she said. "That's exactly what I should do."

He nodded, relieved, and she left him.

But that doesn't mean I will.

TWENTY-TWO

HOLLY SMILED AT the young woman behind Reception. "Hi, I have a reservation. Name of Boland?"

"Of course," the woman said, with the mechanical friendliness of her profession. She checked her computer. "One night, yes?"

To anyone familiar with post-war US colonial architecture, the hotel on the tiny island of La Maddalena could only have been a former military base. The building was long, low and sleek, made mostly of glass and girders, and the floors were polished parquet. Whoever had supervised the conversion into a hotel had spared no expense, trying to soften the vast interior with dramatic chandeliers and murals, but to Holly the result felt like a cross between an airport terminal and a very tasteless nightclub.

Not that the hotel's current clientele would mind much, she suspected. Her journey from Sardinia had been an arduous one, involving a long drive, two ferries and a taxi. But the island's marina was full of sleek superyachts, many with Russian names painted on their bows. And if the lack of conventional access wasn't enough of a deterrent for ordinary mortals, the hotel's astronomic prices would have been. She'd been startled to discover that the cheapest room cost more than three hundred euros a night.

While the clerk checked her in, she turned and watched the lobby. A group of half a dozen men were strolling out of the main doors, dressed in the ubiquitous local uniform of Ralph Lauren polo shirts with sunglasses tucked into the neck, Bermuda shorts and sandals. All were muscular, with military crew-cuts. She recognised them: the soldiers from the airport. They must be remarkably well paid, if they could afford to vacation here.

Turning back to the receptionist, she said idly, "Is there a golf course here?"

The young woman looked apologetic. "I'm afraid the ground's too rocky. But we can offer you some beautiful snorkelling."

At Alghero the men had been wheeling golf bags. Not very smart, to use a golf trip as cover when your destination didn't even have a course.

Abruptly leaving the desk, she followed the men outside. They were boarding one of the yachts, a shiny forty-footer bristling with antennae; expensive-looking even in that company. As soon as they were on board, it began moving towards the marina exit. Beyond the sea wall, the helmsman opened the throttle, and the yacht surged in a graceful arc to the south, its wash bubbling and sparkling in the sunlight.

She went back to the desk. "Look after my case, will you?" she said to the startled receptionist as she grabbed her backpack. "I'll go up to the room later."

Slinging the pack over her shoulders as she ran, she cut across the headland at a fast jog. It was almost twenty minutes before she came to a chain-link fence similar to the one at Capo Marrargiu. But where that one had been rusted through, this was clean and well maintained. It bore the same dire warnings against trespassing in a military zone.

She tracked parallel to it and found a place where animals had burrowed beneath the wire. As she wriggled underneath she caught the sound of gunfire. A burst of around thirty shots, then silence, followed by more firing. Range practice, it sounded like. But as to who would need to come to a place as remote as this for range practice, she had no idea.

She could see the yacht now, moored a little way out to sea, but the firing was coming from the beach, forty feet below her. Crouching down, she took her equipment out of her backpack: a chalk bag, which she fastened round her waist, and her bouldering shoes, tightly fitting slippers of thin rubber with a flat, flexible sole and no tread. The toe of each shoe had a stubby rubber point, for wedging into crevices. They hurt like hell to walk in, but on rocks they made her feel like Spiderwoman.

She crawled towards the edge of the cliff and looked over. There were, she now saw, a total of three yachts moored offshore, and half a dozen rigid inflatables pulled up on the beach. Around forty men were being drilled in groups – some target-shooting, some engaged in unarmed combat, some crouched round an instructor who was demonstrating how to use a rocket launcher. No one was in uniform, but she noted that the soldiers she'd seen at the airport seemed to be the ones doing the instructing.

She edged back, then re-approached the cliff fifty yards to the left, where a bend would mask her from view. Turning onto her stomach, she wriggled her feet down the rock face until she found her first foothold.

In bouldering – climbing without ropes – going down required greater concentration than going up. Climbing up, her eyes and the handhold she was searching for would be in reasonably close proximity. Descending meant she was climbing blind, with gravity trying to make her go faster and further than she could safely control. She took it slowly, reaching into her bag frequently for chalk.

She was about twenty feet into her descent when she heard, above her, the unmistakable squawk of a walkie-talkie. The end of a mountaineering rope skittered down the cliff face to her left, swiftly followed by another to her right.

Shit.

Whoever had been watching her before, at the derelict Gladio base, must have followed her here. She thought she'd been careful, but evidently not careful enough.

Quickly she thought over her cover story. There was nothing incriminating on her, and back at the hotel she had receipts and maps to prove that she was only what she said she was – a US Army officer who preferred her own company when climbing.

She clung to the rock face, conserving her strength, as two men dropped down towards her, one on either side. "Good spot, right?" she asked in Italian, trying to adopt the cheery tone of someone who didn't know she was trespassing.

"Sure," the man on her right said, equally cheerily, swinging something at her.

Just in time she saw that it was a small iron crowbar, the curve ending in a sharp claw. "Hey!" she shouted, pulling back.

The man grunted and swung again, all pretence at friendliness abandoned.

The climber on her left, meanwhile, was fiddling with his line, trying to swing close enough to grab her. It looked like they were simply going to throw her off the cliff. She glanced down. Below her were rocks. If they succeeded, she'd be messed up at best. At worst, she'd be dead.

Instinctively, she went upwards. Men on ropes would always have the advantage going down, but up was a straight race, and she was unencumbered by the gear they carried. The man on her left lunged and succeeded in grabbing her foot as she passed. She went the only way she now could, towards him, jumping into his rope and kicking down at his head. But he was stronger than she was. He tugged and grabbed again, getting a better grip on her ankle.

Looking up, she saw the crampon he was clipped to, just above her head.

It was him or her, and she chose him. Grabbing the crampon's release mechanism, she yanked it from the cliff, then gave one last kick. He fell with a surprised grunt, hitting the rocks below with a sickening thud.

The other man, meanwhile, was using the curved end of the crowbar as a hook, trying to pull himself over to her. She grabbed the claw and twisted. He cursed, surprised, as it slipped from his grasp.

Scurrying up to his belaying point, she levered the flat end of the crowbar into the crampon. It came out easily, and he fell after his colleague, his body thumping off two ledges on the way down. She paused just long enough to see that he was moving, then resumed climbing until she reached the top.

Cautiously, she raised her head over the edge. But there was no one there, just a white Land Rover parked twenty yards off. She ran to it and jumped in, her heart pounding with adrenalin. The keys were still in the ignition. Without pausing to look back, she gunned it back to the hotel to pick up her bags. The most important thing right now was to get off the island before anyone else tried to kill her. Working out who it had been, and why, would have to wait until later.

TWENTY-THREE

KAT SAT AT her desk and went through the websites Cassandre had visited. For the most part, they were a random assortment of newsfeeds, financial information sites and Wikipedia pages. He'd also visited a site called Eurotwinks. She clicked on it, then wished she hadn't. Cute young men with short gelled haircuts and pale hairless chests, having things done to them by older men that made her wince. So perhaps that explained the wife's curious detachment.

Rather more incongruously, he'd also paid multiple visits to the online game World of Warcraft. He definitely wasn't a gamer, that was for sure. She picked up the phone to Malli.

"I know you don't want to get involved," she said. "But just answer one question, would you? Can you think of any reason why a fifty-four-year-old banker should play World of Warcraft?"

Malli hesitated, then said reluctantly, "Do a search for Warcraft and Snowden." He hung up.

She did as he'd suggested, and found an article from the English newspaper that had broken the Edward Snowden story. Titled "NSA Infiltrates Online Worlds", it revealed that the National Security Agency had become aware that in-game currencies were being used to transfer untraceable funds around the world.

She did a quick check through the Wikipedia pages Cassandre had visited. One was headed "1964 Piano Solo", another "1970 Golpe Borghese", a third "1976 Killick Initiative". She clicked on the last one.

In the early 1970s, Christian Democrat party leader Aldo Moro came to the conclusion that the key to preventing outside interference in Italy's affairs lay in persuading the Italian Communist Party to renounce its revolutionary goals and transform itself into a fully pro-West, democratic party. If that occurred, there could be no further pretext for subjecting Italy to Anglo-American intervention under the guise of "anti-communism".[1] Moro therefore developed the strategy of a "*Compromesso storico*" or "Historic Compromise", under which the Communists would join the Christian Democrats in a coalition government of the left.

Far from being reassured, however, the outside powers that had kept a close watch on Italian politics for three decades reacted with alarm. On March 25, 1976, John Killick, the British ambassador to NATO, wrote in a memorandum that, "the presence of communist ministers in the Italian government would lead to an immediate security problem inside the Alliance".[2] A subsequent briefing document added: "For a series of reasons, the idea of a bloodless and surgical coup to prevent the Italian Communist Party from coming into power is attractive. It could come from right-wing forces, with the support of the army and the police."[3] This was similar to the way two previous coup attempts, the Golpe Borghese and Golpe Bianco, had been organised.

The link to the Golpe Bianco page was coloured, showing that Cassandre had clicked on it. She did the same.

The Golpe Bianco or "White Coup" plot was the brainchild of former partisan leader Edgardo Sogno. Sogno conceived the idea of using a combination of political unrest, mass insurrection, the ballot box and military power to force the president to declare a state of emergency, allowing Sogno to form an emergency government – a "white" or "legal" coup.

Kat frowned. Cassandre appeared to have been looking at attempted coups from Italy's violent past. But while a coup might have been conceivable in the dark days of the Years of Lead, surely there was no way the Freemasons could be planning anything like that now?

Her phone beeped. It was her mother, texting an invitation to Sunday lunch. On an impulse, Kat called her back.

"Mamma, would it be all right if I brought someone?" she asked, after the usual pleasantries about her father, *nonna*, and her sister's children.

There was a startled silence at the other end. "You mean – a *boyfriend*?" For Kat to bring a man to meet her parents was almost unheard of.

"Yes, a... My..." Now that she'd started, "boyfriend" seemed the wrong word for a highly distinguished forty-year-old prosecutor. "A man. Someone I'm seeing."

"Of course you can. What does he like to eat?"

"He's not fussy."

"He's not Venetian?"

Kat laughed, though she was aware her mother hadn't meant it as a joke. "No, he's from Bassano." That Flavio was from the Veneto would, she knew, be a point in his favour.

"And is he...?" Her mother left the question hanging delicately in the air.

Kat felt herself getting angry. She couldn't help it: no one could wind her up like her mother. She wished she could pretend she didn't know what her mother was talking about – *What, Mamma? Gay? Black? A Protestant? Muslim?* – but instead, forcing herself to stay calm, she said mildly, "Married? No, this one's single. Although he *was* married, a while back."

"Oh – *divorced.*" Her mother made it sound even worse than being married.

"He's a lawyer." On the plus side, she meant. But her mother chose to misunderstand that too.

"Well, I suppose it's easier for them, isn't it? To divorce. Since they know all the rules, they know how to get round them."

Kat sighed audibly.

"Any children?" her mother added.

"We haven't decided yet."

"No, I meant—"

"I know what you meant," Kat interrupted. "He has two. A little boy, Julius, and a girl, Anna."

Her mother didn't even have to voice her thoughts out loud for Kat to know what they were. *If he's got a family already, he won't want one with you.*

"Though he doesn't see much of them," she added. "They live abroad."

Oh, the heartless philanderer's a bad father as well, is he?

She decided she'd better bring this one-sided internal conversation to an end before she said something she regretted. "So we'll see you around midday, shall we?"

"Of course. I'll see if your sister can come too. You know

how Nonna loves to see her great-grandchildren. And it'll be nice for your... friend, won't it? If he doesn't get to see his own children much."

Oh, joy, Kat thought. She wondered if Flavio was going to be up to this.

TWENTY-FOUR

THE HACKER TRAVELLED to Sicily by ferry, on a stolen passport provided by the cleric. During the crossing he stood at the rail, thinking about the last time he'd made this journey.

He'd been twelve years old when his family had fled Gaddafi's Libya. His father was an educated man, with an American college degree, but when his US visa expired he'd made the mistake of applying to stay in the United States legally, instead of simply slipping underground like so many others. His application was refused. America wouldn't send goods to Libya, because of UN sanctions, but it would send Libyans – unless, that is, they could specifically prove their lives would be in danger.

Pointing out that every Libyan's life was in danger from the mad, murderous dictator who ruled them didn't count, apparently.

By Libyan standards, Tareq's father was reasonably well off. He could afford a laptop, for example – the same laptop that his son discovered when he was six years old. To Tareq, it was like coming across a magic lamp with a genie inside. All human knowledge was contained within it. He didn't have to pester grown-ups with questions any more.

A month or so later he stumbled across a document titled "The Hacker Manifesto", written under the alias "The Mentor".

I am a hacker, enter my world.

I'm smarter than most of the other kids, this crap they teach us bores me.

I've listened to teachers explain for the fifteenth time how to reduce a fraction. I understand it. "No, Ms Smith, I didn't show my work. I did it in my head."

– Damn kid. Probably copied it. They're all alike.

And then it happened. A door opened to a world. Rushing through the phone line like heroin through an addict's veins, an electronic pulse is sent out, a refuge from the day-to-day incompetencies is sought. A board is found.

This is it. This is where I belong.

I know everyone here. Even if I've never met them, never talked to them, may never hear from them again. I know you all.

– Damn kid. Tying up the phone line again. They're all alike.

So there were others like him: young people who existed more fully in the online world than in the physical one. He started to hang out on hacker boards, silently at first, then with growing confidence as he realised that no one knew or cared how young he was. But unlike Mentor, he didn't hate school, or his parents. His father, recognising how gifted he was, had sent him to the best madrasa he could. Tareq studied the Qur'an, but he also learnt algebra and mathematics.

Soon after Tareq's twelfth birthday, his father made a decision.

"Tareq is clever," he told the family one evening after prayers. "He needs to go to a better school. And we need to go to a better country." He looked at each of them in turn. "I've decided. We're going to Italy."

There was silence as they all digested this. Neither Tareq's mother, Zafeera, nor his sister, Faizah, dissented. They all knew Italy would mean a better life. In Libya secret policemen hung round every corner in their leather jackets and sunglasses, watching you. In Libya every neighbour was a potential informant. In Libya people disappeared in the night, never to be heard of again. The only question was whether it was possible to get out of Libya.

Now his father sought Tareq's gaze. "We will have to sell everything to pay for our passage. Everything we have," he said gently.

It took Tareq a moment to understand what he meant. "Not the laptop!" That was unthinkable.

"It's the only way. And soon, when I have a good job in Italy, I'll buy you a better one. I promise."

Tareq bowed his head. "I understand."

Two weeks later they left from a fishing village near Misrata, the smugglers rowing their passengers out in small groups to escape detection. When Tareq saw the ship that was to transport them across the sea he gasped. It was tiny – no more than twenty feet long. A fishing boat. Already the deck was crowded with people.

By the time they sailed, there were so many people crushed onto the deck that he and Faizah had to hold hands to prevent themselves from being separated. Already, some of the passengers were being sick as the vessel rocked in the swell.

The plan was to land at Lampedusa, the most southerly of Italy's islands, and claim asylum. So many people did this, his father had told him, that a military base on Lampedusa had been converted into a holding camp, where they would stay for a few weeks before being taken to the mainland. "It will be like a holiday," he said. "A holiday by the sea."

What his father didn't know, however, was that in the previous few weeks the political climate had changed. The West, having declared war on terror, had decided to make peace with strong Arab leaders like Gaddafi who they believed could act as a bulwark against the threat of radical Islam. President Mubarak in Egypt, President Assad in Syria and King Abdullah in Saudi Arabia were just some of the dictators now being favoured with aid and trade deals instead of sanctions and accusatory speeches in the UN.

In Italy, Prime Minister Silvio Berlusconi seized the opportunity to forge closer links with Libya. Libya had vast reserves of oil, not least because for decades it hadn't been able to sell them to the West. Now pipelines could be laid across the Mediterranean directly to Italy. To smooth that deal, Berlusconi agreed to take care of some minor nuisances that were irritating the Libyan leader. Principal amongst these, it turned out, was the steady drip of Libyans claiming asylum in Italy, whose criticisms of Gaddafi's human rights record were still deterring some – though by no means all – Western firms from investing in his country.

Since Berlusconi didn't want Libyans coming to his country any more than Gaddafi wanted them leaving his, the conversation was a short one. Then the two leaders got on to more important matters. It was Gaddafi, after all, who introduced Berlusconi to the phrase "bunga bunga".

When the wet and exhausted refugees finally reached

Lampedusa, they were met by armed soldiers. All of them, Tareq's father included, spoke the words that should have entitled them to asylum. But the soldiers simply separated them into two groups, one of Libyans and one of other nationalities. The Libyans were bussed to the military port, where a ship was waiting. A few men in the group tried to make a run for it. They were soon brought down by Italian soldiers using their rifle butts.

When the ship reached Tripoli, the refugees were kept on board for several days while the Libyan police interrogated them. Every so often, the police came and took away small groups of people.

"Whatever happens, we must stay together," Tareq's father told his family. But to Tareq he said quietly, when Faizah and Zafeera weren't listening, "If anything happens to me, remember you are the man of the family now. Protect your mother and your sister."

His father was one of the last to be questioned. Almost immediately, he was taken away. Then the policemen came for the rest of the family. They drove them to a police station not far from the docks. "Perhaps they're going to put us with Father," Faizah whispered to Tareq. He nodded, trying to look hopeful, but inwardly he knew it was unlikely. "Keep your hair covered at all times," he told her.

The policemen took them to a room where the walls were stained with brown smears and the fluorescent light tubes overhead were in metal cages. There were two men in leather jackets waiting for them, as well as two uniformed policemen. One of the men in plain clothes asked Tareq why his father had tried to claim asylum.

"Because he believed his life was in danger in Libya," he replied, trying to sound calmer than he felt.

"Why? Do we look dangerous to you?" the man demanded, smiling.

Tareq knew it was a trick question, one with no right answer. But he also knew that whatever these people were going to do to him, they had probably already decided on it. "No?" he said tentatively.

The man laughed. Approaching Tareq, he slapped him hard across the face, knocking him to the floor.

When Tareq could hear again, the man was talking. He was offering him a choice.

"You father has dishonoured your family. I have decided to punish him by dishonouring one of his women. Because he's not here, you can decide which one."

Tareq's head swam. He heard his father's voice. *Protect your mother and your sister.*

"I don't want to choose," he said. "Please…"

"Fine. I'll rape them both." The man clapped his hands. "Bring them in."

"Wait," Tareq said. He was desperately trying to think. Rape would be a terrible thing for either woman, but in Libya's deeply conservative culture, it would destroy any chance his sister had of having a life. "My mother," he said quickly. "If you have to punish one, punish my mother."

The door opened and his mother and sister were brought in.

"Say that again," the policeman said with a smirk. "You want me to screw your mother, is that right?"

"Yes," Tareq mumbled. He couldn't look at her.

"And you're going to screw your sister, you filthy dog."

Tareq stared at him, appalled. "I never said that!"

"I said you could choose which one *I* raped. I didn't say the other one would get off." He glanced at the other men, who were all laughing now. "But if you don't want to do it, I guess we'll just have to do your sister too."

The memory of what happened in that room would always be with him. He remembered their screams, the laughter of the men, the things they did to all three of them, not just with their bodies but with their guns and truncheons and boots. When at last they were done, the men dragged them to a car and drove them at high speed to a sports stadium. Even though it wasn't yet dawn, a small crowd was gathering. Policemen were directing people to their seats.

In the middle of the stadium was a crane. Thirty minutes later, a group of hooded men stumbled out of the changing rooms, barely able to walk. Their hands were bound and they were prodded along by policemen with truncheons. Tareq couldn't even tell which one was his father until the hoods were taken off.

They hanged them three at a time, their wrists still bound, their jerking bodies swinging into each other as the crane hoisted them up, their feet kicking at each other's shins.

When it was over, a policeman standing near the family turned to them. "Now get out. And tell everyone you meet what happens to those who criticise Gaddafi."

But their troubles weren't over. They were tainted now, and who knew if the regime was still displeased with them? The madrassa wouldn't give Tareq his place back. His mother couldn't get a job. They lived off tiny handouts from relatives.

After a month of staring numbly into space, Tareq woke up. He went to an internet café he knew. The owner was a good businessman, but he had almost no technical understanding. Tareq offered to take care of any IT issues that arose. He would do it at night, he said, when there was no one around to see him.

The café owner thought, then agreed. He named a wage that was ridiculously low. But at least it was a wage.

Late at night, when there were no customers, Tareq went online himself. It was a different kind of message board he frequented now. Not just those places in the Deep Web where the most sophisticated hackers lurked, but the even more hidden websites frequented by anti-Gaddafi activists.

After Gaddafi's fall, and the commander's instruction to come up with a plan, Tareq made contact with those hackers again. Some had moved on. But others, he discovered, had made the same journey he had, and were now radicalised. None used their real names, of course, or gave out any details about themselves. But by pooling information, they were soon operating at a whole new level of technical knowledge.

The people he consorted with now taught him how to cover his tracks from the world's security services. Because many had needed to evade Gaddafi's Western-built internet-surveillance system, they already had a working knowledge of how to escape attention. Accordingly, they knew about PRISM, TEMPORA and other Western surveillance programs long before Edward Snowden leaked details of them to the media.

The Snowden affair gave them a unique opportunity, however. Suddenly, the rest of the world was waking up to what the NSA and GCHQ were doing. Countries like Italy were seeking out and removing the wiretaps on their fibre-optic cables.

Tareq reckoned something like the US's proposed opt-in system, VIGILANCE, was probably inevitable in the end. But in this brief surveillance-free window lay his best chance to strike.

It was another hacker called Jibran who gave Tareq his big idea. They'd been on a secure message board discussing the Stuxnet worm, the virus engineered by American and Israeli cyberwarfare specialists to undermine Iran's nuclear programme. In ordinary computers, the worm was almost undetectable. But when it was introduced to a new network, it was programmed to seek out certain centrifuges made by Siemens that were used in the preparation of nuclear material. If it found them, it made them spin at high speed until they broke.

The hackers got hold of Stuxnet and took it apart line by line, looking for what it might tell them about the NSA's cyber capabilities. In fact, the technology inside the worm wasn't particularly new or complex. It was the idea itself that was revolutionary.

A virus that attacks devices instead of computers, Jibran observed. *If you think about it, that's pretty neat. But they should be careful. Once the rest of the world gets into that game, they're the ones with most to lose.*

A lightbulb went on in Tareq's head. He hadn't forgotten the commander's instruction. But only now did he have his first inkling of what his plan might be.

He began researching the Internet of Things.

By now he was regularly using Carnivia to communicate with his fellow hackers. They had all, at some time or another, tried to hack the website's source code. None of them had been able to. And if they couldn't break Carnivia, they reasoned, neither could the authorities.

It was Jibran, once again, who had come closest. He passed some hacked fragments of Carnivia's shell code on to Tareq, who marvelled at their beauty. Every line was written with a brilliant economy that resembled nothing so much as poetry.

Tareq started taking apart every piece of Daniele Barbo's code he could get his hands on. Mostly he did this because he wanted to learn from it. But he also put his knowledge to use. Just as a bomb-maker can learn from taking apart another bomb-maker's work, so Tareq was learning how to walk in Daniele's footsteps.

He used Carnivian encryption to cloak himself when he turned off the Fréjus Tunnel air turbines. That way, even if the authorities realised it was a deliberate attack rather than a freak accident, it could never be traced back to him, only to Carnivia.

As he evolved his plan, though, one thing still worried him. His weakness, as he perceived it, was that he and his fellow jihadist hackers were very few in number. If they attacked a dozen or so devices at a time, they could wreak havoc – but it wouldn't be irreparable. The West would immediately take steps to tighten up security on the millions of other devices he hadn't got around to.

The hacker's ambitions went far beyond mere havoc. He wanted Italy to implode – not just so that Italian voters would demand the removal of the US bases, as the commander had suggested, but because he blamed the country for what had happened to his family. And sometimes, in his wildest dreams, he saw himself achieving even more. He saw the chaos spreading beyond borders, right across the West. If that happened, he might bring about nothing less than an end to the West's reliance on technology. Once that was achieved, the jihadists and the armies of the West would fight each other on a level playing field. And in that war, he believed, the jihadists would win.

And so he changed his plan so that it would involve not just a few attacks but thousands, hundreds of thousands even, simultaneously. To do so required more funds – but whatever he asked for, the commander's invisible backers paid without demur.

Reaching Sicily, he was waved through Immigration with barely a glance. That didn't surprise him. Although Interpol had maintained a worldwide database of stolen passports since 2009, he knew that no government had ever consulted it. It was one of the many snippets of information he'd found online and squirrelled away for future reference.

He rented a room in a quiet suburb of Palermo, well away from the Muslim part of town. Once, Palermo had been the capital of an Arab kingdom. Then, in the twelfth century, the Christians arrived and turned the mosques into churches. But it was said that if you scratched a Sicilian, you still found a Saracen. Perhaps for that reason, there were many thousands of Arab-speaking immigrants there, principally in the poorer parts of the Borgo Vecchio, the old town.

The day after Tareq arrived, he went to a small, rather shabby building on the outskirts of Palermo. A sign proclaimed that this was Palermo Technical College.

He told the receptionist he was enrolled in the IT course that was beginning that same morning. He showed his false identity documents and thirty minutes later found himself in an airless classroom with fourteen other young men. The teacher, also a Muslim, was drawing a network diagram on the blackboard. As it happened, he made several errors, but the hacker kept his mouth shut and assumed an expression of dutiful interest.

He intended to be the second-best student the course had

ever had. not so brilliant as to arouse suspicion, but so far above the standard of the other students that the teacher would give him an impeccable reference.

He kept his other activities for the night time.

TWENTY-FIVE

THEY MET IN a small village up in the hills north of Verona, where the wild asparagus grew. A few elderly men were playing *bocce* in the shade of a plane tree. A ginger cat sunned itself sleepily on one of the metal tables outside the little café-cum-bar. Otherwise, the place was deserted.

Ian Gilroy always chose to meet somewhere he could see her face, Holly had noticed. Not for him a muttered conversation sitting side by side on a park bench, or strolling through a crowd. He'd once told her that, in his experience, assets lied to their handlers at least half the time. The handler's job was to work out which half, and why. That knowledge was often far more useful than whatever raw intelligence they thought they were bringing you.

She wondered if he ever thought of her as an asset, and if so, whether he ever assumed she lied to him.

"So, Holly. How was your trip?" he asked, when the bar owner had brought out their espressos.

"Eventful." She told him about the watchers, the paramilitary training, and the attempt to push her off the cliff. "But as for Capo Marrargiu, there's nothing there any more. Just the remains of some fires and a whole lot of broken glass."

He nodded. "I thought that might be the case. As for your tail... it's possible that was unconnected. After all, you spotted the master sergeants at the airport. If they spotted you in return, they may well have alerted someone to your presence. Say, for example, a wealthy oligarch had hired them to give his staff some freelance small-arms training. Not strictly legal, granted, but hardly a cause for alarm."

"Or maybe your own questions stirred something up, just as you said they might," she reminded him.

He shook his head. "I don't think so. I spoke to some old contacts, as I promised, and your father's report *was* passed up the line, it seems. But no action was ever taken. Once the Gladio network was no longer being run by NATO, it was felt that any activities undertaken by its former members were, strictly speaking, the concern of the Italians, not us. But it seems the report was never actually forwarded to the Italian intelligence services either."

"We washed our hands of it, in other words?"

Gilroy shrugged. "It was a mixture of bureaucratic inertia, I'm guessing, and a feeling that this was a stone we didn't particularly want to turn over. But, Holly, think through the implications. It means your father definitely wasn't the victim of an attempt to silence him. Only a handful of low-level analysts ever saw what he wrote, and none of them could possibly have a reason to want him dead. Your father was a drinker—"

"No," she interrupted. "He started drinking *after*. When he wasn't believed."

"His blood pressure was off the scale," he reminded her gently. "You said so yourself – that he had all the risk factors for a stroke. Far more likely than him being the victim of an attempted *assassination* is that he simply succumbed to his condition."

He gave the word "assassination" a dramatic inflection, as if to indicate how far-fetched that notion was.

"As for what the Freemasons described in your father's report were doing, I think with the benefit of hindsight that's also fairly clear," he continued. "It's no secret that the gladiators were recruited from amongst fervent anti-communists. After the network was rolled up, a number of neo-fascist groups formed from the remnants. Some of them may even have continued to carry out acts of violence. But by the end of that decade the Italians had cleaned up their act and the terror groups had all but disappeared."

"So you're telling me not to rock the boat?"

He shook his head. "I'm telling you there's no boat to rock. Holly, Ted was a good man, and a loving father. Whenever I saw the two of you together, I bitterly regretted not having children of my own, I can tell you. But if he were sitting here today, what do you think he'd advise you to do?"

She sighed. "He'd tell me to drop it. 'Pack up and push on.' That's what he always said."

"Ted was a soldier."

She thought for a minute. "Thank you."

"For what?" His blue eyes regarded her fondly.

"For not letting me turn into some crazy deranged conspiracy theorist."

"It's the least I can do. Not just for an old friend and comrade. For a new friend, too." He was silent. "What do you propose to do now?"

She stared at the distant hills. "Report for duty, I guess. That base newsletter doesn't write itself."

"You'll manage," he said quietly, and they both knew he wasn't referring to whatever trivial tasks would be waiting on her desk.

*

Holly drove down towards Verona. But her attention was only partly on the road. In her head, she was replaying fragments of the conversation with Ian Gilroy.

… It was a mixture of bureaucratic inertia, I'm guessing, and a feeling that this was a stone we didn't particularly want to turn over…

… Only a handful of low-level analysts ever saw what he wrote, and none of them could possibly have a reason to want him dead…

As she came to the junction with the main road into Verona, she waited patiently for a gap in the traffic.

… His blood pressure was off the scale – you said so yourself…

"No, I didn't," she said out loud. "I never said anything about that."

She thought back. If she hadn't actually said it, had she perhaps implied it? Had she perhaps mentioned it in some previous conversation? She didn't think so. But why had Gilroy mentioned it so casually in passing?

Suddenly, her mental landscape shifted, and what was previously white turned black.

Could I have been looking at this all wrong?

The report that had never been passed on to the Italians – was that really just inertia? Or had it been the exact opposite – had someone taken careful steps to ensure that as few people as possible knew of her father's suspicions?

Had it been the US, in particular, who didn't want anyone looking too closely at the Masonic lodge her father had raised the alarm about?

A horn sounded behind her, then another. When she didn't respond, the driver pulled out onto the wrong side of the road to pass her, his hand reaching angrily up to his chin to make the brush-off gesture that was a favoured insult in this part of Italy. The next car did the same.

She sat there, immobile, not caring.

Could it have been Gilroy?

TWENTY-SIX

IN VENICE, DANIELE Barbo looked up as the silence of Ca'
Barbo was interrupted by a click.

It was the sound of his TV coming off standby. He glanced
at the screen. There, in big white letters, it said:

*TURN ON YOUR COMPUTER, ASSHOLE. I'VE BEEN
TRYING TO REACH YOU FOR DAYS.*

Daniele frowned, then smiled as he realised who it was.
Going to his computer, he booted it up and logged onto the
Carnivia admin board.

Pretty neat. How did you do that?

*Smart TV. So smart, it sends data on what programmes you
watch back to LG headquarters in South Korea, so they can
sell it to advertisers. Took me about five minutes to hack the
connection. Why the fuck haven't you been online?*

I decided that maybe being always connected wasn't helping.

He didn't tell Max that he'd also been experimenting with
a twenty-five-hour day, going slowly in and out of phase with
the solar world, or that the walls of the room in which he was
sitting were covered in patches of different colours to help
him synaethesise the numbers they represented. There was
good research to prove the efficacy of such methods when
trying to solve complex mathematical problems, but he
doubted Max would be interested.

Instead he wrote, *What's up? I assume it must be important.*

Something you need to see. A video.

Daniele clicked on the Mpeg Max had uploaded. He was looking at traffic flowing through a road tunnel. The film was grainy – not just because it was from a security camera, but because it was a copy of a copy. Over the image was some Arabic script, its quality already blurred.

Abruptly, a car swerved into the path of an oncoming truck. There was no attempt on the driver's part to brake, or take avoiding action. The truck did try to stop, but only succeeded in jack-knifing into the tunnel wall. Within seconds there was carnage as other vehicles piled into the wreckage.

Where was this?

Jesus, you really have been offline, haven't you? The Fréjus road tunnel. It's been all over the news.

What do those titles at the beginning say?

A jihadist slogan.

And? Daniele knew Max must have some more specific reason for telling him about this.

That's the scary bit. In the video, you can see that the air turbines aren't going round. So I located them online using Shodan. According to the return path history, they were accessed ten minutes before the crash by someone whose identity was masked by our own encryption software. In other words, it was someone inside Carnivia who did this.

TWENTY-SEVEN

"MORE TIRAMISU, FLAVIO?"

"I couldn't," Flavio protested. Then, after a theatrical pause, "Oh, go on then. How can I resist? When it's made properly like this, with *savoiardi* biscuits, and a little bit of salt..."

Kat's mother flushed with pride. "And no Marsala, of course."

"And no Marsala," he agreed. It went without saying that only a barbarian would add a Sicilian fortified wine to a Venetian dish. "But did I detect just a splash of vermouth...?"

There was a crash from the kitchen. Swiftly, Kat's sister Clara handed baby Savina over to Kat and rushed off to see what her toddler, Gabriele, had broken now. Kat's mother tried not to look disapproving. "What a ball of energy that little boy is," she muttered, glancing in the direction of the kitchen.

To Kat's astonishment, lunch with her family had gone rather well. Flavio had talked politics to her father, praised her mother's cooking to the skies, discussed football with her brother-in-law, flirted with her *nonna*, and done a magic trick for Gabriele that left the little boy so impressed he had to hide behind a chair. Now Flavio leant over to where Savina sat on Kat's lap and offered the baby some of his tiramisu. Savina took the spoon in a pudgy fist, sucked it clean, and gave Flavio an adoring smile that made everyone laugh.

Kat felt the sudden surge of an unfamiliar emotion. Lust for the man, the weight of the child in her lap, the laughter of a family… all combining into something new.

My God, she thought. *I want to have babies with him.*

The thought was so unexpected, and so shocking, that she froze.

"What's wrong?" Flavio asked, noticing.

"Nothing," she said quickly. "I was just thinking about the case, that's all."

The case. If she had babies, there'd be no more cases. Not like the Cassandre investigation, anyway. You couldn't run a murder inquiry and pick a child up from nursery the same afternoon. In the last few years she'd lost count of the number of dates she'd let down at the last minute, or family lunches like this one she'd pulled out of.

But in Amsterdam, perhaps, she wouldn't be investigating cases like this one anyway. The thought, which she'd been avoiding, suddenly didn't fill her with quite so much dread.

How strange, she thought wryly: all those male officers who'd called her an ambitious bitch and a ball-breaker behind her back; all that graffiti on her locker accusing her of trying to sleep her way to the top. For all the obstacles they'd put in her way, those people had never managed to derail her career or put her off doing what she enjoyed. But now love, that most traditionally feminine of traits, was going to do it for them.

After lunch was over, the two of them walked to Stazione Santa Lucia for the short hop back to Mestre. The train was delayed by protestors from *No Grandi Navi*, "No Big Boats", the organisation that demonstrated against giant cruise ships in Venice. About a hundred of them were blocking the bridge to the mainland with fishing nets. Kat snuggled into Flavio, too full and sleepy to mind, closing her eyes and basking in the warmth of the sun streaming through the carriage window. The rest of the afternoon would be taken up with leisurely lovemaking, followed by a nap, and then perhaps a *spritz* or two in one of the bars on Piazza Ferretto. There was a time, not so long ago, when Sundays irritated her, because the operations room only ran with a skeleton staff and you had to wait a whole day before things got moving again. But not now. Being with Flavio was changing her.

When they reached the mainland they strolled hand in hand to her apartment. Another thought struck her: he was the only man she'd ever held hands with in public like this. There'd been plenty of lovers, yes; some incredible sex; but it was this simple gesture – one she'd always dismissed in others as mawkish – that she'd reserved for the man she loved.

As they reached her apartment she saw a wiry blonde figure sitting on the steps. In her loved-up state it took Kat a moment to realise who it was.

"Holly!" she said, astonished. "I thought you were still in America."

Holly raised her head and saw them. She looked exhausted, Kat thought. "I'm sorry I didn't call you sooner. Someone wanted my father dead, and now I think I know why."

She'd brought a spidergram, drawn in three colours and cross-referenced.

"The thing is," she told them, "the CIA always denied any involvement in Operation Gladio. Whenever Ian Gilroy talks about it, he makes it sound as if it was a purely NATO-run operation – one the military worked hard to keep secret from the real spies. But how realistic is it that the CIA had no idea NATO was training a guerrilla army of Italian civilians, right under their noses?"

Kat glanced at Flavio. He appeared to be listening attentively, even giving the occasional encouraging nod, but she knew that expression from their own meetings at the Palace of Justice. He was simply storing up his objections until Holly had finished, at which point he might very well tear her theories to shreds. Even to Kat's ears, they sounded far-fetched. And although it was good to see her friend again – the last time she'd seen her had been in the days immediately following her ordeal in the caves – Holly still seemed in a somewhat overwrought mental state. She was talking intensely and very fast, almost gabbling, as she tried to explain.

"What if NATO *thought* they were running Gladio – but actually it had been infiltrated by the CIA? In other words, what if there were effectively two networks: one trained by NATO to act as the resistance in the event of a communist invasion, and another, smaller, group inside that network, a cabal of extremists who carried out acts of politically-motivated violence under the CIA's direction? Then, after Gladio was rolled up, it makes sense that the CIA wouldn't want to lose their network as well. So they got them to regroup, under the guise of Freemasonry."

"Freemasonry?" Kat echoed. She looked across at Flavio to see if he was as intrigued by this coincidence as she was, but he was still wearing the same expression of polite, attentive scepticism.

"Yes." Holly explained about the ex-gladiators infiltrating her father's lodge.

"But not all the acts of violence you've described came from the right," Flavio objected quietly. "The left carried out

Just as many atrocities. The kidnapping and murder of Aldo Moro, to take just one example."

Holly was nodding. "Yes, of course. But it's strange, isn't it, how it was an operation by the supposedly left-wing Red Brigades which stopped the *Compromesso storico* in its tracks, and effectively ended any chance the Communist Party had of sharing power." She looked intently from Flavio to Kat. "Wouldn't it make more sense if the Red Brigades were actually under the control of the same people who were running Gladio all along?"

"A false-flag operation, you mean?" Kat said. She caught the look Flavio gave her. *Don't encourage her.*

"We know the Red Brigades were infiltrated by the CIA," Holly said. "It's mentioned in my father's report – and Gilroy confirmed to me that he was the CIA agent in charge of that. But did it stop at infiltration? Could the CIA actually have been influencing the Red Brigades' choice of targets? A year before the Moro kidnap, the Red Brigades kidnapped someone else." She pointed to the spidergram. "A seven-year-old boy. They cut off his ears and nose when his parents didn't pay up."

Now even Kat's mouth dropped open. "You think *Gilroy* might have been behind Daniele's kidnap?"

"I don't know," Holly confessed. "But what better way to establish the Red Brigades as terrorist bogeymen? The CIA may even have hoped it would provoke so much revulsion that by association it would discredit the whole of the left wing."

"I thought you trusted Gilroy. You always said he was a friend of your father's," Kat said, bemused.

"He was. At least, I thought he was. But, you know, I've only got Gilroy's word for that as well. I mean, I remember him coming round a couple of times when I was a kid, but from what my father wrote in his report, they were more like professional acquaintances than friends. Maybe Gilroy decided to keep me close for a reason. Maybe he's always been concerned that something like my dad's report would turn up one day. I keep asking myself why, if Dad really trusted Gilroy, he made that extra copy and hid it away for safekeeping. Did he have reservations about him, even then?"

"Where are the copies *you* made?" Flavio asked, cutting across Holly's speculations.

"One I gave to Gilroy, and one I emailed to myself from a photocopier at the airport. But when I tried to open it just now, the file was corrupted. I think somehow they must have traced it from the other end and destroyed it."

Flavio raised his eyebrows, but said nothing.

"Which is another indication the CIA could be involved," Holly continued. "Who else would have access to that kind of technology?"

"But why?" Flavio said patiently. "Why would anybody care about a CIA operation from over thirty years ago – even assuming such an operation actually existed?"

"Because it's still going on," Holly said. "I don't understand the how or why, but when I went to Sardinia, I saw soldiers training civilians in the use of firearms and explosives. I think in one form or another, Gladio must still be active. I think after they were exposed, they quietly regrouped under the banner of various Masonic lodges, and they've been carrying out assassinations and corrupting people ever since."

"And no one knows about it?" Flavio said sceptically. "A massive, organised attempt by a foreign power to control Italian politics through violence, dating back over twenty-five years, linked to one of the biggest scandals in Italian political history, and *nobody knows*?"

"Cassandre was researching that period on his computer," Kat pointed out. "Doesn't that seem strange to you?"

Flavio made a small sound, an involuntary *pfff* of disbelief.

Kat fixed him with a look, willing him to understand. *This matters to Holly. And if it matters to Holly, it matters to me.*

"All right then," Flavio said with a sigh. "A conspiracy stretching back to the 1990s and beyond. The *dietrologia* to end all *dietrologie*. Assuming there could be a grain of truth in it, what are you going to do next?"

"I'm going to see what I can dig up on Gilroy's time in the CIA," Holly said. "I'll start with what happened to Daniele. One of the Red Brigades gang that kidnapped him is still in prison. She may talk to me. If not, I'll find someone else. And then, when I've got some evidence, I'm going to bring it to you, so that you can open a formal investigation into the attempt to kill my father."

TWENTY-EIGHT

"*LA MESSA È finita: andate in pace*," the priest intoned.

"*Rendiamo grazie a Dio*," the congregation murmured in response. As the choir's voices soared into the "*Panis angelicus*", Ian Gilroy bowed his head. He rarely knelt these days. His knees were getting too fragile for that. But he genuflected in unison with those on either side of him as the priests and choir filed out.

Unlike the other worshippers, though, he remained seated as the basilica emptied. These moments after Sunday Mass, when St Mark's was closed to tourists, were one of the few times when the great building was almost peaceful. He looked up, drinking in the Romanesque beauty of the great arches. Above his head, gilded mosaics lined the interiors of the five great cupolas, more Islamic than Roman, that surmounted the roof. The Arabic influences were no coincidence: the Venetians had always been acutely conscious of their city's strategic importance as a bridge between East and West.

A few minutes after the congregation had departed, he saw the man he was waiting for.

"Monsignor," he murmured.

"I hope I haven't inconvenienced you." Father Calergi sat down next to him.

"Not at all. You have some news from our Masonic friends?"

Father Calergi nodded. "The Carabinieri are still investi-gating Cassandre's death, despite AISI's involvement. They suspect it must be connected to Count Tignelli and his plans. A view I have done nothing to disabuse them of, incidentally."

"Do I take it that the Curia is becoming concerned?"

"Those of us with Rome's interests at heart certainly have no wish to see Count Tignelli succeed, let me put it that way."

Gilroy gave him a sideways glance. "And yet you only come to me now, after the Vatican itself is safely out of the picture and the banker silenced. A cynic might question your timing."

The priest let that pass. "Can we take it that America shares our concerns?"

Gilroy thought. "Tell your people… that America is keeping a close watch on the situation. And that we will take a view on events as they unfold."

Father Calergi turned his head to look at him. "What ter-rible game are you playing?" he said quietly.

"No game, Father. But things are complicated just now. Timing will be everything. I need to know exactly what the Carabinieri have discovered, and what they intend to do about it. Can you find that out for me?"

"Of course. I'll make some enquiries."

"Good." That was the advantage of dealing with priests, Gilroy reflected: to them, the Sabbath was just another working day.

The two men spoke for several more minutes before leaving by separate exits. Outside, Gilroy took out his cell phone and dialled. There was another matter that could be dealt with today, for that matter.

"Public Affairs," a voice replied. "First Lieutenant Breedon speaking."

"Mike, it's Ian Gilroy. From the Education Centre on base?"

There was a brief pause while Holly's boss placed him. "Yes, of course," he said courteously. "How are you doing, sir?"

"I'm well, thank you, very well... I'm actually calling about Second Lieutenant Boland. As you probably know, I check in with her from time to time, and I just wondered whether you think she's really up to returning to her duties. She still seems in a somewhat fragile state to me."

There was a pause. "Sir, I haven't had any contact with Second Lieutenant Boland," Mike Breedon said. "And I wasn't aware she was planning to return to work. Do you have a date for that? I should talk to the DHR, get things organised for her."

"Do you know what," Gilroy said, "I probably misunderstood. Either that or she took my advice and decided not to rush things after all."

When he'd rung off he turned and looked up at the façade of St Mark's. Despite its familiarity, it never ceased to amaze him. If the interior resembled a gilded mosque, the outside resembled a Moorish palace: Arab minarets atop fantastic Gothic tracery, the whole thing layered with many kinds of coloured stone; porphyry and malachite, amethyst and cornelian, like something from a fairytale.

And His kingdom shall have no end, he thought wryly.

He gave an abrupt nod, almost as if he were saying goodbye.

TWENTY-NINE

"*AS-SALAMU ALAYKUM*," a voice said across the empty classroom.

Tareq looked up. "*Wa alaykumu as-salam*," he replied courteously to the figure who had just appeared in the doorway. Unobtrusively, he reached out and pressed the "CTRL" and "W" keys on his keyboard. A small window on his screen vanished, leaving only a larger window displaying a network-wiring diagram.

"Working on a Sunday?" The teacher came and looked over his shoulder.

"I observed *al-Juma'ah* on Friday. So now I'm catching up."

"Yes, I saw you at mosque." The teacher attended Friday prayers at a moderate mosque near his apartment. Tareq had been careful to sit where he couldn't help but be noticed.

"We must all follow Allah's laws," he said piously.

The teacher nodded. "You know, you are an exceptional student. My brother has a recruitment consultancy for IT professionals. I'll speak to him, if you like. If your work continues at this standard, he'll be able to get you a good job after the course is finished."

Tareq would like that very much indeed, since the teacher's brother was the whole reason he'd come to Sicily in the first place. He'd come across two former students from the course talking about him in a chat room, and immediately seen how it might fit into his plans. "Thank you. That would be very kind."

"You don't mind travelling?"

"Not at all," Tareq assured him.

"Good." The teacher put his hand on Tareq's shoulder. "I'll talk to him tonight."

When the teacher had left, Tareq waited a few minutes before bringing up the small window again. *How many bots?* he typed.

The Ghostnet user he was in communication with replied, *I'll send u a shot.*

Moments later, Tareq received a screenshot showing that the user had control of a network comprising almost half a million home computers. In each case the computers would appear to their owners to be completely normal, if a little slow. In reality, they had become slaves doing whatever the botmaster required, be it sending out spam or orchestrating denial-of-service attacks on a particular website.

How much? Tareq typed.

$5,000 US a day.

What if I want to buy?

Why would u? It's more cost-effective to rent.

I have my reasons.

I wouldn't sell for less than $750,000. This is my livelihood we're talking about.

$500K. You can always infect more.

That takes time. I don't take shortcuts with my code.

Which is why I'm buying it. Do we have a deal at $650K? Final offer.

I accept bitcoins or Ven.

Tareq emailed the funds immediately. The botnet he had

just bought with the commander's money wasn't especially big. The Mariposa net, uncovered in 2009, had controlled over twelve million computers, while the Metulji net found in 2013 had infected about eighteen million. But while the code on which those botnets depended was amateur, the code behind this one was relatively well built. Amongst other things, it was polymorphic, which meant the virus would hide in a different place on each computer, making it extremely hard to detect.

Tareq would have preferred to build his own botnet from scratch rather than buy one and customise it, but there was much to do in a short space of time. Nor was this the only network he would purchase. He and his fellow hackers might be few in number, but by the time the battle started, he intended to command the biggest army in history.

THIRTY

"THANK YOU FOR coming, Mr Speicher. May I offer you some coffee?"

The chairman of Banca Cattolica della Veneziana shook his head. "No, thank you. May I ask whether I am being questioned as an *indagato*?"

Flavio was wearing his lawyer's robes, Kat her Carabinieri uniform, the whole interview designed to appear as formal as possible.

Flavio shook his head. "You are not an official suspect at this stage, no."

"May I ask, then, what specific crime is being investigated here? In addition to the murder of my colleague, of course."

Hugo Speicher spoke calmly, his intelligent brown eyes turning from one to the other. As Kat had predicted to Flavio, this was not a man who would panic easily. But they had concluded he was one of the very few people who might actually give them some insights into Cassandre's death.

"He was courteous, urbane and bright," she'd told Flavio. "But he also seemed to me to have a real distaste for Cassandre."

"And our leverage?"

"The last thing any chairman wants is a scandal. And whatever Cassandre was up to, Speicher must know it could cause the mother of all stinks."

Now Flavio nodded at Speicher. "We can have the Guardia di Finanza take apart your bank with a fine-tooth comb if we need to. But we're hoping that won't be necessary."

The chairman considered. "And my cooperation, if I give it, will form part of the record?"

"Yes, if you wish it to."

Speicher gave a long sigh and some of the stiffness went out of him. He looked suddenly, Kat thought, less like the figurehead of a financial institution and more like a very troubled man.

"Very well. I should warn you, though, that it's quite technical. Most banking is, these days." He gave a rueful smile. "Perhaps that's where it all started to go wrong. Banks don't lend money any more – we conjure with it. We make it vanish and reappear, we transmute it from one currency to another; we send it through the ether in search of tax loopholes and safe havens. And we use it as collateral in ever more complex speculations."

Flavio reached for a legal pad to take notes. "Go on."

"You're aware, no doubt, that one of our shareholders is the Istituto per le Opere di Religione?" Speicher said. "That is, the Vatican Bank."

Flavio nodded. "Yes."

"It's a small stake – no more than three per cent. But that figure probably understates the close nature of the relationship. A relationship that until recently was managed at our end by Alessandro Cassandre. He was very proud of the association. It seduced him, perhaps, into making some unwise decisions." He reflected. "Or perhaps it was the other way round. Perhaps he was always corrupt, and simply saw in the IOR's lax regulatory structure an opportunity to commit financial crimes."

"What crimes, exactly?" Flavio asked quietly.

Speicher held up a hand. "I'll come to that, I promise, but it will only make sense if I give you some background. You've probably read in the papers that, under Pope Francis, the IOR has been under considerable pressure to clean up its act – in other words, to conform to international standards on financial transparency, money laundering and so on."

"I've read some of those reports," Kat said. "It's generally being seen as a big step forward."

"It is. The problem is, there are some past... enterprises, let us call them, that the IOR finds itself somewhat reluctant to be transparent about. Not least of which was its enthusiasm, until very recently, for a controversial financial instrument called a credit default swap."

Kat glanced at Flavio. They'd debated whether to have a financial specialist join them for this interview but had decided that until they knew exactly what they were dealing with, they'd try to keep this to themselves. Now she was wondering whether they'd miscalculated.

"Go on," Flavio said. "But please understand that we don't have any technical knowledge in this area."

"I'll try to keep it simple. Credit default swaps are essentially just an insurance policy against an institution or country being unable to pay its debts. For a tiny sovereign state like the Vatican, which is in the unusual position of having the euro as its currency but not actually being part of the eurozone, it wasn't unreasonable to hold a certain number of euro swaps; particularly during the global recession, when it looked as if the Italian government might default on its debts, which would have caused the value of the euro to nosedive.

"But the reason credit swaps are seen as controversial is that there's no need to hold any of the actual debt you're insuring against. It's a bit like buying fire insurance on your neighbour's house: when does it turn into a gamble that his house really will burn down? There was a point where holding a few swaps as insurance turned into something quite different – a massive bet that Italy *would* default and the euro would plummet. The IOR weren't alone in thinking that, of course. Many of the world's largest hedge funds were betting the same way. Behind closed doors, Berlusconi was saying that debt default hadn't been so very terrible for the Greeks, given what they'd been able to screw out of the rest of Europe in return. If he'd stayed in power, the value of the Vatican's swaps would almost certainly have continued to rise. Instead of which, he was convicted of paying an under-age belly dancer for sex and driven from office."

Kat nodded. Few would forget the scenes during Berlusconi's resignation, when jubilant crowds had sung the Hallelujah Chorus outside his office. An austerity package had been passed within a month.

"So then the Vatican was left holding what bankers call a 'toxic asset'," Speicher continued. "Something listed on the books as massively valuable, but which in reality had become a huge, open-ended liability. Technically, they were probably bankrupt. In similar situations, of course, European governments have created so-called 'bad banks' to hold the assets, to keep them from dragging down the rest of the company. But that was hardly an option for the Vatican. So they did the next best thing – they looked for someone to offload the swaps onto."

"You?" Flavio said.

Speicher nodded.

"But why would your bank want these assets, if they're so toxic?" Kat said, puzzled.

"We wouldn't," Speicher said. "But we – *I* – knew nothing about it. Only Cassandre, the Vatican's link man, knew what was going on. He formed a shell company, owned fifty-fifty by the IOR and ourselves, to which the IOR sold whatever swaps they couldn't close. That company, which was based in Liechtenstein, then sold them to another shell company in a different tax haven, this time owned forty per cent by the IOR and sixty per cent by us. And so it went on... Multiple transactions later, the assets were wholly in our name, and off the IOR's balance sheet."

"And in return?" Flavio asked, his pen moving at speed across his pad. "I assume there must have been something in it for Cassandre."

"In return, the IOR invested in another set of shell companies controlled by Cassandre personally. A payoff, in other words."

"Is the money still there?"

Speicher shook his head. "Cassandre used the funds to make highly speculative investments. Unfortunately, he wasn't nearly as good an investment manager as he was a crook. He lost the lot."

"How did you discover all this?" Kat asked.

"As part of these manoeuvres, Cassandre opened thousands of proxy accounts within the bank." Speicher frowned. "I still don't know why, to be honest. Each account has been numbered and issued with overdraft facilities, chequebooks and so on. But they've not been used. Anyway, one of the assistants in our back office realised something irregular was happening and drew it to my attention. When I looked into it, it became clear that Cassandre had been bypassing the bank's usual processes for years. When I had the evidence, I called him to my office and confronted him."

"What was his reaction?"

"He tried to bluster it out. Said the swaps were all part of some complicated financial strategy that would pay huge dividends to the bank very soon. I told him that was non-sense. Europe has turned the corner now. Only a very few cranks and doom-mongers are still betting the opposite way." He sighed. "I knew I had to fire him. But I also knew that it would almost certainly mean the end of the bank. You can't just sit on something like this – you're required to tell the regulators, who would conduct an investigation. That in turn would spook our institutional depositors. Inevitably, we would end up being swallowed by some larger bank, one better able to accommodate the risk. It would be the end of everything I've worked for. That was what Cassandre was betting on, I think – that these assets were *so* toxic, I'd have no choice but to hush up their existence."

"And?" Flavio said. "Did you?"

Speicher shook his head. "I told Cassandre he was suspended, and called an emergency board meeting."

"That was the board meeting you mentioned to me," Kat recalled. "The last time you saw Cassandre alive."

The banker nodded. "But not actually the last time I spoke to him. I phoned him next morning to tell him the board's decision – that he had to go immediately. By that time he was in a state of high panic. He told me he had a plan. That he now had protection on both sides, whatever that meant; that whatever happened, the bank was safe. He wanted more time, just a few more weeks, and then it would all come good. I told him he was raving and terminated the conversation. Frankly, the man disgusted me. He didn't even have the decency to face up to what he'd done."

Kat looked back through her notes, trying to get her head

round all this. "So your shareholders – the board – must have been furious. Will they lose money, if the bank goes under?" She glanced at Flavio. "That could give one of them a motive to have Cassandre killed, couldn't it?"

"The bank isn't going under," Speicher said.

Kat frowned. "I thought you said…"

"I said it would almost certainly bring down the bank. I didn't say it was a foregone conclusion. The reason I called the board meeting was in the hope that one of our existing shareholders might offer us a rescue package."

"And that's what happened?" Flavio asked. "You have a white knight?"

Speicher nodded. "One of our shareholders, Count Tignelli, has agreed to inject over half a billion euros – enough to cover all our liabilities, should the worst happen. In effect, he's buying us up."

So Tignelli was involved with Cassandre and the bank after all. She'd been certain of it, but at this confirmation she'd been right, Kat felt a familiar throb of excitement. "You didn't mention this when I asked you about him before," she said accusingly.

Speicher looked shamefaced. "Forgive me, Captain, but I was put on the spot and I wasn't sure how much I should tell you. Tignelli had made a verbal agreement to put up the necessary capital, but it seemed to me that the deal could easily be derailed by a scandal and a police investigation."

"You called him," Kat realised. "That's how he knew I was coming to La Grazia. Because you'd warned him."

"I had to tell him Cassandre was dead. Naturally I also told him that the Carabinieri were treating it as murder."

"How did he react?" Flavio asked.

Speicher frowned. "I was phoning to reassure him, you

see. I thought I could break the news about Cassandre in such a way that it would seem like a problem that had fortuitously been solved, rather than one that was being created."

"And?"

Speicher said slowly, "Tignelli's reply was, 'Well, that's one less loose end to be dealt with, isn't it?' Almost as if he were the one reassuring *me*."

Flavio and Kat exchanged glances.

"Is there a possibility that this was a scheme cooked up by Cassandre and Tignelli between them?" Kat asked. "We're almost certain they were members of the same illegal Masonic lodge. Could Cassandre have deliberately lowered the value of the bank, so that Tignelli could buy it up cheap? And that Cassandre was disposed of, when he'd outlived his usefulness?"

"It's crossed my mind," Speicher said. "But the obvious objection to that is, Tignelli *hasn't* got it cheap. He's pouring a huge amount of money into an institution burdened with worthless liabilities. Why on earth would he do that, if he didn't have to?"

"An honourable man," Flavio said when Speicher had left them.

Kat nodded. "It's easy to forget, isn't it, that not all money men are crooks. For every Cassandre there are probably a dozen Speichers."

She got to her feet and crossed to the window. Below her a *topa*, a "rat", a flat-bottomed delivery boat, chugged along the *rio*, its deck stacked high with groceries: tins of Bassano asparagus and San Marzano tomatoes, nappies, and the phosphate-free detergents that were supposed to protect the fragile ecology of the lagoon. The man at the tiller steered it one-handed, with the deftness of a Venetian who had spent all his life manoeuvring these crowded waterways.

"Speicher clearly didn't know about Cassandre's links with the intelligence services," she said. "I wonder if that was the escape plan Cassandre was talking about – a desperate attempt to sell out whatever it was the Masons in the black lodge were up to, and buy himself protection that way?"

"He was clearly a man without loyalties, that's for sure." Flavio came and stood next to her. His arm brushed hers, and she felt the tiny surge of emotion and endorphins that his physical proximity always engendered: a swell of affection, a tiny wriggle of lust. "Just as Tignelli is clearly a man without scruples."

"Is there any way this could relate to the military training Holly saw?" Kat asked.

Flavio turned back to the room, frowning. "I can just about buy that Tignelli's got some complicated scheme that involves taking over Speicher's bank. I can even buy that Cassandre tried to sell him out, and got himself killed as a result. But military training? Plots dating back to the Cold War? Your friend's grasping at shadows. Our own investigation is complicated enough, without trying to link it to fantasies."

Kat said nothing. It disturbed her that, far from becoming immediate friends and allies, Flavio and Holly seemed to have taken an instant dislike to each other. For his part, Flavio clearly thought that Holly was hysterical. He'd told her bluntly that they'd discuss her theories only when she had some evidence, in a tone which made it apparent he thought that was unlikely to happen any time soon.

Kat had waited until her friend had gone before patiently pointing out that Holly was just beginning to entertain a possibility that shattered her entire world view, one that meant re-examining every loyalty and principle she had.

Holly, meanwhile, had been startled to realise how serious the relationship with Flavio was. "What is it with you and sleeping with your bosses?" she'd said incredulously when she'd called Kat later. "I go away for a while and when I come back you're at it again. As if that one mistake with Aldo Piola wasn't enough."

"I'm not actually sleeping with my boss this time," Kat had pointed out. She couldn't help being a little irked at the implication that she was prioritising a selfish relationship with Flavio over loyalty to her friend – not least because there was more than a grain of truth in it.

"Only your prosecutor," Holly had retorted. "How's that going to look in court? It'll undermine our whole case."

"'Our' case? We don't even have a case yet. What do you want me to do? Drop him? That'll hardly help you to find out what happened to your father."

"I just think you might be blinded by your feelings, that's all," Holly said darkly.

And you're not? Kat had thought. But she'd said only, "Give Flavio a chance, will you?"

To Flavio she said, "Give Holly the benefit of the doubt, won't you? At least for a little while. Even if she doesn't come up with anything, we've lost nothing by listening to her."

"For your sake, my love. But you've already got me chasing after one wild conspiracy. Can we try not to add another to the list?"

"Of course. Anyway, now that we've got confirmation that Tignelli was involved with Cassandre and the bank, I think it's time to increase the pressure. Make him think we know more than we do, and that we're closing in. I read that he's one of the sponsors of the grand reopening of the Imperial Apartments at the Ala Napoleonica. I'm going to go along and try to rattle his cage."

THIRTY-ONE

THE WOMEN'S PRISON in the small town of Rovigo was a grim, high-walled building in a run-down suburb beyond the train station. The walls were made so high, Holly had read, after an episode in 1982 when four women awaiting trial on terrorist offences had escaped. Accomplices blasted a hole in the wall, tossed machine guns to the women inside, and kept the guards at bay with automatic fire. Three had later been recaptured, though in one case it had taken over ten years.

That was Carole Tataro, the woman she was there to visit. The same woman who had been part of the Red Brigades gang that kidnapped Daniele Barbo.

Many of Tataro's former comrades had since turned *pentito* and incriminated others in return for lighter sentences. But either because Carole had been amongst the last to be captured, or because she still held firm to the ideology of her youth, she hadn't been one of them. According to what Holly had read online, Tataro had trained in prison as a paralegal and now campaigned against overcrowding within the penal system.

Inside, the place stank of disinfectant and institutional food, and the corridors had the cavernous, echoey quality of a busy train station. Holly was taken to a small visitors' room, itself little bigger than a cell.

The woman who was shown in a few minutes later was surprisingly petite. Next to the overweight female guard, she seemed frail and almost childlike. It was hard to believe she had once fired an Uzi or hurled petrol bombs at policemen.

"Thank you for seeing me," Holly said, extending her hand.

Carole Tataro sat down without shaking it. "I never refuse a meeting. Talking to outsiders keeps my brain sharp. But I have to tell you that if I did refuse anyone, American army officers would be high on my list."

"May I ask why?"

The other woman shrugged. "There are over a hundred US military installations in Italy – more per capita than almost any other country in the world. And Italy pays more towards their upkeep than any other country. Over thirty per cent of the running costs, plus generous tax breaks and provisions to pay for so-called 'improvements' should you ever leave. You're like leeches on our economy." She considered. "No, not leeches. Leeches can be burnt off with a cigarette. You're more like a cancer." She spoke calmly, her dark eyes fixed on the wall behind Holly's head. It struck Holly that her speech patterns were not unlike Daniele's – strangely uninflected and monotonous.

"Perhaps we can agree to disagree about that. I want to talk to you about one particular episode in your terrorist career."

"Former career," Tataro corrected. "My activism is directed at a different target now."

"Former career, then," Holly said impatiently. "I'm talking about the kidnap of Daniele Barbo."

It was extraordinary how Tataro's self-assurance seemed to evaporate at the mention of that name. "Why?" she said bluntly.

"Why do I want to talk about it, you mean? Does it matter?"

"Of course." Tataro had quickly recovered her bravado. "Everyone who comes to talk to me has an axe to grind. A theory they want to prove, an article they've pitched to an editor, a thesis they need quotes for. It would save us both time if you told me what your angle on the Barbo kidnap is, and I'll tell you whether I'm prepared to help you."

Holly looked at her. "I'm a friend of Daniele's," she said simply.

"I... I..." Tataro blinked. "How is he?"

"Still destroyed by what you did to him." There seemed little point in sugaring the pill.

Another pause. "Of all the actions we carried out... That one was a disaster from first to last."

"In what way?"

"You have to understand, we thought of ourselves as disciplined revolutionaries, not criminals. We kidnapped business executives, judges, NATO generals – the class enemy. If the ransom was paid within the stated time, the hostage was returned alive. If it wasn't, he was killed. We had no reason to terrorise the general public, who mostly understood that industrialists and politicians were never going to give up their power unless they were forced to. Freedom for the people meant death to the capitalist hegemony. Communism or destruction: that was the simple choice."

"So why Daniele?" Holly said, impatient with all this propaganda. "Why kidnap a seven-year-old child?"

"At the time, our leadership was in prison and the network was being run by people who hadn't held power before. My cell was led by a comrade called Claudio. Not his real name, of course: we all used *noms de guerre*. Mine was Maria." She hesitated. "There was another comrade called Paolo. There was tension between Claudio and him... Sometimes they egged each other on. Like children, to see who could be the most revolutionary.

"On paper, the Barbo family were a legitimate target. They were wealthy, aristocratic, and they'd recently acquired a large interest in Alfa Romeo cars, which up until that time had been owned by the Italian government. Alfa Romeo was an important part of our strategy. If we could unionise the factory and then radicalise the union, we would have acquired a key political lever.

"Selling a stake to Matteo Barbo was a smart move on the government's part. Although Matteo had been something of a playboy in his youth, he strongly favoured left-leaning, progressive industrial relations, and he was popular with the workers. Claudio argued that by kidnapping Barbo's son, we would force him to sell his stake in order to raise the ransom."

"But it didn't work out like that?"

"Right from the start, everything was fucked up. Don't get me wrong: I'd killed people by that time, many people. Sometimes violence is necessary. But this was a child. A frightened child. And he was... vulnerable, that much was obvious. Not autistic, like they later claimed in court, just a bit unusual. I talked to him a lot, actually. I suppose I wanted him to know that we weren't cruel, only determined, that we had reasons for what we did. And as the weeks went on and the ransom still wasn't paid, I tried to keep him distracted."

"I don't imagine that was easy, given the circumstances," Holly said drily.

"It was, actually. We both liked number games – magic squares and so on." Seeing that Holly didn't understand, Tataro held out her hand for Holly's pen and drew on a page from her notebook. "If you add any column, row, or diagonal of the square, they all come to the same number. He loved that… he started seeing how big he could make his squares so that they still had the same properties. I told him Benjamin Franklin, the US president, once devised a square with sixty-four boxes, and Daniele spent days trying to beat that. Or we'd play age riddles. You know: 'In fifteen years' time I will be the square of my age fifteen years ago. How old am I now?'" She smiled at the memory.

"Very nice. Who gave the order to mutilate him?" Holly asked coldly.

There was the briefest of pauses. "It got very difficult. We knew it was only a matter of time before the police located us. But the parents still wouldn't pay… We had to do something to step up the pressure on them."

"But who gave the order?" Holly persisted. "And who carried it out?"

"The tensions within the group had got worse by then. Claudio was panicking, Paolo was saying that we had to have a new plan. And there were rows – stupid rows about things that shouldn't have mattered." For the first time, Tataro looked embarrassed.

"What sort of things? Oh," Holly said, understanding. "*You*."

Tataro nodded. "Claudio was my lover for almost a year before Paolo came along. It wasn't exactly a normal situation. Going outside of the group for a partner was considered a security risk. Somehow, I came to feel it was my duty to sleep with both of them. I think that contributed to the arguments about what to do with the boy."

"And?" Holly asked quietly. "Who did it?"

"I wasn't there. I was so disgusted by the idea that I walked out when they started discussing it." She shook her head. "Perhaps if I'd stayed... But I doubt it would have made any difference by then."

"What happened to them both?"

"Claudio was killed by Italian Special Forces when they rescued Daniele. Paolo managed to escape. I did too for a while, but in the end I was betrayed... All the other members of our group were killed or captured during the raid. Of course we refused our lawyers, on the grounds that they'd been appointed by the state. Not surprisingly, the trials didn't go too well for us. We all got life imprisonment."

"What if I told you that your group had been infiltrated by the CIA?" Holly said, watching her intently. "Would that surprise you?"

Tataro shook her head. "I came to the same conclusion myself, a long time ago."

"Why?"

"Like I said, the kidnap was misconceived from start to finish. It discredited us in the eyes of the workers – it made us look like criminals, no better than the 'Ndrangheta gang who'd kidnapped the Getty boy a few years earlier. By extension, it discredited the whole radical left. Who benefited? Not us, that's for sure."

"You seem very relaxed about it," Holly said. "I suppose you think that if the CIA were involved, it lessens your own responsibility."

"Don't tell me what I think," Carole Tataro snapped. "I've paid for my actions. I've spent my life locked up with child killers, because what my comrades did to that boy disgusts even the people who are sent to places like this." She gestured around her. "You see how small this room is? I share a space the same size with two other women, neither of whom speak

Italian. We take it in turns to stand up, and when they shit I can hear every sound. That's been my life. I accept it's what I deserve. But don't tell me that I'm any worse than those on the other side of the political spectrum."

Holly waited a moment. "So who was the double agent, then? Paolo or Claudio?"

Tataro laughed hollowly. "Isn't it obvious? It must have been the one who got away. The one who went on to kidnap Aldo Moro. The one I fell in love with, and who told the security services where I would be hiding. Paolo."

THIRTY-TWO

The Ala Napoleonica had one of the best locations of any building in Venice, in the central section of the three enclosed sides of Piazza San Marco. The colonnades on either side had originally been built to frame the façade of San Giminia, one of Venice's most beautiful Renaissance churches. Napoleon had it demolished partly because he thought there were too many churches in Venice, but also because he wanted to bring the Empress Josephine to the city, and he knew she would expect a ballroom.

As she approached the palace steps, Kat wondered at the self-confidence that could lead a man to take such big decisions, and at such speed. Had it been megalomania, ruthlessness, or a bit of both? Napoleon's army occupied Venice for less than nine years, yet during that time the city had changed utterly. Canals had been paved over to make boulevards, whole districts were pulled down to make formal gardens, the political stranglehold of the Venetian aristocracy was destroyed, and dozens of convents and monasteries were dissolved and turned into hospitals, prisons and administrative offices. The Carabinieri's own headquarters at Campo San Zaccaria was one such former convent, just one example of how, in Venice, the past and the present were always intertwined.

Normally, Kat wasn't a great fan of Piazza San Marco. Napoleon had famously called it "the drawing room of Europe", but these days it usually felt more like Europe's sixth-form common room, so crammed was it with groups of bored, milling schoolkids, along with the hawkers who sold them hair braids, glow-in-the-dark yo-yos, fake tattoos, and all the other tat indispensable to an educational visit to her city. Tonight, though, even she had to admit that it was looking spectacular. For the grand reopening of the Imperial Apartments someone had arranged for a double line of flaming torches to snake through the square, guiding the guests towards their destination. On one side an orchestra played, and a red carpet flickered beneath the flashbulbs of half a dozen paparazzi.

She was wearing her latest acquisition for the occasion, a dress by the Venetian designer Laura Biagiotti; a knee-length sheath of diaphanous cotton that could be paired with a belt for elegance or left to flow free for a more sensual effect. Tonight she was wearing it with a belt, along with a matching clutch bag from Malefatte, the leather goods cooperative based in the women's prison. But compared with the other women on the red carpet, she was underdressed. Many were wearing ball gowns. Some were masked; all were plastered in jewels that undoubtedly cost more than she earned in a year. On the other hand, most were at least a decade older than her, the middle-aged men on whose arms they hung exuding the sleek self-importance of the powerful. Tonight, Venice's moneyed classes had come out to see and be seen.

She walked up the grand staircase, an overwrought confection of balusters, pilasters and scenes from ancient history; all of which, she couldn't help noticing, featured famous military triumphs. Doubtless the intention had been to flatter the

French conqueror. At the top, in the throne room, she accepted a glass of *prosecco* from a uniformed waiter. The bottle bore the flamboyant swirling T that marked it out as Tignelli's own brand. It was excellent, the bubbles fine and soft, the nose with a pronounced aroma of peaches and honeysuckle.

She was still looking around, trying to fit names to faces, when a handbell was rung and the waiters began urging the guests into the ballroom. A man with a mop of grey hair stepped onto a dais and started to speak, introducing himself as the professor in charge of the restoration and thanking the sponsors for making the project possible. He saved Count Tignelli's name until last, gesturing dramatically into the crowd as he made the scale of his gratitude clear. Other guests parted to clear a space around the stocky figure of their bene-factor, who acknowledged their applause with a slight bow.

"Napoleon, it is fair to say, will always be a controversial figure in Venice," the professor continued. "Yet his brief tenure here coincided with a necessary rebirth. He dredged the canals and rebuilt the port; he swept away a corrupt, enfeebled gov-ernment and the stultifying effects of the Church; he drove out the gypsies and beggars who were living like parasites off the ordinary people. Above all, he recognised that this part of northern Italy was a kingdom unto itself, distinct from the rest of the Italian peninsula."

That prompted even louder applause.

"We are especially grateful to Count Tignelli for sharing with us some exhibits from his personal collection of the Emperor's memorabilia," the professor concluded, gesturing at the display cases ranged along the walls. "Please enjoy the evening."

As the chatter rose again, Kat drifted over to one of the dis-plays. Tignelli's collection consisted of a mixture of documents and curios: a lock of the Emperor's hair, a handwritten letter to his wife, a military sash worn by him in a battle. There was even a death mask, to which a few of the dead man's hairs still stuck. A little further on, a blue case containing something small and shrivelled caught her eye. A card informed her that it was Napoleon's penis, removed by his doctor immediately after death. It resembled nothing so much as a piece of dried beef jerky.

"You look fascinated, Capitano," a voice said beside her.

She turned. Count Tignelli was standing next to her. "With that?" She indicated the dried-out, twisted thing in the box. "Hardly. No wonder they called him the Little General."

"And yet he was also a legendary lover. Perhaps it just goes to show that stature isn't everything."

You would say that, she thought: Tignelli barely came up to her shoulders. She gestured at the fresco-covered walls. "It all seems a bit like overkill for just one man, doesn't it? Did he really deserve all this?"

Tignelli considered. "He was not only the greatest military leader of all time, but one of the greatest political leaders. His particular genius was to understand that, by itself, power is worthless. Its only value lies in what it allows you to achieve. For those who, like him, wish to leave their mark on history, he makes a useful study."

"Yes? And what have you learnt from him, exactly?"

Tignelli paused, as if to indicate that he knew this was nothing more than a game the two of them were playing, one he wanted to savour. "There's a saying of his I particularly treasure: 'In war, it is better to have one bad general than two good ones.' In other words, it is not always necessary to be right. But it is always necessary to be bold. Does that answer your question, Capitano?"

"Is that why you've bought the Banca Cattolica?" she

asked, watching him closely. "Some people would consider that a bold move, given the state of its finances."

If Tignelli was surprised at how much she knew, he didn't show it. He shrugged. "A business speculation – a somewhat sentimental one, actually. I hate to see a once-great Venetian institution in difficulties."

"Let's hope it doesn't lose any more senior partners, then."

He smiled. "You know, Captain, you're wasted on these small investigations. Someone as notable as you should be taking a more prominent role in this city's administration. Imagine what it would do for the role of women within the Carabinieri if you were its public face."

"That sounds like tokenism to me."

"Well, bear it in mind." Tignelli seemed to assume that such a position was completely within his gift, she noted. "I must admit, I'm somewhat surprised to see you here. Pleasantly surprised, of course. But I understood that the investigation into the death of Signor Cassandre had been transferred to other departments."

"You're very well informed."

He didn't deny it. "And it occurs to me that, now you are no longer part of that investigation, there can be no obstacle to my taking you out to dinner."

She almost laughed at the brazenness of it. "I don't think that would be very appropriate, do you?"

"No," he agreed. "It would be rather deliciously inappropriate." He came closer. "I would like to hear your views, as a Carabinieri officer and a Venetian, on what we can do to clean up the open sewer that our city has become. But I confess that I would also enjoy your company as a woman."

Taken aback, all she managed by way of a comeback was, "I thought you Masons weren't very keen on women."

"And as I told you, Captain, my interest in Freemasonry is purely academic. They're useful sheep, nothing more."

If she'd hoped to put pressure on him by coming here tonight, she realised, she had clearly failed. A hand tapped Tignelli's shoulder, eager for a word with the great man, and he turned away into the crowd without a backward glance.

THIRTY-THREE

AS NIGHT FELL, the hacker's real work began.

He knew there was no such thing as a completely secure internet connection. He had to trust that by the time he came to the attention of the world's security services, he would have moved on, his tracks well covered.

Even so, he took what precautions he could. At the technical college – which was always deserted at night – he first logged onto TOR, then onto a Virtual Private Network service offering anonymous IP addresses, and finally Carnivia. Only then did he access a search engine called Shodan.

Shodan was unique in that instead of searching for websites, it allowed the user to search for devices connected to the internet. Its creator, a twenty-nine-year-old programmer called John Matherly, had said that his aim was to show how large and insecure the Internet of Things had become. His assumption was that if he revealed how lax most devices' security was, manufacturers would be shamed into recalling their products.

Instead, the manufacturers simply ignored Shodan, or at best issued new, more expensive upgrades.

To date, pranksters – one could hardly call them hackers, since no actual hacking was necessary – had used Shodan to turn car washes on and off remotely, accessed a city's traffic control system, and shouted abuse at startled security guards through their own monitoring systems.

It was something rather more than a prank the hacker had in mind now.

Setting one of the parameters to "country: Italy" and another to "architecture: MIPSEL", he searched until he found what he was looking for.

He clicked on the IP address, adjusted a setting, and went off to do something else. When he came back, the readings on the screen confirmed that he'd just managed to raise the temperature in a power plant in Lombardy by one degree.

Immediately he reset the thermostat back the way it had been, before writing a small piece of executable script and adding it to his files. Then he closed the connection and moved on.

Using Shodan, he wandered right across Italy, choosing his targets. A hospital in Friuli-Venezia. The subway system in Milan. A network of seven thousand police-linked burglar alarms in Lazio. A flood-control system in Abruzzo.

At one point he came across a brand of wireless baby monitors that required no password or login. As he considered whether this could be of any use, he found himself looking at a sleeping baby on one of the company's products.

As he watched, the baby's father came into the room, a young man in shorts with heavily tattooed arms. He crouched down beside the sleeping child and, tenderly, planted a kiss on its forehead.

"Sleep well, little fella," he whispered in English.

The baby stirred, opened one eye, then began to yell.

"Shit!" the father said heavily. Resignedly, he reached down into the cot to pick it up.

Involuntarily, Tareq laughed. The young man froze, then

stared incredulously at the baby monitor. Holding the baby to his shoulder, he went out of shot. Over the baby's squalls, Tareq heard him calling to his wife.

"Janey! Hey, come here!"

When his wife came in, scolding him for waking the child, he pointed at the monitor. "That thing just *laughed* at me."

"Rufe, what are you *talking* about?"

"The monitor. I just heard it laugh."

Janey was wearing very short boxer briefs and a tank top, no bra. As the two of them peered at the baby monitor, Tareq couldn't resist saying, "Boo!"

"Fucking A!" the man yelled, jumping back. The baby yelled even louder. His wife, with rather more presence of mind, reached round the back of the monitor and yanked out the lead. Tareq's screen went blank.

Still laughing, he scrubbed the baby monitors from his list and moved on.

It was as he was investigating the capabilities of Yale's new internet-connected deadbolts that he thought again about that family. If he was successful in his plans, he would destroy a major part of the life they currently took for granted. He might even kill them. How did he feel about that?

He had never killed someone at close quarters. But he felt no more remorse about destroying that baby, he realised, than he would about picking off an opponent in a video game. It only reinforced his resolve to unleash a wave of destruction that would annihilate technology itself.

A level playing field.

He moved on from the locks, and spent rather more time examining supermarket supply chains. These were more sophisticated than most networks. When a customer purchased, say, a pear, the scanner at the till sent the information back to the store's own inventory system. If it looked as if the store might run out of pears in the next twelve hours – based on a complex algorithm factoring in variables such as the price of pears at rivals' stores, the fact that shoppers tended to consume more fresh fruit at the weekend, any special offers on bananas coming up that might tempt people away from their usual fruit, and whether there was a surplus of melons in the back that needed to be got rid of – it would automatically order up more pears from one of the huge Central Distribution Centres, or CDCs, dotted around the country. If enough people bought enough pears, a stock-control program at the CDC would inform its opposite number at the grower's, and inside a vast ripening warehouse a sprayer would adjust the mixture of nitrogen gas and carbon dioxide in the atmosphere, speeding up the ripening process.

As a distribution system it was both incredibly efficient and incredibly fragile. Effectively, it meant that tens of millions of people were never more than a week away from starvation.

Most of Europe's big supermarkets used encryption systems to move data around their networks. Unlike manufacturers of baby monitors, they had a powerful commercial interest in maintaining security: their sales information could be useful to their competitors. What they were unaware of, though, and the hacker knew full well, was that the world's data encryption standards had been designed by a team of American software engineers that had been infiltrated by agents from the National Security Agency, as part of an operation called BULLRUN. The agents deliberately built weaknesses into the protocols, so that the NSA would be able to spy on companies without their knowledge.

Tareq set to work finding a way into the supply chains, using an exploit left behind by BULLRUN. It was intricate, absorbing work, and he didn't notice the time passing. He jumped as a voice at the door said, "*Sabah el kheer*."

Quickly minimising his working window, he looked up. Somehow, night had turned to day. "Good morning."

"You're here early," the teacher said, smiling. "Still keen, then?"

"Of course."

"I spoke to my brother. It's all arranged – I'll forward you the details. Of course you'll have to start at the bottom. But if you have the right attitude and work hard, it's a good life." The teacher came and leant in close. "Americans like to tip, he says. Even for the most stupid things. If you mend their wi-fi, or show them how to get their emails, they'll shower you with dollars."

The teacher looked at the taskbar along the bottom of the screen, where Tareq's window was minimised. "What's this?" Before Tareq could answer, his hand had gone to the mouse and opened it.

Tareq had hacked into the mainframe of Esselunga, Italy's largest supermarket, and given himself root privileges to access the servers controlling stock levels. "It's nothing," he said quickly. "That is, I was just curious."

The teacher gave Tareq a startled look. "This is hacking, you realise that? There are laws about this. You could be arrested. We could *all* be arrested – they can trace it back to here."

"It's secure. I'm using TOR—"

"TOR? Why?" The teacher stared at Tareq. "What else have you hacked?"

"Nothing," Tareq lied.

"Listen," the teacher said, more gently. "I did some stupid stuff myself, when I was your age. I understand the appeal. The feeling that you know more than they do, so why shouldn't you go wherever you want? After all, if their security is so feeble, it's their own fault, right?" He wagged his finger. "Wrong. There is private property on the internet, just as in the real world, and the penalties for going wherever you want are much, much greater. We'll talk about this today, in class."

When the other students arrived, the teacher initiated a discussion about computer ethics. Tareq did his best to look like a shamefaced kid who'd been carried away by all the knowledge the teacher had imparted in his lessons.

"What other damage can hacking do?" the teacher asked, towards the end of the talk.

A student raised his hand. "Hacking can kill."

The teacher raised his eyebrows. "Would you like to give us an example?"

"The Fréjus road tunnel."

Tareq stiffened. How did anyone know about that?

"There's film of the air turbines, just before the crash," the student was saying. "They're saying it was a hack."

While the others studied network protocols, Tareq surreptitiously did a search. The student was right: the film of the Fréjus demonstration had been posted online, along with some stupid slogan. So far it was only posted on a few jihadist websites. But those websites were exactly the kinds of places the West's security services monitored.

Which meant, in turn, that the NSA would pick up on it. Even without those splitters on the fibre-optic bearers, their eavesdropping capabilities were formidable. Electronic ears and eyes at listening stations in Cyprus, Bermuda, Great Britain, New Zealand and Gibraltar would even now be swivelling in his direction, trying to sniff him out, to isolate his digital footprints from all the other billions of computer users around the world. He was fairly sure they wouldn't be able to trace him immediately, but it was a risk he couldn't afford to take.

At the back of the classroom, unseen by any of the other students, he logged onto an internet dating website. Going to an account he had set up months before, he wrote a message to the commander, then saved it as a draft.

He logged out, then logged in again under a different name and sent a message to a Muslim girl in Morocco. The girl had never received any dates from the site, which was perhaps not surprising since her face was entirely covered by a hijab. The commander would get the message, realise there was a draft waiting for him, and log into the other account using the same credentials Tareq had used. Then he would reply the same way.

As Tareq closed the window, he glanced up. Across the classroom, the teacher was looking at him with a troubled expression.

While the class began an exercise, the teacher stayed at his own computer, clicking repeatedly. Every so often his eyes would stray towards Tareq, his expression ever more troubled.

He's checking up on me, Tareq thought. *Following my trail.*

He wondered how quickly he would be able to finish what he had to do there. It looked as if he was going to have to accelerate his plans.

THIRTY-FOUR

DANIELE BARBO TAILED the cloaked female figure along the narrow canalside pavements of Carnivia, hanging back so that she was only just in sight. It was only a precaution: he had used his administrator privileges to become invisible, as had Max.

That's her, Max said, using a private mode of speech that only Daniele could see. *Domino9859.*

Are you sure?

Certain. Max's administrator privileges also allowed him to search Carnivia users' activity logs. *This is who changed the settings on the Fréjus tunnel turbines. Who she is in RL, I have no idea, of course.*

Domino9859 was going into the area of San Polo just beyond the Rialto bridge. Centuries ago, the city fathers had designated this as a place where prostitutes could walk around bare-breasted, to prove that they were genuinely female and not transvestites; almost seven hundred years later, the effects of that decree still shaped what happened here, both in the real Venice and its digital equivalent. For Carnivians seeking pleasure, this was Party Central.

It was the first time Daniele had been in Carnivia since stepping down. The streets were more crowded than he remembered them. Election posters hung from balconies, and more were being towed up and down the canals on barges. They bore slogans that made no sense to him: "Carnivia Libre"; "Oldtimer Alliance"; "Taxback Now".

As they passed through the crowds, an avatar in the basic, uncustomised cloak and mask of a new user suddenly shrieked: *LOOK AT ME! LOOK AT ME!* Ripping off his clothes, he stood there naked, writhing strangely. Daniele saw he was wearing a kind of sash. On it were the words: "I VOTE TO FLOAT".

What the…? Daniele muttered.

Newb-hazing, Max explained. *Oldtimers test for specs by offering them a float badge. If they accept, they find themselves running a prank script.*

"*Specs*"? "*Oldtimers*"? They were terms Daniele wasn't familiar with.

"Specs" are the speculators who've only joined Carnivia in the hope of cashing in on a stock flotation. Oldtimers think only pre-Abdication members like themselves should be eligible to vote. But the most successful party, according to all the opinion polls, are the Taxbacks. They're offering a straight deal: five bitcoins per vote, to be paid for by taxes on the whole user base after the election. When you think about it, that's a pretty neat formula. Nobody wants to be liable for the tax but not get the bribe.

You warned me this would happen, Daniele said sadly. *I didn't listen.*

Even I never thought it would be as bad as this.

Ahead of them, Domino9859 turned into a courtyard and up some steps. Following her, they found themselves in an elegant *loggia*. Half a dozen people, male and female, stood around chatting.

Looks like some kind of soiree, Max said.

As Domino9859 took her cloak off, Daniele saw that she was wearing an unusual band round her neck, like an iron collar. To his right, another woman was kneeling in a position of supplication, offering a wooden cane to a seated man.

I'm not sure we should be here, Daniele wrote.

Even so, he couldn't help but watch as Domino9859 lay over a man's lap. The man began to spank her buttocks with a paddle. Daniele could hear the thwack of wood on flesh; the tender skin reddened more deeply with each blow. Except that it wasn't flesh, Daniele had to remind himself. This was role play, not the real world. But somehow the distinction was easy to forget.

All around them, similar scenes were being enacted. Two men were taking it in turns to thrash a female avatar. Another was being roughly taken by a group of three men who were accompanying their thrusts with a stream of abuse. Yet another was being flogged with a cat-o'-nine-tails, each slap of the leather plaits followed by a realistic-sounding gasp of pain.

This makes no sense, Daniele said.

Like so many things in Carnivia.

No – I mean a jihadist, a hacker, would never get involved in something like this.

Well, if you want to examine her without her knowing, you'll never get a better chance, Max observed.

Daniele switched to a different view. The lifelike 3D rendering of avatars and buildings that was the ordinary user's experience of Carnivia vanished, replaced by wireframe and lines of code. To most people it would have been incomprehensible. But just as a musician can read a score and hear the music in his head, Daniele could still visualise every feature of the scene in front of him as he searched quickly through the code.

Isolating Domino9859's avatar, he went through it line by line. He felt bad about doing it – far worse than he did about watching her enact a sexual fantasy. The code contained her entire digital footprint. Even though it was encrypted, it was personal to her.

Eventually he found what he was looking for. A tiny anomaly, so small he would have overlooked it had he not specifically been searching for it. It was a worm – a virus designed to take up residence in the user's computer and stay there, dormant and unnoticed, until some specific event or command woke it. Typically, worms were linked to botnets, networks of hijacked computers that were used to send out spam.

He realised now what must have happened. Domino9859 wasn't a hacker. But her computer had been infected by someone who was. Effectively, she had become his proxy, doing his bidding without even being aware of it. And because her real identity was masked by her Carnivia username, there was no way of tracing that computer in the real world.

How are you doing? Max asked privately.

Almost there.

Daniele made a copy of the worm to study later, then switched back to normal view and made himself visible.

I need to speak to you, he said to Domino9859.

Who are you? she said, not stopping what she was doing.

An administrator. I think your computer has been taken over by a virus. If you're prepared to tell me your real-life identity, I can send you some tools that will disinfect your hard drive—

He found himself talking to empty air. Domino9859 had vanished.

Disconnected, Max observed.

I thought she'd appreciate our help.

What makes you think she's even a she?

It was true, of course: here in Carnivia, gender was a matter of personal choice. Perhaps to Domino9859, revealing his or her true identity was more frightening than having a virus.

This is a real problem, Daniele said.

The authorities had been looking for an excuse to close down Carnivia for years. To date, every legal challenge had failed, but terrorism legislation was far more draconian than the anti-pornography and anti-drugs laws that had been used against them in the past.

So what do we do?

This was just the sort of conundrum that had made Daniele decide to walk away from Carnivia. He believed absolutely in the right to privacy. For him and the small, close-knit group of hackers who first colonised the internet, back when it had to be accessed with a dial-up connection and a modem, it was a fundamental article of faith. But the principle, so unimpeachable in theory, seemed to become increasingly difficult and fuzzy when translated into practice.

One thing he was certain of, though. If he simply informed the authorities, they'd shut the site down – but that wouldn't stop this hacker.

Only he, Daniele, had the skills to best him. And it should be done here, on Daniele's home territory, in a world he knew better than anyone.

Not that he had changed his mind about leaving. If anything, this proved that looking after Carnivia wasn't a part-time job. But this last threat would have to be tackled before he could put Carnivia behind him.

THIRTY-FIVE

KAT WALKED INTO La Colomba just after one o'clock. The restaurant wasn't the kind of place she normally frequented: the customers were almost exclusively male, grey-haired, and wearing dark, handmade suits, while the waiters wore formal uniforms and black bow ties. But it was the walls, not the clientele, that drew the eye here. A century ago this had been an artists' hang-out, and the owners would sometimes accept a small painting in lieu of cash. Picasso, Vedova, de Chirico and Morandi had been among those who paid their bills this way, and the walls were stacked with priceless artworks.

She spotted her host, seated at a discreet table in a corner. He got up as she approached, kissing her on each cheek, his fingers fluttering down her back in a way that was not quite a caress, but not quite innocent either.

"Captain Kat," Vivaldo Moretti said, taking her hands in his and moving them apart so that he could look her up and down. "You are looking, if I may say so, more beautiful than ever."

"Thank you." She was wearing a dark pleated dress that ended just above her knees. Though formal, it was also a little more feminine than she normally chose for work.

He smiled at her fondly – not that one would have known it from his expression, which was almost immobilised by his

many facelifts, only by the mischievous twinkle in his eyes
and beckoned to the waiter as they sat down. "I've ordered a
bottle of the Valentini. Needless to say, I'm hoping to get you
a little bit drunk."

Vivaldo Moretti was a politician, a gossip and an incorri-
gible flirt. For all three reasons he was an unlikely friend, but
friends they somehow were. At some point over lunch he
would undoubtedly make a pass – it was no coincidence that
they always met in the dining rooms of grand hotels: he
would, she knew, already have reserved a room upstairs, just
in case. Yet she also knew that when she turned him down he
would roar with laughter, accept it gracefully, and tell her
what a terrible mistake she was making; knew, too, that if she
ever did take him up on his offer, the room would turn out to
be the finest in the hotel. She couldn't help liking the old
rogue, and although she had no intention whatsoever of giving
in to his advances, she suspected she'd be a little disappointed
if he ever stopped making them.

He was also the least corruptible politician she knew. It
was this, as much as his unerring ability to sniff out political
rumours and gossip, that had made him one of the first people
she'd called when putting out feelers about Tignelli.

They ordered – *sarde in saor* for him, *schie* for her, with a
grilled bass from the lagoon to share afterwards. Knowing
that it was the nature of gossip that it must be traded, she told
him about her relationship with Flavio. And, both because he
would relish it, and because she couldn't tell anyone else –
certainly not Holly – she also dropped in a few choice titbits
about her visits to Flavio's office.

"So he shouted through the door, 'Tell the judge I'm
coming'," she concluded. "And you know what? He was."

Moretti laughed so hard he had to wipe his eyes with his

napkin. When they moved on to speak about the investigation, however, his mood grew sombre.

"I never imagined," he said, "when you asked me to find out whether Count Tignelli has any political ambitions, that it would be such a difficult task. Had the request come from anyone but my favourite *capitano donna* of the Carabinieri, in fact, I might well have concluded after a few conversations that he had none, and abandoned the quest. But rather than disappoint you, I persevered, and found to my surprise that there were still some secrets in this city to which I was not yet privy."

"Such as?"

"That man has bought himself more influence, and in a shorter time, than anyone I have ever come across," Moretti said bluntly. "He's throwing money at everyone from city councillors to your own Carabinieri. And it's not just local influence he's after. There are four senators in Rome under his direct control."

"Why? What does he want?"

The waiter stopped by to refill their glasses, and the politician waited until they were alone again before continuing. "On the face of it, separatism."

"Separatism? Like the Liga Vèneta, you mean?"

For decades now, a majority of the inhabitants of the Veneto had been in favour of breaking away from the rest of Italy. In a recent poll in which over two million people voted, almost ninety per cent had supported independence, and the separatist Liga Vèneta or LV was the biggest party by far in the regional assembly.

"Like the LV, yes," he agreed. "There's a feeling, you know, that separatism might be an idea whose time has finally come. Scotland was a close-run thing; Crimea managed it; Catalonia and the Basque Countries are hoping to be next... Everywhere, independence movements are gaining momentum, while conventional politics have been discredited by scandals and apathy."

"But the separatist parties in the Veneto all want different things," she objected. "The LV want us to become a completely new country, but stay in the European Union. The Lega Nord want us to be part of a new region called Padania. The North-East Project are libertarians, the LVR are republicans, the PNV are federalists…"

"Indeed. But if a real leader emerged, someone who could bind the various factions together," he said. "What then?"

"And that's Tignelli's role," she said thoughtfully. "He sees himself as the leader. The new Napoleon."

Moretti nodded. "The other big obstacle, of course, is the lack of a referendum. Opinion polls are one thing, but a majority at the ballot box would be quite another. Article One of the United Nations Charter guarantees a people the right to self-determination. Once there's cast-iron evidence of what the people want, it becomes a lot harder to refuse it." He leant forward. "And I have it on good authority that one of Tignelli's tame senators in Rome is going to propose exactly that – a formal, binding referendum on Venetian secession, to take place this autumn."

"So it will happen?"

"That's the curious thing. Of course it won't. The Veneto isn't like Scotland or the Basque countries – we're the wealthiest part of Italy. Rome would be mad to allow a referendum to take place, because the separatists would surely win, and Rome would lose the greater part of the country's tax revenues. So they'll block it, just as the bastards always do."

She glanced at him. "You sound as if you're on the separatists' side."

He shrugged. "Like all northerners, I resent seeing our

taxes go to prop up failing regions in the south, while our own schools and hospitals don't get the funding they need. But personally, I think the answer is reforms, to force the other regions to balance their books."

Their food came. Moretti, like many men his age, was a traditionalist when it came to matters of cuisine, and the food in front of them now was as classically Venetian as it was possible to be. *Sarde in saor*, cold sardines with vinegar, raisins and pine nuts, was a dish that had evolved in order to preserve fish before the advent of refrigeration. Outsiders often professed not to like it, but to Venetians who had grown up with its tangy, gelatinous flavours, it was the taste of home. Kat's *schie*, too, were something of an acquired taste. Tiny mudshrimps from the lagoon's edge, they looked like nothing very much, whilst the white corn polenta on which they were served had a mouth-filling, sticky texture that was very different to pasta or gnocchi. But they were fresh and juicy, each one an explosive mouthful of fishy brine.

She said curiously, "Earlier, when I asked you what Tignelli wanted, you said, 'On the face of it, separatism.' Why 'on the face of it'?"

Moretti spread his hands. "He must know perfectly well his referendum won't happen. There has to be more to it than that."

She thought for a moment. "What will happen if a referendum is proposed, and Rome vetoes it?"

"If people have their hopes raised and then dashed again, you mean? Some will argue that Rome is already in breach of Article One. Undoubtedly, tensions will run high."

"A good moment, then, to unilaterally declare an independent republic? With Tignelli's tame Freemasons ready to move into all the key positions?"

He considered. "Perhaps. But there would still be huge logistical challenges. For example, you'd have to persuade businesses to stop paying their taxes to Rome. And since the government can take the money directly from their bank accounts..."

"But what if you already owned a bank?" she persisted. "A nice, Venetian bank?" Another thought struck her. "I bet that's why he got Cassandre to open all those accounts. He wants to be ready on day one – the moment he announces his independent republic of Veneto, or whatever it's to be called, he'll say that every business has a bank account waiting for them."

"Even so... People have tried to break Italy apart before. Even at times of crisis, it isn't an easy matter. And this isn't a time of crisis, is it?"

"Unless he means somehow to create one." The waiter took away their empty plates and she drank a mouthful of the white wine. It was delicious: cool and rich and savoury. "The dead Freemason, Cassandre, was reading up on the internet about the Golpe Bianco, the 1974 White Coup plot. The plan back then was to get the government to declare a state of emergency and use that as a pretext to seize power, wasn't it? Perhaps he saw parallels between that and what he'd learnt of Tignelli's plans."

"That's often how these things are done," he agreed. "The instigator demands powers to tackle some pressing issue, then simply refuses to relinquish them once the crisis is over. Greece, Thailand, Pakistan, Peru... they all followed a similar pattern. Tignelli hero-worships Napoleon, you say?"

She nodded.

"Coup by consent was how Bonaparte came to power, in the putsch of 18 Brumaire. And the fall of the Venetian Republic was a coup in all but name."

"That makes sense. He's modelling this as closely as possible on what worked for Napoleon. He told me himself that he'd been studying him."

"If this is true, it's a very serious matter," Moretti said thoughtfully. "Not just for the Veneto, but for Italy too. Without us, I should imagine the country will be bankrupt within a year."

The full brilliance of Count Tignelli's scheme only then dawned on her. "Of course – the deal with the bank. That's part of it too."

"What deal?"

"He bought the Banca Cattolica della Veneziana cheap, because its books are burdened with a huge pile of apparently worthless credit default swaps that have been unloaded onto it by the Vatican Bank," she explained. "But they're not actually as worthless as they look. As you just said, if the Veneto becomes independent, the chances of Italy defaulting on its sovereign debts will go up, and the value of those swaps will go up with them. He's not bankrolling independence for political reasons, or not alone. He's set it up so that it'll make him a fortune."

"And the crisis you think he may intend to manufacture to make all this happen? Do you have any idea what that might be?"

"None whatsoever," she confessed. "But whatever it is, I suspect it will be something dramatic. Tignelli isn't a man to do things by halves."

THIRTY-SIX

ON THE WALL of Holly's apartment, the spidergram was spreading.

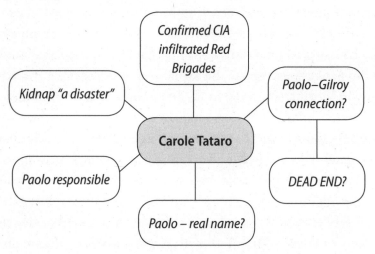

She decided to flip things round and take a look at Gilroy's side of the operation. Not surprisingly, there were no references to him anywhere on the internet. It had been too long ago, and the spy had for obvious reasons kept a low profile during his professional career.

She did, however, come across the name Hannah Proost. Proost had been an administrative assistant in the CIA's Milan Section – competent, hardworking, but certainly not what most people thought of when they used the word "spy". She'd been doing her job for more than twenty years when, in 2003, she was asked to assist a visiting team from Langley.

The team were there to snatch a radical Muslim cleric called Abu Omar from the streets of Milan. After several weeks of planning, they intercepted him in a quiet street, bundled him into the back of a van and drove him to the US Air Force base at Aviano. He was then flown to Egypt, where he was tortured by the security services on the CIA's behalf. It was just one among dozens, possibly hundreds, of similar renditions carried out in the post-9/11 years.

What made this one different was that a determined Italian prosecutor decided to charge the CIA officers involved with conspiracy to kidnap. Since most of the snatch squad had stayed in Italy only long enough to carry out the operation, and had in any case used false names, being convicted *in absentia* wasn't any great hardship. For Proost – resident in Italy for over two decades, married to an Italian, and now forced to flee to the US, unable even to visit her sick mother in Holland – it was very different. The CIA refused to confirm or deny that the operation had taken place, thus preventing her from claiming diplomatic immunity, and also refused to confirm that her involvement had been limited to providing administrative and translation services. She resigned in order to issue her employers with a lawsuit; as a result, her government pension was withdrawn. Pretty soon her only occupation was giving interviews to journalists.

The Abu Omar story had been picked over by the world's press until there was nothing left, but it seemed to Holly that a twenty-year CIA staffer might well know something useful about her quarry. She contacted a journalist who'd done a recent interview with Proost, asking him to pass on her details. To avoid scaring off either party, she used her private email.

Within hours she had Proost's answer. *I'll talk to you for a fee of $1,000 US.*

She wired the money by PayPal.

Thank you. I don't like taking money for this, but it's my only source of income. Please understand though that I can't and won't discuss anything relating to operational security. Would you rather do this by Skype or Carnivia?

Skype, Holly wrote. She still found something a little disconcerting about conversing with the masked denizens of Carnivia.

Details exchanged, she found herself looking at a dumpy middle-aged woman sitting on a suede La-Z-Boy settee. A cat was curled up next to her, on a cushion embroidered with the words "Dogs have owners, cats have staff".

Holly introduced herself as a writer doing research for a book about the CIA in Italy.

Proost snorted. "Another one?"

"This is a slightly different angle," Holly said. "I'm writing an appreciation of one of the Section's most senior agents – Ian Gilroy. I imagine you must have known him?"

There was a pause. Skype lag? No: when she spoke, Proost's voice was guarded. "Ian Gilroy. He's still going, is he?"

"Well, he's retired from the CIA, of course. He has a part-time role in education at Camp Ederle." The other woman's face was expressionless. "I'm just after some background. What kind of guy was he, what kind of operations he ran..."

"We didn't overlap by much."

"I know." Holly glanced at her notes. "By my reckoning, Gilroy would have come to Italy towards the end of the 1960s. The Section Chief then was a man called Bob Garland. From what I can gather, Garland took Gilroy under his wing."

Proost shook her head. "Whoever told you that got it wrong. The talk when I arrived was that Garland and Gilroy were rivals, not protégé and mentor."

Holly frowned. Gilroy had always given the impression that, whilst he'd been alarmed by some of his predecessor's methods, they had been close. "So Gilroy tried to clean things up, and Bob didn't like it?"

"Wrong again. My understanding was that there'd been concern back at Langley about the way things were heading when Garland ran the show. There was an initiative from the Italian socialist party to share power with the communists—"

"I know about that. The Historic Compromise," Holly interrupted. She wanted to focus Proost on the stuff she couldn't find in the history books. "What was Langley's response?"

"Well, panic, pretty much. From what people said to me later, the seventh floor decided Garland had been too soft. Gilroy was sent to sort things out."

"Meaning what, exactly?"

Proost shrugged. "I do know that there were hundreds of operations in those years. The cryptonyms went all the way from A to Z."

"Could those operations have included infiltrating the Gladio network?"

A long pause. "Even if I knew that, I couldn't discuss it with you."

Holly mentally parked that response for later analysis. "Let's assume for a moment that it did. What I still don't understand is that the gladiators were generally seen as being on the right wing of Italian politics. Yet the only public record of Ian Gilroy's career has him involved in an operation to penetrate the left wing, the Red Brigades. Why would one agent be involved in both operations?"

"Like I said, I don't know any details. But I do know that after the collapse of the Historic Compromise, Gilroy was seen by Langley as the man who'd delivered the goods. That was when Bob was eased into retirement."

So personal ambition, and America's strategic objectives, had somehow coincided. Gilroy had achieved what his bosses wanted, and profited as a result. But what exactly had that been? And more to the point, by what methods had it been achieved?

"America was working for the collapse of the Historic Compromise, then," Holly said. "And Gilroy was the man who made it happen. But why would that require the death of someone who found out about it?"

"Death?" Proost frowned. "Whose death?"

"Major Ted Boland, at Camp Darby. He and an Italian neighbour stumbled across evidence suggesting that part of Gladio was being run as a network of *agents provocateurs*—"

"Wait a minute." Proost stared at her. "Boland is your name."

"Major Boland is my dad."

"Oh my God," Proost said faintly. "You're *that* Boland."

"What Boland?" Holly said, suddenly alert. "What do you know about my father?"

"Nothing." Proost shook her head emphatically.

"Did Gilroy try to have him killed to protect his operation?

Was it the CIA who authorised it? If you know anything –
anything at all—"

Proost leant forward to the screen. A message appeared.
Call ended.

THIRTY-SEVEN

DANIELE HAD SPENT many hours examining the worm he'd found in Domino9859. Because it was written in Carnivia's site-specific programming language, any information that might have enabled him to trace its creator was encrypted. There was one part, though, that was in clear text. When he'd designed the encryption, Daniele had deliberately excluded numerals. In any code, numbers written as numerals were easy to crack, since there was no disguising that they continued to behave according to the immutable rules of mathematics. For that reason, most cryptographic systems required the sender to write out numbers as words: five, twenty-five and so on.

Deep within the Carnivia worm was the number 10-12-1437.

In some way, he believed, this had to be significant. The Stuxnet worm, for example, had contained the number 06-24-2012. It was part of an instruction to the virus to start deleting itself on the twenty-fourth of June, 2012.

It seemed likely to Daniele that 10-12-1437 was also part of an instruction – in this case, for the virus to activate. But even though it wasn't encoded, the hacker had somehow managed to disguise it.

Unless…

Daniele turned to the internet and did a little research. The one thing he knew about the hacker was that he was a radicalised Muslim.

He soon discovered that whereas each new year in the Western calendar began on the solar anniversary of Christ's birth, the Muslim calendar was a lunar one. In that calendar, the current year was 1437. And the current month was Dhu al-Hijjah, the twelfth month of the year. It was the most blessed and propitious time in the calendar, the time of *haj*. It also signalled the end of Dhu al-Qa'ada, the Month of Truce.

If the last six digits indicated the month and year, did "10" indicate the day?

The tenth day of Dhu al-Hijjah, he discovered, was an especially significant day in the Muslim calendar, because it marked the celebration of Eid al-Adha. The words meant "The Day of Sacrifice".

This year, Eid fell on the eleventh of September. Or, written another way, 9/11, the anniversary of the attack on the World Trade Centre.

That had to be the worm's zero-date. Exactly seven days away. And, coincidentally, just a few hours before the elections within Carnivia were due to take place.

The Fréjus attack, Daniele was sure, had been nothing more than a trial run. But in one week's time, any of Carnivia's users who were infected with the worm would become a zombie army, their computers under the hacker's control.

He was still considering the implications when Max popped up on his screen.

How's it going? Max asked.

Gnarly. You?

I've been counting worms. They were pretty sure Domino9859 wasn't the only user to be infected, but they had no way of knowing how widespread the problem was.

Daniele had asked Max to take a random sample of three hundred avatars and examine them, to see if any of those were infected too.

And?

In my sample of 300, I found 52 nasties.

Daniele stared at the screen. Over seventeen per cent! It barely seemed possible. If you scaled up from Max's sample to the number of registered users, it meant that even on a conservative estimate, around half a million Carnivians had been infected.

How could that happen and us not know about it?

That's what I thought. So I did a recount.

And?

And by the time I'd finished, there were 58. It's growing all the time, Daniele. In some way we haven't yet worked out, the virus is jumping between our users' computers.

It must be spreading socially, inside Carnivia. Every inter-action, however brief, between Carnivians involved a small exchange of code. The worm must have a tiny self-replicating payload that attached itself to an infected user's keystrokes. Essentially, the hacker was using each Carnivian he compromised to recruit others. A part of Daniele couldn't help but admire the neatness of it.

This was no ordinary denial-of-service attack the hacker was planning, he realised. When you put all the parts together – the attack on Fréjus, the jihadist slogans, the sophistication of the worm, the date – there could be only one conclusion.

This was cyberwarfare, and his website – Carnivia – was where the battle lines were being drawn.

THIRTY-EIGHT

FLAVIO HAD BEEN working late, and Kat was making *risotto alla sbirraglia*, risotto with diced chicken and carrots, which had to be stirred with every ladleful of hot stock or it would not become creamy, and then they were in a hurry to get into bed and enjoy each other before it was time for the bodyguards to come back. Only after their lovemaking was over and they lay tangled in each other's limbs, the backs of his fingers lightly stroking her shoulder, did she tell him what she'd learnt – that Count Tignelli's goal appeared to be independence for the Veneto, and as much for personal gain as political belief.

"Vivaldo says there must be more to it than just a referendum that's proposed and then denied, though. That might make people in the Veneto angry, but it wouldn't be enough to make them break with Rome. He thinks Tignelli will do something to provoke a state of emergency." She hesitated. "Avvocato Marcello mentioned that AISI's interest in Cassandre was linked to terrorism. Could *that* be the pretext – some kind of terror attack?"

"I thought you were insisting that AISI were part of the Masonic conspiracy themselves."

"Yes, well maybe I was wrong about that," she admitted. "The more we find out about Tignelli, the more it looks as if he's trying to break away from Rome, not cosy up with them."

We still don't have any evidence of that," he warned. "On the other hand, there probably is enough now to question Tignelli in connection with Cassandre's murder. He had a clear motive to make that deal with the Banca Cattolica, and thus to get rid of anyone who got in the way." He glanced at her. "It's difficult. Not least because I have to be absolutely sure that personal feelings have played no part in my decision."

"I understand." Aroused by the absent-minded touch of his hand on her arm, she reached around and started rubbing his stomach, feeling the lattice of muscles beneath the skin.

"I'll sleep on it," he decided. "And let you know first thing in the morning."

By way of answer, she kissed his chin, working up the line of his jaw to his earlobe. She could sense him becoming aroused, and moved her hand lower. On the bedside table his phone buzzed and flashed, as if in protest. Groaning, he reached for it.

"They're here," he said, looking at the screen. "Damn."

She didn't need to ask who. The bodyguards were like the wife in this relationship: duty and security, calling him away from her.

He swung his feet onto the floor. As he reached for his shirt, she stroked his back, for the simple pleasure of touching his skin for a few seconds longer.

He said quietly, "When I said I had to be sure that personal feelings weren't a factor..."

"Yes?"

"It works two ways, you know. That is, I obviously feel a certain pressure to see things from your point of view. But I also feel the exact opposite, a need to keep our heads below the parapet. To keep you safe. If we were simply to ignore what Vivaldo Moretti told you... No one would ever blame us for not pursuing it."

"I know," she whispered.

"We could be in Amsterdam within a couple of months."

She said nothing. She didn't tell him that she wouldn't respect him if he dropped the investigation now, because it wasn't true. She trusted him to do the right thing, and who was to say, in a situation like this one, what that might be?

"The point is, I mustn't be influenced either way." He stood up, then leant down again to kiss her goodbye. "I'll let you know first thing."

THIRTY-NINE

HOLLY'S SPIDERGRAM WAS begetting a whole family of baby spiders now.

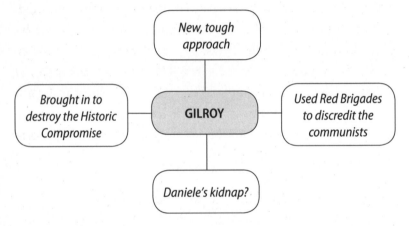

Something Carole Tataro had said to her in the prison interview room came back to her. She added:

> *"But please don't tell me I'm any worse than those on the other side of the political spectrum."*

And then:

> *Was he doing the same thing on the right, with Gladio? Proost refused to answer that.*
>
> DEAD END?

But it wasn't a dead end, she realised; not quite. The regular internet might not have been much use, but she had access to something many times more powerful.

She went to Camp Ederle late that night. But even after midnight, a US base is rarely quiet. The MP on the gate told her it was good to see her back, ma'am; and just walking from the parking lot to the building where her own section, Civilian Liaison, was based, she encountered several other people who recognised her.

The main thing, though, was that her boss, Mike Breedon, wasn't around. Her desk was much as she'd left it months before, bare and neat, apart from a pile of accumulated mail.

She slid her Common Access Card into the card reader by her computer and booted it up. After entering a clearance code, she was able to access NIPRNet, the Department of Defense's own intranet, and CREST, the CIA's Records Search Tool. Because the information she was looking for was more than twenty-five years old, she was hoping it would be readily accessible.

She typed in "Gilroy, Ian".

For a moment, nothing but the response

Searching.

Then:

ERROR. No records relating to that term.

Frowning, she tried SIPRNet, the NSA's secure equivalent. Nothing there either.

As a last resort, she logged into JWICS, the Joint Worldwide Intelligence Communications System. Where SIPRNet was cleared for material up to "Secret", and could be accessed by up to four million trusted allies around the world, JWICS was FAEO, For American Eyes Only.

Gilroy, Ian. 798 records. Refine your search?

She typed "operations". That got it down to seventy-four documents. She clicked on the first one.

ERROR. You do not have clearance to access this material. Please contact your network administrator or chain of command.

Going back, she typed "personnel, location, based at".

54 records.

Opening the first document, she found that it was a simple note of which CIA office Gilroy had been working out of in 1974. She clicked the next one. That gave her the same information for 1979.

A thought occurred to her. Using the regular internet, she made a timeline of all the atrocities and assassinations that had characterised the Years of Lead. Then she highlighted the locations.

19 November 1969. *Antonio Annarumma, a policeman, was assassinated during a riot by far-left demonstrators in* **Milan.** *There was immediate public revulsion, with many commentators denouncing the left.*

12 December 1969. *Four separate bombs were planted in* **Milan and Rome,** *killing 16 and injuring 90. The Red*

*Brigades were initially accused of what became known as
the Piazza Fontana massacre. Later, officials admitted
that there was no evidence for this.*

In 1969 the young Ian Gilroy, newly arrived in Italy, had
been based at the Milan Section, where – according to JWICS
– he was assigned to something called Operation Amethyst.
By the end of the year, however, the same records showed he'd
been travelling regularly to Rome, for something called
Operation Beachcomber. The dates corresponded to the
period immediately preceding the Piazza Fontana bombing.

31 May 1972. *Massacre of three policemen at* **Peteano,**
north of **Venice.** *Although the Red Brigades were accused
of the killings, over a decade later a right-wing activist
admitted having planted the explosives.*

By 1972 Gilroy was stationed at Venice, where he was
running an operation codenamed Clockhouse. All records for
Clockhouse ceased abruptly at the end of May.

28 May 1974. *Bombing at Piazza dell Loggia,* **Brescia,**
west of **Venice.** *Killed 8 and wounded 100.*

Again, May 1974 saw a flurry of activity in the Venice
Section for something called Operation Emerald.

Gilroy had continued to be stationed at Venice during the
summer of 1977, when Daniele Barbo had been kidnapped by
the Red Brigades. Then, in 1978, he'd moved to Rome.

March 16, 1978. *Christian Democrat leader Aldo Moro
kidnapped by the Red Brigades in* **Rome.**

Coincidence? Or an indication of something more sinister?

After the end of the Cold War, and the enforced termination of the Gladio network, the Red Brigades had also fallen silent. Until, that is, almost a decade later, when they'd made a sudden resurgence. The last assassination they carried out was as recent as 2003. Shortly afterwards, Ian Gilroy retired from the CIA's payroll.

Again, was it a coincidence that terrorists were killing people on Italian soil just as America was calling for its allies to join a global war on terror?

Excitement prickled her skin. *I may not have the evidence yet. But I'm building a picture.*

She sat back, thinking. Then she pulled a memory stick out of her pocket and downloaded everything.

A message flashed up.

SECURITY WARNING. Downloading classified material may only be carried out with the express permission of your Command. In no circumstances may such material be removed from NSA-approved facilities.

She clicked "Continue".

Was it just the insubstantial weight of the memory stick in her pocket making her jumpy as she walked back to her car? Every shadow seemed to hide a figure, watching her; every surveillance camera seemed to swivel in her direction. She jumped when a horn blared behind her, but it was only a group of men heading out of the base at high speed and in high spirits for some late-night R&R.

She took a right out of the camp and drove slowly along Viale della Pace, scrutinising her rear-view mirror. There was no one coming after her. But she found those words of her father's favourite poem echoing in her head, all the same:

> *This season's Daffodil,*
> *She never hears,*
> *What change, what chance, what chill,*
> *Cut down last year's;*
> *But with bold countenance,*
> *And knowledge small,*
> *Esteems her seven days' continuance*
> *To be perpetual.*

Had it been a warning? A prophecy? Or just a statement of the obvious: *with knowledge comes fear?*

Back in the centre of Vicenza, she parked her car in the usual place, an underground multi-storey. As she got out, she heard footsteps coming up behind her, rubber soles scuffing on rough concrete. She turned, panicking, her hand reaching automatically for the can of pepper spray that, ever since the events in the caves of Longare, she'd carried everywhere she went.

"Hai qualche monetina?"

It was just a young beggar, a junkie, asking for money. She shook her head. He started to push forward into her personal space, still muttering demands, then backed off rapidly when she showed him the spray. Even so, the adrenalin was pumping as she walked to her building.

She let herself in. The hallway was quiet, but the door to the ground-floor apartment where Alberto, the handyman, lived was open. She heard voices. As she pressed the button for the tiny lift, Alberto hurried out, beaming. In his hand was a glass of grappa.

"Ah, Signorina Boland! C'è qualcuno che aspetta di vederla."

She'd never had anyone wait to see her here, let alone at this time of night. She was about to tell Alberto he must be mistaken when a tall, lean figure stepped into the hallway behind him.

"Good evening, Holly," Ian Gilroy said. "I hope you don't mind. It seemed like the easiest way to get hold of you."

Sharing the tiny lift as it lurched upwards to the fifth floor, she looked at the wall rather than meet his eye. She could feel him examining her thoughtfully, but he chose not to say anything until they were inside her apartment. She saw his eyes flick over to the spidergram, and his eyebrows raised briefly, but he turned to face her without comment.

"Why are you here?" she said without preamble.

"Holly," he said gently, "I understand why you're suspicious of me."

"What do you mean?"

"You've been checking up on me. Perhaps you're wondering if *I* had anything to do with what happened to your father." His candid blue eyes met hers, unflinching. "Indeed, I can see why you might think I did."

He placed the bottle of grappa on the table. "It's time I told you the truth, Holly. Hear me out, and then decide whether I'm the monster you think I am."

Eventually she consented to have a drink with him. They sat on her tiny terrace with its views over the Berici Hills, the lights of Vicenza twinkling in the foreground.

"What I'm about to tell you is highly secret," he began. "In 1968, I was sent to this country for the first time. My orders were simple: to stop the communists from getting into power. Langley felt that there were new challenges in Italy that required a new approach... I was told I would even have political cover to overrule the Section Head, Bob Garland, should it become necessary."

"You came in with orders to kick ass, in other words."

He nodded. "The strange thing, though, was that I didn't have to. Instead, it was as if my arrival had galvanised Bob. He responded with a flurry of initiatives, new operations, special-access projects... I had my hands full just deterring him from the most extreme. Frankly, it would have taken very little for our work in Italy to go down the same path we had already taken in Greece and South America. Certainly there was no one back in Washington trying to rein us in."

He was silent for a moment, collecting his thoughts. "Quite early on, it became clear to me that the Red Brigades were going to be a particular problem. They were vicious, well organised and highly disciplined. I was determined to under-mine their influence... and that was when an asset by the name of Mariano Cardillo fell into my lap.

"Cardillo was a natural – he took to a life in the shadows like a duck to water: one might almost say he was addicted to it. He was also a dangerous right-wing extremist who wor-shipped power and violence – those were his only true gods, I think, although he liked to talk about restoring the honour and prestige of the Catholic Church as well. He had been recruited to Gladio in the usual way, by NATO, and given paramilitary training, but he was never going to have the patience to wait until the communists' tanks were rolling across the Dolomites before he got involved in the action.

"He had decided, in fact, to infiltrate the enemy, on his own initiative. When I came across him, it was in the guise of

a low-level Red Brigades fellow-traveller, a part-time anar-
chist who helped them out with bomb-making, gun-running,
that kind of thing. I thought I was turning him, but to my
surprise, during that initial, wary conversation, it became
clear that he was interested in using *me*.

"Working entirely on his own, he had succeeded in gaining
the trust of the Red Brigades' leadership. Now he wanted my
help in getting right to the heart of the organisation, from
which position he could, he assured me, help me to destroy it
completely.

"It was almost too good to be true. For several months I
remained suspicious, looking for a trap. But he proved himself
again and again. He had acquired the *nom de guerre* of Paolo
by then." He looked at her to see if she had remembered that
was the name of one of Daniele's kidnappers. Satisfied, he
continued, "And in that guise, with a little help from us, he
rose rapidly through the terrorists' ranks. The only difficulty
was the perennial one with all double agents: to what extent
do you use the information they give you, when doing so may
blow their cover? It's an irony of these situations that the
more valuable the asset's information, the less one is inclined
to risk acting on it."

"So you did nothing?"

"Oh, we did what we could. This isn't some elaborate mea
culpa for standing on the sidelines, Holly. But it was clear that
we were going to have to be smart, if we wanted to both
disrupt the Red Brigades and protect Paolo's identity.

"Above all, though, we had to stop Moro's Historic
Compromise, his plan to bring the communists into a coalition government." He grimaced. "The strategy we hit on was
a beautiful one, though I say so myself – beautiful but terrible.
We realised that, if we could only persuade Moscow that the

Historic Compromise would take the Italian Communist Party out of Moscow's control and into that of the Christian Democrats, they themselves would order the Red Brigades to undermine it in any way they could. And in Paolo, we believed, we had the means to make that happen.

"And so it proved. Paolo fed back certain titbits of information suggesting the Historic Compromise was all a plot on behalf of the moderates; some judicious leaks from within the Christian Democrats reinforced the illusion, and within a remarkably short space of time we were in the fortuitous position of having an agent at the heart of a terrorist organisation which was now dedicated to exactly the same tactical objectives as ourselves."

"A terrorist organisation as your asset?" she said ironically. "What could possibly go wrong?"

He nodded. "The problem, of course, was that there was now absolutely nothing restraining Paolo from pursuing his own right-wing agenda. Every action he carried out, no matter how barbaric, had the effect of impressing his supposed masters in Moscow with his brutality, his Red Brigades colleagues with his ideological purity, and Langley with his usefulness as a double agent. Effectively, Bob and I had lost control of the situation. Paolo did what he chose. The rest of us were just along for the ride."

"And Daniele's kidnap?"

"The first we knew of that was when we read about it in the press."

"So that's why you feel guilty about Daniele. Without you, his mutilation would never have happened."

He inclined his head.

"And how does this relate to my dad? Where does he come into the picture?"

After the Red Brigades assassinated Aldo Moro, it was clear to me that Paolo had to be stopped at any cost." He shrugged. "A cynic might say that we had achieved our objective: with its principal architect dead, the Historic Compromise soon died as well. But I swear that if Paolo was ever given a direct order to do such a thing, it came from Moscow, not us. In any case, we made a concerted effort to round them up – all of them, even Paolo. But somehow he got wind of it and slipped back into the old Gladio network from which he'd come. There were plenty of right-wing Italian border officials, secret service officers and so on eager to help him. He was spirited away; first to Argentina, I believe, and later to Japan.

"But he didn't lie low for long – as I said, terror was a kind of addiction for him; and while both America and Russia might have been satisfied now the power-sharing proposal was dead, for Paolo and the other fascists that had only ever been a stepping stone. At some point he returned and resumed his former activities within Gladio. Only now he suited himself as to whether he claimed his atrocities in the name of the Brigate Rosse or some right-wing terror group."

"And then Andreotti revealed Gladio's existence."

Gilroy nodded. "A setback for them. But, as your father discovered, not one that they intended to be derailed by. They quickly found ways to regroup, either by infiltrating existing Masonic fraternities or by setting up their own illegal ones. I was aware it was happening, even before your father wrote that memorandum – I'd been trying to track Paolo ever since he'd returned to Italy – but his report was the first time I realised that they were operating a lodge at Camp Darby."

"So when he came to you..."

"What I told you – that I simply thanked him and passed the report up the line – was a lie, Holly," he said quietly.

"I knew it."

He held up a hand. "Wait. I think this is where you have perhaps jumped to a wrong conclusion. When you raised it, I thought – forgive me – that it would be better for all concerned if we were able to leave the past well alone. It was selfish of me – I was prioritising my own feelings of guilt over your right to know the truth." He hesitated. "The fact is, I asked your father to see what else he could find out."

She stared at him. "You *recruited* him? You sent him back into that nest of vipers…?"

"I'm sorry," he said simply. "It was a misjudgement. You must understand – what he was describing had Paolo's fingerprints all over it: exactly the same organisational structure as the Red Brigades, only with Masonic lodges instead of revolutionary cells. And there was no one else I could use."

She thought a moment. "What exactly did he do?"

"The gladiators already believed that, as a NATO officer, your father must be sympathetic to their ideology. I thought that if he appeared sufficiently enthusiastic, he could get close to the ringleaders, along with whichever Italian or NATO officers were abetting them. Then we'd go in and roll them all up in one swoop – not just Paolo, but the entire network."

"He would have gone back to Mr Boccardo, the neighbour who first alerted him. He'd have asked him to get them both inside the group."

Gilroy nodded. "He was getting results – we spoke about it on the telephone, guardedly of course, but he sounded positive. He hinted that he'd been able to keep some kind of record – names, dates, details: all the small stuff that allows a case officer to piece together what's really going on.

Unfortunately, before he could deliver it to me, he suffered that stroke."

"In his report, he mentioned someone called Caesar."

"Yes. I'm guessing that was Paolo himself. Or an invention of Paolo's, to make it seem as if he was in touch with some higher and even more powerful authority. If anyone questioned his orders, all he had to do was say that Caesar agreed."

She was silent, thinking it all through.

"So you see," he said gently, "it isn't only Daniele I feel guilty about. It's you. I admit it: when I saw an opportunity to support your application for a transfer to Italy, I seized it. I wanted to make amends, as well as to see what sort of person Ted's daughter had become. I never imagined that we'd become friends as well."

If we are friends.

What Gilroy had just told her had the ring of truth. No one, surely, could invent a story that fitted the facts so well, right down to the tiniest detail. And yet something made her hold back from saying that she believed him.

"No doubt you want more proof, Holly," he said, reading her mind. "And believe me, I've been asking round all my contacts from those days, trying to find something – anything – that might convince you. But it's all too long ago. And I'm concerned that the more people I remind about activities they believed were safely hidden away a generation past, the more likely they are to decide that one or both of us would be better out of the picture."

She thought. "You say my father kept some kind of record."

"That's right, I believe he did."

She said softly, "You want me to look for it, don't you? It isn't just to convince me. Even after all this time, you still want to know what happened."

"I do, yes."

She nodded slowly. "And I will. If those notes can be found, I'll find them. And then we'll know the truth."

FORTY

IN SICILY, TAREQ was woken by the sound of his phone ringing. He reached for it immediately. Only a handful of people had this number, and none of them would use it except in an emergency.

When he glanced at the screen, he expected to see a caller ID starting with 00 218, the dialling code for Libya. But, oddly, there was no number on the screen. It didn't say "Blocked", or "Unknown": it was simply blank.

"Hello?" he answered hesitantly.

The voice that replied was also speaking English, but in a strangely mechanical monotone.

"You - need - to - move - immediately."

It was a text-to-speech converter, he realised. The caller wasn't speaking, he was typing. "Who is this?"

"A - friend. You - have - been - betrayed."

"The teacher? Was it him?"

There was a long pause. Tareq could hear the clicking of a keyboard. Then the voice said, "Those - who - recruited - you - are - in - the - pay - of - infidels. Do - you - have - an - escape - plan?"

Tareq's mind was racing with questions. The commander a traitor? Could it be true? But he knew that in this shadow war they were fighting, men could be turned by many means, fair or foul. So he only said, "Yes. I have a plan."

"Do - it." There was a click, and the voice was gone.

FORTY-ONE

SLEEP WAS IMPOSSIBLE.

After several hours, Holly abandoned the attempt and got back in her car. In the pre-dawn darkness the Ponte della Libertà was deserted. The lights of Venice glowed through a faint sea-mist, a haze like tracing paper, through which she could just make out the skyline of Cannaregio.

She left the car at Tronchetto for the ten-minute walk to Calle Barbo. Venice at this hour was like an Escher labyrinth, eerily deserted: more than once she found her way blocked by a canal that had somehow turned a corner in front of her.

She pulled on the brass bell handle next to the lion's-head postbox. To her surprise the door opened almost immediately. Daniele was wearing his normal daytime garb: T-shirt, sneakers, jeans. In his hand was a fork.

"What do you want?" he said. "I was just having lunch."

"Daniele, it's four o'clock in the morning."

"Not in São Paulo," he said reasonably.

"What does São Paulo have to do with it?"

"Nothing. I'm just illustrating that time is a man-made construct. I suppose you want to talk to me?"

"Well, I certainly haven't come all this way to listen to you talk about man-made constructs."

"There's nothing to discuss, Holly. We're not together any more."

"I know," she said impatiently. "That doesn't mean we never speak to each other again."

He hesitated. "You'd better come in, then."

He took her to the vaulted old kitchen at the rear of Ca' Barbo. Although she knew that he was an excellent cook, capable of following complex recipes to the letter, today he was eating the simple cold pasta dish Venetians call *salsa aurora*: a sweet-and-sour mix of fried peppers, tomatoes, courgettes and slices of peach.

Watching him eat, she discovered she was hungry too, and reached for a fork. "I know you've always thought I was crazy to trust Ian Gilroy," she told him between mouthfuls. "And if you'd asked me six hours ago, I'd have said you were probably right. But now I'm not so sure."

She related her earlier conversation, and his face darkened.

"But this is what he does," he said. "Gilroy's genius, I realised many years ago, is that he tells stories. Brilliant, shiny stories that somehow seem to offer you whatever it is that you most want in the world. In your case, he knows you want to believe him, because the alternative is just so unthinkable."

The speech was so unlike Daniele that she only looked at him, wondering.

"I saw him throw his magic dust into my father's eyes," he explained. "I'm not saying it was easy for my parents after my kidnap. But, somehow, every conversation seemed to begin, 'Ian Gilroy says…' or 'Ian agrees…' And after my father died, Gilroy was left as the principal trustee of the Foundation. He'd convinced my father it was the only way to prevent me from selling off his art collection. But if that lever hadn't been available to him, he would have found some other lie. I'm sure of it."

"I heard you accuse him of it once. He asked me to wait behind a screen at his house, when you came to speak to him. He wanted me to hear how unreasonable you were being."

"It was him who pushed us together, wasn't it?" he said sadly. "You and me... that was always part of his plan."

"No," she said firmly. "I made my own decision about that. One I don't regret, by the way. The point is, I've been trying to figure out if there's any way of proving whether or not Gilroy's version of events is correct. And it seems to me you're the only person who might be able to help."

"Me? How?"

"It all comes down to your kidnap. If Paolo *was* the mastermind, as both Gilroy and Tataro claim, then perhaps you saw something to corroborate their version of events?"

He shook his head. "You know I don't remember anything about the kidnap. Not after the first few days, anyway."

"Which in itself is strange, don't you think? I looked up memory loss due to psychological trauma on the internet. It's almost always temporary."

"Believe me, my parents tried everything. I was dragged from doctor to doctor for years. Most decided it was linked to my..." He hesitated. "My other condition."

"But that's another thing," she said. "When I spoke to Carole Tataro, she told me she used to play number games with you. She said that you seemed a little strange, vulnerable even, but not autistic."

"My parents believed the same thing. That the kidnap somehow triggered, or at any rate worsened, whatever was wrong with me."

"But don't you see the implication?" she persisted. "If what you have is actually not high-functioning autism at all but some trauma-induced condition that closely mirrors it... True autism is incurable. But a condition which mimics its symptoms might, in theory, be reversible. There are papers describing children brought up in Eastern-bloc orphanages, for example, who appeared to display autistic behaviours but who grew up to be indistinguishable from other kids."

"Some of them," he corrected. "Those who were taken out of that environment young enough. I read those papers too. But even if that were once applicable to me, it isn't relevant now."

"I've been doing some research. There's a relatively new technique called EMDR – Eye Movement Desensitisation and Reprocessing. No one seems to know exactly why or how EMDR works. But studies have shown that, when combined with hypnosis, it's the most effective treatment for post-traumatic amnesia there is." She hesitated. "I already spoke to Father Uriel," she said, naming the psychiatrist who'd treated both herself and Daniele in the past. "He's familiar with it."

"I'd like to help, really. But I don't have time for this right now." He ran his hand through his hair and for the first time she saw how exhausted he was. "There have been… problems. With Carnivia. A kind of virus. I'm getting to the bottom of it, but it's difficult."

In fact, he was understating the scale of the clean-up he and the other administrators had been undertaking. He had written a piece of software that would remove the worm, but it was an operation that had to be carried out on an individual basis, user by user. And more users were being infected all the time. It was a race between the virus and the wizards; one they were currently losing.

"If there's at least a chance that your condition could be cured, wouldn't you want to take it?"

"Why would I want to be like other people? I'm happy the way I am."

"You wouldn't be like other people," she insisted. "You'd still be Daniele – still brilliant, still strange. Who knows, perhaps you'd simply be more you. Perhaps you'd be capable of even greater things than you already are."

He was silent a moment. The idea that treatment might actually unlock his abilities rather than stifle them was one he hadn't considered before. And it was true what that professor at MIT had written: his best work appeared to be behind him. He needed to do something different if he was to get a different result.

Sensing his hesitation, she added, "Daniele, it would mean a lot to me if you would at least try this. I have to find out what happened to my dad, and at the moment I'm getting nowhere."

There were many people, she knew, who thought that Daniele Barbo was impervious to such emotional appeals. But she had never believed that to be the case. His emotions might be different from other people's, but they existed nevertheless.

"All right," he said at last. "I'll try. I suppose I've got nothing to lose."

FORTY-TWO

IT WAS FIVE thirty in the morning when Kat's phone rang. Scrabbling for it, she saw Flavio's name on the screen. "Yes?"

"I've authorised a warrant," his voice said. "You're to bring Count Tignelli in for questioning."

"What charges?" she asked, reaching for a pad.

"Conspiracy to murder, conspiracy to overthrow the state, organising an illegal group, and conspiracy to manipulate the financial markets. We'll throw the lot at him, make him fight us on every front."

"You won't regret this," she said, scribbling.

"Actually, I suspect I might. But I'm also sure it's the right thing to do. And Kat? Be careful which *carabinieri* you take with you. I'd rather Count Tignelli didn't know anything about this until you knock on his front door."

As soon as he'd rung off, she called Aldo Piola. He too answered immediately, and with much the same hope and expectancy in his voice, she realised, as there had been in hers when she'd picked up the phone to Flavio.

"Kat? What is it?"

"I need to get a team together who definitely aren't Freemasons." She explained her problem, the phone tucked under her ear so she could pull on clothes as she spoke.

"Let's meet at San Zaccaria in thirty minutes. We'll go

through Hapadi's list and Cassandre's, cross-checking them against the available officers. In the meantime, what about Panicucci? He's good, and I'd swear he isn't the Freemason type."

"Good idea. I'll call him now."

"And Bagnasco? We can be pretty sure she isn't a Mason. Like you, she doesn't have the first qualification."

"She may be a woman," Kat said, "but I have absolutely no doubt she'd be on the phone to her uncle before we even got into the boats."

There was a silence. "I think you're wrong. But it's your operation. Your call."

"Thank you." Besides, she thought, she intended to go in fast, and there would be no room in the boats for an officer who got seasick.

Venice was still shrouded in mist as the twelve-man team roared away from the pontoon at Rio dei Greci. It would burn off later, but for the moment it gave the city an eerie, insubstantial translucence, water and stone blending seamlessly into each other in the chilly, muffled grey.

They used no sirens and as they approached La Grazia she gave the order to turn off the blue lights as well. She glanced at her watch. Twenty past six. It seemed unlikely the staff would still be asleep, but if they could catch Tignelli himself in bed, so much the better.

She noticed the absence of La Grazia's launch as they tied up. As the *carabinieri* streamed up the immaculate lawn towards the house, the only sign of life was a water sprinkler, spinning like a radar antenna over the lush green grass.

"Ring the bell or break down the door?" Panicucci asked.

"Both."

"No need," the lead *carabiniere* said, pushing the door. "It's already open."

Inside, the great house was eerily silent. A portrait of Napoleon stared down at them haughtily as they milled in the grand hallway.

"Count Tignelli?" Kat shouted. There had still been no response to the bell.

"Is it possible there's no one here?" Piola asked quietly.

He was right. As they fanned out through the ground-floor rooms, it became apparent that neither Tignelli nor any of his staff were at home.

"Capitano?"

One of the *carabinieri* was calling to her. She followed his voice into a dining room. On the table a light meal was laid out: some fruit, slices of ham and *carpaccio*, an unopened bottle of *prosecco* in an ice bucket. Flies lifted off the meat and circled, droning angrily, as she approached. She lifted the bottle out of the bucket and felt it. It was barely cool, the ice long since melted.

"It seems strange to leave the food out," the *carabiniere* added unnecessarily.

She looked again at the table. It was laid for two, but neither plate had been touched. A sudden foreboding came over her. "Search upstairs," she commanded. "Every room. Sottotenente Panicucci, come with me." Heading outside, she ran down the gravel path that led through the gardens.

Panicucci caught up with her. "Where are we going?"

"The *peschiera*," she panted.

The huge seawater basins also appeared to be deserted. Looking down into the nearest one, she could just make out the eels' silvery, undulating shapes, clustered around something under the surface. She walked along the ancient stone wall to get a better look. When she was directly above the spot where they were congregating, she found a rock and dropped it into the water.

The mass of eels parted briefly and a man's face peered up at her. A ravaged, torn face, surrounded by flickering, Medusa-like tails... As she watched, sharp teeth bit into Tignelli's cheeks, and half a dozen more darted forwards, fastening their mouths onto his lips and chin, tearing and pulling.

She turned. "The sluice gate," she shouted to Panicucci. "Open it!" He understood, and ran to do as she'd said. She looked round for more rocks, but there weren't any. Cursing, she jumped feet first into the water, which was cold and slightly greasy, whether from the presence of the body or the eels, she couldn't have said. Some of the smaller creatures darted away, but the larger ones were more aggressive, taking advantage of the space left by the more timid to force their way even closer to their meal. She splashed and kicked, driving them off. A long, thin shape slid from Tignelli's shirtsleeve; another backed out from his trouser cuff. A commotion under his shirt, in the region of his chest, showed where another was panicking; a moment later, it flickered from his open collar, sinuous and silvery as a knotted necktie, and was gone. The water level was falling now, Panicucci having got the sluice open. On and on she beat at the water, shouting at them in choice Venetian – it was only later she realised that she might as well have saved her breath, since they couldn't hear. Soon the wriggling mass was breaking the surface of what little water was left, and then it was slipping away, tumbling into the next basin.

By her feet, the plundered, ripped-apart face of Count Birino Tignelli, would-be conqueror of Venice, emerged from the receding waters like a nightmare.

*

"You did well," Hapadi said. "Another hour or so and they'd have destroyed any indication of how he died. Even so, don't expect much in the way of forensic evidence."

She nodded. She was wearing white microfibre overalls instead of her wet clothes now. Despite Hapadi's caution, it was clear that Tignelli had been murdered: the two bullet wounds in his chest left no doubt.

A second forensic team was examining the former convent's chapel, which turned out to be decorated with flags bearing the symbol Father Calergi had identified as the *carità*, along with other Masonic paraphernalia. It seemed likely that was where Cassandre had been killed: the search team's ultraviolet lamps had revealed faint traces of blood on the flagstone floor.

Whoever had murdered Tignelli, she reflected, had hit on a far surer way of ensuring no evidence was left behind.

"We need a word, Capitano."

She looked up. Aldo Piola was standing ten yards off. Behind him she saw the trim, dapper figure of Colonel Grimaldo of AISI.

"I suppose you've come to order us off this investigation as well," she said bitterly as they walked back to the house.

"On the contrary," Grimaldo said. "I have some evidence that I believe may be useful to you."

"What kind of evidence?"

"A wiretap." He pulled out a miniature recorder and a pair of earbud headphones. "It's probably easier if you use these. The quality isn't perfect."

She put the buds in her ears and pressed "Play". There was some interference, then she heard Tignelli's voice. "*Pronto.*"

The voice that spoke next was strangely robotic. "Good - evening - Count - Tignelli. We - need - to - meet."

"Who is this?"

"An - interested - party. One - who - is - aware - of - your - plans."

"I have no interest in discussing any plans I might have with you," Tignelli said brusquely.

"Then - they - will - not - succeed."

Tignelli's voice became more cautious. "If you have some-thing to say to me, then say it."

"This - phone - is - being - tapped - by - the - Italian - Intelligence - Service. I - will - be - with - you - in - one - hour."

"Alone?"

It was clear that Tignelli was asking if the visitor would be unaccompanied, but the voice chose not to take it that way. "Yes. Just - you. Send - your - staff - away." There was a click as the caller disconnected.

She pulled the earphones from her ears. "What time was this?"

"Nine o'clock last night."

"And you didn't do anything?"

"I was engaged on another operation at the time. I was only alerted to it this morning." He gestured at the search teams. "It seems you beat me to it."

Her eyes narrowed, and he sighed. "Capitano, I'm aware you've been speculating that AISI might somehow have been involved with Count Tignelli's plans. I'm here to assure you that isn't the case. I can also promise you full cooperation in what will now become a joint investigation."

"What makes you think I was speculating about anything of the kind?"

"Avvocato Marcello authorised us to tap your phone as

well as Count Tignelli's," Grimaldo said matter-of-factly. "Along with that of Avvocato Li Fonti. You see, we were initially just as suspicious of you as you were of us. Given what Cassandre had told us, we couldn't take any chances."

"And what *did* he tell you, exactly?" She pushed out of her mind that anyone tapping her and Flavio's phones would have heard the most intimate details of their relationship.

"As you quickly realised, Alessandro Cassandre was an unscrupulous chancer. He'd worked out why Count Tignelli thought the bank's apparently worthless credit default swaps would become valuable, and decided to ingratiate himself into the Count's organisation to try to profit from it further. Then, when his own corrupt financial dealings were discovered by the bank's chairman, he decided to save his own skin by coming to us and offering to betray Tignelli and his co-conspirators instead. Needless to say, he wasn't offering cooperation for patriotic reasons. He wanted immunity from prosecution, as well as a substantial payment."

"Did you agree?"

Grimaldo shook his head. "We told him he'd have to get closer to the conspirators before we even discussed a deal. It seems Tignelli chose not to trust such an obviously self-serving ally after all."

"So what will happen to Tignelli's plans for an independent Veneto now?"

"Thanks to you, we have the list of names from Cassandre's computer – almost certainly his fellow Masons. We'll round them all up and make sure they understand that this particular enterprise is to go no further." He hesitated. "Unfortunately, some aspects of Tignelli's plan may not be so easy to stamp out."

Something in the darkness of Grimaldo's tone made her frown. "Why not?"

"The separatist coup, if that is what we may call it, won't happen. But the events that would trigger it... they may be a different matter."

"What events?"

"He was planning an atrocity," Grimaldo said quietly. "A terrorist attack on Venice. His intention was that it would be foiled in advance, at which point he would use it as a pretext to declare that Rome was no longer capable of protecting the city. That would have been the signal for the regional assembly to declare a state of emergency, swiftly followed by a local referendum on independence."

"Can you stop it?"

"We thought so – that was the operation I was involved in last night. We had a name: a radicalised Muslim, currently studying in Sicily. Cassandre had been transferring money to him, on Tignelli's instructions. But when we sent a GIS squad to arrest him, we were just hours too late. It seems he'd been tipped off."

"Where could he have gone?"

"We don't know. It's possible he's slipped out of the country altogether, in which case he might no longer pose a danger. But until we know for sure, we're keeping the threat level at red."

"Are there any leads?"

"Just one. Shortly before he left, a teacher at the college where he was studying was killed. The local police have it down as a hate crime. But it's surely a remarkable coincidence that one of the very few people who could help us to identify the terrorist is now dead."

FORTY-THREE

DANIELE TOOK A taxi to the Institute of Christina Mirabilis, the private hospital deep in the Veneto countryside where Father Uriel was based. This was the region where the grapes for *prosecco* were grown, and every spare inch of land was covered in neat rows of vines.

The Institute itself, a former monastery, was so hidden away that, if it weren't for a discreet sign by the roadside, it would have been easy to miss the tall metal gates. On either side of the long driveway, men in brown monastic robes and women in blue habits worked the Institute's own vines, or bustled to and fro between the sprawling buildings. But a keen eye would have noticed that it was the nuns who were doing the bustling, while many of the men had a listless, medicated air. The former were nurses, while the latter were patients. Father Uriel's psychiatric work principally involved treating that small but notorious subset of the priesthood who had committed acts of sexual abuse. He believed some of them could be cured; perhaps more importantly, he believed that all of them could be redeemed. It was not only to avoid controversy that his hospital was so tucked away. For him, contemplation, confession and prayer were at least as beneficial as psychotherapy and medication.

He also saw a few patients with other conditions, and for

a time had worked with Daniele on developing his ability to empathise with other people.

"I'm glad you've come to see me," he said when Daniele was shown into his treatment room. "It's been a while."

Daniele shrugged. "I saw no point in continuing our previous sessions."

"Because the therapy wasn't working?" the psychiatrist asked. He left the briefest of pauses. "Or because it was?"

"Because I realised that your definition of working may not be the same as mine," Daniele answered coolly. "It's too late for me to change who I am. But if by remembering what happened during the kidnap I can clear up some unanswered questions, that's different."

Father Uriel got Daniele to lie down, then placed a pair of lightweight foam headphones over his ears and a small egg-shaped pulser in each hand.

"When you hear a click in your left ear, or feel a pulse in your left hand, I want you to look to the left," he instructed. "When the click and the pulse come from the right, look right. I'll guide your eye movements to begin with, but after that, just keep them going by yourself. If at any point the process becomes too painful or traumatic, I'll stop and take you to a safe place in your mind where no one can hurt you. Do you understand?"

"Yes."

"Good. Now focus on the end of my pen." Father Uriel held up a retractable ballpoint and clicked the end twice. "I want you to tense and relax each part of your body in turn, starting at the toes. Tense… and relax. That's it."

By the time he had relaxed his entire body, Daniele was feeling mentally clear-headed and physically lethargic, his whole attention locked on the end of Father Uriel's pen.

"I'm going to move the pen to the right now," Father Uriel said in a calm, low voice. "And to the left... Good. Now I want you to think about a sensory memory from your kidnap. Back then, at seven years old, in the room where they held you... It could be a sight, a sound, anything."

"I remember the lines between the bricks on the wall," Daniele heard himself saying. "I remember the pattern they made. I used to count the uprights between each brick."

"How many uprights were there?" Father Uriel continued to move the pen from side to side. In his palms Daniele felt the small, rhythmic pulse of the clickers, the sound swinging from one ear to the other, as steady as a metronome.

"Four hundred and seventeen."

"Good. What can you hear, when you're in that room?"

"Goats. There are goats outside. Sometimes I smell them too. We're in the countryside, somewhere remote."

"Who's keeping you here?"

"There are three whose names I know. Claudio, Paolo and Maria. Claudio is meant to be in charge but the other two discuss everything with him before they let him make the decisions."

"How long have you been here?"

"A week. When they brought me here they said it wouldn't take this long. All my parents have to do is send the money and they'll let me go. Maria says it can't be much longer now. She's been saying that for days."

Father Uriel lowered his pen. But Daniele's eyes still swung from left to right and back again.

"Who do you like most out of the kidnappers? Who do you trust?"

"Claudio seems all right. Paolo I'm not sure. Maria's nice. Sometimes she comes and sits with me."

What do you talk about?"

"About what they believe. What they're fighting for. They're against rich people like my father. They want a society where everyone's the same. Where no one can be better than someone else because of what family they come from."

"I'm going to take you forward a week, Daniele. What's happening now?"

"They're arguing."

"What about?"

"Why my parents still haven't paid. Claudio's angry. He shouts at me. 'What kind of brat are you? Why don't they want you back?'" Daniele gulped. "He… he…he… he…"

"It's all right, Daniele. You don't like being shouted at, I understand that. What else does Claudio say?"

"He says they're going to kill me," Daniele shouted. He started, and dropped the clickers. His back arched. Reaching up, he tore off the headphones in a panic.

"You're in a safe place now," Father Uriel said, careful to ensure that his own voice held no echo of the stress in Daniele's. "A calm, quiet place where they can't hurt you."

He spent five more minutes calming Daniele before bringing him out of the trance.

"It didn't work," Daniele said flatly, sitting up.

"On the contrary," Father Uriel said. "It's working extremely well, for a first session. You have unreasonably high expectations, that's all."

FORTY-FOUR

KAT STEPPED OFF the Alitalia flight to Palermo to be greeted by the unmistakable smell of Sicily. The last time she'd been here, years ago, it was springtime and the air had been thick with *la zagara*, the scent of orange and almond blossom. Today, the sun was so fierce that the runway seemed blasted a dazzling white, and heat-haze made the distant mountains shimmer and melt; but the scent was no less heady: a pungent mixture of jasmine, citrus, aeroplane fumes and the spicy, African smell of carob trees.

A *sovrintendente* from the local Polizia was waiting for her in the terminal building. "Hi. I'm Turi Russo," he said, saluting laconically.

Only when they were in his car and driving towards the city did he raise the reason behind her visit.

"Frankly, I don't know why the Carabinieri are interested in this one." A motorist pulled out in front of him without warning; Russo gestured angrily and leant on his horn, but made no attempt to pull him over. "Let alone AISI. It's a hate crime, pure and simple. We had it wrapped up within a day."

"Wrapped up? You mean you arrested someone?"

"No," Russo admitted. "I mean we got the investigation finished and the paperwork sorted. But the signs could hardly have been clearer. The victim was Muslim. When we found him, his carotid artery had been severed just below the wind-pipe. The jugular veins to the heart were also cut, on both sides." He glanced at her to see if she understood.

"So?"

"That's the method halal butchers use to kill an animal," he said bluntly. "Ergo, hate crime. It's hardly surprising. Palermo's a racial powder-keg right now. We've got an official unemployment rate of twenty-five per cent, but the real figure is much higher. Meanwhile we're straining at the seams with Arabs, Albanians, gypsies… And that's before you even get to the *mulignane*."

"The what?"

He laughed. "Don't you have that word up north? Aubergines. It's what we call the Africans. Senegal, Gabon, Ivory Coast, Congo, Somalia, Liberia… We don't need to read the newspapers here. We can tell where the civil wars are just by the colour of the *clandestini* climbing off the boats. We're meant to stop them coming in, but until the politicians decide to get serious, how are we meant to do that?"

Irritating though Russo's racism was, in truth his opinions weren't much different from those Kat sometimes overheard in the Carabinieri bar at Campo San Zaccaria. "Was anything stolen?"

"Not that we could tell."

"What about computers?"

Russo looked sideways at her. "That's AISI's interest, I take it?"

"We picked his name up in the course of another investiga-tion," she said blandly. "You know how it is. Every lead has to be checked."

In fact, the murder of the teacher, Jabbar Riaz Karimi, was still the only lead AISI had. They'd discovered that shortly before his death he'd been searching online for any information linking the Fréjus road tunnel disaster to jihadists. When that hadn't turned up much, he'd tried adding a name – Hafeez Bousaid – and the words "identity theft".

Hafeez Bousaid, they quickly established, was indeed the name from a stolen passport. Meanwhile, the agencies investigating the Fréjus road tunnel disaster were, Grimaldo had told Kat, starting to entertain the idea that it could have been some kind of cyber attack.

None of this, though, was to be shared with Russo unless it was absolutely essential. The Italian police had a long history of ending up on the wrong side of investigations: Grimaldo was determined to limit knowledge of this one to as few people as possible.

"I'll need all the paperwork and the crime-scene photographs," she said now to Russo. "And I'd like to examine the crime scene myself."

"No problem. The files are in the boot, so we'll head straight there."

Despite his words, she suspected he made a slight detour in order to take her through the very centre of Palermo, "so you can see what it's really like down here". He was quite right: she was taken aback. In Venice, as in most Italian cities, the *centro storico* was the cultural heart of the city, the focus of its nightlife and its smartest shops. In Palermo, the centre was a sprawling, crumbling *medina*, an African souk housed in semi-derelict *palazzi*, where the throb of African music and rows of makeshift stalls had ousted any semblance of Italy.

"I couldn't stop here," Russo said as he drove slowly down the street. "Usually we come in a convoy of three vehicles." He gestured into an alleyway. "There's probably only a few hundred *clandestini* living here permanently. The rest stay just as long as it takes to get a *permesso di soggiorno*, then they move on."

She gave him a sideways glance. "How do they get hold of the residence permits?"

He shrugged. "They all want to go north, where the money is. We don't encourage them to stay here, put it that way. If that means turning a blind eye to officials selling permits, so be it."

"Do they give you much trouble?"

Russo laughed. "Not exactly... These Africans, they describe this area as *tranquillo*. Know why?"

"No." It certainly didn't sound quiet to her.

"Because nobody bothers them. Nobody asks for their papers, nobody from the electricity company looks too closely at where their power comes from, nobody chases them when they steal a purse or lift a tourist's phone. So while it might be a little noisy at three o'clock in the morning, in all the ways that matter to them, it's quiet." He hooted his horn to clear a group of dark-skinned young men out of the way. They scattered languidly, eyeballing him. "We've got a saying down here, '*Fatti i cazzi tuoi*' – you know it?"

"I know it," she said. "'Take care of your own dick.'"

"Even when one of their own is murdered, don't expect anyone to come forward and tell the Polizia they've seen something. They're all too busy taking care of their own dicks."

He drove her across town to an area he referred to as "Zen". She thought he was being sarcastic, until she saw the signs to "Zona Espansione Nord". It was less claustrophobic than the centre, but bleaker. High-rise apartment blocks, covered in graffiti, were surrounded by waste ground and stinking piles of refuse.

"Believe it or not, this is a relatively good area if you're an immigrant," Russo said as he got out of the car and began picking his way through the litter. "To be fair, the rubbish strike isn't their fault. That's the council. Turns out there are more people in head office paid to supervise the rubbish collectors than there are actual rubbish collectors. Someone tried to do something about it, and they all promptly went on strike. So there you are – you can either have clean hands or clean streets. Not both."

Up on the fifth floor of one of the high-rises – Russo didn't even bother to see if the lift was working – they found a door covered in police tape. "The door's still here, anyway," he said cheerfully as he produced the key.

Inside, she was surprised to discover a pleasant if rundown apartment – the view alone, over the sea to the north, would have made up for the lack of amenities. There was a stack of microfibre overalls and gloves in the hallway, along with a police logbook. Kat suited up while Russo signed them both in. She noticed he didn't put on overalls himself.

"That's where the body was found." He pointed towards the balcony. "When we checked with the people downstairs, blood was running down the outside wall into their kitchen. But they still claimed not to have seen or heard anything."

She went through the photographs in the file. It was as he'd described, although she was struck by the way the bloodstains seemed to indicate that the body had been moved onto the balcony while the victim was still bleeding out.

She went and stood on the spot where the body had lain, looking out over the sea. She was in shadow now. So Jabbar Riaz Karimi had died facing south-east, she thought.

Getting out her phone, she brought up Google Maps.

"He was facing Mecca as he died," she said, showing him. "The killer positioned him that way. Not just the general direction, either: the exact orientation. Still think it was a hate crime?"

He shrugged. "OK, so maybe it was another Muslim. A pious one with a grudge. It's not going to make any difference. Whoever did it wore gloves and cleaned up anything that might incriminate him. Cheeky bastard even looked it up on the internet."

"What do you mean?" she said, puzzled.

"When our scene-of-crime people got here, they found the victim's own tablet computer open on a page about how to clean up crime scenes."

"He didn't wear gloves," she said slowly.

"What do you mean?"

"Look." She got out her phone again. "When I used this just now to look up which way Mecca was, I had to take my glove off – it doesn't work with the touch screen. At some point he must have taken his gloves off to use the tablet. He may well have wiped it afterwards, but even so there could still be a partial or a smudged print."

"Very well," Russo said grudgingly. "I'll get the specialists to dust the tablet again."

She shook her head. "I'll take it with me when I go back to Venice. The fewer people touch it, the better. And now I think I'd better see the technical college."

The college was little more than half a dozen rooms in a run-down municipal building. The students were mostly non-Italian: Chinese, Middle Eastern, a smattering of Africans.

Kat spoke to one of Jabbar Karimi's students, who

confirmed the impression she'd already formed: the teacher was a mild, pious man, good at his job. He even helped some of the students get employment after the course was over, through his brother, who worked in IT recruitment.

A technician was working on the computers in Karimi's classroom. When she asked what he was doing, he told her that one of the students had downloaded a piece of freeware called Boot and Nuke. It had completely erased the hard drive of every single machine on their network.

Kat could feel the trail running cold. The killer had slipped into this place, then slipped away again, leaving not a single lead. That was unusual: most people left something. This man was either very lucky or very smart.

She turned to Russo. "Has there been any strange activity around here recently, anything that could be connected to computer hacking?"

"No," he said immediately. Then, "Well…"

"What is it?"

"It's probably nothing, but… last week there was a businessman in Palermo who almost crashed his BMW. He had some crazy story about the car's on-board computer suddenly malfunctioning, switching the engine off and locking the steering when he was doing sixty kilometres an hour."

Her interest quickened. "Was the car connected to the internet?"

"How did you know that? Apparently it was one of the newer models that has a built-in mobile broadband uplink. Anyway, the officers put it down as an ingenious story to avoid being charged with careless driving and referred the case to the prosecutors. I only heard about it because someone was joking about it in the canteen."

Just like Fréjus, she thought. *He's trying things out on a small scale, getting the technology just right.* "Let me know if anything else in that line comes up, will you? And I'd better talk to the dead man's brother, the one who works in recruitment."

FORTY-FIVE

"LIVIA? LIVIA BOCCARDO?"

As the teenagers streamed out of the classroom, chattering amongst themselves, the teacher looked up. "Yes?" Then, a moment later, "*Minchia!* Holly Boland? I don't believe it!"

"It's really me," Holly assured her, as amused by the fact that her childhood friend was a teacher as by the profanity she'd just uttered in front of her students. "Do you have ten minutes? We could grab a coffee."

Livia consulted her watch. "I have to go and supervise a conversation class in a minute. And the coffee here's undrinkable. But we could sit outside."

"Why are the kids in school?" Holly asked.

"Oh, it's a summer school. The local council's almost bankrupt, so they rent the school buildings out during the holidays. Most of the teachers are happy to earn a little extra. Besides, these foreign kids are generally well behaved. They don't have the drugs problems our local kids do."

"*Pisa* has a drugs problem?"

"Everywhere in Italy has a drugs problem. But tell me, what are you doing here? Last I heard, you were at college in America."

"I live in Vicenza now." Holly explained that she'd followed her father into the military. "It was our dads I wanted

275

to talk about, actually. I'm looking into that period when... when all the bad stuff happened."

"Why?" Livia said bluntly. Leading Holly to a small playground, she pulled out a packet of cigarettes.

In the vaguest terms, Holly explained that she was considering the possibility both men had been put in danger because of their involvement with the Masons. "I know your father died in a car crash, but I'm just wondering – was there anything suspicious about the circumstances?"

Livia laughed hollowly. "You could say that."

"In what way?"

"My mother told everyone it was a car crash because that's what she wanted us children to think. But before she died, she admitted to me that wasn't actually what happened. Papà was found with his throat cut, on the beach at Tirrenia."

Holly stared at her. It was too similar to the way Kat's victim had been found to be a coincidence.

"She wanted to protect us from the truth, but I think she also felt it was something to keep quiet about. So she pretended it was just a traffic accident."

"But he was definitely a Freemason?"

Livia nodded. "I found some of that weird regalia they wear when I was clearing out my parents' stuff."

"You still live in the same apartment, then?"

Livia exhaled smoke. "Yes. 87A. Why?"

"I have an idea that my father was keeping some kind of record or notes, some evidence of what he and your dad discovered. Could we take a look at your apartment? Just in case it's there, and you never spotted it?"

Livia shrugged. "If you like. Come by in an hour, and we'll have some lunch as well."

*

If Holly had been there for a different reason, having lunch at Livia's apartment would have been a fun occasion. She'd forgotten the Pisanese's amazing ability to throw food together for an impromptu meal. Yesterday's bread, torn into chunks and sprinkled with water, and a couple of roughly chopped tomatoes sprinkled with salt and oil from an unmarked bottle and garnished with basil leaves, turned into a *panzanella* salad, while the fridge yielded a thin booklet of greaseproof paper which unfolded to reveal a dozen slices of *prosciutto crudo*. There was red wine too, of course: Sangiovese, also from an unmarked bottle. Livia said she got both that and the olive oil filled up by the tobacconist down the street. "I don't ask where it comes from. It's a state secret. But it's always excellent."

As they ate, they caught up on old times. Most of Holly's old classmates, it turned out, were still living in or around Pisa. "Alessia Abbado's gay now, she's living with a female fitness instructor. Tiziano and Elide got married. And Tomas Mazzi and Sofia Trentino were together for five years, then he went off with an Australian divorcee." Not for the first time, Holly found herself wondering what her life would be like now if she'd stayed here instead of joining the US Army. She'd thought that by coming back to Italy she was coming home, but the truth was that to the Pisanese, anywhere outside Tuscany was still a foreign country.

"So what is it we're looking for?" Livia said at last. "A shoebox? A file? A trunk of papers?"

"I don't know," Holly confessed. "At a guess, some kind of folder or notebook. But it could be anything."

"OK," Livia said dubiously. "There are a couple of places we could try."

The apartment was so small that after twenty minutes they'd exhausted all of them.

"What happened to the picture that used to hang just here?" Holly asked, pointing at an alcove.

"We had a burglary. They didn't take much, but everything got broken."

"When was this?"

Livia thought back. "It must have been soon after Papà died. I remember because they took some of his things – Mamma was really upset."

"What kind of things?"

"Personal stuff from his desk, I think she said. I don't really remember—" She broke off. "You think it could have been connected?"

"I don't know. But it's a coincidence, isn't it? He's killed – then the apartment gets broken into?"

"In which case, do we assume they found what they were looking for?"

"Well, they didn't come back. So either they got it, or they were satisfied it wasn't here in the first place. I guess we'll never know."

FORTY-SIX

IAN GILROY SLIPPED into the gloomy interior of Santi Apostoli in Cannaregio and looked around. The man he was meeting wasn't there yet; but then Gilroy hadn't expected he would be. Gilroy always turned up to a meeting thirty minutes before his asset.

While he waited, he put some coins in the meter that controlled the lights in the side chapel and Tiepolo's *The Last Communion of St Lucy* jumped out of the darkness. He was still examining the painting when the church door opened briefly. A slight, stooped figure was silhouetted for a moment against the brightness of the day. Gilroy glanced at his watch. The other man was early too.

He waited at the altar rail. The newcomer nodded in greeting, then, by unspoken consent, they both turned to look at the painting.

"I imagine you know the story of St Lucy?" Gilroy said at last. "She was a wealthy young noblewoman who took a vow of celibacy and poverty. The man she had been promised to took exception to both, but particularly the latter, and had her committed to a brothel as punishment. When she still resisted, he had her eyes put out. Look, you can see them there, lying on that plate in the foreground."

The other man only grunted.

"Second Lieutenant Boland is looking for her father's records," Gilroy added.

"Is that wise?"

"I judged it best to let her see what she can find out. If there is anything, she'll bring it to me. Then we'll take a view on what to do." He paused. "My point is, Generale, that nothing should happen to her in the meantime. The very worst outcome would be for her to have an accident and leave a half-finished trail for a diligent prosecutor to follow. There was nearly such an accident in Sardinia, I understand. We must have no repeat of that." He spoke quietly, but there was no doubting the anger in his voice.

The other man shrugged. "She was poking her nose in. She was lucky not to lose it."

"No accidents," Gilroy insisted.

"Very well," the other man said languidly. "Not until she has either found the files or established that they don't exist. But no longer. Speaking of prosecutors, I suppose you've heard that Flavio Li Fonti is now looking into the other matter… They'll find nothing, I take it?"

"There's always something. But I doubt it'll be anything conclusive. Steps have been taken."

"Then we have nothing to fear." The man Gilroy had addressed as "Generale" turned away impatiently. It was a courtesy title: he had been retired for many years. Once, he had been one of the most powerful men within the Gladio network.

"There's always something to fear, Generale," Gilroy called after him silkily, his voice carrying in the reverberant air. "The Italian courts become both less forgiving and less susceptible to influence with each passing year. Those without a foreign passport or diplomatic immunity do well to remember that."

The general stopped, then turned and came back to where Gilroy stood. "Are you *threatening* me?"

"Leave the Boland girl alone. Believe me, there are good reasons why we don't want any unwelcome publicity just now."

"She may be less reliable than you think. As well as less useful."

Gilroy turned back to the painting of St Lucy. "Do you recall the last bit of the story? After her eyes were put out, they tried to carry her into the brothel by force. But somehow she became so strong that ten men couldn't move her." He paused. "Never underestimate the power of a determined woman, Generale."

FORTY-SEVEN

JABBAR KARIMI'S BROTHER Aslam had an office near Taormina, further down the coast. Kat knew the town only by reputation: a photogenic tourist magnet, made affluent by visitors from all over the world. Russo had declined to come with her, but at least he'd loaned her a car. She took the *autostrada* from Palermo before turning off it and winding up smaller roads to a craggy plateau hundreds of feet above the sea. On either side lay peaceful orange and lemon groves, dotted with the ancient, gnarled trunks of well-pruned olive trees. Almost every lay-by held a farmer, seated in the shade, selling cantaloupes and watermelons out of the back of a rickety three-wheeled van. In the distance, the massive cone of Mount Etna was capped with white despite the summer heat.

She hadn't been able to make contact with the brother: his phone was switched off and there was no answer from his office. When she reached the address, in a suburb of Giardini Naxos, she soon discovered why. His business consisted of no more than a single Portakabin, locked. The windows were barred; peering through, she saw two desks with computers on them, a wall-mounted air-conditioning unit and a large map of the world.

"So you've come at last."

She turned. A dark-skinned man in his thirties was walking towards her. "Signor Karimi?" she asked.

He stopped and frowned. "He's the one that's dead."

"I know." She gestured. "I'm sorry for your loss. I just came from Palermo, from your brother's apartment. I'm working with the local Polizia—"

"Wait a minute," he said. "Are you saying *Jabbar* Karimi is dead as well?"

"Yes," she said. "As well as who? Jabbar was your brother, correct?"

He shook his head. "I'm not Aslam Karimi. I'm his business partner. Aslam died in a car accident two days ago. Until you told me, I didn't even know his brother was dead too."

"Their business is IT recruitment," she told Flavio on the phone that evening. "Specifically, they place qualified IT people on ships – Giardini Naxos is a stopping-off point for big cruise liners visiting Taormina. Most of their recruiting isn't even done face to face. They look at a person's qualifications, check their references, then forward their CV to the shipping companies."

"Any idea what name our suspect's travelling under now?"

"None whatsoever. Aslam Karimi dealt with all the recommendations passed on by his brother, and guess what? It turns out his computer's been wiped too. His business partner is contacting all their clients to see if he placed anyone in the last few days, but it'll take a while to get a response."

"So...?"

"So it looks as if Colonel Grimaldo was right, and our man has slipped out of the country."

"What will you do now?"

"Come back to Venice. The Polizia here can follow up the remaining leads. Besides, I miss you."

He laughed softly. "I was wondering if you'd say that."

"Well, it's true," she protested. But she knew that a part of her had been resisting admitting, to herself as well as to him, just how much she needed his presence. She'd got on and done the job, but there had been a dull ache in her heart the whole time she'd been in Sicily. "What about you?"

"Unlike you, I have no problem admitting that I'm in love," he said, amused. He grew more sombre. "You know, I'm beginning to think there might have been something in your friend's wild fantasies after all."

It took her a moment to work out that he meant Holly. "Oh?"

"Tignelli's death – it wasn't just some lone gunman, Kat. It was a *raid*. They found marks left by two rigid inflatables, deep footprints in the mud from boots with identical treads, and explosive charges were used to knock out the house's surveillance systems. There's a partial image from one of the security cameras just before the explosion. It shows four men in black balaclavas running towards the house."

"A military-style operation, in other words?"

"It certainly looks that way."

"By who?"

"There are no indications yet. In the meantime, we're rounding up all the names on Cassandre's list, and guess what? Not one of them will admit to being part of Tignelli's lodge, even though we found cards on some of them with that *carità* symbol. But compared with what happened to Cassandre and Tignelli, a tough interview with a prosecutor looks like a walk in the park. I'm not saying your friend is right and it's all part of some massive fifty-year conspiracy. But it does seem like there are plenty of people who think they can just close ranks and refuse to talk to us."

"Be careful," she said, anxiety thickening her voice.

"I'm always careful. But you know, Kat, we only have the law. In the face of corruption, organised crime, interfering foreign powers, politicians who line their own pockets, bureaucrats who only care about preserving their pensions, and governments that are worse than all the rest put together... The law may not be perfect. But it's all we've got."

"Only if people like us fight to keep it that way."

"Yes," he agreed. "I'm not changing my mind about leaving, Kat. This will be my last investigation. But I won't duck it. And then... Amsterdam. I promise."

"Amsterdam," she whispered. It was starting to sound more and more like a talisman, a mythical place of peace and protection. Or, perhaps, a safe word, to be invoked in times of danger.

FORTY-EIGHT

BACK IN VICENZA, Holly poured herself a glass of wine and considered her options. On the coffee table was a note she'd found in her mailbox.

I've bought you some time. How much, I don't know.

Gilroy. But time to do what? The leads she'd had led nowhere.

It suddenly struck her that she'd neglected to speak to the most obvious person of all about this. She checked the time. It would be still be early evening in Florida.

"Hi, Mom," she said when her mother answered. They chatted for a few minutes before Holly moved on to the reason for her call.

"You know that document I found in Dad's old footlocker? I'm not sure I've told you this, but I think it related to the death of Mr Boccardo. Did Dad ever mention working with him – with Mr Boccardo, that is? Some kind of investigation or plan they were doing together?"

"Oh, Holly," her mother said heavily. "You haven't got mixed up in all that, have you?"

Her ears pricked up. "All what?"

"Your father said something very bad had happened to Mr Boccardo, that maybe it hadn't been a car crash like they were saying. I don't know the details, but after that he spent all his time at work. He said he was trying to find out how it had happened – 'going through the tapes' was how he put it."

"Tapes? What tapes?"

"I don't know. He didn't really talk about his work at home. None of the men in his unit did. Even when they got together, it was all acronyms and codewords – Autodin and OL9, and something called the tropo that was always breaking down."

"And that was when he started drinking?"

"I guess. He couldn't sleep. Drinking was the only thing that helped him relax."

"Did he ever bring anything home? Any notebooks or records?"

"Not that I know of."

"Could there be anything like that stored with his old army stuff?"

"The trunks? I gave everything that was left to the recycling service. They came by a couple of weeks ago – knocked on the door and said they had a special rate. And when I told them he was a veteran, they brought it down even more. You said you'd taken everything that mattered, so…"

"Don't worry, Mom." She didn't think her father would have kept a second document at home in any case, let alone a box of tapes or other records. "Tell me, though: was there anything special about the days immediately before his stroke? Anything out of the ordinary?"

"Well, I don't recall exactly – it's so long ago now. But I do remember that he stopped going into work so much. He said…" Her mother's voice was thoughtful, as if she was only just remembering this. "He said he had to decide."

"Decide what?"

"I don't know. But whatever it was, it involved a bottle of whisky. After his stroke, I forgot all about it."

"You think maybe he could have found out who killed Mr Boccardo?"

"Maybe." Her mother sounded doubtful. "But I don't see that would have been such a big deal, would it? He would just have told the police. That wouldn't have called for a bottle."

"Of course," Holly said. "He'd have reported it. That was the kind of person he was."

There was only one kind of crime her father would need to agonise about, she thought: a crime that had been committed by his own countrymen.

As if reading her thoughts, her mother said, "Promise me, Holly…"

"What, Mom?"

"If there was something he did – something disloyal – promise me you won't make the same mistake."

"I'm not sure he *did* make a mistake, though," she said. "I think maybe he was the only one who found out the truth. And that's why they were so frightened of him."

FORTY-NINE

"AS BEFORE, DANIELE," Father Uriel instructed. "When you hear a click in your left ear and a pulse in your left hand, look to the left. When the click and the pulse come from the right, look right. Ready?"

"Ready," Daniele said. His voice seemed to come from very far away.

Father Uriel guided Daniele's eyes with the tip of his pen for a few moments. It puzzled him that Daniele was such an easy subject to hypnotise. All the literature suggested that those with Asperger's syndrome – that is, high-functioning autism – were almost immune to hypnosis, possibly because their minds were so analytical. The fact that Daniele didn't easily fit into that category made him wonder if there was anything in the theory that Daniele's condition could be something more complex.

"Where are you now?" he asked quietly.

"In the room. The same room. The one I'm always in." Daniele's voice had taken on the truculent inflections of a child.

"What's happening?"

"They're shouting. Paolo and Claudio. Not *at* me this time. But about me. Paolo's saying they've got to do something. Move locations. Ask for less money. Anything to resolve it. 'If we stay here, we'll die,' he says. And then—"

"What is it, Daniele?"

"He's got a gun," Daniele whispered. "He's waving it at Claudio. I'm scared. And then he's walking towards me. He gets hold of my hair and pulls my head back. He's saying... He's saying they should cut their losses and shoot him. He means me. And Claudio says, 'All right then, do it.' Then... Then..."

"Yes?"

"Maria shouts at them both to shut up. Claudio storms out. Maria goes and takes the gun from Paolo. She kisses him. At first I think she's hugging him, but they lie on the floor and start wrestling. Wrestling and kissing."

"What then, Daniele?"

"She says, 'Not in front of the boy.' They go into the other room. But they leave the door open and I can still see them. Taking their clothes off. Wrestling and kissing again." With a start Daniele woke up. "Fucking each other," he said disgustedly in his normal voice. "Like animals."

"Can you recall anything else?"

Daniele thought, then shook his head. "I can sense shadows – glimpses – but it's as if they're on the periphery of my vision. When I try to reach for them, they're gone."

Father Uriel noted the jumbled synaesthesia of Daniele's speech, as well as how tired he sounded. "As I said at the outset, EMDR can take multiple sessions to be effective. You're making good progress."

"You also told me this was the only treatment," Daniele said. "But that isn't true, is it? I did some research. There's ECT. Electroconvulsive shock therapy."

Father Uriel shook his head. "ECT is regarded as an absolute last resort in psychiatric medicine. Passing an electric current across the brain to provoke a seizure is the equivalent of hitting a faulty computer with a sledgehammer—"

"Doctors don't understand how EMDR works, either."

"EMDR is *safe*. As for the literature you may have found on ECT and amnesia, it's little more than conjecture. Because patients who are given ECT almost always experience a period of temporary memory loss, it's been theorised that blocked memories might return along with the others. But it's only been tried on a handful of subjects. Most ethics committees aren't prepared to risk the potential downsides."

Daniele regarded him calmly. "If you don't give me ECT, I'll give it to myself."

"What do you mean?"

"There are sites on the Dark Web where you can find all the information. Not that I want to resort to that. I'd much rather have it done here, in a medical setting."

Father Uriel was so angry he could barely reply. "You think you're the first patient to play mind games with me? I've had men in here who've done evil acts beyond your comprehension. You can't manipulate me, Daniele."

"I'm not trying to," Daniele replied evenly. "But I am determined to try every treatment there is."

FIFTY

ONCE AGAIN HOLLY drove south. Usually this was a journey that lifted her spirits, the flat plains of the Po giving way to the soaring mountains beyond Bologna, tiny fortified towns clinging to their sheer sides for protection. But today she barely noticed them.

She was thinking about her mother's words. *Autodin and OL9, and something called the tropo that was always breaking down...* They'd stirred up half-forgotten memories: conversations between her father and his friends that had been less guarded than usual because only the kids were around.

When she reached Camp Darby, tucked away in the sleepy pine woods that stretched between Pisa and the sea, she showed her CAC card at the gate. "Know where you're going, ma'am?" the soldier on duty asked politely.

"Recycling centre. Straight down towards the beach, then left past the missile silos. That right?"

"Yes, ma'am," he said, saluting.

The recycling centre was a vast hangar set amongst the pine woods. Half a dozen trucks were lined up neatly outside, each one at a precise forty-five-degree angle to the building.

"Whadda you want?" a voice shouted suspiciously. She turned to see a grizzled, limping figure stumping stiffly towards her, his paunch straining at the buttons of his uniform.

Staff Sergeant Kassapian might be only a year or so off retirement, but he ran the recycling facility with old-school rigour.
"Ma'am," he added as an afterthought.

"Staff? It's me. Holly Boland."

"Well, so it is." He gave her a stare which might have contained the faintest ghost of a smile. "Now, whadda you want?"

"Pick your brains, Staff."

He grunted. "If I had any of those, would I still be here?"

"We're talking about some stuff that happened back in the
day. I don't think there's anyone else from my dad's time left
to ask."

"No, there ain't," he agreed. He gestured at the thirty-foot-
high mounds of paper scattered across the inside of the hangar.
"You're not going to sneak any of these papers out, are you?
'Cos I got into trouble last time you did that."

"What I'm looking for won't be in here," she assured him.
"The thing is, I don't know where it would be. I'm looking for
some records, tapes maybe, that my dad put in a safe place."

He thought for a moment. But she got the feeling he wasn't
so much racking his brains as debating whether or not to tell
her something. Then he shook his head. "Nothing comes to
mind."

She said curiously, "What did my father do here at Darby,
exactly? I know he ran a unit that was something to with
Autodin. That was a codeword, presumably. But what exactly
was Autodin?"

He snorted. "Kids today. Think you know everything when
you don't know anything. Autodin wasn't a codeword, it was
the Automatic Digital Network. The secure comms system for
the whole US military. Back when we didn't have email, and
a computer was the size of a truck, that's how we got information around."

"How did it work?"

He shrugged. "Microwaves, I was told. Not the kind inside your oven, the kind that bounce round the sky. You wanted to send a secure cable, you took it to the hut and an operator typed it into the computer for you. No satellites or internet then. Everything went through the tropo."

"What was the tropo? Part of the same system, presumably?"

He nodded. "The troposcatter was the transmitter, the bit that linked everything together. The tropo at Darby was the forwarding hub for the whole of Italy."

"So my father would have had access to all the cables that were sent to and from Washington? Even cables from other bases?"

"They'd have passed through Darby, sure," he said cautiously. "But I'm not saying he'd have looked at them. Why would he? Most of that stuff was classified."

She recalled her mother's words. *Going through the tapes, was how he put it.* "And the CIA? Would they have used the same network?"

"Sure. Only one Autodin. And it was maintained by the military."

"So that was why my father was involved in Gladio," she said thoughtfully. "He'd have overseen their training in operational communications." Her father had held a unique position, she realised: right in the centre of the US's global web of clandestine communications. A man like that, if he started digging, would have no shortage of material to dig through. "What happened to the Autodin system? Is it still in use?"

Kassapian shook his head. "It was decommissioned in 2000. Most folks were amazed it had lasted that long. But that old kit was built tough. They used it mostly as a backup by then, but eventually it wasn't worth anyone's while keeping on the maintenance crew."

"So the equipment's gone too?"

Again he hesitated. "Pretty much. There's a few bits and pieces in one of the storage hangars."

"Could I take a look?"

He scratched his head. "Don't see why not. I'll take you there."

She'd have walked, but he climbed into the driving seat of a meticulously clean army jeep.

"This area's ordnance storage, mostly," he said as he drove, indicating the long, low buildings that stretched away as far as the eye could see, half-hidden amongst the woods. "ICBMs and chilled munitions. There's eight thousand tonnes of HE in our fridge just now." He chuckled at her reaction. "You get used to it. Anything happens here, they reckon it'll make a bigger bang than Hiroshima. But it won't. We got procedures coming out of our ears."

"How many are there?" she asked, twisting to look.

"Hangars? One hundred and twenty-four. Remember the Gulf War? Every missile and bullet came from one of these. Plus trucks, rations, construction materials, tents... The mission challenge here is to be able to send a brigade of five thousand men anywhere in the world within forty-eight hours, with everything they need to fight a war. Right down to clean underwear. Here we are." He'd pulled up next to a hangar. Leaving the engine running, he got out and slid the doors open just wide enough to admit the jeep.

Inside, a concrete floor sloped downwards. On either side were lines of cargo containers, some covered in canvas drapes. Kassapian paused to turn on some lights – parallel rows of industrial downlighters that walked into the darkness as they flickered into life, like beacons down a runway. Getting back in the jeep, he drove them towards the rear of the building.

They stopped next to a low island of metal cabinets, each the height of a man. It was only when she looked more carefully that she saw they were bits of ancient computer equipment. All had been crudely ripped from wherever they'd been installed and were now trailing bare wires. Some of the cabinets were buckled and damaged. Yet somehow they triggered a memory, a flashback of some long-ago visit to her father's workplace.

She blinked, and the memory was gone.

"This isn't it," she said, frustrated. "Whatever my father found, he'd have put it somewhere safer than this. Isn't there anywhere else?"

Kassapian said nothing, chewing his lip. She recalled how he'd hesitated earlier. "There *is* somewhere, isn't there? Somewhere secure, that my father had access to."

"Well, there's the old C3," he admitted. "We weren't meant to talk about it, back then. But I guess there's no harm now."

"C3? A Command, Control, Communications centre?"

Kassapian's squat face almost cracked a smile. "So you haven't forgotten everything your dad told you."

"Not everything. But where is it? Not round here, surely?" During the Cold War, C3s were situated in bombproof bunkers, far underground.

He shook his head. "Not here, no. Sea's too close, and in any case they wanted it a long way from the ordnance."

He drove her out of the camp and north along the coast road. It was crowded with Italian holidaymakers eating ice creams and carrying bottles of water. It was strange to think of these bikini-wearing tourists casually strolling only a mile or so from eight thousand tonnes of high explosive.

"I remember my dad taking me to a radio station round here," she shouted over the noise of the wind as they joined the motorway. "Just a couple of huts, and these big signal dishes. He said it was where Marconi sent the first radio transmissions."

Kassapian nodded. "Coltano. That was where the main troposcatter dishes were. It's all falling down now."

After twenty minutes he took the exit to Pietrasanta. Almost immediately, they started winding up into the mountains. A truck thundered past in the opposite direction, its trailer piled high with white stone. "Marble," Kassapian said, pulling over to give it room. "Good stuff, apparently. This is where Michelangelo came when he wanted something special."

Eventually they turned onto an unmarked track that led straight towards the sheer face of the mountain. Clearly, this had once been a quarry. Only a military guard tower, discreetly set back from the road, gave any clue to its more recent purpose.

"I don't know why they mothballed this place, instead of decommissioning it like they did Sorrate and West Star," he commented. "Someone comes out every few months, makes sure the badgers haven't got in. But it's pretty low-maintenance. The stone keeps the humidity down. Maybe that's why they didn't close this one. Or maybe they just forgot about it."

In front of them was a hangar similar to the ones at Camp Darby, built against the mountain. When Kassapian produced a key and slid the door back on its runners, however, it became clear that the hangar was there purely to conceal the bunker's real entrance, a round disc of blastproof iron the height of a truck.

Even though the door was counterweighted, it took all their combined strength to pull it open. "We'll take the vehicle," he said when they'd done it. "Takes a while to get anywhere otherwise."

He got back in the jeep and waited for her to join him. For a moment, though, she stood there, peering uncertainly into the tunnel's dark mouth.

"What's up?"

I'm terrified, she wanted to say. *I can't do it*. She realised she was shaking. It had been in an underground facility, entered through a door much like this one, that a man had stripped her naked and tortured her, physically, mentally and sexually.

Kassapian grunted. "You're a US Army officer, aren't you, Boland? 'Cos you've sure as hell got the pips on your shoulder. Nothing to be scared of down there but a few spiders." He hauled himself out and went to a fusebox. "Maybe this'll help." Lights flickered on ahead.

"Sorry, Staff. I was just taking a moment." She climbed back into the jeep.

The further they drove into the mountain, the more frequent the lights became. Every few hundred yards they passed through another set of blast doors. It was very cold.

"It was all self-sufficient, of course," Kassapian said. "Got its own hydroelectric plant, sewers, the works. And there's half a mile of rock above us now. Russians could nuke Camp Darby to kingdom come, this place would still be functioning." He nodded towards a side tunnel marked "Roosevelt Drive" in peeling stencil. "Sleeping quarters are down there. Moleholes, they called them. Two hundred bunks for six hundred men."

"What about families? Was there any room for them?"

He shook his head. "No room for anyone who wasn't essential."

She thought about her father. Could he have done it, if he'd been ordered to come here at a time of nuclear crisis? Could he have said goodbye to his wife and children – to *her* – with deliberate casualness, so as not to let them know anything was wrong, and then retired behind these blastproof doors to wait until the deadly radiation storms had killed every living thing above?

She supposed he could. An order was an order. And what would have been the alternative? To die with one's family instead of fighting the enemy would have been the greatest dereliction of all.

Kassapian pulled up and switched off the engine. "We'll walk from here."

They went through a smaller blast door, past an alcove marked "DECONTAMINATION/SHOWERS". Open-fronted metal cases held racks of radiation suits and masks. The ceiling now was only a little higher than a submarine's. She felt claustrophobia clutch at her, panic fluttering in her bowels.

It's just psychological. Like he said, you're a US Army officer. Deal with it.

More peeling stencils on the walls. "MESS" on one side, "LATRINES" on the other. To her surprise, there was even a tiny two-seat barbershop, the electric trimmers still dangling neatly from a metal arm. Even during a nuclear conflict, it seemed, the US military hadn't been about to tolerate long hair.

"In here," Kassapian said, opening a door marked "COMMAND". Inside, a viewing gallery overlooked a triple-height room, the far wall of which was dominated by a huge map of the world. Major cities were marked, as were US bases. Facing it were four long desks, each designed to seat a dozen men. By each place was a heavy Bakelite phone. Some of the desks had what looked like radar screens and ancient computer monitors built into them. Even the chairs were somehow redolent of her childhood: solid and wide-armed, they spoke of the physical presence of big, burly warriors.

"The Autodin op sat down there. But the equipment's right in here. This is where your dad would have been."

Kassapian opened another door and flicked on the light. The room was perhaps twenty feet by thirty, crammed with the same kind of computer equipment she'd seen in the storage hangar. But where that had been trailing wires, disassembled and neglected, this had been left neat and tidy and ready for battle. She half-expected Kassapian to press another switch and for all the relays and tape decks and cathode-ray screens to flicker silently into life, filling the room with the quiet, purposeful chatter of combat.

"Does it still work?" she asked.

He shrugged. "I guess. If you could ever figure out how to turn the damn thing on."

On one of the desks was a neat stack of operating manuals. She picked up the top one and opened it.

Autodin circuit facilities are constructed using the RED/ BLACK protocol, in which unencrypted data lines (RED side) are kept physically separated from the encrypted circuits (BLACK side). A typical data circuit is connected from the Accumulation and Distribution Unit to the RED patch panel in Technical Control.

There was no way she'd ever figure it out. Besides, it looked like it would need a small army of technicians to operate it.

A doorway marked "TAPE SEARCH" to one side led to a small alcove. The walls were lined with shelves of tape reels and diskettes.

"This here's the vault," Kassapian said, following her in. "Like your 'Sent Messages' folder, only probably with a lot less storage capacity. The switch automatically made a copy of every message. If it got lost, the operator could track it down here and resend it."

She looked along the neat rows of boxes. Some were labelled with the names of long-ago missions. "Operation Angel Fire"; "Operation Mountain Cross"; "Operation Sea Freedom"...

"This is the safest place, isn't it?" she said, almost to herself. "Safe from nuclear attack. But more to the point, safe from anyone who came looking. Only a handful of people even knew this facility existed. If my dad had to keep something hidden, this is where he'd have brought it."

Kassapian shrugged. "Maybe."

She continued to look along the shelves. "Operation Hollow Road"; "Operation Open Sea".

And then she saw it.

"Operation Unconsidered Earth".

And as if he were standing just behind her, she heard her father's voice, reciting those lines from Kipling:

> Cities and Thrones and Powers
> Stand in Time's eye,
> Almost as long as flowers,
> Which daily die:
> But, as new buds put forth
> To glad new men,
> Out of the spent and unconsidered Earth,
> The Cities rise again.

She reached for the box. Inside was a reel of magnetic tape and a stack of half a dozen eight-inch floppy diskettes.

Whatever it was her father had almost died for, she was now holding it in her hand.

They were walking back to the jeep when she heard a muffled clanging sound echoing down the corridors. Kassapian gave her a sideways look. "Badgers, most like."

Another clang, louder this time. "A badger that can kick open steel doors? I don't think so." She quickened her pace. "Is there another way out of here?"

He shrugged. "In theory. These tunnels go right through the mountain."

"Why 'in theory'?"

"I doubt anyone's used the secondary exits for a while. They may even have welded them shut when they mothballed the place." He waved his hand dismissively in the direction of the noise. "It's probably just someone saw us on the CCTV, thought they'd better check us out. We'll speak to them."

There was another clang, then another. "No!" she said. "I can't take that risk."

He frowned at her jumpiness. "We should really get permission before you take those disks, as well. They'll probably have to be signed for."

She looked at him. In his sixties, soft on beer and pizza. He was too proud to show it, but he wasn't in any condition to get into a fight. Instead, he'd take the easy option and play things by the book.

"Staff Sergeant Kassapian," she said desperately, "what sort of man was my father?"

"Well…" He considered. "Ted was solid. One of the best."

"He hid these disks because he didn't want anyone else to

find them. And now his daughter's got them. You think if he was here, he'd want us to go talk to whoever's up there? Or would he say, 'Let's try that other way out'?"

He sighed. "I'm too old to be getting into stuff like this."

"Then let's stay out of it," she said, heading for the jeep. "And I've got a strong feeling the best way to do that is to get out of here before whoever that is comes and finds us."

They drove down another long tunnel. The air was musty from disuse, and cobwebs brushed Holly's face.

Eventually they came to another blast door. It seemed to be unlocked, but it was too stiff for the two of them to open.

"Let's use the jeep," she said.

Kassapian shook his head. "Can't risk scratching the fender."

From somewhere deep in the tunnels behind them she caught the growl of a vehicle. "I'm real sorry if you get a dressing-down, Staff," she said, climbing into the driving seat. "Just blame me, OK?"

She edged the jeep up to the door, then pressed down on the gas. The back wheels spun, and oily smoke poured out of the exhaust.

"If you're going to do it, do it right," Kassapian shouted over the din. He pointed. "Put it in four-wheel drive, then low range."

She did, and tried again. The blast door creaked open on rusty hinges.

"Women drivers. Women *kid* drivers. One year off my pension, and I get this," he muttered as he got in beside her. "That's if they don't take my goddam pension away from me."

*

At the base she switched back to her own car and left Kassapian, still grumbling, to his mounds of shredded paper, though not before she'd embarrassed him by giving him a big hug.

Was it her imagination, or did the guard who swiped her card to let her out of the main gate take a few moments longer than he needed to? Was that some message, flashed onto his screen, that caused him to turn his head for a moment, before turning back to her and saluting, his face impassive?

She took the coast road home, scanning her rear-view mirror. Up the A12 to La Spezia, then the A15 inland. She varied her speed constantly, to help identify any watchers. More than once she thought she'd spotted a tail, only for it to drop away or overtake.

Which either meant she was just being paranoid, or that the watchers were professionals. Not that the *real* professionals would need a tail. She knew she'd never spot the drones from Sigonella or Aviano, criss-crossing the skies at ten thousand feet; much less the orbiting Atlas V and Delta IV satellites, several miles above that.

When she was near Venice she stopped at a service station and took out her phone. To her surprise, Daniele answered straight away.

"Can I come and see you? There's something I need you to take a look at."

"OK."

He rang off without saying goodbye. And this time it surely couldn't have been just in her imagination that she heard a whisper-quiet echo of his voice, bouncing back from the other side of the world: the chatter of satellites on a disconnected line.

FIFTY-ONE

DANIELE HEARD HER out, frowning occasionally. When she'd finished, he held out his hand. "Give me your phone."

She handed it over and he took out the battery.

"Your CAC card too."

He wrapped both in kitchen foil, then walked to the fridge and put them in the freezer compartment. "Follow me."

Upstairs, he disconnected his television, then went to his computer and accessed his router.

"What are you doing?"

"I'm turning off my wi-fi. Do the same in your apartment. And get yourself some burner phones – there are booths round Santa Lucia where you can buy a pay-as-you-go SIM with no questions asked. Have you ever left your phone unattended?"

She thought back. "I don't think so."

"Well, that's something. But they don't actually need the physical phone any more. The NSA have a piece of spyware called DROPOUT JEEP which gives them remote access to every application on your iPhone. They can turn on the camera, activate the microphone, even track your location via the GPS."

"Maybe my burner better not be an iPhone, then."

"Or an Android, or a BlackBerry. If it's called a smart phone, chances are it's a dumb choice."

"What can be on those disks that matters so much to them?"

"I don't know. If I had an eight-inch floppy drive, I might be able to read them. Unfortunately, I haven't seen one of those for decades."

"Any way you can get hold of one?"

"Let's try eBay." He went to his computer and did a search. "There are still a few around second-hand," he reported. "Amazing the prices this old hardware fetches."

"What about the tape?"

"That may be harder. I'm guessing, though, that the tape and the floppies contain the same data. He would have stored a copy in each medium, for safety. But bear in mind that all magnetic material decays over time. The disks may have dried out, or their contents may be encrypted. There are no guarantees."

It struck her that Daniele seemed different from the last time she'd seen him: his speech patterns more fluent, his eye movements less evasive. "How have the sessions with Father Uriel been going?" she asked.

He shrugged. "I've persuaded him to give me electric shock treatment."

She stared at him. "Isn't that rather… barbaric?"

"Only in the movies," he said calmly. "These days it's done under general anaesthetic. And they're very sparing with the current."

"Even so, it doesn't sound like the kind of thing Father Uriel usually goes in for."

"It isn't." He didn't explain how he'd persuaded the psychiatrist to give it to him.

"I should go." She crossed to the window. Scanning the *calle* below, she caught sight of a beggar in a doorway, his hoodie pulled up to hide his face. A junkie, by the looks of him.

She remembered the kid in the multi-storey car park near her apartment. "It's the same guy," she said slowly.

"Who is?"

She showed him. "I wouldn't forget him. I almost sprayed pepper in his face."

He glanced at her. "You can stay here if you want. Actually, I'd like that."

She hesitated. It was true that she'd rather not be on her own. And having faced down her fear at entering the bunker earlier, she felt more ready for what he was suggesting than she had done in months. But she also knew from experience that with Daniele, you couldn't always rely on inference or assumption. "Just so I'm clear, if I stay… are you asking me to sleep with you?"

He considered. "I think it would be good for you if you did."

She laughed out loud. "You have some great chat-up lines, you know that?"

He looked puzzled. "Why? Am I wrong?"

"No," she said. "I think you're probably right."

Four miles away in Mestre, Kat's arm ached from mixing olive oil into shredded cod. She'd already prepared *seppie in nero*, cuttlefish cut into thin slices and simmered in its own ink with onion, white wine and garlic. It had been plopping gently on the stove for forty minutes now, almost as long as she'd been stirring her *baccalà*.

What did it mean, she wondered, that she was cooking for Flavio the two dishes that, for her, most epitomised the Venetian cuisine of her childhood? True, the cod came not from the lagoon itself but from the Lofoten archipelago in Norway, high in the Arctic Circle, where the fish were caught and then hung out to dry in the cold summer breezes. But

Venetians had been traders for as long as they had been fisher-men, and there was no more traditional dish in the city than *baccalà mantecato*. She'd already boiled the cod in milk until it was soft. Now she had to beat it with the olive oil, drop by drop, as if she were making mayonnaise. Usually she employed an electric mixer for this part, but real traditionalists like her *nonna* always insisted that a wooden spoon was best.

She'd tell Flavio she'd used a mixer, she decided, so that he wouldn't expect her to use a spoon every time. Plus, if he believed she'd done it this well with a mixer, he'd never nag her to do it the more time-intensive way.

The thought of deceiving him so cleverly over a culinary matter made her smile. Their life together – she still couldn't quite bring herself to use the word "marriage" – was going to be a battle of wills as well as a meeting of minds, she knew that. She found she relished the prospect of fighting with him almost as much as she looked forward to being loved by him. And how many men could one say that about?

She looked at the clock: it was past midnight. He'd phoned earlier to say he'd be working late. "It's going well," he'd said. "I've developed some compelling leads. This goes right to the heart of power, Kat. There are some very important people who had good reason to make sure Tignelli didn't succeed."

"Rome?" she said softly. Ever since she'd found the ravaged body, half-eaten by eels, in the *peschiera*, she'd been asking herself the investigator's most fundamental question: *cui bono?* Who stood to benefit most from Tignelli's death? And the answer, surely, was to be found in the point that Vivaldo Moretti had made to her, over lunch at La Colomba. If Tignelli had succeeded in removing the wealth of the Veneto from Italy's coffers, Italy would have been bankrupt. She doubted any government minister or official would have given a direct order on such a matter, but Tignelli's assassination had all the hallmarks of a convulsion by Italy's *stato profundo* – the "deep state", the shadowy and ever-shifting alliance of politicians, security services, industrialists and white-collar criminals for whom influence and corruption were simply two sides of the same coin. With a single bullet, Italy had been saved – which was perhaps the greatest irony of all; the whole corrupt mess had been saved from its would-be cleanser, who was, in any case, no better and no worse than the rest.

"Not exactly. I can't talk on the phone. I'll tell you all about it when we meet," he'd promised.

"I'll have the food on the table at ten past twelve, and not a minute later."

He'd laughed. "Then I'd better not be late, had I?"

Usually, *baccalà* was served on grilled polenta or even bread, but tonight she was doing it the Istrian way, with some ribbons of pasta, a few chopped anchovies and a handful of bread-crumbs. It was the dish her *nonna* had made every Christmas Eve, when they were supposedly fasting before the big day.

She opened a bottle of cold Tocai and tasted the *baccalà* one last time. It was, she thought with satisfaction, perfect. Her phone buzzed. Glancing at the screen, she saw he'd sent a message.

With you in two. xxx

Humming, she filled a saucepan with water for the pasta, then crossed to the window. Flavio's car was just drawing up in the street. She watched him get out, and her heart skipped a beat. He bent down to speak to the bodyguard, then slapped the car roof, telling the man to drive on.

He looks energised, not tired, she thought. *It's been a good day*. But the thought was barely forming in her mind when a flash lit up the street. She couldn't tell at first where it had come from – lightning! A camera? – but even as she was wondering, the sound reached her – a low pressure-punch, like water crashing up a borehole, that forced in her cheeks and squeezed her solar plexus, followed by a brilliant pulse of petrol-orange flame that erupted upwards from the car's buckling roof like some savage, monstrous jellyfish. She was dimly aware of metal shrieking and spinning through the air. All around her, windows collapsed, liquid as waterfalls: the pane she was looking through shattered as a fragment of tarmac whistled past her head, burying itself in the wall behind. Cars piled up in the street, higgledy-piggledy – she thought for a moment it must have been a traffic accident, a collision of some kind, but as the ring of thick black smoke cleared, she saw the vehicles had simply been hurled out of their parked rows by the force of the explosion. Where Flavio had been standing – where the car had been, the bodyguard, everything: *my love, my whole life* – there was now only a crater. Debris still rained down, thumping and bouncing on the roofs of cars and buildings; and after that, in the ringing silence of her deafened ears, there was just some rather beautiful grey ash, fluttering down on the whole scene like cherry blossom blown off a tree by a strong wind.

FIFTY-TWO

AND THEN, IN the aftermath, everything was chaos. The street filled with people, rushing from their beds to help. There were at least a dozen wounded, from the ground-floor apartments mostly, cut by flying glass as they'd slept. Car alarms shrieked, and then sirens: Carabinieri and Polizia, fire engines and ambulances.

She had no recollection of running down the stairs. She found herself walking the street in a daze, back and forth, trying to locate his body, or what was left of it, anything. She fixed on that one, urgent task as if her whole life depended on it. *I have to hold him.* She found a man's Corvaro shoe, its sole slightly worn, blown off by the explosion. And then, a few minutes later, she saw his leg, crooked, under a parked car, the foot bare. She bent down to haul him out, expecting the weight of a body. But the leg came easily, attached to nothing, and she sat down in surprise.

She was still holding the leg, nursing it against herself like a baby, when the ambulance people came and gently tried to prise it from her.

"No!" she said, or tried to say. "Help the wounded first." Nothing came out of her mouth. But perhaps it was her ears that weren't working, not her voice, because she saw the paramedic mouthing that he *was* attending to the wounded: her.

She let him wipe blood from a gash below her ear she
hadn't even been aware of and fix a temporary dressing. She
closed her eyes. A great, numbing weariness washed over her.

He's dead. He's dead. He's dead.

Grief hit her like a hammer blow, the enormity of it sweeping away the last remnants of adrenalin. When they returned
ten minutes later to take her to hospital, she was still holding
the leg, rocking back and forth over it, as if she would send it
to sleep. She continued to hold it like that all the way to the
emergency room, where she finally passed out.

They came sometime in the night to take a statement.
Carabinieri, two of them, a colonel and a female *sottotenente*.
She didn't know them, but they clearly knew who she was;
knew, too, that Flavio Li Fonti had been her lover.

Were you expecting him, they asked gently but firmly. Had
he visited you at your apartment before. How often. How
long. They wanted dates and times, but the grief and shock
had knocked her powers of recollection out of her.

Afterwards, she slept. When she woke, she thanked the
nurse for giving her something to help. The man shook his
head. "I didn't. That's just nature taking its course."

Her limbs and brain felt like glue.

By midday they told her she could go. But not back to her
apartment, which was still sealed off. Of course: the explosives team would be searching it for fragments. She hoped
someone had turned off the water for the pasta. The saucepan
would have long boiled dry by now.

At the thought of the meal she would never now eat with
him – at the thought of the hundreds, thousands of meals that
would now go uncooked and unshared – she lifted her face to
the ceiling and howled like a dog.

The nurses let her cry, and when she was done, gently asked if she had anyone to be with.

She didn't.

There's someone waiting for you, they told her. A Carabinieri officer. He didn't want to come in before, with the others.

It was Aldo. She wrapped her arms around his big solid chest and howled out more tears, until as quickly as it had come, all her energy was gone and she collapsed again.

"You can come with me, if you like," he said gently.

She shook her head. "No." She felt obscurely that it wasn't right. "Thank you. But I need to be alone."

FIFTY-THREE

HOLLY DROVE DANIELE to the Institute of Christina Mirabilis. The nun at Reception directed them to a day ward, where Daniele was given a surgical robe and had a cannula inserted into the back of his hand. Only then did Father Uriel appear, his expression sombre.

"As you know, I have serious doubts about this procedure. However, I've consulted with my ethics committee and they have decided that when a patient is threatening self-harm, then it is reasonable to provide it, so long as he fully understands the risks involved."

Holly gave Daniele a puzzled look. He hadn't mentioned anything about self-harm to her. But he only nodded calmly.

What those risks were, Father Uriel was now explaining. "You may have sore muscles from the seizure. You may suffer a dislocation of the jaw or shoulders. You may remain disorientated or confused for up to a week. More specifically, it is highly likely that you will suffer from some degree of amnesia. This could last for a few hours or a few days. In extreme cases, it could be months." He paused. "There may be more significant side effects as well. First, the seizure might become permanent – what we call status epilepticus. If this happens, your risk of mortality is around twenty per cent. Secondly, it may affect your brain in some other, more unpredictable way.

A small number of those receiving ECT develop cognitive problems—"

"Wait a minute," Holly said, alarmed. "By 'cognitive problems', you mean brain damage?"

"He's trying to scare us," Daniele said calmly. "Don't worry. I've researched the risks." He reached for Father Uriel's consent form.

"And you're quite certain you want to do this?" Holly said.

"Whatever happened to me in that room, I need it to end." He looked at her and attempted a smile. "There's a part of me that's still locked up, Holly. I want to be free."

They wheeled him away after that. Even though he'd told her it wasn't like the movies any more, she couldn't help picturing Daniele as if in an electric chair, a rubber bit between his teeth, his body jerking and spasming as the current sent his brain into overload.

To take her mind off it, she went outside and switched her phone on. There were two messages from Aldo Piola. She frowned: she hadn't spoken to Kat's former lover for many months, since he'd led the team that rescued her from the caves at Longare.

Please call me. It's urgent.

She dialled his number. "Aldo? What is it?"

"You haven't heard?"

"What?" Fear twisted her guts. "Is Kat all right?"

"She's OK – she's taken a blow to the head, but it's only superficial. But Flavio's dead. He was blown up outside her apartment. Kat saw the whole thing."

"Oh, my God... Where is she now?"

"I don't know. She needs to be with someone."

"I'll find her," she promised. Ringing off, she went back

inside. "Is he in the recovery room yet?" she asked the nurse.

The nun shook her head. "Not yet."

She was torn. Daniele would be expecting her to be there when he woke up. But Daniele had nurses and doctors to look after him, while Kat was walking the streets of Venice in turmoil, alone.

"Can you give him a message for me when he wakes up?"

Kat went back to her desk at Campo San Zaccaria. She saw the startled looks her colleagues gave her, but she ignored them.

Sottotenente Panicucci came over. "Capitano... Are you sure you should be here?"

"Where else should I be?" she snapped. "I want a full update. On everything." She looked at her emails. To her surprise, there were only a handful: only a single night had passed since she'd last checked them. Such a short interval of time, yet it seemed forever. *When I last checked my emails,* she thought, *he was alive.*

Suddenly it seemed impossible, quite impossible, that he was dead.

"Fuck it!" she shouted out loud. "Fuck it! Fuck all of it!"

Some concussed part of her brain was trying to make her continue her life as normal, but the simple truth was that she had no normal now. Nothing was ever going to be the same.

"You're right," she said to Panicucci, defeated. "I shouldn't be here."

Holly found her sitting on a bench on the *riva*, staring out at the lagoon. A hundred yards away, a giant cruise ship slid slowly towards the terminal at Tronchetto, towering over its pilot boats, its upper decks sparkling with camera flashes. Kat looked at it with unseeing eyes.

"I was going to marry him," she whispered as Holly sat down.

"I know." Holly reached for her hand. For a long time they sat there without speaking, in a place beyond the reach of words.

FIFTY-FOUR

IN THE PERIOD that followed, Holly divided her time between her two friends, trying to look after them as best she could. Daniele, dazed and withdrawn after his ECT, and Kat, who flipped between lethargy and mania as she struggled to process her lover's death.

Disappointingly, Daniele had recalled nothing further from his kidnap. In fact, he seemed to have forgotten why he'd undergone the treatment in the first place, or any of the conversations the two of them had had in the days preceding it.

And if he remembered sleeping with her that night, or the long, whispered conversation that had followed, he showed no sign of that either.

An inquest was opened into Flavio's death and immediately adjourned. His wife flew back from London, where she'd been living with their children. In a newspaper interview she spoke of moving back to Italy permanently. Kat felt no desire to meet her.

She was summoned to a meeting with the other prosecutor, Benito Marcello. He started by saying that he was sorry for her loss. Then he asked her to sign a written version of the statement she'd given to the investigators in the hours after the bombing.

She took it and read it. The statement, and the accompanying report, made it clear that Avvocato Li Fonti had visited her apartment more often, and more regularly, than security protocols permitted. One of his bodyguards had apparently remonstrated with the other, only days before the explosion, saying that they should report the situation to their superiors. He was the one who had died alongside Flavio.

According to the report, the explosion had been traced to a plastic recycling bin in her street, where traces of C4 explosive had been found. A row of those bins had made a kind of lay-by among the parked cars: a natural place to pull up when dropping someone off.

They're blaming me, she thought.

But, with a sudden shock, she realised they were right. Not only had Flavio bent his security protocols for her; their texts and conversations had been full of arrangements and locations.

Will you come back to Venice now?

I think so. The local Polizia can follow up the remaining leads.

And, even worse:

I'll have the food on the table at ten past twelve, and not a minute later.

Then I'd better not be late, had I?

And finally, as his car turned into her street: *With you in two.*

I helped them kill him, she thought. *I was as much a part of it as the people who planted that bomb.*

"It seems unfortunate," Marcello was saying, "that a man known to be at risk of assassination by ruthless organised criminals could allow himself to become so careless." He let his eyes travel over her body. "But perhaps not inexplicable.

A man grows tired of such constraints. Of being alone, perhaps. He allows himself to get caught up in unwise, even reckless, situations."

Guilt turned to anger as she realised what else he was trying to do. "Wait a minute. 'Criminals'? Are you trying to say he was killed by the Mafia?"

He looked surprised. "Of course. They'd been pursuing him for years. That was why he had bodyguards in the first place." He looked at her questioningly. "Unless you have other evidence you wish the inquest to consider?"

This goes right to the heart of power, Kat. There are some very important people who had good reason to make sure Tignelli didn't succeed.

And before that, when she'd called him from Sicily:

I'm not saying your friend is right and it's all part of some massive fifty-year conspiracy. But it does seem like there are plenty of people who think they can just close ranks and refuse to talk to us.

She shook her head. "Nothing."

"According to the established procedures, I am therefore transferring the investigation into Avvocato Li Fonti's death to the Direzione Investigativa Antimafia," he continued. "A prosecutor with appropriate security measures in place will now take over."

"What about the investigation Flavio was working on when he died?"

"That will also be transferred to another prosecutor. But it seems in any case the trail has run cold. If there ever *was* a terror plot, it appears to have been averted. The excellent work you yourself did in Sicily, I understand, points to the conclusion that the suspect has left Italy by sea, no doubt hoping to evade the stricter border controls at the airports.

The relevant international authorities have been alerted. But it is no longer Italy's problem."

This is how it works, she thought. *If you kill enough people, eventually those who are left get the message.*

Everything was being wrapped up and placed neatly into files. And there it would stay, alongside all the other unclosed files that detailed her country's dark, hidden history.

Aloud she said, "He was never too scared to investigate."

He nodded. "Of course. He was a brave and determined prosecutor who will be sorely missed by all those who worked with him."

"Unlike you, I mean," she said pleasantly. "You're terrified, aren't you? Underneath that fine suit you're just a squirming, sweating ball of fear." She stood up. "You know what Flavio said to me not long before he died, Avvocato? He said, 'The law is all we have.' But until people like you grow a pair of balls, we don't even have that."

FIFTY-FIVE

THEY SAT IN the music room at Ca' Barbo. Kat, Daniele, Holly. Each of them, for different reasons, utterly defeated.

Holly recalled previous times when everything had seemed lost: how it was always Kat, with her energy and good-natured bossiness, who had pulled them out of despondency and assigned them tasks. But now she seemed quite broken.

It's up to me now, Holly thought.

She turned to Daniele. "Daniele, could I borrow a whiteboard?"

He waved his hand at the boards covered with mathematical formulae that lined the walls. "Be my guest."

"I'm going to write down what we know," she said as she wiped the boards clean. "One of us may spot something the others have missed. We'll use red for Carnivia, blue for my father, and green for the terror plot. OK?"

It might have been her imagination, but she thought she heard a faint sigh escape Kat's lips.

"I'll go first," she said, scribbling. "I believe my father was silenced by corrupt Freemasons who had previously been part of NATO's Gladio network. According to Ian Gilroy, he'd asked my father to find out more. But according to Staff Sergeant Kassapian, my father ended up making copies of the US's own secret cables to and from Washington. Why, I don't yet know. And I can't read them until the floppy-disk drive we've bought off eBay gets here. Kat?"

Reluctantly, Kat took the green pen and stood up. "I started out investigating the murder of a banker who'd betrayed his fellow Masons' plans for an independent Veneto. The Masons' Grand Master, Count Tignelli, was financing a terror attack by a jihadist hacker, but that seems to have been averted."

"Wait a minute," Daniele said, looking up. "Did you say a jihadist hacker?"

She nodded. "That's right. He was enrolled at a technical college in Palermo. Why, I have no idea, as his skills were clearly far in advance of the other students'. In any case, he seems to have slipped out of the country—"

"He's the one who's created the virus in Carnivia," Daniele interrupted. "He must be. And it's not true that the attack's been averted. In just over twenty-four hours' time, he intends to launch a coordinated attack on the Internet of Things, using a botnet of Carnivia users. It'll be like a hundred thousand Fréjuses all happening at once."

"Hang on," Kat said, trying to get her head round all this. "I know there's speculation that what happened at Fréjus might have been a hacker, but what's this about a botnet?"

Daniele explained about the worm inside Carnivia, and the zero-hour that would be triggered at midnight the next day.

"Can you prevent it?" Kat said when he'd finished.

"I specifically designed Carnivia so that kind of intervention is impossible. The only way would be to create a virus of my own, and wipe Carnivia."

"To temporarily shut it down, you mean?"

Daniele shook his head. "That wouldn't be enough to disrupt the instructions the hacker has sent to each user's computer. I need to write a piece of code that will wipe every-thing – my servers, our users' identities, their own computers, the lot." He smiled ruefully. "Websites that deliberately fry four million people's hard drives aren't too popular. There'll be no coming back from that."

"But you'll do it?" Kat asked. "You'll stop the attack?"

"Yes," Daniele said. "It's my site. My responsibility. Besides, I've been looking for a way to extricate myself from running it. Might as well go out with a bang."

Holly wondered at the apparent lack of emotion with which Daniele spoke. She knew his relationship with his website was a complex one, but she guessed that, whatever he said, destroying the world he'd created would be no easy matter for him.

"And then Flavio died," Kat said, turning back to her board. "I've got no absolute proof that it's linked to the Tignelli investigation. But the last time we spoke, he said he'd found something – something significant. I think he must have tied Tignelli's death back to a person or group, in Rome perhaps, with a vested interest in blocking Venetian independence."

"Any idea who?" Holly asked.

Kat shook her head. "But I think that was why they killed him that night. Whatever it was he'd worked out, they didn't want him repeating it to me." Something else occurred to her. "Though the time *before* that, when I was in Sicily, he said something about you. How perhaps you weren't as crazy as you seemed."

"What could he have meant by that?"

Kat shrugged. "Who knows?"

"Could he have come across a connection between the two cases?"

"Well, I can hardly ask him now, can I?" Kat snapped. There was a long silence. "Sorry," she muttered.

"No, I'm sorry," Holly said with feeling. "This is a shit time for you."

"For all of us," Kat corrected. "You and your father. Daniele and Carnivia… It's all shit. So what do we do now?"

"I think we have to go right back to the beginning," Holly said. "In Daniele's case, that means his kidnap. For me, why my father was so interested in those Autodin transcripts. And for you, perhaps, establishing who was powerful enough to kill not only Tignelli but Flavio too, and what it was he found out before he died."

FIFTY-SIX

"I NEED MORE ECT," Daniele told Father Uriel. "A higher current, a longer seizure – whatever it takes to shake my memories loose."

Father Uriel regarded him over folded arms. "No," he said quietly.

"If you don't…"

"I don't care what threats you make, Daniele. You wanted ECT, and we've tried it. We won't be doing it again." He paused. "However, that's not to say I'm giving up."

"What do you mean?"

"There's a new therapeutic technique I've started using recently with some of my other patients. It's unproven, but I think you in particular might find it effective."

"Why me in particular?"

"Because it involves your own website," Father Uriel said. "Tell me: you built Carnivia – could you build a replica of the room in which you were imprisoned by your kidnappers?"

He built the four hundred and seventeen uprights in the bricks along one wall, the two hundred and four along the other. He built it eight paces by eleven, and then remembered that he had to go back and adjust for the fact that, at seven years old, his strides had been a lot smaller.

It was many years since he'd created Carnivia, but the language in which it was coded was as familiar to him as his mother tongue. Even so, constructing the room took him several hours, building up every tiny detail, pixel by pixel.

When he had finished he showed Father Uriel.

"Good. Now I want you to create an avatar for each of the principal kidnappers."

That was easier. He made avatars for Claudio, Paolo and Maria. To each of them he gave a mask. It meant he didn't have to spend time getting their faces right, but he dressed them in the clothes he remembered each one wearing – Paolo's denims, Claudio's beret, Maria's leather jacket.

"And I want you to make an avatar for yourself, as you were at the time you were kidnapped," Father Uriel said.

Daniele made himself very small, and placed himself in the room.

He was more used than most to living his life through the medium of a screen. But even he was surprised at how quickly the real world seemed to melt away as he manipulated the avatar. With a part of his brain he was back there again, a kidnapped child. "You say you've done this before?" he asked.

"A little," Father Uriel said. "It was after I first started working with you, in fact, that I began to wonder about the possibility of using virtual worlds in psychotherapy. I soon discovered I wasn't the only one exploring that area – there are psychiatrists treating victims of sexual abuse, for example, using avatars to help them re-enact what happened in a non-threatening environment. I simply flipped that process on its head. So I might get sex offenders to re-enact their assaults, while simultaneously asking them how they could have done things differently. Because they're in a more controllable version of the world, they don't feel the same pressure they would if it were real."

Daniele frowned. "You think that could be why I built Carnivia? Because I needed a more controllable version of the world?"

"It's crossed my mind. If you think about it, it's a remarkable feat of dissociation. Some people use alcohol or medication to block out trauma. You just went ahead and rebuilt the universe the way you wanted it to be."

When Daniele was ready, Father Uriel put him into a light trance. After a few minutes he felt himself drifting into the same state of mental focus and physical lethargy he'd experienced in previous sessions.

"It's the final week of your kidnap," Father Uriel's voice said from a long way away. "You've been here a long time now – thirty-three days. What's going on?"

"They're arguing." Daniele indicated the avatars. "Always arguing. And they're scared. We're all scared."

"What are you scared of, Daniele?"

"Of them killing me."

"Why will they kill you?"

"Because my mummy and daddy still haven't paid the ransom."

"Why haven't they?"

"Because they don't love me," he whispered. "Because I'm strange."

"Who says so?"

"Paolo."

"Are you scared of Paolo?"

Daniele nodded, his eyes wide.

"I want you to be Paolo now, Daniele. Control his avatar for me. Make him say the things he says to you."

As Daniele slipped into the persona of his kidnapper, Father Uriel saw how he became stronger and more assertive. When he took him back into Daniele's childhood avatar again, his hands no longer shook.

He made Daniele role-play each kidnapper in turn, then moved on a day.

"What day is it today, Daniele?"

"Day thirty-four."

"How are you feeling?"

"I'm scared but I'm excited."

"Why are you excited?"

"Because these are the best numbers. Thirty-four is a Fibonacci number and a semiprime and a heptagon. If you make a four-by-four magic square, the numbers always add up to thirty-four."

Uriel raised his eyebrows. "I didn't know that."

"Maria showed me. Maria isn't her real name, but I'm not allowed to know what her real name is. It's like she's wearing a mask." He paused. "That's cool, isn't it? For people never to know who you really are."

"Indeed." Father Uriel mentally tucked Daniele's comment away for future discussion. "It sounds as though you quite like Maria."

"She likes numbers too. She teaches me. She's better than the teachers at school."

"Is that confusing for you? That someone who kidnapped you is also an effective teacher?"

"I don't know. Thirty-five is a good number too. It's the highest you can count on your fingers using base 6."

Father Uriel took him forward one day at a time, probing for anxieties. When he reached day thirty-six, Daniele fell silent.

"Why are you quiet, Daniele?"

"I'm thinking about the thirty-six officers problem. It's a puzzle set by a man called Euler. He wanted to know how you could arrange six regiments of six officers in a grid so that no rank or regiment gets repeated. I've drawn it on my wall."

"It sounds very difficult."

"Euler thought it was impossible. But he wanted to prove *why* it was impossible. That's interesting, isn't it? Not just saying it can't be done, but showing why numbers can't work that way."

"What are the kidnappers doing while you're thinking about your puzzle?"

"They argued this morning. Then Claudio went out in a rage. Paolo went to sleep. I think Maria went out for a while too, but not for long. Then she comes into my room. She's got a bottle of medicine."

"What kind of medicine?"

"She says it will make me sleepy. But I don't want to sleep. I want to think about the puzzle. She says I have to drink the medicine to please her. So I do. But I don't get sleepy, not really. And then she comes back. She's got a knife. It all happens so fast I don't... don't..."

He screamed: the high, piercing scream of a child. His hand flew to his left ear. Then, moments later, his other hand went to his right, his eyes locked onto some unseen terror in front of him.

"It's her!" he shouted. "It's her!"

"Daniele, it's all right. I'm going to take you to a safe place..."

But the child kept on screaming.

*

It took a good half hour, and all Father Uriel's skills, to calm Daniele down.

"Do you remember everything that just happened?" he asked when he'd brought him out of the trance.

Daniele nodded numbly. "It was her. The woman I knew as Maria... Carole Tataro. The one I trusted. Who understood numbers like I do. No wonder I didn't want to remember."

FIFTY-SEVEN

WHILE HOLLY SCOURED the internet for anything that might explain her father's interest in the Autodin transcripts, Kat dug out the copy of Cassandre's hard drive that the Carabinieri technician, Malli, had made. She went through the files a second time, looking for anything that might give them a lead.

After two hours her head was aching and her vision was starting to blur. "This is hopeless!" she exploded. "Let's go out for a coffee."

"Give me a couple of minutes," Holly murmured. "I'm right in the middle of some really technical stuff about troposcatter relays."

While she waited, Kat brought up Cassandre's web history. She hadn't looked at it since she'd found the Wikipedia articles about coup plots.

On the page about the Golpe Bianco plot, she noticed a paragraph she'd skimmed last time.

> In his memoirs, the instigator of the coup, Edgardo Sogno, recalled that he visited the CIA station chief in Rome in July 1974 to inform him of his plans. "I told him that I was informing him as an ally in the struggle for the freedom of the West and asked him what the attitude of the American

government would be. He answered what I already knew: that the United States would have supported any initiative tending to keep the communists out of government."[5]

Sogno maintained that he would have succeeded had he not been betrayed by his co-conspirators: "It is possible that too many people knew of our plans."

She clicked on another page Cassandre had visited, this time about the 1970 Golpe Borghese coup attempt.

The military attaché at the US embassy was tightly connected with the Borghese coup organisers. US President Richard Nixon closely followed the preparations for the coup, of which he was personally informed by two CIA officers.[10] These facts were confirmed in 2004 through a Freedom of Information Act request by the Italian newspaper *La Repubblica*.

However, the FOIA request also revealed that only a few marginalised sectors of the CIA were in favour of the coup, while the main response was to not allow major changes in the geopolitical balance in the Mediterranean.[11] The plot was eventually aborted after Borghese received a phone call, reportedly from the American Embassy.

"I'm done," Holly called from across the room. "Want to get that coffee now?"

"Not right now. I think I may have found something interesting."

Senator Giovanni Pellegrino, in charge of a subsequent parliamentary inquiry, said, "Somebody in Italy claimed they had support overseas. But, once informed of what was going on, the relevant people immediately blocked Borghese and his people."

"Is it significant," Kat said thoughtfully, "that after several of the failed coup attempts in Italy, someone's pointed at the CIA as being the ones who stopped it?"

"Well, of course they do. If they couldn't blame the CIA, it would be aliens and flying saucers."

Kat glanced at her. "You said yourself you thought the CIA had infiltrated Gladio," she reminded her. She gestured at the screen. "Besides, these people aren't cranks. They're senators, investigative journalists, even the heads of intelligence agencies."

Holly came to read over her shoulder. "Then let's say it's true. We believe in democracy. So?"

"*Cui bono*," Kat said slowly.

"Meaning?"

"Meaning, who benefits? Look, I've been assuming that it's the Italian government in Rome that doesn't want to see the Veneto split away from Italy. But there's another geopolitical player in this region, isn't there? The US. Your government wouldn't want Italy to break up any more than Rome would."

"Because?"

"How many US military installations are there here in the Veneto? How many American nuclear weapons silos? How many listening posts? How many radar stations and runways and drone hangars? What would happen to those if the Veneto became independent? If the decision were up to local voters, they'd all be gone within a year. Far easier, perhaps, just to despatch Tignelli, and close his plans down that way."

Holly was silent. Kat tapped a name into Google Maps.

"Aviano US Air Force base," she said, pointing. "Seventy kilometres north of Venice. A helicopter could reach La Grazia in fifteen minutes, and if it dropped an assault team over the lagoon, no one would ever see. Camp Ederle in Vicenza is about the same distance, as is Camp Del Din. If the CIA wanted to stop Tignelli, they had no shortage of Special Forces stationed nearby to help them do it."

"We don't operate like that," Holly said. "Not in Italy, anyway." But in her heart, she knew what Kat said was possible. Who could now deny, after the countless drone strikes around the world, that America wouldn't stoop to assassination to achieve its aims? Who could claim, after the abduction of Abu Omar and others, that her country would respect the laws and institutions of its allies? Wasn't this in effect what she herself had been saying to Kat all along – that America had been secretly influencing Italy's affairs since her father's time and beyond?

"I think Tignelli, like Sogno and Borghese before him, was a former gladiator who got too big for his boots," Kat said. "A gladiator who, along with many others, used Freemasonry as cover after Gladio was exposed. But instead of simply causing terror and chaos, Tignelli decided – whether from greed, political conviction, or a mixture of both – that he was the one to bring stability. I think Tignelli was cleverer than those earlier plotters, though. He didn't commit the mistake of asking the CIA for their blessing. But, thanks to Cassandre, they found out anyway. And, just as they did with those earlier coup plots, the Americans decided to stop him."

"And your proof?" Holly said at last.

"I don't have any yet. But I'm absolutely certain of one thing. What you've been saying all along is right. What happened to your father, what happened to Daniele, what happened to Tignelli and Cassandre and Flavio, what will happen to all of us if Daniele doesn't destroy Carnivia – it's all connected."

There would be a time to mourn Flavio, and mourn him she would. But first she needed to ensure that he hadn't died in vain.

"There's someone I have to talk to," she said, standing up. "Someone I think can tell me more about what's really been going on."

FIFTY-EIGHT

DANIELE SAT PATIENTLY in the small room. He had gone straight there from Father Uriel's treatment room, and the person he wanted to see was keeping him waiting.

Automatically he calculated the number of bricks in the wall opposite. Two thousand one hundred and fifteen, if you assumed that the average mortar gap was ten millimetres.

He recalled the famous anecdote about the mathematician G. H. Hardy, when he went to visit his fellow mathematician Srinivasa Ramanujan. Hardy had remarked that he had come there in taxicab number 1729, which was a very dull number.

"No," Ramanujan replied, "it is a very interesting number. It is the smallest number expressed as the sum of two cubes in two different ways."

Such was the small talk of mathematicians.

He was just considering what interesting properties 2115 might have when Carole Tataro was shown in.

He didn't stand up. Neither, for a few moments, did she sit down.

"I don't know whether to call you Carole or Maria," he said at last.

"You can call me 1853602 if you prefer," she said, taking a seat opposite him. He noticed how she moved the chair as far away as the small room would allow.

"Is it nice, to have a number of your own?"

She gave him a sharp look, but saw that he wasn't mocking her. "The novelty wears off." She gestured at the walls. "I suppose you've counted them?"

"A rough approximation. 2115."

"2187," she corrected him. "The builders skimped on mortar, and the door is a non-standard size."

"That's interesting," he said. He meant the number, not the reason. "Three to the power of seven."

She said, curiously, "Do you remember something you once said to me? You said, 'Every number is infinite.' You meant every number is interesting, I suppose, but it was an unusual way of putting it."

He shook his head. "I've had amnesia about most of what happened during the kidnap. I'm only just remembering things now."

"Such as?" she said carefully.

"I've remembered what you did to me," he said quietly. "That it was you who cut off my ears and nose and sent them to my parents."

There was a long silence "Here's another number," she said at last. "Twenty-four. The number of years I've already spent in here for being the person I was then."

"I just want to know why you did it. I think I know why you tried to pin the blame on Paolo. To do what you did, and to a child... The Italian prison system isn't kind to people like that."

"You think I'm a monster."

"Aren't you?"

She sighed. "Perhaps. But that wasn't the reason I told everyone it was Paolo."

"Why, then?"

"I was ordered to say that, if I was ever challenged."

"Ordered? By who?"

"My… handler, I suppose you would say. I never knew his real name."

"Describe him for me," Daniele said softly.

"Tall. Blue eyes. Wide shouldered, in that rangy American way. His Italian was excellent, though he spoke with a strong Venetian accent he didn't always seem aware of."

Daniele nodded. "His name is Ian Gilroy."

She shrugged. "If you say so."

"And how did he convince you to mutilate a small, frightened child who trusted you?"

"He persuaded me that it was the only way to save your life." She looked at him. "I know that must sound extraordinary. But he told me the Italian authorities were panicking. They were no closer to finding us, but at the same time they were insisting the parents didn't pay a ransom. He was afraid Claudio or Paolo would panic and kill you to get rid of the evidence; or that the Italians would mount a hastily arranged raid as soon as they located us and we'd all be killed. He said the only way to save you was to do something to break the stalemate, something that would give your parents a reason to insist on paying the ransom."

"And meanwhile he was telling my parents not to pay, that everything would turn out for the best if they just stayed strong," Daniele said bitterly. "That's Gilroy, all right. Weaving his stories, so that everybody hears what they want to hear."

"I cared for you by then, Daniele. And I could see – or thought I could see – the truth of what he was telling me. Paolo and Claudio were at each other's throats. That was partly my fault…"

"It was Gilroy who'd encouraged you to sleep with both of them, presumably?"

"He'd impressed on me how important it was to get close to each of them, to have some leverage, yes. And I suppose I was panicking too by then. I would have done anything to get you out of there alive, anything."

He only looked at her. The silence dragged on.

"There isn't a day when I haven't thought about what I did. I still hear your screams in my sleep. But I told myself that it wasn't your ears or your nose that made you who you were. It was your mind. You were so clever, so quick... I wanted to save that part of you."

"My mind was not unaffected too, as it turned out," he said drily.

"I know. I've read about you, Daniele, over the years. Every article or reference I could get my hands on..." She paused. "The word 'sorry' doesn't do this situation justice. Nothing can. But I'm saying it anyway. I'm so sorry."

He said sharply, "How did you become Gilroy's asset in the first place?"

"He simply approached me one day in the street. Said he knew who I was and that he had a proposition for me. At that time, the Historic Compromise between the communists and the socialists was just a rumour. Gilroy confirmed that it was happening. We were against it, of course – it would have meant the end of the revolutionary struggle; our own people sharing political power with those we most despised. He said his lot were against it too, that it wasn't in either side's interest to have Italy ruled by a stable, moderate coalition. Temporarily, we had a shared objective."

"For once I don't think he was lying," Daniele said. "Chaos in Italy *did* suit both Washington and Moscow."

She nodded. "He arranged for us to receive explosives, guns, information on possible targets... But I also started to notice how operations that we *hadn't* carried out were being attributed to us as well. Sometimes because it turned out we were all using the same batch of explosive."

"He was bolstering right-wing terrorists with one hand, and left-wing terrorists with the other. Infiltrating both sides – not to bring them to justice, but to coordinate the terror. And if people ever started to work out what was going on, he had a convenient screen to hide behind. Gladio. A NATO network gone rogue. Nothing to do with the CIA at all."

She shrugged. "I guess."

"But there's one thing I still don't understand. Why are you here? If you were such a precious asset... couldn't you have bargained for your freedom?"

Tataro laughed hollowly. "Precious at the time, perhaps. But after the collapse of the Historic Compromise, I'd served my purpose. Besides, too many of my former colleagues were turning *pentito*. The last thing the American wanted was for me to disappear into a witness-protection scheme and start spilling the beans. In here, I can be given quiet reminders from time to time that they're still watching me."

"If they're so dangerous," he said, "why are you talking to me now?"

She looked him in the eye. "Because I always promised myself that if you ever turned up here, you were the one person who deserved to know the truth."

FIFTY-NINE

FATHER URIEL USHERED his patient out of the consulting room and began writing up his notes. He had twenty minutes before his next appointment: a rare gap in the middle of the day.

The patient, a Catholic priest from Belgium, had finally started to make progress. For over a month he'd talked about sin and repentance and forgiveness. He was a dissociative narcissist whose deeply held belief in his own spirituality had enabled the terrible abuse he had inflicted on a nine-year-old girl. "God brought her to me," he would say, or "God sent her to comfort me." After several weeks of therapy, that had changed to "God sent her to tempt me," or "God wanted me to know the nature of sin." Whenever a question was too tough, or reflected badly on him, he would simply start praying. Father Uriel had been treating him with an avatar therapy similar to the one he had used with Daniele. In the priest's case, he allowed him to role-play the sexual encounter with the girl he had abused. When he'd made the priest perform the role play again, whilst at the same time playing an audio recording in which the victim described the scene from her point of view, the man had finally started to cry, the first tears he'd shed that weren't self-pity.

At the end of the session the priest hadn't prayed, as he usually did. That wasn't uncommon after a breakthrough, either. Many of Father Uriel's patients lost their belief at precisely the same point at which they acknowledged the evil within their own natures. Father Uriel didn't worry overmuch about that. It always seemed to him better to save a man's soul than to save his faith.

When he had finished his notes he stared through the window at the Institute's grounds. Then, with a sigh, he lifted the phone.

"Some time ago we had a discussion," he said when the other man answered. "About your ward."

"Indeed. I remember it well."

"You asked me if there was anything you could do to help his recovery... And you were kind enough to make a generous donation towards our work."

"Which, as you know, I consider very valuable. I've since sent some other sponsors in your direction, incidentally."

"I'm aware of that. I'm very grateful."

"How *is* Daniele?"

"Improving, I think. That is, he has remembered some details about his kidnap." Father Uriel hesitated. "Specifically, which one of his kidnappers mutilated him."

There was a short silence. "Could it be a... confabulation, I think is the medical term? A made-up memory?"

"I don't believe it could, no. But in any case he has gone to see the woman in prison, to confirm it. I thought, as his guardian, you would want to know. He may be disturbed or upset by what he's discovered."

"Thank you."

"Perhaps it would be better if you didn't tell him that we've spoken. Strictly speaking, as a patient..."

"Of course not. Go in God, my friend. And if you ever find yourself in need of anything for your work, anything at all, please be sure to let me know."

"Thank you."

There was a click, and the conversation was over.

SIXTY

KAT BUZZED AT the morgue door until Dr Hapadi came to open it. His green plastic apron, and the length of time it had taken him to answer, suggested that despite the lateness of the hour he was still working.

"I'm sorry to disturb you," she said. "It's important."

He showed no surprise. "You'd better come in."

He led her into his office. Beyond, through the glass wall, she could see his assistant removing the liver and spleen from a corpse, weighing them on a pair of scales.

"There are things people haven't been telling me," she said, turning her attention back to the medical examiner. "Right from the start. And it seems to me that you were more involved than you've been letting on. You were the first Freemason on the scene, when you were called to Cassandre's body. It had to be you who made the call to Saito."

"I spoke to General Saito, yes," he said quietly. "It was clear to me as soon as I saw the body that the death was connected to Freemasonry. Clear, too, that it must be Tignelli's black lodge that was responsible. We all knew what he was up to – there was no way he could have declared a state of emergency without Carabinieri support. For months he'd been putting out feelers, sounding out which Freemasons might support his plans, offering bribes or positions of power in the new administration."

"And Saito immediately called me."

"He decided it had to be investigated by someone who didn't know what had been going on – someone who wasn't a Mason. But it also had to be an officer who wouldn't find out too much."

"Thanks a lot."

He shrugged. "General Saito said you weren't popular within the Carabinieri, that you'd put a lot of backs up and people would have no problem refusing to talk to you. He said there was no way you'd ever get to the bottom of it. For what it's worth, I told him he was wrong. I've seen you at work. I thought trying to block your investigation would only make you more determined."

"So Saito put his niece on it, to keep an eye on me. And he spoke to the other Freemasons working on the case and warned them, too. I'm guessing that included Guiseppe Malli, our IT technician."

Hapadi nodded. "When Malli found that list on Cassandre's computer, he removed all the names of serving Carabinieri officers before he sent it on to you. We hoped you'd have enough to stop Tignelli without dragging our own people into it."

"And yet it was you who put me in touch with Father Calergi. And Father Calergi who gave me the idea that Tignelli's plans were political."

"Those of us who are loyal Catholics as well as Freemasons were always uneasy about Tignelli's plans," Hapadi said quietly. "Venetian independence might have been a good idea for the Veneto, but what would it have done to the rest of the country? And in particular, to the Vatican? If Italy fell apart, the Vatican could have been bankrupted. Tignelli didn't care about that. He simply wanted power for himself."

"That was Cassandre's motive too, I'm guessing," she said.

"He had a photograph of himself with Pope Benedict on his desk… He wanted to save his own skin, for sure, but when he finally had to choose a side, he chose Rome over Tignelli. But who told the Americans about all this? Who was it that decided I couldn't stop Tignelli on my own?"

His eyes gave nothing away. "What makes you think anyone did?"

"When Tignelli died, I didn't think to ask myself how he came to be killed on the very night that Flavio and I had been discussing whether or not to issue a warrant for his arrest. Later, when I did think about it, I assumed it must have been a leak within AISI, particularly since Colonel Grimaldo told me they'd been tapping our phones. But Tignelli was already dead by the time Flavio called me to say he was issuing a warrant. So it couldn't have been AISI. That only leaves the US. They must have been bugging my apartment. But why? Who told them we were getting close?"

"Father Calergi does have some longstanding contacts in that area, I believe," Hapadi said reluctantly. "But it was inconceivable that the Americans wouldn't find out sooner or later. They know everything that's going on in this country. They always have. Every time you use your laptop, every time you do a search on Google, every time you make a call – it's all accessible to them."

"But if that's the case, why didn't they do a better job of it? How come they could stop Tignelli and his black lodge, but not the hacker?"

Hapadi shrugged. "There I can't help you. Maybe he was just too clever for them."

"No," she said. "That hacker might be a technical genius, but he's no political strategist. There's something more going on here. Something I'm still not seeing."

SIXTY-ONE

HOLLY RECEIVED A text from Daniele. It read simply: *It was Carole. Everything Gilroy told you was a lie.*

She hadn't wanted to believe it. Even as the evidence against Ian Gilroy mounted, she'd found herself hoping against hope that it was all a mistake.

The man she'd trusted. The man who had become, in so many ways, a substitute for her own father's presence in her life. A man who, it turned out, had so much blood on his hands all the water in Venice couldn't have washed it away.

Her father... Daniele... And those were just the two closest to her. How many other Major Bolands had there been? How many other Daniele Barbos? How many Boccardos and other innocent victims, ostensibly killed by terrorists claiming to represent this ideology or that, by gunmen or bomb-makers, in so-called traffic accidents or fake suicides, or who'd simply disappeared without trace?

Many hundreds, she guessed; possibly thousands. In the great scheme of America's global powerplays, it was a tiny, almost insignificant number. But each one had been a life, snatched away in a war they'd barely realised was being fought all around them.

Her whole identity, her sense of self, was based on a falsehood: the lie that America's presence in Italy was benign. That you could simultaneously be Second Lieutenant Boland, US Intelligence Analyst, and Signorina Holly, from Pisa.

The reality she thought she knew dissolved, and in its place was the simple conviction Kat had voiced.

It's all connected.

She picked up her car keys.

SIXTY-TWO

CAROLE TATARO SAT on her bed for a long time, thinking. Then she went to the door of her cell and banged on it until a guard came.

"What do you want?"

"I demand solitary confinement for my own protection."

The guard eyed her contemptuously. "I'll pass the message on."

"I need it now."

The guard didn't bother to reply as he swung the hatch shut.

Later, at supper time, she found a piece of paper, folded in two, tucked under her plate. Inside a razor blade and the words: *You can do this the easy way or the hard way. You have until 10 p.m.*

Going back to the door, she banged again. When the guard came she showed him the note. "Still think I'm making this up? I demand to see the governor now."

He barely glanced at it. "The governor's gone home. You can make an appointment to see him in the morning."

She went and sat down on the bed again. After a few minutes she noticed one of the women she shared with, Sophia, stand up and gesture to the other, Fatma.

Fatma was the larger of the two. It was she who held Carole Tataro down, while Sophia wielded the blade that had been provided with her own dinner tray.

SIXTY-THREE

HOLLY DROVE TO the base. The throb of rock music echoed across the tarmac from the direction of Joe Dugan's, the biggest of the on-base bars. Returning troops, no doubt, celebrating the end of some overseas deployment.

"Have a good evening, ma'am," the MP at the gate said, clearly assuming the bar was where she was headed too.

She went down Main Street, then took a left. The armoury was dark at this time of night. She let herself in with her CAC card, then walked through to the firing range at the rear. As an officer, she was entitled to practise her marksmanship at any time, day or night.

Going to a locker, she entered a code and took out an M4 carbine with M68 close-combat sight – the standard issue, shoulder-fired weapon of the US Army, with a telescoping stock and short barrel to aid close-quarter combat. Its rounds were so powerful, they were capable of piercing body armour.

She laid it carefully on the floor, then reached inside the locker again for the magazine and ammunition. Behind them, at the back, was a handgun in a worn leather holster, a Sig Sauer P229 from the seventies. The 19mm rounds were of the type named Parabellum, from the Latin motto "*Si vis pacem, para bellum*": "If you seek peace, prepare for war."

Holly Boland prepared for war.

Taking a laundry bag from her pocket, she unrolled it and

pushed the M4 inside, then strapped her father's Sig inside her fatigues where it wasn't visible.

Going back to the desk, she signed herself into the shooting range. Under "Reason for Visit" she wrote "Target practice".

Then she turned and headed the other way, towards the exit.

SIXTY-FOUR

DANIELE BARBO SAT at his computer and logged into Carnivia.

He felt strange, but in a way that was not entirely unpleasant. Since his session with Father Uriel and the conversation with Carole Tataro, it was as if a fog had lifted from his mind.

He wandered the streets of his creation, looking at the buildings on either side, marvelling at their intricate design. But the person who had built them so obsessively, pixel by pixel, wasn't him. Somehow, the impetus to reimagine the world had dissipated along with his amnesia.

But he felt, even so, a great sadness that something so extraordinary, so bizarre, must now be destroyed.

Nothing we build is permanent, he reminded himself. *Everything must fall. Why should Carnivia be any different?*

He wrote the code that would erase the website. It took only a few minutes. Even the functionality that would reach out to his users' computers and wipe those too was barely more than a footnote. Every user granted the site perpetual access to their data, in order to interact with contacts and friends anonymously and to read or post gossip about them. It was an option, but one that almost nobody refused.

He wondered how this action of his would be perceived after he'd done it. People would say he must have been planning it all along, that Carnivia had been the most elaborate hack in the history of the internet.

How ironic that it was him, not the unknown cyber-terrorist, who would be seen by posterity as the villain.

He looked at the clock on his computer. There were still two hours until midnight, when the botnet worm would activate. Now that the wipe code was written, he might as well use the remaining time to try to find an alternative solution. Perhaps when he'd created Carnivia's encryption, all those years ago, there'd been something he'd overlooked, some tiny chink or weakness he could exploit to hack his own website instead.

SIXTY-FIVE

KAT SURFED FROM link to link, following winding trails through the back pages of the internet. Much of what she found was nonsense, the delusional ramblings of conspiracy theorists. Yet right alongside the nonsense she found articles by academics, investigative journalists, even former Gladio agents, all attesting to the same thing: for the past seventy-five years, ever since the beginning of the Cold War, the CIA had been intervening in Italy's affairs. To begin with the meddling had been political, certainly, aimed at keeping the country out of the hands of the communists, but as the decades went on, the corruption had gone far beyond that.

She found a statement under oath by one General Maletti, head of Italian Military Counter-Intelligence from 1971 to 1975, saying that the CIA had foreknowledge of right-wing terror attacks, and that on at least one occasion had supplied a Gladio cell in Venice with explosives.

She found that an American archbishop, head of the Vatican Bank for eighteen years, had used his Vatican passport to successfully fight off extradition proceedings in connection with CIA payments to terrorists.

She found articles offering evidence of the CIA working with the Mafia to break trade unions; of the CIA working with American corporations to take control of Italian markets; of the CIA planting stories in the Italian media through corrupt journalists, or even buying those media outlets outright.

She found a quote by a former member of Propaganda Due, the black Masonic lodge in Rome, saying that becoming a member was "the only way to have a sort of cosmic clearance with Anglo-American institutions".

She found that it was forged intelligence originating in Italy which had resulted in the false claim that Saddam Hussein possessed weapons of mass destruction, subsequently used as a pretext by the US to initiate the second Iraq war.

She recalled her own previous cases: one in which she'd discovered that American military contractors had been secretly involved in the civil war in Bosnia and Croatia; another in which a US officer had used Italy as a staging post in the illegal rendition of prisoners from Afghanistan.

Most recently, she found allegations that Italy was being specifically targeted by the NSA as a base for cyber-surveillance, with more secret listening stations than any other European country. From Italy, the US could eavesdrop on internet traffic right across Europe, North Africa and the Middle East.

VIGILANCE, she read, the Virtual Intelligence Gathering Alliance, was America's answer to the Snowden revelations. Instead of spying covertly on friendly nations, America was now inviting them to opt in to a massive "Golden Shield" covering the whole of the Western world. So far, only Britain had joined up.

She saw, finally, what this cyber attack Tignelli had put in motion would do, and why America had been in no hurry to stop it.

Just as in the darkest days of the Cold War, terror in Italy would be a lesson delivered to the rest of the world: without our protection, see what might happen. Violence that furthered America's political agenda would be quietly facilitated, not curtailed.

That was the reason Tignelli died when he did; why Flavio had been silenced; why the hacker had been forewarned. It was simple, cold-hearted *realpolitik*.

She called Daniele.

"Those attacks from within Carnivia," she said. "I think it's possible that America wants you to be the one responsible. That it isn't just jihadists they mean to take the blame – it's sites like yours, along with the very nature of the free internet. From their point of view, it's a win-win situation: either you take down Carnivia yourself, or it's utterly discredited. Either way, they get what they want."

There was a long silence. "I'm working on it," he said at last. "Leave it with me."

He rang off.

SIXTY-SIX

HOLLY WENT BACK to her apartment and collected the other things she'd need. In particular, she took out a small carton from under the sink.

Then she called home. As she waited for her mother to pick up, she walked out onto her little balcony. The night was a warm one, but there was always a breeze up here, looking over the rooftops towards the hills south of Vicenza.

"Hey, Mom. What's up?"

"Hi, Holly." Her mother's voice turned curious. "What time is it with you? Isn't it late over there?"

"Not too late. How are you?"

They chatted for a while before she said, "Put Dad on, would you?"

"Sure. I'll put the phone by his ear so he can hear you, OK?"

"Hey, Dad." She waited, as always, for him to answer before continuing. "Well, I found out who did this to you. Found those Autodin records as well, though I haven't been able to read them yet. I don't know exactly what you were planning to do with them. But you'd already written one report that had been buried, hadn't you? So I figure whatever it was, it was going to be something no one could ignore."

Was it her imagination, or did the even pace of his

358

breathing quicken slightly? Could he even recognise who was speaking to him?

"You had all their top-secret cables, didn't you?" she said, her voice cracking. "Every dirty operation the CIA planned, every bribe they paid out, every debrief and update, they all passed through the Autodin on their way back to Washington. I think you were going to put it all out there, Dad. I think you were going to blow the whistle on the whole corrupt mess."

She waited, listening. No: his breath was as regular, and as peaceful, as a sleeping child's.

"I'm going to finish it, Dad," she whispered. "I'm going to see it through."

Per il miglior papà del mondo.

SIXTY-SEVEN

HE TRIED ALL the obvious things, the tools of the modern cryptographer – differential cryptanalysis, XSL, the sandwich attack, mod-n. But it was as he'd expected: nothing worked. He had made sure Carnivia was proofed against such methods when he created it.

The only way asymmetric encryption like Carnivia's could be penetrated was by a process known as complex integer factorisation – breaking down large numbers into many smaller, more workable divisors. But no one had ever devised a way to do that on a large scale. The only mathematician who'd come close was a man called Peter Shor, and his algorithm was so complex that it required imagining an entirely new kind of supercomputer, a quantum computer, to run it.

It came back to the old conundrum of P=NP: you could look at a solution and quickly tell if it was correct, but you couldn't do it backwards to create the solution.

Even so, Daniele tried. He scribbled formulae, put together theorems, tried variations on Shor, all to no avail. The problem lay within the very nature of numbers themselves.

A phrase drifted back into his mind. Something Carole Tataro had reminded him of. *You said, "Every number is infinite..."*

It was true, in a way: every number not only represented a finite quantity, it had other properties too. There were prime numbers, Gaussian numbers, transcendental numbers, Fibonacci numbers, Pell numbers... the list went on and on. And, as Ramanujan had pointed out to Hardy, even those few numbers that were apparently without any interesting features were so rare that they became fascinating in themselves.

Suppose that instead of writing 1, 2, 3, 4, you wrote... what?

One is the only number that is both its own square and its own cube.

Two is the only even prime number.

Three is the only number which is both a Fermat and a Mersenne prime.

Four is the smallest squared prime.

And so on – every number unlocked, not by what it was, but by what was contained within it. It was like breaking an atom down into its neutrons, or a cell into its DNA.

DNA.

He thought about the spiral pattern within DNA. And he glanced at the wall.

Many years ago, his father had hung the walls of Ca' Barbo with modern paintings from his collection. Although the Barbo Foundation had put most into storage, a few still remained. It amused Daniele to cover them with Post-it notes bearing his favourite mathematical formulae. To him, the equations were just as beautiful, and far more expressive of genius, than the art underneath.

Near his computer was a portrait of a woman by the Italian modernist Modigliani. Its only merit, as far as Daniele was concerned, was that the artist had clearly understood that the symmetry of a human face was determined by the laws of the Golden Section, or phi. So Daniele had stuck over the woman's face a note depicting the ratio that phi expressed.

And then, quite without warning, he saw it. It was so simple, obvious even, that he almost laughed out loud. Of course numbers had their own DNA, just as cells did. And of course they followed the same graceful, endlessly repeating pattern that characterised the whole universe, from the tiniest seeds to the mightiest galaxies.

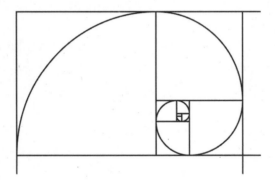

P=NP was not a theorem, but a shape. It was phi.

It will be beautiful.

He allowed himself a brief moment to savour this triumph. He had solved a puzzle that had baffled the world's greatest mathematicians. Or perhaps, he admitted to himself, he hadn't so much solved it as hit upon a solution. Like Einstein's theory of relativity or Newton's gravitational constant, a single moment of creative insight had illuminated everything, and inspiration had tumbled unbidden into his head.

But there was no time to think about that now. He set to work turning his discovery into an algorithm that would tear the masks from Carnivia's millions of users.

SIXTY-EIGHT

HOLLY DROVE THROUGH the dark Veneto countryside to the villa where Ian Gilroy lived. Once, it had been where the Barbo family spent their summers, away from the stink and humidity of Venice. But somehow, when Daniele's father had transferred his art collection to a charitable trust, the villa had been transferred along with it.

She wondered if that had been planned as well, or whether it was a happy accident. She doubted that much in Gilroy's life was accidental.

Leaving her car by the big wrought-iron gates, she slung the laundry bag over her shoulder and walked up the lawn towards the house. For the first time she pondered the apparent lack of security. Was it there, but hidden? Or was Gilroy simply the sort of spymaster who preferred crypsis and misdirection to tripwires and alarms?

She thought how appropriate it was that he had chosen Venice as his stamping ground. A place of mists and watery reflections, of shifting surfaces and deceptive, glittering façades. An ambiguous, impossible city, one that had dreamed itself into existence in defiance of all reason or logic.

It wasn't only Daniele Barbo who had created his own version of reality. Ian Gilroy had done it too.

Twenty yards from the house, she took out the M4, slotted

the magazine into place, and pulled the first round into the chamber. The handgun and holster she fastened around her waist.

She tried the front door. It wasn't locked.

He was sitting at the back of the grand entrance hall, in an antique wooden chair that looked as if it might once have been the throne of some doge or duke. Watching her, his eyes hooded. One hand cupped his chin. The other, his left, lay casually across his lap. On either side, on the painted panels that lined the walls, *trompe l'oeil* nymphs and mischievous fauns eyed her lasciviously.

She raised the carbine. "Show me your other hand."

He raised his left hand and waved it ironically. Unarmed.

"You were expecting me, then."

"Oh, Holly," he said, his voice cracking with what sounded strangely like relief. "I've been waiting for this moment for many, many years."

SIXTY-NINE

"I THINK I'VE done it," Daniele said to Kat. "But there's a problem."

He had written his algorithm and sent it into Carnivia. He'd watched, appalled, as the hacker's chosen targets spilled across his screen. Power plants, hospitals, hydroelectric dams, air-traffic-control systems... An elevator in Milan's tallest building that would have crashed to the ground, killing everyone inside it. A cooling fan in the electrical substation of a subway system that would have burst into flames. A vulnerability in the Italian stock exchange that would trigger automatic selling. The tram system in Rome. He'd been astonished to discover just how easy it had been for the hacker to line up so many simultaneous acts of destruction.

One by one, his own code extracted the botmaster's instructions from the infected computers, like pulling out a weed along with all its roots.

And he had seen, too, what kind of users Carnivia had. Stripped of their anonymity, he had glimpsed pornographers and the consumers of pornography; drug dealers and drug buyers; gossips and trolls and cyberbullies. But he had also seen a network of gay men in Saudi Arabia, using it to share information that would get them three years in jail and five hundred lashes if done openly; an underground democratic movement in Egypt; an endangered Christian congregation in Iraq. He saw whistleblowers using it to denounce corruption and abuse of power around the world; celebrities using it to escape the pressures of fame; the shy using it to speak out and those who were burdened with secrets to confess.

"So you've beaten it?" Kat said.

"Not quite. I've been looking for the master computer, the source of the infection. And I think I've found it. But I can't access it."

"Meaning what, exactly?"

"Meaning it's probably the hacker's own computer. For some reason, this one target is so important that he's taken personal charge of it. That implies it's something highly complex that needs to be controlled moment by moment, rather than just by turning off a few switches."

"Any idea what?"

"At first I thought it could be a plane – if he were on board, and had found a way to hack the on-board electronics, he could override any attempt by the captain to resolve the problem. But since 9/11, aeroplanes have had additional countermeasures to prevent that from happening."

"What about a ship?" she said slowly.

"Why do you say that?"

"It's always bothered me that the hacker was enrolled at that technical college, when he quite clearly knew more about computers than all the other students put together. When he disappeared, we assumed he'd slipped out of Sicily by getting a job on board a cruise ship. But what if getting on board that ship was the whole point of going to Sicily in the first place?" She paused. "What if he's somehow found a way to hijack it?"

SEVENTY

IT WAS PAST three in the morning when Kat called Aldo Piola. She asked him to wake General Saito and Prosecutor Marcello and get them to come to Campo San Zaccaria.

"What else do you need?"

"About a dozen *carabinieri*. A major incident room. And a technical expert, someone who knows about ships and explosives. But the most urgent thing is a couple of bright young officers to help me identify which ship the hacker could be on."

"Who would you like?"

"Panicucci and Bagnasco," she answered without hesitation. There was silence at the other end when she mentioned the second name.

"I don't like her, but she's clever," Kat explained. "And she's thorough. She won't panic."

"All right. I'll speak to General Saito and Marcello."

The explosives expert, Major Tasso, reached Campo San Zaccaria at the same time she did.

"Is what I'm suggesting feasible?" she asked him. "Could one man hijack a cruise ship?"

"It depends how technically sophisticated he is," he replied cautiously. "But assuming he's found a way to evade the ship's own security systems, it's certainly possible, yes."

"And then what? Could he threaten to sink it? Run it aground? Blow it up?"

"Again, it depends on a number of factors, such as what kind of fuel it uses. Some of the most modern cruise ships burn gas oil, which is more environmentally friendly than heavy fuel. The downside, though, is that it's much more explosive."

"How explosive?"

"Think back to 9/11," he said quietly, "and remember what around seventy tons of airplane fuel exploding inside a skyscraper looked like. Then consider that a fully laden cruise liner might be carrying over two thousand tons of gas oil, which is just as flammable. If that went up, it wouldn't be a question of fires or sinking. The ship itself – the hull, the sides, the plating – would be like the nails in a nail bomb. They'd add to the blast, not contain it."

"Wait a minute," she said, doing the maths. "Are you saying an explosion on a passenger ship could be *thirty times* bigger than the ones that brought down the Twin Towers?"

He nodded. "And if by some miracle a passenger did survive the blast, that kind of explosion creates a thermobaric vacuum – it's effectively a fuel-air bomb, one that would rupture the lungs of anyone within range. What that range would be, it's hard to say, but we're certainly talking hundreds of yards, even in the open sea."

"*Porco Dio.*" She thought of the behemoths she saw daily chugging in and out of Venice. Campaigners worried about the environmental damage, but why had no one thought about the security risks?

Suddenly her blood ran cold. "And what would happen," she said slowly, "if the explosion *weren't* in the open sea? What if it took place in a more confined space?" She gestured

In the direction of the waterfront, fifty yards away. "Somewhere like the Bacino di San Marco?"

He shrugged. "Let's just say, I doubt if any of us would still be standing here afterwards."

She was following a simple train of logic, but even so, she couldn't quite believe where it was taking her. Grimaldo had told her that Tignelli's plans involved positioning himself as the saviour of Venice. And Tignelli had mentioned to her himself, the first time she went to La Grazia, just how much damage cruise ships had done to his eel farm. You could hardly find a more emotive subject for Venetians, or one that better symbolised the need for change.

Panicucci and Bagnasco arrived. She explained the situation in a few sentences. "I need you to find out if any of the cruise ships currently in the Adriatic run on gas oil. Look for references to 'green' or 'environmentally friendly' on their websites. And then look at their schedules, and see where they're headed. In particular, see if any of them have Venice as their next port of call."

She turned back to Major Tasso. "You mentioned 9/11, Major. I think it's possible this man doesn't only want to hijack this ship, or even just to blow it up. I think..." She hesitated, reluctant even to put the thought into words. "I think he may mean to use it to attack Venice as well."

SEVENTY-ONE

"WON'T YOU SIT down, Holly?"

"I prefer to stand." She kept the carbine trained on him.

"Are you going to tell me what I'm supposed to have done?"

"Really?" she said incredulously. "You can't remember? Or are you simply wondering which bits I know and which I don't?"

He regarded her calmly. "I'm not going to lie to you, Holly. I have taken some hard decisions in the service of my country. That was my job."

"You ordered the mutilation of a child in order to grab newspaper headlines and demonise the Red Brigades. You had a former prime minister assassinated to stop him entering into a power-sharing coalition with the communist party. You summoned up atrocities like marketing executives book advertising campaigns. Even recently, you had Count Tignelli killed, and Kat's boyfriend blown to pieces in front of her when he got too close to finding out why."

"Yes," he said simply. "Yes, I gave those orders. Sometimes not in so many words, but those were my wishes, and they were carried out."

"And you arranged for my father to be given blood-thinning medication, in the hope that it would kill him."

"No," he said, raising his hand. "No, that's the irony in all this, Holly. I never ordered that. I took his report and told him I'd pass it on, that's all. We don't kill Americans."

She saw then what he was going to do – admit everything she was certain of, but deny the one thing that would make her pull the trigger.

Words; always words. He used them as a musician used notes, or a magician a deck of cards. The one thing he would never do was tell her the truth.

As if reading her mind, he said, "There's no such thing as history, Holly. Only competing points of view. Why don't I give you my perspective on all this? And then, if you don't like it, you can go ahead and shoot me."

More words. She feared them – feared his skill: that he would use them to dazzle or bewitch her. But it was ingrained in her nature to allow an accused man his say.

She gestured with the gun. "Go on."

"As you know, back in the seventies we had a major job on our hands, stopping the communists from getting into power," he began. "Even as a junior partner in a coalition government. Once voters elsewhere saw Italy making a success of euro-communism, who knew where it might end? The Italian peninsula; a Russian satellite; the contagion spreading to Spain and France... So we pursued a two-pronged strategy. One: turn the people against the communists. Two: make sure that Italy *wasn't* a success."

"Generating bloodshed on both sides, you mean. With Gladio as your instrument. But it wasn't the gladiators themselves who came up with those initiatives, was it? It was you. The puppet master. Pitting Punch against Judy, Judy against Punch."

"That's overstating it a little," he said mildly. "The truth is, no one was in complete control of the situation. But yes, for a time I and my colleagues had the tiger by the tail, and we did a pretty good job of making sure it bit the other guy instead of us." He shrugged. "It worked, I guess. After all, we won the Cold War."

"But you didn't stop then. It would have been the logical time to call a halt. But by that time you were addicted to it."

"Or, to put it less hysterically, we had a very efficient, expensive asset – an entire country at the heart of Europe that was set up to work as a client state of the US in all but name. Of course, we'd always been careful to maintain the outward appearance that Italy was still a functioning democracy. But effectively there was a whole parallel system of government, shielded from public view. We had our ruling council, our sub-committees and executive bodies, our central bank, our police, our civil servants and bureaucracy. The world knew them as charitable organisations, Mafia families, Masonic lodges and private financial institutions. But in reality, they were all extensions of our control. And, don't forget, we had filled that country from top to toe with military installations. Once it became clear that the end of the Cold War wasn't the beginning of some grand *pax Americana*, we still needed a base in the Mediterranean from which to project our military capability into Asia, into Africa... Into the rest of Europe too, should that need ever arise. Being the world's policeman means being ready to put boots on the ground, wherever that ground might be."

"You're not the world's policeman," she said bitterly. "Policemen uphold the law. Policemen carry out arrests, not assassinations. You're the world's vigilante, acting in no one's interests but your own."

"Perhaps. But what's good for the US has generally been

pretty good for these little European countries too. Take Tignelli, for example."

"Stopping him was your doing, I suppose?"

He nodded. "It's nothing we haven't done before. Every so often one of our gladiators gets drunk on his own success, starts believing he's the answer to the mess he's helped us create. In Tignelli's case, he had the resources to set up an entire black lodge to support his plans. But the last thing America wants is for Italy to break apart. That could be a real impediment to the free movement of our troops."

It took her a moment to realise he wasn't joking.

"We soon realised, though, that disrupting Tignelli's ambitions gave us access to some very useful levers," he continued. "There's only one player in Italy besides the US, and they've been misbehaving of late. This Pope has been rather critical of the war on terror. Seen in that context, that shady deal between the Vatican Bank and Cassandre to offload their toxic assets is gold dust. At the right time, a quiet word will be had in the right ear, and the Pope's policies will drift back in our direction. That's how it works."

"And the attack Kat and Daniele have been trying to foil? Is that how it works as well?"

He shrugged. "As you know, Europe's been squealing about the extent of our cyber-surveillance programmes. They need a gentle reminder of just how risky the world can be right now if you don't have US protection. After this, every government in Europe will be begging to be allowed to sign up to VIGILANCE." He nodded thoughtfully. "It's a rather brilliant system, actually. Someone noticed that terrorist activity in Europe actually decreased after Snowden revealed the extent of our spying activities. At first we thought the bad guys had just learnt how to evade our scrutiny. But then we realised: knowing you're being watched actually makes you behave better in the first place. It was a philosopher called Jeremy Bentham who discovered the principle, back in the eighteenth century. He used it to design a self-regulating prison in which every inmate believed himself secretly observed by the guards. He called it the Panopticon – the All-Seeing. VIGILANCE is our Panopticon, Holly. And pretty soon everyone in Europe is going to walk inside it of their own free will."

"At what cost?" she said, appalled.

"Oh, well." He considered. "Venice will burn, I imagine. But is that such a terrible thing? The place is sinking anyway. Don't worry, we'll help them rebuild it. Only this time it'll be six feet above the water level, there'll be proper sewers, fire exits, service roads... For the first time in ten centuries, it might actually *work*."

"You'll turn it into Disney World," she said. "Vegas-on-Sea."

"Disney World is a damn well-run business. They could do a lot worse." He sighed. "And yes, some people will die, in the panic and the fires. A few thousand, I estimate. If you look around the world right now – at Syria, at Lebanon, at almost any African country – that's an almost insignificant figure, although the fact that this conflagration will headline every news channel across the world will make it seem so much more important. I'm not defending it, Holly. The decision not to give the Italians more details of the attack was the wrong one, in my opinion. It's one of several things that's persuaded me it's time to retire – *really* retire, that is, as opposed to just leaving my official post."

"You're Caesar, aren't you? The man on the ground who calls America's shots."

He nodded. "A purely honorary title. My predecessor, Bob Garland, was the first Caesar, I was the second. Italy has had sixty-two official governments in seventy years, but only two real rulers. You'll be the third."

"Me!" she said, astonished. "What makes you think *I* want anything to do with this?"

"What makes you think *I* did?" he retorted. "When I brought you over here, Holly, it was because of your father, just as I told you. But the more I've seen of you, the more I've realised that you're exactly what this place needs. There are some who think you might have been contaminated by your Italian upbringing. But I look at you and I see a brave, patriotic American, a logical thinker who puts her own country first, but who loves this ridiculous nation enough to want to save it from itself. Am I right?"

She didn't reply.

"The point is, all these difficult decisions will now be yours to make. Have we been too heavy-handed? Should we be allowing men like Flavio Li Fonti to unearth our secrets, if the price of that is worldwide revulsion against America and our policies? Which is more important, the lives of a few Italian troublemakers or the safety of US troops around the world?" He leant forward. "You want to do good, Holly? I'm offering you the power to do unlimited good. Be my conscience, my advisor, whatever you like to call it. And then, when I've shown you how it works, I'll step back and you'll take over."

"Just like that," she murmured.

He shrugged. "Or you can shoot me. I'm not sure I care any more. I certainly won't try to dissuade you, if that's what you choose."

"And – just so I'm clear about the options – is there any other choice here?"

"Of course. If you decide not to kill me, but you don't want the position I'm offering, you can walk away with no hard feelings. I could probably even arrange for you to do good somewhere else. What would you like, Holly? Humanitarian work in Sierra Leone? Peacekeeping in Darfur? Preventing genocide in Iraq? If you really have no stomach for the harsher realities of American power, there's always the flipside – the positive work it allows us to do around the world. If that's more to your taste, you only have to say."

"And then there's a fourth option," she said.

He raised his eyebrows. "Which is?"

She pulled the laundry bag from her shoulder and, without taking her eyes off him, reached inside for the objects she'd brought from her kitchen.

A carton of rat poison. And a sharp knife.

"The fourth option is that I make you swallow the contents of this carton. It's Warfarin – the same blood-thinning agent I believe was used on my father. And then I cut off your ears and nose, just like you had Carole Tataro do to Daniele. The shock might bring on a stroke like my father's, or it might not. But either way, the anti-coagulants should mean you bleed to death."

She watched him carefully, but the pale blue eyes barely flinched.

"Yes," he said softly. "Yes, that would be another option, wouldn't it? So, Holly, which is it to be?"

SEVENTY-TWO

THE CARABINIERI HELICOPTER flew fast and low over the sea. Soon the coast of Italy was only a series of twinkling pinpricks behind them.

It had taken Bagnasco and Panicucci only a few minutes to identify the most likely ship. Not only was *Serenity of the Seas* a colossus of a vessel, carrying up to 3,750 passengers and 1,300 crew, but she was also gas oil powered, and Venice was the next destination on her itinerary. The clincher was the state-of-the-art technology she boasted, from free on-board wi-fi via the ship's own satellite, to the facial-recognition apps, location tracking and special RFID wristbands that replaced conventional security systems.

Prosecutor Marcello, though, had been unconvinced, particularly when Kat requested that Venice be closed to all shipping and a general evacuation organised immediately.

"Close Venice?" he echoed, appalled. "Do you have any idea, Capitano, how many cruise ships visit our city each day? And how many visitors those ships bring in?"

"Twenty thousand tourists a day, about a quarter of the total," she said impatiently. "But the safety of the other three quarters, not to mention Venice's own citizens and its buildings, must be our priority now."

"There has to be a reasonable balance between security

378

and letting people lead their normal lives. We can't be seen to be panicking at every fanciful suggestion." Marcello had sat up a little straighter, clearly enjoying the unfamiliar sensation of casting himself as the champion of personal liberty. "Your request is refused."

"Wait," Saito said. "The ship in question is currently in international waters. So long as the ship's captain agrees, no Italian warrant is needed to board it. The request isn't yours to refuse or accept, Avvocato." He looked at Kat. "I'm over-ruling the prosecutor. On my authority, you're to take two officers and search that ship. If you find anything, anything at all, we'll discuss further what to do."

"Thank you, sir." She'd been out of the door before he had a chance to change his mind.

Right now, *Serenity of the Seas* was sailing up the Croatian coast. By dawn, those lucky enough to have outside cabins on the starboard side would have a direct view of the scenic bays of Losinj, while even those on the inside could watch them slip by on their "virtual porthole", a round television screen above their bed.

Around midday, *Serenity* would turn north-west and cross the Adriatic. With any luck, the late-afternoon sun would be bathing Venice in a magical glow as she sailed through the Bacino di San Marco and up the Giudecca Canal, towards the terminal at Tronchetto. Passengers could then plan to disembark for dinner, or join one of the walking tours laid on by the ship.

In practice, though, most would eat in Qsine, *Serenity*'s own fine-dining option, or one of the other on-board restaurants. It was the approach itself, through the Bocca di Lido into the lagoon, that would have all 3,750 passengers crowding the rails with their cameras as the ship towered over Piazza San Marco, the Doge's Palace and the basilica.

"There it is," the helicopter pilot shouted over his shoulder, pointing. Kat looked down. There were three or four islands in view, their lights just visible in the darkness. One seemed especially built up. Then she realised it wasn't an island at all, but a ship.

She'd seen supertankers and had marvelled at the vast empty length of them, the crew quarters and bridge just a small structure on the endless deck. *Serenity* was nothing like that – although almost as long as a supertanker, its seven storeys towered above the deck, crowded with cabins, atriums, tennis courts, climbing walls, water slides... The bridge itself was a visor's eyepiece, a glass slit, tiny in proportion to the rest, that ran the whole width of the ship and even jutted out a little from each side.

That isn't a floating skyscraper, she thought as the helicopter hovered carefully over the landing pad, matching its own speed to the ship's. *That's a floating city.*

She checked her handgun, and saw Bagnasco and Panicucci do the same.

Two officers were waiting to greet them and hurry them down to the bridge. It was bigger than it had appeared from the air, a double-height gallery forty metres wide. There was little in the way of what Kat, used to smaller boats, recognised as navigation equipment, only a cockpit like that of a jumbo jet situated dead centre, containing two seats surrounded by banked rows of screens and computer consoles. The ship's wheel the nearby helmsman was holding was no bigger than a motorboat's. It was extraordinary to think that such a monster could be controlled by something so tiny.

"I'm Captain Lozano and this is my First Officer, Daryl

Valasco," the captain said, getting up from one of the cockpit seats. "How can I help you?"

"We're looking for a terrorist suspect we believe may be hiding amongst your IT crew," Kat replied.

"I'll assemble them now." The captain nodded to the first officer, who moved swiftly towards a phone. "Is my ship in any immediate danger?"

"I don't know," she said truthfully. "Have you noticed anything strange since leaving Sicily? Particularly with your computer systems?"

He shook his head. "Absolutely nothing. It's been a very smooth voyage."

"Well, as a precaution, I suggest you disable any equipment accessing the internet."

The captain frowned. "It's not quite as simple as that. Our passenger-biometric-recognition systems all use the same network. But I'll have someone run some checks."

While they waited for the men to be brought up, Kat found herself looking at Bagnasco and remembered that the *sotto-tenente* suffered from seasickness. "How are you feeling?" she asked quietly.

"Oh." Bagnasco looked surprised. "I'm fine. I've got used to it, I guess." Well, that was something, Kat thought.

Soon eight men were led into the bridge, still rubbing the sleep from their eyes.

"Is this all of you?" the captain demanded.

One of the men glanced down the line. "All except Mustaqim. He's on night duty."

"Where is he?"

The man went to a computer screen mounted by the door and typed something. A map of the ship appeared. A small blue dot was flashing on Deck 3. Looking around, Kat noticed that each crew member was wearing a coloured bracelet. Those must be the trackers she'd read about on Bagnasco's computer.

"He's in the gaming centre," the man reported.

"First Officer Valasco, would you be so kind as to go and get him?"

"I'll go too," Kat said. "Keep the rest here, would you? My officers can start checking their identities."

She accompanied the first officer into a glass lift. It descended into an atrium three floors high, lined with shops.

"Follow me." Valasco led the way across the floor and through a fire door. A sign announced that this was Casino Royale, the largest on-board gaming facility in European waters. On every side lights flashed and machines beeped. Even though it was the middle of the night, it was crowded with people.

He opened another fire door and they entered another windowless, beeping space. Only this time the machines were video games and the clientele mainly teenagers.

He pulled out a tablet and consulted the map again. The flashing dot was only a few feet away now. "Over here," he said, leading the way towards a dance mat.

The teenager gyrating on the mat barely glanced at them, all her concentration fixed on the screen.

"Get me a picture of this Mustaqim," Kat said. "As quickly as possible, please. And I need to speak to the captain again."

"We have to search the ship," she said.

"Very well. But we can't disturb the passengers. They'll be sleeping."

"Wake them all, and search every cabin," Kat said forcefully. "This man is dangerous."

The captain frowned. "Forgive me, Capitano, but what

exactly *is* the intelligence that leads you to that conclusion? This is just one man. The engine room is securely guarded. He has achieved nothing so far, nor has he shown any signs of attempting anything criminal. Isn't it possible that he's simply used his technical skills to conceal the fact that he's gone off for a sleep when he should be on duty?"

"That's just the point. He's a hacker. And this is a ship controlled by computers." Kat gestured at the technology on the bridge. "He could be planning anything at all."

The captain looked a little amused. "But the passenger wireless network has no link to the systems that control the ship. All these machines uplink directly to the company's own satellite."

"Then there's your weakness, Captain. If hacking a satellite is what it takes to control your ship, then believe me, that's what he'll have done."

"But he doesn't control my ship," the captain pointed out. "I do. Here, let me show you." He turned to the man holding the ship's wheel. "Helmsman, bring her about three degrees."

"Aye aye, sir."

The captain turned back to Kat. They waited. Kat saw the confidence in his eyes flicker, to be replaced by doubt and then alarm. He turned back to the officer. "What's the problem?" he said sharply.

"I don't know, sir." The helmsman pressed some buttons rapidly. "Everything's working normally. But the ship isn't responding."

Under their feet, Kat felt the slight increase in vibration as the engines picked up speed.

"Well, it responded to the throttle," the captain said reasonably.

"Sir, I didn't increase throttle."

There was a short silence. "Reduce speed to seven knots," the captain said.

"Aye aye, sir." And then, "Engines are not responding, sir."

"Search the ship," Kat repeated. "Every cabin. He's hiding here somewhere with a laptop, controlling it all."

SEVENTY-THREE

THEY ORGANISED THE *Serenity*'s crew into search teams. As they went down to the first deck, the lights went out.

The emergency lighting immediately came on – dim LEDs in the floor and ceiling, designed to guide passengers in the event of a shipwreck. But suddenly the vessel looked less like a floating four-star hotel and more like a vast, fragile container crammed with humanity.

Even from the bridge, Kat could hear the shouts of panic. "You may need to start thinking about evacuating the ship," she said to the captain when no one else was listening. "We should get as many people off as we can."

He shook his head. "Unfortunately, that isn't an option. Our lifeboats are designed to be launched when the ship's stationary. Any more than five knots and they'd be dragged under by our wake." He glanced at a screen. "At the moment, our speed is fourteen knots. And it's increasing all the time."

The full horror of the situation was only just starting to dawn on her. "How long until we reach Venice?"

"At this speed, around four and a half hours."

"And can we tell exactly where we're headed?"

"My navigator tells me that the GPS coordinates correspond to the Campanile di San Marco," he said quietly.

The *campanile*, the famous bell tower in the middle of

Piazza San Marco. Almost equidistant between the Doge's Palace and the basilica, and more than a hundred metres from the seafront.

"It seems that he intends us to crash at full speed into the *piazzetta*," the captain said. "What will happen then, we don't know for certain. But with full fuel tanks, it seems likely the ship will explode."

"Can't you empty your fuel into the sea?"

He shook his head. "There's no mechanism for doing that."

It's a floating bomb, she thought. The ship was a huge, seaborne missile, aimed at the very heart of Venice. She thought of the pictures that would be on the front pages of tomorrow's papers. The *campanile* would be toppled, the twin columns of San Marco and San Teodoro smashed to nothing, the stone lions on which children played and visitors posed for photographs lost forever. And the square where genera- tions of her ancestors had gossiped and strolled and bought cold drinks from the wine sellers who lingered in the shade of the colonnades would have become a scene of destruction, reclaimed by the sea, a second Ground Zero.

But it was more than that. The Doge's Palace, famously, had a wooden roof: it had been constructed by the shipbuild- ers of the Arsenale as a kind of upended hull, using the same techniques that had made Venice's fleet the envy of the world. The five golden domes of the basilica – designed in the thir- teenth century so that the symbol of Venice's power would be visible from far out to sea – were also made of wood. Fire had long been the threat which most exercised Venice's authori- ties, to the extent that, even today, restaurants had to apply for a special licence to install pizza ovens. Fire could jump the narrow waterways in an instant, consuming cramped apart- ment buildings and grand *palazzi* alike. If *Serenity* exploded in Piazza San Marco, how far would the destruction spread? To the rest of the San Marco district; perhaps as far as Cannaregio and Castello… She felt a cold fury that she pushed to one side.

She called Piola to update him. "Can *you* still get off?" he wanted to know.

"I don't think so. The pilot says the helicopter can't take off at this speed. But in any case, I couldn't leave the passengers."

He said quietly, "If you find him, and you have the option, shoot to kill. Promise me, Kat – don't think twice."

"I will." She hesitated. "Are they evacuating the city yet? In case we're not successful?"

"We've been discussing it all night." He sighed. "Nobody in authority wants to be the one to take that decision. You know what the Ponte della Libertà's like at the best of times. Even if we had the means to communicate a general evacuation, how could we possibly get three hundred thousand tourists across one small bridge in just a few hours? There would be panic."

"Even so, we have to try."

"I'll keep working on it. But Kat, let's hope it doesn't come to that. He must be somewhere on that ship. There's still time to find him."

As night turned to day, Daniele finished disinfecting the last of his users' computers. There had been a few he'd failed to get to in time. In cities up and down Italy traffic lights failed, and the morning rush hour was even more gridlocked than usual. Hundreds of internet-connected cars – those using Ford's SYNC technology, BMW's ConnectedDrive, Audi's Connect, and Mercedes' COMAND – had crashed, adding to the chaos, while some drivers' garage doors simply refused to open. In several government buildings, water sprinklers came on for no reason, whilst the servers of Italy's three biggest banks suddenly uploaded all their customers' details onto the internet.

So far as he could tell, though, none of the attacks had resulted in any loss of life. By 10 a.m. there was only the hacker's own computer left.

By half past ten, newsfeeds across Italy were reporting the situation. Some were already speculating that it could have been a cyber attack.

Daniele thought for a moment, then posted a message on Carnivia's login page.

Dear Carnivians,

Over the last few weeks, Carnivia has been compromised. A hacker succeeded in spreading a virus among the site's users. His aim was to create terror by causing hundreds of thousands, possibly even millions, of internet-connected devices to malfunction simultaneously.

The only way to prevent these attacks was for me to remove Carnivia's encryption systems and disinfect the site. The encryption will be restored shortly, but in the meantime you should be aware that nothing you do or say on Carnivia will have the usual level of anonymity.

In the circumstances, today's elections have been suspended for twenty-four hours.

Daniele Barbo

He pressed "Publish" and sat back. He had no doubt there would be howls of protest; accusations, too, that he'd misled his users when he'd said the encryption couldn't be broken even by him. Others would seize the opportunity to argue that he should never have allowed his users to be anonymous in the first place.

But for the moment he had more pressing things to think about, and an important decision to make.

SEVENTY-FOUR

BY MIDDAY, THE search teams had gone through every one of the 1,650 cabins. They'd searched the Aqua Park, the Colonial Club, the virtual golf course, the three restaurants and the discotheque. They'd searched the Balinese Spa and the Raj-themed solarium, the Hawaiian Palm Court and the Latte-tudes Coffee Shop. They'd searched each of the passenger decks before descending to the clanging, echoing galleys below, the crew quarters and engine rooms.

Of the hacker, there was absolutely no sign.

Kat took personal charge when they searched his berth, looking for any clue. They found a battered Qur'an, two mobile phones, and three passports with the same photograph in all of them. The oldest passport was Libyan, in the name of Tareq Fakroun. He was twenty years old. She didn't recognise either the face or the name, but that was hardly surprising: there had been no matches on any of their databases to the fingerprint recovered from the tablet in Sicily.

Recalling the tablet prompted her to look for a computer. "No laptop," she said. "That *must* be what he's using." She turned to the captain. "If he wanted to access the computer network, where would be the best place?"

He shrugged and looked helplessly at the IT officer.

None of us really knows how all this stuff works, Kat thought. *We think we control it because we can use it, but really it's a mystery to us.*

"Probably the server room," the officer said. "But it's already been searched."

"Take me there anyway."

The server room was another level down into the bowels of the ship, a hot, enclosed space full of equipment. Thick clusters of cables ran through ducts in the roof. Racks of computers flickered silently beneath them.

"Is there any way of turning off the parts he's using?" she asked.

"We've tried," the IT officer said. "It doesn't seem to make any difference. If I had to guess, I'd say he's bypassed our network altogether, and written his own skeleton program to run the ship."

She didn't know computers, but she did know ships. "He'll still need the GPS to lock onto his destination. If he wanted to hack into the satellite upstream of all the other electronics, where would he do it from?"

It was the captain who answered. "There's an antennae enclosure right on the top of the ship. You can only access it by climbing up the side of the radar tower."

She took Panicucci and Bagnasco, hurrying up service stairways that led from deck to deck. Finally they were at the foot of the radar tower, and there was only one metal ladder left to climb.

As she climbed, rung after rung, the sun bounced off the painted metal into her eyes. Looking down, she saw that the sea was at least seventy metres below her.

The steps of the ladder disappeared through the floor of

what looked like a small observation deck, the highest point of the ship. Gingerly, she raised her head through the hole and looked around.

A dark-skinned youth was sitting cross-legged by the radar antenna, a laptop nestled between his knees. He was wearing what looked like a sleeveless padded jerkin. Then she saw the wires protruding from the seams. A suicide vest.

He met her eyes, and his hand went towards his pocket.

"Stop!" she called, her hand going to her gun.

He didn't. As he pulled out the detonator she shot him in the face. There was no time for thought; no time for anything as conscious as a decision. She realised, even as she did it, that she had always been intending to do this, ever since Piola had cautioned her not to hesitate. The boy's head exploded, blood spraying the side of the tower, the computer jerking out of his lap as his body first bucked, then slumped to one side, his dark hair smearing his own blood spatter as he fell. The recoil knocked her backwards too, so that she swung sideways on the ladder, her left hand clinging on for dear life as she fought desperately to regain her footing.

Then she was springing up onto the platform. He was still alive, still twitching, then suddenly he wasn't. She checked his airway and fastened her lips on the mangled jaw to give him the kiss of life, just as instinctively as, moments before, she'd pulled the trigger.

Panicucci and Bagnasco came to crouch silently beside her. It was only when she saw blood pooling around their boots that she realised it was hopeless.

"Get the laptop," she said, standing up.

She looked in the direction they were heading. A shimmering sliver beckoned on the horizon; gilded domes, spires and cupolas catching gold under the sun's blaze, the ship's prow pointing towards it as neatly as an arrow.

Venice.

They took the laptop back to the bridge for the specialists to examine.

"Every command is password-protected," the IT officer said at last. "We can't even work out what it's doing."

"Then turn it off," Kat said. "At least that way we can make sure it's not controlling the ship any more."

The IT officer turned the laptop over and sprung out the battery. As he did so, there was a groan in the depths of the ship, a hum that rose in pitch from the engines beneath their feet. She felt her body leaning backwards as the vast vessel surged forward.

"A dead man's handle," the officer said quietly. "He must have rigged it so any disconnection would make the engines revert to full speed."

"How long to Venice now?"

The first officer consulted a screen. "At this speed, less than thirty minutes."

She grabbed her phone. "Daniele," she said when he answered. "I need your help."

She summarised the situation in a few sentences. "So what I need to know," she concluded, "is whether you can hack the shipping company's satellite and reset the GPS coordinates."

He considered. "Yes and no. I can probably knock out the satellite link. But the ship itself will still be locked onto the old coordinates. Unless you can find some way of making it change course, it will simply follow the old bearing until it either hits something or runs out of fuel. Is there no steering at all? No way of overriding the electronics?"

She looked over to where a group of officers were conferring. "They're working on it. But, Daniele, I don't think we should rely on them. The ship's simply too big and complex."

"A boat's a boat. There must be some way of making it change course."

An idea floated into her brain.

"You'll think this is crazy," she told the captain. "But I've been around boats all my life. And I know that big boats behave just like small ones, when it comes down to it."

He nodded cautiously.

She said, "What if we take the hacker's suicide vest and blow a hole in the port bow, just below the waterline? The ship will list, and the drag will pull it round." She pointed at the chart. "We'll start sinking, obviously, but in the meantime we'll veer to port, away from the Bocca di Lido. And if we don't pass through the *bocca* into the lagoon, at least Venice will be safe. In the best-case scenario, perhaps the sand will bring us to a halt slowly enough that the fuel tanks don't explode."

"How do you know the vest will blow a small hole rather than a big one?"

"I don't. But I don't think he'd have wasted his time building a bigger suicide vest than he needed. I'm betting that bomb contains just enough explosive to destroy him, his laptop and whoever came after him."

"I pray to God you're right, Captain," he said faintly. "Because I certainly don't have a better idea."

They pored over a plan of the ship, debating exactly where to place the explosives. But she knew that, right or wrong, the time for thinking was almost over. They could see Venice's skyline quite clearly now, behind the long line of the Lido. She could make out the tops of individual buildings: the terrace bar on the roof of the Stucky hotel; the glittering domes of St Mark's itself; the white cupola of Santa Maria della Salute.

She had a sudden memory of a dark January night: *aqua alta* flooding La Salute's steps; snow falling; a corpse washed in from the lagoon. Her first case with Aldo Piola. How long ago all that seemed now.

"I'll detonate it here," she said, interrupting the discussion. She pointed to a spot halfway down the bow.

"Those are the crew quarters. I can take you there," the first officer said immediately.

"Get the passengers assembled in their life jackets," the captain said to one of his men. To Kat and the first officer he simply said, "Good luck."

Another officer had rigged up a detonation line. As Kat carried the vest gingerly down the endless gangways, it seemed to her that rather than blowing a hole that was too big, the opposite was more likely. Could a few pocketfuls of explosive really punch a big enough hole in a hull as thick as *Serenity*'s?

She was glad First Officer Valasco was with her: below the waterline it was easy to become disorientated in the identical corridors. The vibration of the vast engines seemed stronger down there, too: more than once she found herself bouncing off the metal walls, careful not to let the vest make contact as she did so.

Eventually he opened a door. "In here."

There was little preamble. They laid the vest in a bunk to focus the blast outwards, then played out the detonation line and retreated into the corridor. While Kat crouched down and set the fuse, the first officer stood by, ready to help her away.

Kat was already running when the crack and boom of the explosion sounded behind her. *Too soon*, she thought. *It's gone off too soon*. For a moment she was back in her apartment, frozen to the spot, watching through the window as Flavio was blown up. Instinctively she flinched and stumbled, but the first officer had her by the arm and was half pulling, half propelling her along the corridor. Crew members sealed bulkheads behind them as they retreated along the ship; behind her she heard a second, slower explosion as the sea, snarling and savage, charged in to reclaim the space that man had briefly usurped.

The passengers were lined up on deck now, silent in their life vests. On the bridge, she and Valasco found the other officers peering anxiously down at the bow.

"Anything?" she asked. One of the men shook his head.

Daniele called her back. "I've spoofed the satellite's telemetry and tracking."

"Meaning?" she said impatiently.

"It's temporarily out of operation. What's happening your end?"

"I'm not sure." But even as she said it, she felt the deck under her feet shifting, tilting infinitesimally to port. She held her breath.

They were only a few hundred yards from shore, the ship's prow pointing like a colossal battering ram at the gap in the Lido. As the deck listed to the left, the ship followed it round, like a skateboard with all the rider's weight on one side. It wasn't by much, but the prow was now definitely pointing away from the gap, and at the Lido instead. She could see the ornate façade of the Hôtel des Bains, and the rows of blue-and-white *capanne* where this had all begun. She could see the sunbathers, lined up behind the police tape that was keeping them away from the beach. And she could see the soft yellow sands waiting to embrace *Serenity of the Seas*; could feel them clawing already at the ship's belly. *Serenity* slowed, lurched and swung over onto her starboard side all at once, more dramatically this time. Kat found herself charging in a group of officers towards one end of the bridge, now ten feet lower than the other; then she took a tumble, executing a perfect waltz step and cartwheel into Panicucci's arms before they both crashed to the floor, which had taken on the angle of a children's slide. With a sudden, spasming shudder, the great behemoth was beached and could go no further, towering at a crazy, drunken angle over the empty sunloungers, as if she would simply tip her passengers onto them and be done with it.

SEVENTY-FIVE

DANIELE BARBO WAITED in a quiet corner of a bar near the Rialto. The barman, along with most of the customers, was masked. There were others, though, whose faces were bare. For many of those who had been part of the Unmasking, as it had become known, it was now seen as a badge of honour not to hide their identities. Daniele had therefore introduced a new functionality to the site: users could choose whether or not to go incognito.

Hi, Daniele.

The avatar who dropped into a seat next to him was one of those not wearing a mask, but Daniele would have known who he was in any case.

Hello, Max. My congratulations.

Yes, everything turned out all right in the end, didn't it? In the aftermath of the Unmasking, entrusting the safety of Carnivia to an administrator – and not just any administrator, but the one who had helped Daniele Barbo to identify and neutralise the virus – had seemed like the only sensible choice. When the elections were reinstated, Max had won by a landslide.

That's what I wanted to talk to you about, actually. My decision to stand aside from the site... I'm reconsidering it.

There was a long pause. *Oh? Why?*

In part, because of your success, Daniele answered.

I don't understand.

When I thought about what the hacker had done, there were a few things that still bothered me. Such as how he'd been able to achieve so much on his own. So, while Carnivia was unencrypted, I took a closer look at his history. It turns out there was someone who helped him... another hacker, who called himself Jibran on message boards. It was Jibran who suggested targeting the Internet of Things. And it was Jibran who suggested Carnivia as the way to do it.

A smart guy, then, Max responded.

Yes... Although, strangely, it was also Jibran who leaked the video of the Fréjus tunnel attack. Had you not drawn that to my attention, Tareq Fakroun might well have got away with it. Why did Jibran do that, do you suppose, if he was so smart?

Perhaps he couldn't resist the urge to show off.

Perhaps. But I started to wonder if there could be more to it than that. So I took a closer look at Carnivia's administrators too.

And? What did you find?

It all made sense, Daniele wrote sadly. If only there was a better way to express his feelings at that point than through some stupid emoticon. It was something else he would have to add; now that they could remove their masks, avatars should be able to laugh, or cry, or show anger, or look disappointed. *The fact that you were so keen to become elected. The way Carnivia's oldtimers and newbies were being set against each other. The security scares, to which the only possible answer would be ever-higher levels of scrutiny.*

I don't know what you're talking about.

What are you, Max? Or should I call you Jibran? Are you part of USCYBERCOM? The Cryptologic Division? Tailored

Access Operations? Or some other group deep within the NSA, something so secret we haven't even heard about it yet? Maybe you're not even a single person any more. Maybe the entity I've been calling "Max" is actually a team, working in shifts out of some anonymous building in Fort Meade or Palo Alto.

This is crazy.

When did they recruit you, Max? And how? Was it about money? Women? Or simply the chance to be someone important: the person who helped the US military get control of Carnivia?

There was a long silence before Max responded. *It's you that became the monster, Barbo, not me. You refused to see where all this was going. That the internet isn't just some cool game any more, where kids can prank each other without anyone knowing who they are. This is the real world now. And in the real world, there are bad guys who will stop at nothing to destroy everything that matters.*

Indeed there are, Max. And you know what? You're one of them.

Abruptly, Max's avatar disappeared.

Goodbye, my friend, Daniele typed into the empty air. *I hope you thought it was worth it.*

He pushed back from the screen and turned to watch Holly. She was sitting at another computer, transferring the contents of the Autodin disks from the floppy drive to a memory stick. Once Daniele had nursed the data from the ancient disks, they'd given up their secrets without a struggle.

She'd known by then roughly what to expect; even so, the sheer number of incriminating documents her father had amassed had taken her breath away. Gilroy had used euphemisms even when sending secure cables back to Washington – whether to protect himself or his superiors, she didn't know. It was tempting to believe that he'd been a lone wolf, left to run his private fiefdom as he saw fit, but surely it beggared belief that the CIA's high command could have been completely ignorant of the blood that was dripping from its most senior Italian agent's hands. But euphemisms or not, by comparing the date of a cable to actual events it wasn't difficult to work out which dark episodes in Italy's history had actually been instigated by him. There were nearly two thousand files, and every one of them was damning.

Daniele hadn't asked her what condition Ian Gilroy was in when she left him, and as yet she hadn't told him. But from her focused, hurried movements he guessed that for one reason or another she didn't think she had much time.

"That's all of them," she said at last. "Now what?"

He showed her how, once inside Carnivia, it was possible to place a document in a locker that anyone could read but no one could delete.

"Are you sure?" he said as she copied the files across. "This won't be reversible, you know. Once they're out there…"

"I know what I'm doing." She was very pale, however, and a vein throbbed just below her ear. She added, more quietly, "I know what they'll do to me, too. I'm ready for it."

He nodded. "Press 'Enter' and it's done."

She pressed without hesitation and he saw his happiness winging away into the ether, never to return.

"Can I use your phone?" she asked. He passed it to her.

"Kat," she said when it was answered, "you need to send a scene-of-crime team to Ian Gilroy's villa, and then come and pick me up at Ca' Barbo." She listened, then said, "No, I'm fine. But send a forensic examiner to the villa too. Gilroy's dead."

They sat and waited for the Carabinieri. "Do you know what he said, before he died?" she said reflectively.

Daniele shook his head.

"He said, 'I love you, Holly. I've loved you like you were my own, ever since the barbecue where we played that game, the one where you stood on my feet and I walked you round the garden. Perhaps if I hadn't loved you so much, I would have stopped them from trying to kill your father. But he had so much, and I had nothing.'"

"A last, desperate lie to try and gain your sympathy."

"Perhaps. But I like to think there was a glimmer of humanity left in him, after all."

She found, though, that she couldn't tell even Daniele about the very last words Ian Gilroy had spoken; his voice barely louder than a whisper as he closed his eyes and waited for the end.

"*Ego te absolvo a peccatis tuis.*"

Had he been speaking to her, or to himself? Or had it been nothing more than the automatic reflex of a Catholic facing death?

I grant you absolution for your sins.

Whatever the reason, she felt a curious sense of peace, as if the two sides of her nature had finally been resolved. Perhaps even more curiously, she found herself hoping that in some way Gilroy had felt it too.

She looked at Daniele. "Did you know he tried to get you away from Venice, when he heard there was to be an attack? He wrote to you, saying Ca' Barbo was falling down and that you'd have to move out. Apparently you never replied."

Daniele grunted. "I wouldn't read too much into that. He probably just wanted me out of the way."

She was silent for a moment, thinking. "What will you do with the algorithm? Keep it for yourself, or publish it?"

"It's already out there." He gestured at the window. "Literally. I tore it up and dropped it in the *rio*."

"Why?"

He said slowly, "It would have meant a world without secrets. A world where everything that is mysterious, or complex, or creative, could be replicated by a piece of software. I decided I didn't want to live in a world like that after all."

"On the plus side," she said, "it would have meant shorter queues at Disney World."

He smiled at that, then said, "How did you do it?"

"Gilroy? I shot him with my father's pistol. It seemed the most appropriate thing. A single bullet, for all the Years of Lead. He would never have stood trial for what he's done. His paymasters would have seen to that."

He heard no remorse in her voice; only a terrible, steely determination. He nodded. "You did the right thing."

There was a sound below the window. Getting up, she crossed to it. "Kat's here, with Colonel Piola. Have the files all uploaded?"

Kat opened the door to the music room and saw her friends sitting there, their heads together, bent over the computer. For a moment she held back, watching them, before she stepped into the room.

"Holly," she said. "Oh, Holly…"

Behind her, Piola said gently, "Let me do this."

Kat shook her head. "It should be me." She took a breath. "Second Lieutenant Boland, I am arresting you on charges of murder, of espionage, of accessing classified information without authorisation…" The tears came then, flowing down her face and choking her throat; the first tears she had shed, she realised, since Flavio had died. She cried for her friend, and she cried for her lover; she cried because Venice was saved, and because it was doomed, and she cried because Italy would probably be no better off with Gilroy dead than it had been when he was alive. She cried for the youth whose life she had taken, and for Daniele, who was about to lose the one person who truly understood him; and she cried because she knew that the Americans, with their zealous hatred of whistle-blowers, would leave no stone unturned in their quest to wreak revenge. But most of all she cried because it was true what Flavio had said, almost the last time they had spoken; and yet it was too tiny, too fragile a truth to ward off injustices like the one she was committing now.

All we have is the law.

And so she spoke the formal words of the arrest as carefully as a prayer through her tears: a prayer for the safety, and the soul, of Holly Boland.

HISTORICAL NOTE

The Traitor, like the rest of the Carnivia trilogy, is fiction. But it draws on a number of historical events.

Many of the facts about Operation Gladio, for example, are now well established. Prime minister Giulio Andreotti did indeed reveal to the Italian parliament in 1990 that NATO, for the previous forty years, had been training, resourcing and running a secret paramilitary network of civilians, drawn from the far right of the political spectrum, which was intended to form an armed resistance in case of a communist invasion. It wasn't long before evidence began to surface that some gladiators had, in addition, used their training and their NATO-supplied explosives to commit atrocities and assassinations, part of a coordinated "strategy of tension" that, they believed, would make the public demand tougher security measures from the government. A small number of gladiators were subsequently convicted of these crimes by the Italian courts.

Many commentators believed that these attacks had been carried out with the tacit approval of, if not at the actual behest of, the CIA. To take just one example: General Gianadelio Maletti, former head of Italian Military Counter-Intelligence, testified under oath that "the Americans had gone beyond the infiltration and monitoring of extremist groups to instigating acts of violence" – a claim that was dismissed by the CIA as "ludicrous".

It is also well established that NATO, and in particular the British and American security services, did all they could to prevent Christian Democrat party leader Aldo Moro from brokering a "historic compromise" with the Communist Party, even going so far as to contemplate orchestrating a "bloodless coup" should the coalition take place. Moro himself, his widow recalls, was warned by Henry Kissinger when on a visit to Washington that there would be dire consequences for him personally if he did not abandon the plan.

The deal with the communists was eventually scuppered when the ultra-left wing Red Brigades first kidnapped Moro, then murdered him. When a subsequent Italian parliamentary enquiry asked the US about possible CIA infiltration of the Red Brigades, the request came back with the comment that the CIA could "neither confirm nor deny the existence of documentation relating to your enquiry". Readers wishing to learn more about the murky politics of the time should see *NATO's Secret Armies: Operation Gladio and Terrorism in Western Europe* by Daniele Ganser.

More recently, the story of the CIA operation to kidnap a Muslim cleric, Abu Omar, from the streets of Milan, and the efforts of a determined Italian prosecutor to bring the agents responsible to justice, has been told in *A Kidnapping in Milan: The CIA on Trial* by Steve Hendricks.

Propaganda Due, as Kat Tapo mentions in *The Traitor*, was a "black" or unaffiliated Masonic lodge that existed in Rome from about 1950 to 1980. It has been called "the government within the government" of Italy. The Grand Master, Licio Gelli, fled abroad to escape arrest and was later convicted *in absentia* of conspiracy against the state. Another member was Roberto Calvi, known as "God's Banker", who was found hanged underneath Blackfriars Bridge in London in 1982.

Since then there have been several other instances of Masonic lodges in Italy being used as cover for criminal and political conspiracies.

References to US government cyber-surveillance programs such as BULLRUN, PRISM, MUSCULAR, TURBINE and so on are as accurate as I can make them. However, VIGILANCE is fictional – my attempt to bundle all these separate capabilities into one package. My accounts of the vulnerabilities inherent in the Internet of Things are also, I believe, correct at the time of writing, although I have no evidence that such vulnerabilities could extend to the systems on cruise ships.

Ian Gilroy is a composite figure, inspired by – amongst others – Hung Fendwich, ostensibly an engineer at the Selenia Aerospace and Defence Company during the seventies and eighties, but actually one of America's most senior Italian analysts; and Captain David Carrett of the US Navy, subsequently indicted by a Milan court on terrorism charges.

The independence movement in the Veneto has the support of the majority of the local population: in a 2014 poll in which two million people voted, almost ninety per cent were in favour of breaking away from the rest of Italy. The Regional Council of the Veneto has since voted to instigate a binding referendum. There has been no official response from the national government in Rome.

There have been many proposals to ban large cruise ships from Venice, some of which have been voted into law only to be overturned on appeal. At the time of writing, the issue remains unsettled, and the biggest cruise ships continue to pass within a few hundred feet of Piazza San Marco.

For links to further reading, and information about the other books in the Carnivia trilogy, go to www.carnivia.com.

ACKNOWLEDGEMENTS

Special thanks to Philip Baillieu for explaining the intricacies of credit default swaps, to Matt Styles for advice on strokes and to Anna Coscia for correcting my Italian. Any errors that remain are of course my own.

My thanks too to Laura Palmer, my editor and publisher, for maintaining her enthusiasm from the very first page of book one to the very last page of book three, and to Lucy Ridout for a mammoth feat of fact-checking and copy-editing.

I'm especially grateful to all those in Venice, Vicenza and Verona, from a full colonel of the Carabinieri to numerous peace campaigners, who made me welcome and helped with my research, and whose generosity of spirit right across the political spectrum reminded me why I love Italy so much.

And finally to my family, who for the last four years have lived with all these crazy conspiracy theories.